Noelle Holten is an award-winning blogger at www.crimebookjunkie.co.uk. She is the PR & Social Media Manager for Bookouture, a leading digital publisher in the UK, and a regular reviewer on the Two Crime Writers and a Microphone podcast. Noelle worked as a Senior Probation Officer for eighteen years, covering cases of domestic violence and abuse. She has three Hons BA's – Philosophy, Sociology (Crime & Deviance) and Community Justice – and a Masters in Criminology. *Dead Secret* is the fourth novel in a new series featuring DC Maggie Jamieson.

www.crimebookjunkie.co.uk

twitter.com/nholten40
facebook.com/noelleholtenauthor

Also by Noelle Holten

Dead Inside

Dead Wrong

Dead Perfect

DEAD SECRET

NOELLE HOLTEN

One More Chapter
a division of HarperCollins*Publishers*
1 London Bridge Street
London SE1 9GF
www.harpercollins.co.uk

HarperCollins*Publishers*
1st Floor, Watermarque Building, Ringsend Road
Dublin 4, Ireland

This paperback edition 2021
First published in Great Britain in ebook format
by HarperCollins*Publishers* 2021

A catalogue record of this book
is available from the British Library

ISBN: 978-0-00-838368-8

Printed and bound in Great Britain by
CPI Group (UK) Ltd, Croydon CR0 4YY

For one of the strongest women I know –
My mother, Irene Quinn.

Chapter One

He was out of breath, knuckles swollen and throbbing from the repeated punches thrown. He wanted it all to stop – it was too much. He couldn't do it any more.

'You'll never get away with this.' The words were out of his mouth before he could stop himself. He had followed every instruction, but his nerves were shot.

What the fuck have I got myself into?

The woods were quiet, except for the sound of a fire crackling in the distance. A whisper of voices from the drunken youths sailed through the air.

Would they hear him if he screamed?

The sky grew dark, hinting at the storm approaching, casting a shadow that made the trees look like a menacing crowd of people surrounding him. He glanced around and then looked down at the screen on his mobile.

There's still time to stop it …

The blow to the back of the head caught him off guard. It wasn't supposed to be this way …

He reached up and felt the back of his head. When he pulled his hand away and looked, it was covered in blood. Then the dizziness hit, and he fell to the ground. His eyes rolled. He looked left and then right. The leaves rustled behind him.

No escape.

He didn't know how long he had been unconscious. When he woke, the pain was crippling. He felt weak, could barely move – he needed to get help. He reached his hand out and grabbed at the ground, looking for some leverage to pull himself forwards.

He tried to push his body up from the ground, but he couldn't. His arms shook; he was too weak. If he could get to his phone, he might be able to get help. He reached under himself, into his jeans pocket; a searing pain shot through his head with every movement, but he had to ignore it. It was fight or die time now.

His pocket was empty.

Then he remembered it had been in his hand just before he was struck. He lifted his head and looked around, biting his lip, and holding in the scream that desperately wanted to escape. His phone was a few feet ahead. If he could get to it, he could call for help.

His nails dug into the leafy, cold ground and he used what little strength he had left to pull his way towards his mobile – it was like a beacon of hope taunting him with every agonising pull he managed.

A noise behind him.

He nearly had his phone. Just a little bit more.

He looked up, facing the threat with pleading eyes. Just as he was about to wrap his hands around the device, a sharp pain caused him to cry out. He saw the hammer as it hit the ground and then the world went black.

Chapter Two

Lucy Sherwood never imagined she would be dealing with a client even before her refuge had officially opened, but the battered and semi-conscious woman in her doorway said otherwise.

She knelt beside the woman, checking that she was breathing while her other hand searched in her oversized pocket for her mobile phone. When she finally found it, her hands shook as she dialled 999 – situations like these often triggered her own experience of domestic abuse, but she pushed those thoughts to the back of her head as she focused on what the control room operator was saying down the line.

'Hi. My name is Lucy Sherwood. A woman just knocked on my door and collapsed when I opened it. Her face is cut, and her eyes are swollen. I'll need an ambulance here as soon as possible.' Lucy gave the call handler the full address to the haven and waited on the line as the operator asked her to confirm the female was breathing. Lucy noticed the woman's eyes flutter and, although her lips were moving, no sound was coming out. She told the operator to hold on as the woman began to come around.

'Hi, sweetheart. I've called an ambulance. They're on their way.' She shook the woman gently by her shoulders, not wanting to harm her but hoping it would keep her conscious.

The unidentified female's eyes widened, and she bolted upright. She had a short, jet-black pixie-like haircut, and Lucy noticed what looked like a hearing aid behind her ear. Her clothes were damp; it had been raining intermittently and Lucy figured she must have got caught out in the showers.

The female scrabbled to stand up, but Lucy held her shoulders, being careful not to use too much force. 'Hey, it's okay. Just sit here. You're safe.'

The young woman stared at Lucy as she shook her head. There was desperation in her eyes – a look Lucy was all too familiar with. Lucy heard the ambulance in the distance. 'Here they are now. Can you tell me your name?'

She shook her head, and Lucy looked at the large satchel she clutched to her body. It was large enough to hold some clothes and toiletries but not so big as to hinder an escape.

'Okay. That's fine. We can sort all that out later. Sit still. I don't want you to hurt yourself any more than you already are.' The ambulance pulled up outside the security gate and waited for Lucy to open it. 'I just need to go and open the gate. I won't be a minute.' Lucy stood and ran to the office. She flicked on the light and found the fob, pressing the button as she returned to the young woman. The ambulance drove up the driveway and Lucy went to go and meet them halfway, but the girl grabbed her hand. 'Okay, hun. I'll stay.'

'So, what do we have here?' The female respondent knelt down and began to unload some equipment from her bag.

'She turned up at my door and collapsed when I answered. I can't get her to speak.' Lucy looked the other woman in the eye and signalled at the satchel still being held tightly by the young female.

A male paramedic stood back as his colleague asked the woman some questions. 'Can you tell me where it hurts, hun?' They watched as the young girl pointed to her face, her head, and her arm.

'Okay. Let's have a look at that arm. Tell me if it hurts when I touch you here.'

The woman shook her head.

'How about here?' The female paramedic squeezed her forearm.

Again, she shook her head but there was a large bandage with bloodstains seeping through at the top of her arm. 'Did this happen today?'

The woman nodded.

'I'll just check it over and give you a clean bandage. Okay?'

Reluctantly, the young woman allowed the paramedic to change the dressing.

When the paramedic reached her wrist, the young female winced and tried to draw her hand back. 'That's sore? Well, the good news is you can move it, so I don't think it's broken but we should probably get it X-rayed at the hospital.'

The young girl yanked her arm away and winced while shaking her head furiously.

'Okay. Stay calm. You don't want to injure it any further now, hun. How about I bandage it for now, and we'll revisit the X-ray in a little bit. Are you okay to stand? You might be more comfortable lying down in the ambulance.'

Lucy noticed the woman staring intently as the paramedic spoke. She could read lips.

The woman shook her head and clung to Lucy with her free hand.

'It's okay.' Lucy knew exactly how the woman felt. Once you go to the hospital, you have to face questions from more professionals and acknowledge the abuse … or lie. 'Do you want to come inside? You can lie down on the couch.' Lucy pointed to the communal lounge door.

The young girl nodded.

They helped her up and carefully walked the mystery woman to the couch. Easing her down gently, the emergency services continued to check her out while Lucy stood back, waiting for the police to arrive. As if on cue, the buzzer for the front gate sounded. Lucy left the paramedics and opened the front door; pressing the key fob, she waited as the police drove in. They exited their vehicle and when they reached the door, she introduced herself, explaining that the woman was lying down on the couch while the paramedics looked her over.

She whispered to the officers, 'She won't speak and doesn't want to go to the hospital, so I'm not sure how much information you'll learn but follow me.' Lucy showed them to the communal living area.

The two officers identified themselves to the woman on the couch, and Lucy noticed her body stiffen as they approached. The woman turned away from them and wouldn't answer any of their questions.

'She's been through quite an ordeal and may be a little nervous. How about you leave your details and when she's able and willing to talk, I'll give you a ring. I have plenty of rooms here and she's free to stay until we figure this all out.'

While Lucy waited for a response, she sent a quick text to her friends, Sharon and Mark. They were due to come around, but given the situation, Lucy didn't think more people would be a good idea, especially as Sharon Bairden was an advocate for domestic abuse victims and Mark was a police officer who she used to work with in the Domestic Abuse and Homicide Unit (DAHU).

The officers looked at each other and nodded. One handed Lucy a card. She walked them to the door. 'I used to work in the DAHU at Markston Police Station. I'm a Probation Officer, so I do have some experience. I don't get the impression this is a random assault.'

'Well, she is in safe hands then. We'll log this into the system in case anyone reports anything about the assault or a missing female.' Lucy handed the officers her card from the stack on the side table by the door and thanked them as she watched them leave.

The paramedics were wrapping up the woman's wrist. 'Other than the swelling and cuts, there doesn't appear to be anything broken. Did I hear you say that she can stay here overnight?'

Lucy looked at the female paramedic. 'Yes, that's if she wants to. I don't want to assume …' She smiled at the stranger. 'Do you have anywhere else you can go?'

The young woman shook her head and patted the couch.

'You want to stay here then?' Lucy wanted to be sure the woman didn't feel she was being forced into staying, while reassuring her that she would be safe.

The woman nodded as she tucked her feet underneath herself.

'Okay.' Turning back to the emergency services, Lucy

smiled. 'I'll keep an eye on her and if her situation changes or I have any concerns, I'll bring her in to the hospital. Perhaps she'll feel differently in the morning.'

Lucy showed them to the door. It was going to be a long night. She'd decided that she would stay in the communal room with the woman so she could keep an eye on her. 'I'll get some blankets.'

Lucy went to the cupboard in the hall and pulled out a large fleece throw. 'That should do.' She grabbed a thinner one for herself and hoped she was hiding the concern she felt.

Why is she so afraid to speak?

Chapter Three

Lucy looked at the vulnerable young woman for a moment when she returned to the communal living area. 'Do you think you can tell me your name now? Everyone's gone, it's just us.' She wondered whether the woman was fearful of disclosing her details while other professionals were at the property.

There was no response. Of course there wouldn't be; the woman was staring into space – she hadn't heard her.

Lucy sat down beside her, and the female jumped. 'Sorry. I didn't mean to startle you. Are you okay to talk?' Lucy noted the woman once again staring at her lips as she spoke. 'Can you hear me, sweetheart?'

The woman's hand wavered side to side and then she tapped the hearing aids. So, she was deaf or at least partially. The young woman held out her hand and mimicked writing.

'Okay. I'll get you something you can write on and then how about we get you some warm clothes, a nice cuppa, and hopefully some sleep. Do you sign?' Lucy wondered if she would need to get an interpreter in.

The woman shook her head.

Lucy stood and went to the metal cabinet at the back of the room. She still had boxes to unpack but remembered that she had put a load of notebooks and pens in the cupboard earlier that day. 'I know I have some … ah, here they are.' She pulled a notebook out of the box and reached into her own pocket for a pen.

She handed them to the woman and waited.

The woman didn't take long before passing the notebook back to Lucy. It had only one thing written down.

'Ronnie'

'Your name is Ronnie? What about your last name? Would it be easier for you if I wrote my questions down?'

Ronnie shook her head and covered her mouth as she yawned. Lucy noticed her fiddle with her hearing aids.

'You're tired – in fact, you must be exhausted. How about I show you to your room?'

Ronnie shook her head and tapped the couch.

Lucy pointed to the stairs. 'I have a vacant room you can use. It might be more comfortable. You can put your stuff away and I can give you something to change into.' Lucy had been collecting donated clothing for a few months in anticipation of the haven's opening. 'I'll be back in two secs.'

She stood and went to the room she had kitted out with the donated items. Her plan had been to turn this room into a shop of sorts – the residents could purchase things with tokens. She hadn't worked out all the details but that would come in time. She found a pair of black leggings and a sweatshirt that looked like it would fit Ronnie and walked back into the communal lounge. She handed the clothing to the young woman.

'We don't have to go up just yet. Shall I turn on the telly for a bit?' Lucy picked up the remote and turned on the television.

They sat in silence staring at the screen, and Lucy noticed the woman had removed the hearing aids and placed them on the side table. She put the subtitles on so that Ronnie could follow the programme, but when she turned and looked at the vacant stare in the woman's eyes, she didn't think she really cared what was on.

What happened to you, Ronnie?

Chapter Four

DC Maggie Jamieson had been looking forward to a weekend off after having to say goodbye to Dr Kate Moloney and finalising the case against the person the papers had called 'the Living Doll Killer'. She was mentally exhausted.

Kate had returned to Ireland with her parents when her near-death experience of being abducted by her stalker had left her shaken. She'd asked Maggie to watch Salem, her black cat, and Maggie hoped that after having a little time away, Kate would return and start working alongside her in the Major and Organised Crime Department (MOCD). Kate's time in the DAHU was nearing an end, and DI Rutherford was finalising a proposal for a profiler consultant within their team.

After her shower, Maggie went downstairs and called out to the cats. Although Scrappy still wasn't happy having another furry being in his presence, he tolerated Salem. It was nice to have an extra cat for company and Maggie toyed with the idea of adopting another, as Scrappy was getting older.

Then she remembered how much time it took for a kitten to adapt and quickly dismissed the idea. She was far too busy for that level of commitment at the moment.

Maggie tapped the tin of cat food and listened for the patter of feet. 'There you guys are.' Scrappy hissed at Salem as Maggie put down his bowl of food. 'Hey! Be nice.' She wagged her finger as she put a separate bowl down for Salem on the opposite side of the door and clicked on the kettle. As she reached in the cupboard to grab a mug, she heard her mobile ring.

Maggie ran into the living room and unplugged the phone from the charger and saw DS Nathan Wright's name flashing on the screen.

'Oh shit.' She swiped to answer. 'Hey, boss.' He hated when she called him that, so she did it anyway. 'Don't you have better things to do than ring me on a Saturday? You do remember you gave me the day off, right?' She hoped he was calling for a personal rather than work-related matter.

'I do, but unfortunately crime never stops and you can probably guess what's coming next.'

She heard him sigh down the earpiece.

'Oh crap.' Her shoulders slumped. 'I don't have the weekend off after all, do I?'

'Good work, detective.'

Although Nathan was trying to make light of the situation, Maggie could tell he was just as pissed off as she was. The last case had hit them all pretty hard.

'When do you need me?'

'As soon as you can get here. I'll text you the address. I'm at the crime scene now. It looked like it could just be a serious assault, but the victim died before the ambulance crew arrived.'

'Okay. I'll get changed and be with you as soon as I can.' Maggie raced upstairs and put on some comfortable clothes after seeing the address she was heading to. Chances were, after last night's rainfall, the ground would be muddy and her work trousers weren't going to cut it.

Maggie's brother was still in bed; he'd some time off and had been talking about going away on holiday soon. She hated to disturb him but needs must. She knocked gently on his door.

'Andy. Sorry to wake you, but I need to take the car.'

She heard him groan.

'Uh, yeah, no problem. It's your car to be fair. I'm off today anyway. I thought you were too?'

'So did I, but someone had other plans. Have to head out to a crime scene. I've fed the cats and I'll let Scrappy out before I go. I think Salem is in Kate's … I mean the spare bedroom.'

'Okay. Catch you later.' He rolled over.

She closed the door and jogged down the stairs. Maggie unlocked the cat flap and called out to Scrappy. 'Time to go now. You have three seconds before I lock it again, Scrapps.' She tapped her foot on the floor. She swore her cat understood her, as he came bolting from the living room and out the flap at record speed and locked the flap after him.

Maggie grabbed the car keys from the bowl on the table, threw on her coat, and headed out the door.

Chapter Five

Maggie arrived at the scene, pulling up behind the string of cars that were gathered at the location. She unbuckled her seatbelt and stepped out of the car, taking a deep breath as she looked around at the property. There was something familiar about the area. Directly in front of her was a large grey building. It looked like rented offices – the kind where different companies were in and out every other week. She took out her phone and texted Nathan.

I'm here. Where is everyone?

Her phone rang.

'Hey. You have to walk behind the building. There's a small wooded area. You'll see it when you walk around.'

Nathan sounded breathless.

'Are you okay?'

'Yeah. I tripped over a big branch. After the storm last night there's a few littered on the ground, so watch where you're going.'

'See you in a minute then.' Maggie disconnected the call and walked around the side of the building. Nathan was right, branches littered the ground. She could see the crime scene tent in the distance. She jogged over to the crime scene manager and signed herself in.

'Where can I get a forensic suit?' She hadn't spotted the vehicle until the officer pointed it out on the far left of the lot. Maggie nodded a 'thanks' to him and made her way over. Once kitted out, she followed the path towards the tent, making sure not to disturb anything on the way, as well as keeping an eye out for anything she might trip over; the last thing she wanted was to find herself face down in the muddy grass.

The crime scene tent was set up just on the edge of where the grass met the wooded area. The mix of wet leaves and mud wafted a stale smell in the air. Maggie stepped into the tent and headed over to Nathan.

'What do we have then?' She looked at the body on the ground. Dr Fiona Blake's forensic assistant, Charlie, was holding the victim on his side, while the doctor looked to be examining a wound on the back of the victim's head.

Nathan leaned in and whispered. 'Unidentified male. Dr Blake was just about to turn him back over.'

'Nice of you to join us, DC Jamieson.' There was a curtness in her voice. Dr Blake's assistant lay out a sheet of plastic and Dr Blake then proceeded to turn the victim over, carefully laying him down on the sheet.

Maggie ignored the hint of sarcasm in the pathologist's voice. Dr Blake hadn't been the same with her since Maggie had briefly identified one of the forensic team as a person of interest in the Living Doll Killer case, without even so much as a heads-up to the pathologist. Maggie refused to rise to the bait this time, believing if she ignored the pathologist's jibes, she'd eventually grow tired and things would get back to normal.

'Thanks, Fiona. Good to see you.' Maggie smiled as she kept things friendly.

She looked down at their victim now that he was on his back. Another wound could be seen where his hairline started – the left side of his forehead. His face was covered in cuts and bruises and there were four marks on his left cheek.

'What are those?' Maggie pointed at the four black dots on the victim's cheek. If the dots were joined, they would form a right-angle triangle. Maggie made a mental note of the image.

'Some sort of ink marker or pen, I'd say, as there are a few smudges. As for what it means,' she shrugged, 'your guess would be as good as mine. Looks like he could be between sixteen and twenty-four years old. Other than the gash here,' she pointed to his forehead, 'there don't seem to be any deep wounds on his face, just the superficial cuts, some swelling, and bruises …' She looked into his eyes with her penlight. 'No petechial haemorrhaging. Don't take this as gospel, but as he died just before the ambulance arrived, I suspect we'll find that the blows to the head is the cause of death – a slow internal bleed perhaps. I'll know more when I get him back to the lab.' Dr Blake checked the victim's pockets. 'Nothing here to help with your ID, I'm afraid. Do you need anything else from me or can I make a move?' She looked past Maggie, directly at Nathan.

'Thanks for that. Nothing more from me. What about you, Maggie?'

Maggie shook her head. The face markings were stuck in her head. Where had she seen marks like that before?

'Right then. I'll be in contact when I know more. Bag him up, Charlie.' Fiona directed her assistant and left them standing in the tent.

'Who found him?' Maggie scratched her chin.

'Let's step outside and let them get on with their work.' Nathan swivelled around and walked a few feet ahead of Maggie. He stopped and turned to her. 'A security guard was out having a fag when he said he noticed the victim on the ground. Bethany has more of the details. You can catch up with her in a moment.' Nathan stared ahead.

'What time was that? Have statements been taken?'

'Who knows how long the poor kid has been there. Dr Blake may be able to shed some light on that, but he was found only a few hours ago. I got a call from DI Rutherford at about six this morning. Called you not long after I arrived. Bethany had been working the night shift and arrived with some of the field team. Last I saw her, she was taking down the statements and may still be in the building actually. I'm going to head back now. See if you can find her and, once caught up, head back to the office. Sorry to ruin your weekend plans.'

PC Bethany Lambert rarely ventured out of the office. Her computer skills and logical thinking had her tasked mainly with working analytics alongside a civilian analyst, but it was nice to see her come out of her comfort zone now and again.

'Oh shit.' Maggie looked at her watch.

'What?' Nathan turned back.

'I'm supposed to go over to Lucy's later today. I better just message her and let her know before I get too absorbed and she thinks I've brushed her off.'

'Right, I'll be off now.' Nathan walked towards his car.

Maggie took out her phone and messaged Lucy.

Really sorry but I've been called in to work so I won't be able to drop by.

Speak later. X M

Maggie headed towards the office complex when her phone beeped.

I should have messaged you. Have a crisis of my own, but nothing to worry about. Hope it's nothing too awful on your end. I'll catch you up later. X Lucy

Although Lucy's message intrigued her, she pocketed her mobile and hoped that Bethany managed to find out more from the security guard. As selfish as it sounded, Maggie wanted this to be one of those quick cases – culprit easily identified and order restored. But nothing was ever that simple.

Chapter Six

When Maggie walked towards the building, she spied PC Bethany Lambert talking to a security guard through the large windows that surrounded the bottom floor. Maggie assumed he was the witness whom Nathan had told her about. She entered the building from the back door that had been propped open and walked over to the pair. She introduced herself to the man. He smiled and continued his conversation with her colleague.

'As soon as I saw that kid's head caved in, I called the ambulance. I can't believe he died. Never been that close to a dead body before this.' The man rubbed his forehead.

'Did you notice anyone else in the area?' Maggie was curious whether or not there had been any teenagers drinking in the woods, as it was a Friday night when the assault must have happened, and youths often gathered in the area.

'Nope. I saw the claw hammer on the ground, not far from the lad. I didn't touch it though. Figured it was probably what did the damage.' He shuddered. 'I don't know what else I can tell you. Do you think he could have been in a fight or something? I wasn't outside much last night, but I've heard a few fights in the past.'

'It's possible and certainly an avenue we'll explore. Thanks so much for your time. PC Lambert will leave her details with you and we'll be in contact if we need anything further.' Maggie walked away and waited by the door for Bethany.

'I'm shattered. I was hoping to at least get a few hours' sleep before the next shift, but it doesn't look like that's going to happen.' Bethany sighed.

'You may be able to catch a nap in the break room once we get all the info on the system.' Maggie knew it was unlikely but sometimes a reassuring word could give you that boost of energy you needed to get through. 'Did you get anything useful from the witnesses?' Maggie held the door open.

'Not really. Though I'd like to follow up and see if there were any call outs about fighting or youths in the area. I'll get on that when I get back to the office. Is Kat here?'

Maggie wondered where DC Kat Everett was too. 'No, I haven't seen her. She may well be at the office.'

They both headed to their own cars, and Maggie drove to Stafford Police Station. Considering it was a Saturday, the drive into the town centre was fairly clear. Maggie parked her vehicle in the back lot of the station and made her way up to the office. DC Everett was at her desk and waved to Maggie.

'Just about to make a cuppa. Do you fancy one? Nathan said to let you know there'll be a briefing in an hour.' Kat stood and stretched her legs.

'I'd love one. Thanks. Is Bethany not back yet?'

'She was here a second ago, but I think she went downstairs to talk to some of the field team.'

Maggie nodded, and a flash of the victim popped into her head. 'Poor kid. Any ID yet?'

'Not at the minute. There's a message on your desk. Your journalist friend wants you to call her back.' Kat inclined her head in the direction of Maggie's workspace.

'What does she want? I swear she has a wiretap set up somewhere. How the hell does she know so quickly when something has happened?'

Kat laughed. 'Your guess is as good as mine.' She headed towards the kitchen, and Maggie laughed as she heard her humming some tune off-key.

Maggie picked up her phone and dialled the number to the *Stafford Gazette*.

'Julie Noble speaking. How can I help?'

'Hi. It's DC Jamieson. I got your message.'

'Oh, so are we back to formalities now, DC Jamieson? I'll cut to the chase, as I am sure you're busy – any ID on the male found at Castle Bank Industrial Estate? I heard someone cracked his skull. That true?'

After the last case, Maggie and Julie had formed a strange friendship. There had been a spark of chemistry between the two but only Julie played on that. Maggie preferred to keep things professional.

'Ms Noble, I'm not sure why you think you have any special privileges – you know I can't discuss the details of an ongoing investigation with you. Who told you about this anyway?'

'I have my ways.' Julie paused. *'Look, I just want to know if you can give me a little headline – something short – do you think this was a one-off attack or the start of something more?'*

'Something more?' Maggie rolled her eyes. 'Not answering

that. In fact, I think I should just end this call at this point before I say something you misconstrue and I end up in the shit. I'm sure there'll be a press conference in due course. You'll just have to wait.'

'You're no fun, Maggie.'

'I never said I was.' Maggie disconnected the call. The last thing she wanted was for someone to claim she was feeding the press information. With Stafford being a small area, Julie often juggled two roles – her main job as the local news reporter but she also contributed to the *Stafford Gazette* with features on crime in the area. Maggie knew, however, that Julie Noble was not one to give up so easily – she just hoped that she kept Maggie's name out of anything she did report. Even mentioning that she had spoken to the reporter could be taken out of context.

Out of the corner of her eye, Maggie spotted Nathan returning to his office. He motioned for Maggie to join him.

'What's up?' Maggie loosened the bun in her hair. Her head was beginning to hurt.

'We'll have a briefing shortly …' Nathan shuffled some papers on his desk. 'I've just filled in DI Rutherford. She can't get a hold of DCI Hastings, so she's a bit frazzled. I'm giving you a heads-up that today is not the day to piss her off.' He motioned for Maggie to sit.

'What's up with DCI Hastings? He seems to be all over the place lately. I'm not surprised the guv is losing her patience, she hasn't had much support from him.' Maggie pulled out a chair and sat down. Hastings had been missing work and distant recently. There had been rumours that he wanted to retire early to spend time with his family but hadn't been allowed. Maggie's own relationship with the DCI blew hot and cold over the years. When she had first started in the MOCD, he had been reluctant to listen to her theories, but as she proved herself with excellent conviction rates, he gave her the space she needed – for the most part. At times he had reminded her of her father. Praise didn't come often, but when it did it was brief and awkward.

'Yeah, I noticed that too, but if Rutherford knows what it's about, she's keeping it close to her chest. Just watch your step, okay?'

Maggie cocked her head to the right, but the frown on Nathan's face told her to leave the conversation for another time. 'I've just been on the phone with Julie Noble. She had left me a message, so out of professional courtesy I called her back. I'd really love to know where the hell she gets her intel?'

Nathan shrugged. 'Maybe she has a contact in this office. Who knows? What did you tell her?'

'Nothing. Not even a hint, and I want that on the record.' Maggie tapped Nathan's desk. 'Though she knew enough herself. I said she'd have to wait for the press conference like everyone else.'

'Smart response. I know you wouldn't share details with the press, so stop being so paranoid. They'll have something from us later today. If the vic is in the system, we'll get an ID and inform the family – that's the priority – but we're as much in the dark as the press.' He looked over her shoulder and gestured. 'Kat's waving a cuppa this way. Go, drink up and I'll see you in the briefing room soon.'

Chapter Seven

An hour later, Maggie followed behind Kat and Bethany as they headed into the briefing room. The whiteboards were being set up and a few officers from the field team had joined them. Maggie caught her breath when she saw DI Rutherford. The guv had dark circles forming underneath her eyes, and Maggie knew then that there was more going on at the office than was being said, as it looked like Rutherford hadn't slept in a week.

'Thank you all for coming. Let's get through this as quickly as possible. We've a young male at the mortuary waiting to be identified and a family to share some horrendous news with – not the way any of us saw our weekend going, I'm sure. Due to the nature of the injuries, we can safely say he's been killed under suspicious circumstances. For those of you who weren't able to attend the crime scene, a hammer was found and it's with forensics for testing. As an aside, DCI Hastings is … off sick, so I'll be taking the lead until he's back and I'll fill him in on where we are at. What do we know so far?'

Bethany spoke up. 'Well, guv, I interviewed the security guard, but he couldn't tell us much, as he stumbled across the body during a break. The site is a common meeting place for youths from the area to go and get pissed and occasionally there have been some punch-ups – I verified this with the Neighbourhood Police Team. The witness initially thought that our victim was one of the regular teenagers who passed out, so didn't pay much attention at first. He said they normally just wake up and go on their merry way home. But when he'd finished his fag and the lad still hadn't moved, he decided to investigate further. Once he realized it was more serious, he called it in straight away.'

'Any CCTV in the area?' DI Rutherford queried as she wrote the information on the whiteboard.

'Yeah. I still have to go through it, but the security guard wasn't convinced it would be much help, as it mainly covers the exit, entrance, and not much beyond.' Bethany shrugged.

'How shit is that security? I mean why was the kid found so late? Don't they do regular checks?' Kat blurted out. Maggie smiled inwardly as DI Rutherford held her hand up to Kat. Her point was valid, but the guv clearly wanted to get the facts out before any wrong conclusions were made.

'What about you pair? Anything to add?' Rutherford looked over at Maggie and Nathan.

'My initial thoughts are that the location where the victim died was not where it all started. Before I caught up with Bethany, I had a chat with the first responder and with the way the body was positioned, and the marks in the dirt behind him, it seems to me that he either dragged himself there before the final blow to the head or someone else dragged him. He wasn't a big guy, so it's possible someone pulled him out of the forest

– maybe something spooked them? What I don't get is that there was no ID left behind, or even a mobile phone – but the hammer was …' Maggie knew Bethany would be tracing the mobile signal once they had an ID to see if it was still active.

Nathan interjected. 'Maggie's right. He was initially attacked deeper in the wooded area. There was dirt under his nails and leaves and mud stuck to his clothes, so I'd rule out the idea of someone hauling him that distance – I think he tried to get away and ended up at the secondary scene where he was found.' Nathan stood and went to the giant map of South Staffordshire that was tacked on the wall. He pointed to the location of where the body was found and then dragged his finger before stopping and tapping on an area within the forest. 'Crime scene officers followed the trail which ended around about here. So, the next question is: was it a bunch of college kids, drunk, maybe things got out of hand? Or was our victim targeted? A robbery gone wrong?'

Kat jumped in again. 'From what I've heard so far, it doesn't sound like a well-planned assault though, does it? I mean, our vic's face was pretty beat up but he was able to drag himself out of the woods. He was what? About eighteen years old, maybe younger? I have a few ideas about that. What if he stumbled across some kids dealing weed, they threatened him, maybe he got a bit gobby – they hit him with the hammer a few times, not realising how bad his injuries were? Then bricked it when they saw the kid was unconscious. Wonder if we speak to Comms and ask the public to come forward with information – you know, maybe someone's son or brother came back and was acting a bit weird? Washed their clothes but don't normally? You know, that kind of shit.'

Maggie agreed with Kat. Her scenario sounded plausible,

but something was bothering her about where the victim was found. She just couldn't put her finger on it yet.

'All good theories and lines of enquiries to follow up on. The door-to-doors might get us some answers before we have to start involving the press, so other than confirming a body was found and asking for any witnesses to come forward, we're going to hold back on any specifics.' DI Rutherford rubbed her chin. 'I'm hoping it is local kids, rather than a stranger outside of the area – and given what we know, it being a fairly secluded industrial site, it is likely to be someone who knows the area. Let's focus on that avenue first. Did the security guard notice any strange vehicles around?'

'No, guv.' Bethany looked through her notes to confirm. 'Said his car was the only one in the lot, actually.'

'Big area for only one guard, isn't it?' DI Rutherford looked on the map.

Maggie eyed the map. The guv was right – a site that large would surely have more than one security guard. Kat's comment about shit security earlier was well placed.

'Apparently there are usually three of them. One was a newbie and complete no-show and the other called in sick at the last minute. But the guard said it wasn't really unusual for them to be on their own some nights,' Bethany called out.

'Talk to those people then confirm their whereabouts so we don't waste any more time on them than is necessary. Not much else we can do today – make sure you've recorded everything and ...' DI Rutherford looked at her watch, 'then go home and I'll see you all back here in the morning.'

Before leaving for the day, Maggie asked if Kat would contact the security guards who had failed to attend work and arrange for them to come in for an informal chat. Her head was pounding, as she'd had no time between the last case and this new one to de-stress. She needed some alone time to process the events of the day before heading home. She knew exactly what would fit that bill.

Chapter Eight

Outside, Maggie looked up and noticed the dark clouds forming – rain wouldn't be too far off. She started to compartmentalize the crime scene in her head as she walked over to the café at the end of the road from the police station.

Inside the café, Maggie sat down at a table that gave her a good view of the street while not making her the centre of attention. When the waitress came around, she ordered herself a cappuccino and then began to clear her head by staring out the window at the drizzle of rain that had just started. Droplets landed on the glass, blurring her view. The bleak weather matched her own mood today, though she did her best to hide it from her colleagues.

Maggie's thoughts immediately drifted to Kate's decision to go on indefinite leave after the last case they worked on. The pair worked well together, and she never imagined how lost she would feel with her friend not being around to bounce her theories off. She had met Kate when she had been seconded to the DAHU and worked closely on bringing the killer of domestic abuse perpetrators to justice. When Maggie had returned to the MOCD, Bill Raven's case had knocked her confidence and then the Living Doll Killer had made things personal. Too personal. Maggie shook her head. Those cases were closed, and Kate wasn't here. She had worked on her own successfully for many years without a criminal psychologist on board – she'd do it again.

Maggie wasn't the type of person who spent much time on general hobbies or interests, but lately her job was having an impact on her mental well-being. Well over ten years as a detective working murder cases could take its toll, but Maggie loved her job and knew she was a good detective. Her success lately was due to her colleagues, working with Kate and other agencies, because they made her strive to be the best she could be and reminded her about all the things she loved about her job: justice, protecting the public, and the feeling that she had accomplished something. She was making a difference.

She'd still been speaking with Kate since she had left, but the conversation was generally casual or about their cats. Now that the team had a new murder investigation to work on, Maggie wondered whether Kate would mind her bringing up work, as the last thing she wanted to do was trigger her friend and ruin any recovery or healing Kate had managed to achieve so far.

Maggie was still drowning in her own thoughts when there was a 'tap tap tap' on the table. She looked up and didn't know whether to smile or scream.

'What are you doing here?' Maggie raised a brow.

'Oh, DC Jamieson, you're always so welcoming. It's a coffee shop. What do you think I'm here for?' Julie Noble pulled out a chair and sat opposite Maggie.

'Did I ask you to join me?'

'Not directly, but I could see you wanted me to, so I made it easier. Have you ordered?' Julie waved at the waitress and asked for a coffee. She looked at Maggie and waited, but Maggie ignored her, turned away, and looked out the window.

'Suit yourself.'

'Why didn't you just go up and order? You'll be getting it to go.' Maggie glanced at the journalist before she returned to watching the people outside run for shelter as a flash of rain came pelting down.

Julie leaned across the table and whispered: 'I just love your flirting, Maggie. It's a wonder you aren't swamped with requests for dates. Why the long face?'

Maggie knew that Julie was trying to get a rise out of her and straightened up in her chair. 'You sure are full of yourself, aren't you? What makes you think I'd share anything with you? You're not exactly discreet.'

Julie leaned back and faked being surprised. 'Oh c'mon! Your private life is hardly newsworthy. I thought we had passed all that bullshit. You know, all was forgiven. Anyway, I promised you a coffee after all that mess with the Living Doll Killer, so this one's on me.'

Maggie could see Julie was offering an olive branch. She wanted to accept it, but a part of her still didn't believe the journalist's motives. Julie Noble was attractive, annoying, and a complete enigma but at least Maggie knew that she wouldn't be barking up the wrong tree, like she had been with Kate. 'Fine.' She huffed. 'One coffee, but can we not talk about work? I'd feel much better knowing that you're not mentally taking down every word we say and filing it away to be used in one of your stories.' Maggie pursed her lips.

'So suspicious. As you wish, DC Jamieson.' A smile crept across her face. 'Or can I start calling you Maggie again? How's your friend – Kate, isn't it?'

Maggie frowned. 'I said I didn't want to talk about work.'

'Kate doesn't work with you any more, does she? I'm actually interested in how she's doing. I know what it's like to not get the justice you feel is deserved when …' Maggie noted the frown on Julie's face before she continued. 'Never mind. Why don't you tell me what we can talk about so that I'm not putting my foot in it every five minutes?' Julie twirled her fingers around the locket which hung around her neck.

Now Maggie's interest was piqued. 'What do you mean by that?'

Julie leaned forwards. 'Why don't we save that for another time?'

The waitress came over and placed Maggie's cappuccino in front of her. She handed Julie a takeaway cup. Julie stood and handed the young woman some money before looking back at Maggie. 'Next one's on you, Maggie. Call me.'

Chapter Nine

Maggie left the café shortly after Julie did, and when she walked into her house, the aroma hit her nostrils and she smiled. She threw her jacket over the bannister and dropped her bag as she headed into the kitchen.

'That smells delicious! What's the occasion?' She picked up a chopped pepper and popped it in her mouth.

'No reason. I wasn't sure what time you'd be back and figured you wouldn't make anything for yourself. After that last case, you were wasting away. Need my sis back – you're all skin and bones.' Andy poked her in the belly.

Maggie started opening up the cupboards and looking inside. 'Hello? Where's my brother? What have you done to him?'

Andy laughed. 'The bloody cheek! I can stop now if you'd prefer?'

Maggie held up her hands. 'No way! My tummy would never forgive me if I didn't eat that!' Her stomach growled to back up Maggie and she laughed. 'See? Have the cats been fed?'

Andy nodded. 'Fed, watered, and probably snoring in sync upstairs. You know, I'm surprised at how quickly Salem's adapted. If he stays much longer, I'm not sure I'm going to let Kate have him back.' Andy went on to tell Maggie that he'd been waking up to find the black moggy curled up on the chair in his room.

'I think you'll have a fight on your hands – not sure I'd like to be on the wrong side of Kate.' She popped another pepper in her mouth.

'Has she said anything to you about coming back?'

'Not yet … I've been avoiding the topic when I speak to her … shit friend, aren't I?' Maggie's shoulders slumped.

'Totally shit.' He smiled.

Maggie didn't want to think any more about the possibility of Kate not returning, so she changed the subject.

'How long is that going to be?' She pointed at the pot.

Andy lifted a lid and looked in. 'Another half hour, at least.'

'Well, if you don't need any help, I'm going to try and catch the last half of the news.'

'Go ahead.' Andy picked up the peppers and added them in.

Maggie stretched her arms as she walked into the living room. She kicked off her shoes, curled her legs underneath her, and turned on the TV, but when she saw Julie Noble's face and listened to the reporter's words … she wished she hadn't.

'What the actual fuck?'

Chapter Ten

Maggie stared at the screen and listened as Julie Noble stood in the car park of the crime scene she had left only hours ago. She wondered if this was why Julie had been so friendly at the café; perhaps she had hoped that buying Maggie a coffee would soften the blow. It was still daylight, so the footage must have been pre-recorded. Maggie turned the volume up and felt her jaw tighten as she watched.

Why the hell did I expect anything more of her?

Maggie had worked hard to get past the journalist's passive aggressive reporting of the news after the Raven case and had begun to believe that Julie had changed her ways when she had helped Maggie and the police bring Kate's stalker to justice. She should have known better.

'Does South Staffordshire have another serial killer on the loose? Today the body of a young man, said to be in his late teens, was discovered at the edge of the woods on Castle Bank Industrial Estate. Battered and bruised, my sources tell me he sustained numerous

blows to the head and died before the paramedics had arrived. Is this a robbery gone wrong or should residents be more concerned?

'The police have no leads and are investigating the death as suspicious. Are you waiting for your son, brother, or boyfriend to come home? If you know anything about what happened here in the early hours or think you may know who the victim might be, you can call the Stafford Gazette *anonymously and speak to me. You have my promise to do whatever I can to help the police bring the perpetrator to justice. Let's hope we don't have another Ripper on the loose …'*

'That bloody cow!' Maggie was furious and turned off the television to stop herself from throwing the remote at Julie Noble's face. The victim had only just been discovered and already the reporter was stirring up the community's fear by comparing the killer to the Yorkshire Ripper. If this wasn't contained, they could have a load of vigilantes on the loose.

Maggie looked around the room for her mobile phone. There was no way Julie would get away with reporting fake news. She stomped out into the hall and rummaged through her bag. A text wouldn't cut it this time. She wanted the journalist to know exactly what she was thinking. She scrolled through her contact list and hit call.

'Well, this is an unexpected but pleas—'

'Save it, Julie. What the hell are you trying to do?'

'Whoa. Back up – can you tell me what I've allegedly done this time to get those hackles up?'

Maggie bit her tongue to hold back what she really wanted to say. If she could have reached down the phone line and grabbed this woman, she would have done so without any hesitation or concern for the consequences.

'Your bloody news report. Who's your source?'

'DC Jamieson, you know I can't tell you that. Have I touched a nerve … again?'

'Your story will only serve to raise people's anxieties and, on that note, what the bloody hell possessed you to hint that we have a serial killer on the loose? We'll have vigilantes to contend with next – is that what you want? We have no …' Maggie stopped herself before she said anything further.

'You have no what?' Julie waited, but Maggie wasn't going to give her anything she could twist into a story.

'Don't push me, Julie. While I have you on the line,' Maggie paced the hall as she tried to calm herself down, 'can I offer a little advice?' Maggie didn't wait for a reply this time. 'Before you start spouting your mouth off, you should get your facts right.'

'Well why don't you tell me what I've got wrong and I'll be sure to update it in my next report?'

'I'm not pissing about here. Do you ever think of the victim's family or the unnecessary fear your sensationalistic bullshit raises? I thought you classed yourself as a journalist with integrity. Isn't that how you want people to see you, especially when you have the power to work with agencies to do some good? But noooo. Instead, you report fiction to get the juiciest story – like one of those rag papers … You should have been a crime writer not a news reporter.'

'Oooh ouch. Should I be offended by your rant? How about you use all that anger and energy towards finding the guilty party and leave **me** *to do* **my** *job?'*

Maggie was about to respond when she heard dead air. She threw her phone back into her bag. 'The bloody nerve!' she screeched.

Andy came running out into the hallway, his eyes wide. 'Hey. What's happened?'

'Argh. Sorry. I was just speaking to that reporter from the *Stafford Gazette* – that woman infuriates me.' Maggie's fists were clenched by her sides. She had to keep them there or she would be tempted to punch the wall, but she wasn't about to ruin her décor for Julie bloody Noble.

'Is that all?' He laughed. 'Dinner's ready. Go have a seat and you can tell me all about *that woman* as we eat.' He winked.

Maggie ignored the implications of the wink, and her mood changed for the better when she saw the dining room table. Andy had set the table using the plates he had bought her with his first pay cheque after he moved into the house. She ran her finger over the ridge of the plate. It was the little things that brought her back to earth when her anger levels rose. The plates were white with the Wonder Woman logo in the middle. Andy used to call her that when they were growing up because Maggie always looked out for everyone while trying to get through her own stuff. Sometimes she didn't know how she even kept going.

'So why are your knickers in a twist then?' Her brother knew her better than anyone and he wasn't wrong. Had it been any other reporter, Maggie wouldn't have let them get under her skin. But this one had, and Maggie didn't know what she wanted to do about it.

'I'm just pissed off that every time I think I've made some headway with Julie, she does something to really piss me off. I bumped into her earlier today at a café and she bought me a coffee. I'd kind of given her a lecture but … I don't know. I thought we had moved forward, I guess. Then I see the news and she must have known that would grate on me – but she didn't even warn me.' Maggie reached across and put some potatoes on her plate as her brother dished out the stew he had made.

'You have that look you used to get when you had a crush on someone. Sounds to me like you're really fond of this Julie.' Andy smiled. 'And it's about time you had a bit of fun. You work so hard, and I feel like a broken record but what's the harm in asking her out, unless she's straight?'

'No, she's not straight but that's beside the point. Have you heard anything I said? She gets on my nerves. She's always messing up my cases … and … and …' Maggie slumped. 'I think she's pretty clever, exciting and there's something about her that intrigues me. Okay. You may not be wrong.' She stuffed her dinner in her mouth before she said anything else. Maggie was tired of hiding her feelings all the time. There had been a spark the first time she had met Julie Noble and, although the journalist knew how to push her buttons, Maggie couldn't help how she felt. She took risks at work all the time – maybe she needed to do the same in her personal life.

Andy raised his hands in the air and cheered for himself. 'So, you'll ask her out?'

'Ask her out? Too soon for that … or … maybe I will, but not tonight – I need to calm down. I have a case to concentrate on and the timing just isn't right. How can someone so interesting be so infuriating at the same time? Don't answer that.' She laughed. 'Anyway, I promised Kate I'd call, and I'd rather hear about your holiday plans. Spill.' Maggie listened as her brother waffled on about places he wanted to go but her mind was definitely elsewhere.

A new case would be just the thing to focus on so that she

didn't have to deal with her own feelings – everything else would have to take a backseat for the time being.

Chapter Eleven

After dinner, Maggie settled herself on the couch while Andy went upstairs to search the web on her iPad for some holiday destinations for him and his friends. She hoped she could do the same in the not-so-distant future. Salem nestled beside her while Scrappy glared at him and Maggie from the chair opposite. 'There's plenty of room for you too, Scrapps. Don't be such a grump.' She patted a space beside herself, but he wouldn't budge. Her brother often joked with her that she and Scrappy had a similar personality. She couldn't see it herself though.

Maggie pulled out her mobile, swiped the number and waited as the phone rang at the opposite end. Hearing Kate's voice, she smiled.

'Hiya! I've got someone here who wants to say hello …' Maggie put the phone on speaker and held the device next to Salem. After Kate said a few words, Maggie returned the phone to her ear. 'You should see the eyes I am getting from Scrappy.'

'Ah bless. Thanks for that. I'm missing him madly. I know it hasn't been that long, but it feels like it has been ages since I've been able to snuggle with him. Anyway, it's great to hear your voice too. How's things?'

Maggie briefly updated Kate on the events of the day and the clash she had with Julie Noble earlier.

'Another case to keep you busy. As for Julie – I thought I noticed a spark there. Why not put aside the professional Maggie and spend some time focusing on your personal side? It's all work, work, work with you. I didn't want to say anything about Julie before because I know how you are about your private life.'

'Not you too!' Maggie sighed.

'Oh really? Who else agrees with me then?'

'Andy. He thinks I should ask her out. I mean do I even want a relationship? I'm not lonely – never have been. And work keeps me out for long hours.' Maggie tried to think of some more excuses before Kate used some logic and knocked her back.

'Why can't you just have a bit of fun? And by the way, a relationship isn't about filling a void of loneliness you know. You can be perfectly happy but want someone else to share your life with. You've always struck me as the type of person who won't pursue anything unless you felt there may be a future in it.'

'You know, I sometimes hate how good you are at reading people.' Maggie's lip curled. 'But with a new case, and Julie's bloody news reports – the woman can't separate fiction from fact – I don't think now is the right time to even go there.'

'It's far easier to see things in others, and I'd be shite at my job if I couldn't read people, wouldn't I? You'll always have an excuse. Just bite the bullet and go for it.'

'If I say okay, can we drop it and talk about something else?

How have you been?' Maggie tried to hide how annoyed she was that both her brother and Kate seemed to know more about what she should do than she did. Once again, she was allowing negative thoughts to invade her head – her father sitting on her shoulder reminding her that two women being together is wrong. She knew that people wouldn't understand why she cared so much, but she did. She wanted her father to be proud of her. Maggie shook her head and listened as Kate directed the conversation to the investigation.

'Can you tell me any more about the new case?'

Maggie noticed how quickly Kate ignored the question about how she had been. As much as she wanted Kate back in Stafford, she knew it had to be in her own time. The fact that she was interested in discussing the case could be taken as a good sign, but Maggie wouldn't push her.

'A teenager was found with head injuries at Castle Bank Industrial Estate. Looks like it could be a robbery that went wrong, as the victim had no phone, wallet, or ID on him, and the suspected weapon was left at the scene. Hopefully forensics will find some prints and it will be an open-and-shut case.'

'Without knowing more specific details, I'd agree from what you said. Probably of similar age. As soon as you started talking, I remembered that there had been a spate of those type of robberies in Markston. Might be worth calling the Integrated Offender Management Unit and make some comparisons.'

'Oh really?' Maggie paused. 'Do you recall how long ago they were?'

'I'd say a couple of months, maybe a little more, but don't quote me on that. My memory still needs a bit of work.'

'Thanks for the tip. I'll give them a call and run it by

Nathan tomorrow. Before I forget, seems DCI Hastings has gone AWOL. Rutherford says he's off sick, but something about her caginess doesn't sit right with me.'

'Well, that is curious. Maybe he is genuinely sick but asked her not to say anything; it could be more serious than a cold. Hey! Didn't you say you were going over to Lucy's tonight? Please say hello to everyone for me.'

'I was but she said there was something happening at the haven and we'd catch up later. To be honest, I'm a bit shattered anyway, so it probably worked out for the best. Think I'll go have a hot bath and crash. We'll speak soon.' Maggie ended the call.

Before heading for the bath, Maggie sent Lucy a quick text to make sure everything was okay. Lucy sent her a thumbs-up emoji and then wrote:

Will catch you up later. X Luce

Maggie wasn't going to pretend she wasn't relieved. Right now, all she wanted was the bath and her bed.

DI Rutherford had asked them all to come in early and she wanted to make sure she was well rested.

Her gut was screaming at her and she just wished it would shut the hell up. They had barely moved on from the last case – she didn't need another one on her plate so soon.

Chapter Twelve

Lucy woke with a start and rubbed her neck. Her phone bleeped and she reached across and grabbed it off the side table. The nightmares about her abusive ex-husband, Patrick, still hadn't stopped but at least they weren't every night any more.

She looked at her phone. Three new messages and they were all from PC Mark Fielding.

Mark was always checking up on Lucy, not as a police officer but as her friend; she had been keeping him at arm's length despite her feelings. It was still too soon – too raw – but one day she knew that her emotional scars would heal, and she hoped that Mark would still be in her life. She smiled when she opened each message and cursed herself for not getting back to him sooner. He'd probably been worried all night. She fired a quick text back to let him know she was fine and mentioned she'd call him later to update him. She wanted to speak to him anyway to see if there had been any DV call outs in the area over the last few days. It may help in putting together Ronnie's story without having to press her for information. Ronnie's complete denial was concerning but not uncommon, and Lucy wouldn't be the one to push her over the edge. When Ronnie was ready, she would talk.

It was still early, and Lucy wanted to be dressed and ready before Ronnie woke up. She looked over at her, tossing around but still asleep. Lucy could easily imagine what she was thinking about. She shuddered. Lucy wouldn't let any more memories of her ex-husband invade her thoughts today.

Lucy stood and crept out of the communal lounge. Her own room was on this main floor and she went in, grabbed a T-shirt, cardigan, and a pair a jeans from her wardrobe and threw them on before heading into the kitchen. She filled up the coffee maker and waited as the smell of fresh brewed coffee teased her nostrils.

The creak of the floorboard just outside the kitchen door alerted her to the fact that her guest was up. Lucy couldn't help but wonder *who* was she running from? As concerned as Lucy was for Ronnie, she couldn't deny that she was also concerned about the abuser coming to the haven. Yes, she had panic alarms everywhere, but that didn't mean the police would arrive in time if someone came around to finish what they had started. She shook the thoughts from her head, as the only way the haven address would be known would be if a person was referred by an agency and she wasn't accepting referrals for men at the moment. She still had some work to do in that area.

Lucy remained straight-faced despite her shock at seeing Ronnie when she walked through the kitchen door. The bruises on her face, her fat lip, and cut arms brought Lucy back to a place she didn't want to be. A horrible thought came to her then.

Had she been too ambitious in opening the haven when her own experience of domestic abuse still bobbed on the surface of her mind?

Ronnie waved weakly, and her eyes quickly averted to the floor.

Lucy removed her cardigan and draped it over Ronnie's shoulders. 'Here, take this – I'll get another one. Help yourself to some coffee. I'll be back in a minute.'

Lucy watched as Ronnie pulled her arms through the sweater and wrapped the belt around her. There was something peculiar about the girl's demeanour, but Lucy cast her suspicions aside and put it down to whatever it was Ronnie had just experienced. Lucy ignored the little alarm ringing in the back of her head.

I just can't put my finger on what it is ...

She shuffled back to her room, rubbing her neck because it was still sore from sleeping on the small two-seater, and she grabbed her hoodie off the back of the door. When she returned to the kitchen, Lucy sat across from the girl and smiled.

'My friend, Vicki, will be here shortly. She'll be working here when I finally get this place open, and I know she wouldn't mind me telling you but she had a very traumatic background too. Abusive partners. Drug and alcohol issues.' Lucy admired how far Vicki had come in the last year.

The woman's eyes widened, and she got up to leave. Lucy reached out and gently grabbed her hand.

'Hey, there's no need to run off. Vicki won't bother you. I just wanted you to know so you aren't surprised when she arrives, in case I'm not around. I promise. But if you did want to speak to someone, she's a very good listener. And if you want to go out, get some fresh air or anything, you're free to – don't feel you have to hide away. All I'd ask is that you take one of the haven's mobile phones, so that if you get lost you can call – the number for the house is stored in the phone and I can come get you. My personal mobile number is also there. Okay?' Lucy let go of her hand, and she sat back down but wouldn't look at Lucy and she took that as her cue.

'I'm going to jump in the shower; the hot water may help this crick in my neck.' Lucy tapped Ronnie on the shoulder. 'Will you be okay if I leave you for a bit?'

Ronnie nodded, and Lucy returned to her room. She unplugged her mobile and sent a quick text to Vicki to explain the situation.

Thanks for the heads-up. I'll tread carefully.

I should be there in a minute or two. X Vicki

Lucy smiled. Hiring Vicki was a great decision. Although Lucy had personal experience as a domestic abuse survivor, she was still a Probation Officer and those who came to the haven for help would always feel reluctant in case Lucy broke their confidence. One of the rules to stay at the haven was that there was a possibility that police or other agencies would be contacted if any staff member felt that either the person, the public, children or someone else was at risk of serious harm.

Lucy heard the front door open.

'I'm here, Luce! Thought I would check the emails – then grab myself a coffee,' Vicki called out.

'Just jumping in the shower. I won't be long!' Lucy smiled.

She didn't like the idea of leaving Ronnie alone for too long – that's when a person's thoughts could consume them. Vicki would make her feel at ease soon enough.

When Lucy had finished her shower, she walked into the office and saw Vicki's crutches against the wall. She sat in the spare seat beside Vicki and gave her an update on Ronnie's situation.

'Sounds like she's had a horrendous experience, but she'll open up when she's ready. You know how this works.' Vicki squeezed Lucy's arm.

Movement in the kitchen caught their eye on the video monitor. They watched as Ronnie walked to the sink, flicked the kettle on, and stared out the window. When the steam came out of the spout, Ronnie picked up the kettle and then poured the boiling water on her arm.

What the hell?

Ronnie didn't even flinch. It was like she didn't feel any pain. She placed the kettle back, used a tea towel to dry her arm, and covered it up with the sleeve of the cardigan. Vicki turned and looked at Lucy. They waited until they saw Ronnie leave the kitchen, and Lucy stood and headed to the kitchen.

Maybe I was wrong.

At the counter she touched the kettle.

Ouch!

She sucked her index finger and turned on the cold tap, holding the sore digit beneath the running water. Lucy looked up at the camera and raised a brow. She knew Vicki would be watching.

Lucy returned to the office. 'I had my suspicions about self-harming, but I wasn't sure. I'm going to leave some bandages and cream in her room. In case she needs them—'

Vicki stopped her.

'I don't think you should. She'll feel like we're spying on her. Maybe just tell her where things are, like an induction to the haven. Then she'll still feel like she is in a safe place. If it were me, that's what I'd want.' Vicki shrugged.

'You're right. I'll do that. By the way, can you leave one of the resident mobiles by the door with a spare set of keys? I told her she was free to come and go – I think if she feels confident enough to go out and about, she might be ready to open up soon. I've got to contact the DAHU and do some work for Probation. I'll be in my room if you need me, okay?'

Vicki nodded. Lucy needed to know more about Ronnie's background, and if the woman wouldn't tell her, there might be something in the system that could.

Chapter Thirteen

Maggie observed the faces of her colleagues in the incident room as DI Rutherford waited for everyone to find their seats. They'd been told earlier that though forensics had been working around the clock to ID their victim, their findings had been confirmed when the parents of a missing teen called in after seeing the reports on the news. According to Rutherford, the initial description of the young man had matched, and the parents advised he hadn't been seen since early Friday morning, which fit their timeline. Maggie hated to admit it, but Julie's report may have helped them identify the victim sooner than they would have otherwise.

When Dr Fiona Blake had arrived at the office earlier, Maggie had tried to get some hints about what she would be discussing, but unusually the forensic pathologist kept quiet. Not even offering a small morsel of information for Maggie to mull over. Maggie wished she would just get over whatever grudge she was holding about the police questioning Charlie when Kate's stalker had been still unknown. It irked her that Fiona couldn't see that the evidence they had at the time fit Charlie – they were just doing their job and she would have done the same if the shoe were on the other foot.

When the room quieted, DI Rutherford cleared her throat. 'Thank you all for coming in when I know some of you were scheduled to be off. Dr Blake wanted to be here today to go through her initial findings and give feedback to you all directly. I'd ask that you listen to what she has to say first and at the end, she'll gladly answer any of your questions. As you can imagine, she's very busy so we don't want to hold her up any longer than necessary.' DI Rutherford then nodded at the pathologist before leaving the room.

Dr Blake took the floor.

'Good morning, all. I always find that going through my findings first-hand saves a lot of time and although this is not always possible, on this occasion, in the hopes of a swift resolution, I thought we'd all benefit. So, I'll go through everything my team and I have done. As you can imagine, I'm shattered so the quicker I can get through this, the better.' She looked around the room before continuing.

'As some of you are not familiar with the processes my team and I go through, I'll talk you through it from beginning to end, starting with the arrival of the body at my lab in Staffordshire Police HQ. As per normal practice, we took photographs of everything in situ – and then Charlie searched through the body bag for any trace evidence. For anyone who doesn't know Charlie,' she shot Maggie a look, 'he assists me in the lab, and you may have come across him at crime scenes.'

Dr Blake opened the laptop in front of her and a presentation appeared on the screen. There seemed to be a mix of the actual crime scene pictures as well as photos of what she had just been discussing.

'Next step.' She pressed the clicker and a new slide appeared. There were a few gasps in the room – the image before the team was not something they were used to seeing on a Sunday morning. 'Sorry. Perhaps I should have warned you first.' Maggie was sure she saw a sly smile creep across the pathologist's face. 'After I removed the clothes of the male vic, more photos were taken.' She flicked through a few more slides. 'And the evidence collected was bagged and documented. Biological samples were taken from his hair; we scraped the fingernails and swabbed the head wounds. After this, we took his fingerprints.'

'Sorry for interrupting.' Kat waved to get the pathologist's attention. 'I may be jumping the gun, but you haven't said anything about the marks on his face – kinda looked like a triangle.'

Dr Blake reached into the case she had brought with her and pulled out a handful of small booklets. 'I was going to pass these around at the end, but since DC Everett has raised the query despite what was asked at the start …' she glared at Kat, 'I may as well pass them around now. It's just a summary of what I'll be talking through today. The final report will be sent to your DI.' Dr Blake waited until the booklets were distributed before continuing. 'The facial markings were made from a black permanent marker – like a Sharpie. I have no idea what they mean – one of my colleagues wondered if it had to do with gangs? But that will be up to you to determine.' The pathologist fiddled with her earring before continuing.

Gangs! That's what had been bothering Maggie at the crime scene. She was sure she had seen those markings before but there was definitely something different about the one on the victim. She made a mental note to follow this up and returned her attention to the pathologist.

'All scars, birthmarks, and any unusual physical features were documented. It was because of this and after returning a call to the parents who rang in about their missing son that we now believe that our victim's name is Timothy Griffiths. We're still waiting for the fingerprint confirmation but we're fairly certain based on what the parents told us.' She shook her head. It was never easy to speak to parents of missing children when a body turns up. 'When we asked if Timothy had any markings on his face, possibly something he had done to himself, they confirmed that when he left the house Friday morning for college, there was nothing there other than a smile.' Dr Blake poured herself some water and took a few sips before she carried on.

Dr Blake walked over to the enlarged photo and pointed at the screen. 'I inspected the neck, looking for broken cartilage which might indicate strangulation, but there were no signs of this.' Maggie thought the pathologist looked pleased with herself and wondered if this was a bit of payback for the Charlie incident.

'My initial findings are that this was a young, healthy male who didn't appear to have an ongoing health issue that contributed to this death.'

'Sorry to interrupt, but did the parents tell you the age of Timothy?' Maggie waited for the sarcastic answer to come. But Dr Blake surprised her.

'Yes, he was eighteen. A few months shy of his nineteenth birthday, actually … and he preferred being called Tim.' She turned back to the screen, brought up another morbid picture, and continued. 'Based on the preliminary findings, I think it is safe to say that the head trauma, caused by a blunt object – possibly the hammer, which was found in situ – was the cause of death. It was a slow death, unfortunately. The injuries caused a slow internal bleed. The first blow to the back of the head, had he been found earlier, may have left him with some serious but nonfatal injuries. However, the second blow to the front caved in his skull and, after dragging himself out of the woods, he bled to death. Now, time of death is never something I like to guess on, but in my opinion, he could have been struck anytime between 2pm and 8pm on Friday. He probably drifted in and out of consciousness before he was eventually found by that security guard. By then, it was already too late.' She looked past them all at the back wall. For someone who spent most of her time around dead people, it was clear that Dr Blake was still affected by the deaths that came across her table. For Maggie, young victims were always harder to deal with, so much life ahead of them. Death was never easy to accept but when a person had lived a good, full life, you felt a little less emotional – at least that's how Maggie felt.

Back in work mode, the pathologist continued. 'And there you have it. Any thoughts, ideas, or theories on who may be responsible? Although I usually leave the detective work to you, the experts, I think it would be valuable if we pool our ideas about what looks suspicious or needs to be followed up and fed back into the inquiry. I can answer the pathology side of anything you come up with now or we can chat later when you've had time to digest everything.'

Maggie smiled. She liked this addition to their briefing and hoped it was something that would become a regular occurrence. It seemed that her suggestion of having more multiagency involvement in their investigations was being listened to by DI Rutherford.

The room was silent.

'Why don't I leave you all to process what I've said and once all the reports are back from the other experts, I'll add it to my own findings for the coroner; DI Rutherford has left an open invitation for me to attend these briefings, so we can discuss it all then.'

Nathan stood and thanked Dr Blake for attending. As she packed up, he spoke to the team. 'Right, so there's some food for thought. I'd like you all to go away, make sure you cross-reference what was discussed today with everything already on the system, and come back tomorrow with some focused lines of enquiry. We can bring some peace to Tim Griffiths's family as quickly as possible. The Family Liaison Officer is going over there today, and I believe …' He glanced at Dr Blake and she nodded. 'We should have more information by the time you all return tomorrow.'

The robbery theory leapt out at Maggie, still a strong possibility, but what else could have been at play here? Maggie had been to so many similar crime scenes of this kind – something else niggled at her brain. The black dots on Tim Griffiths's face – four dots – what did they mean?

Chapter Fourteen

Maggie had collapsed when she got home on Sunday evening and when she woke up, her body felt like she had been through an assault course. Although she didn't feel stressed, the aches were an indication of the pressure she was already feeling. She used the train ride into work to get into the right headspace.

She hated Mondays, especially ones which meant she had to be in the office before the sun rose. Lately, she didn't feel she had had any time to recharge herself and vowed that once this case was over, she would take a leaf out of her brother's book and organize a holiday. She still hadn't got back to her parents when they asked if she would be visiting anytime soon. A trip to Glasgow might be just what she needed. As Maggie took out her phone to set a reminder to call her parents, DI Rutherford stormed into the open-plan office and called out. 'Nathan! Maggie! In my office.'

'Be right there, guv. I'm just—' Maggie turned to face her boss.

'Did I not make myself clear? My office – now!' The DI turned on her heels and stalked out of the room.

Maggie gathered her notebook; the look on their guv's face hinted that she wanted them for more than just a casual discussion about the weather.

'Do you have any clue what this is about?' Maggie followed Nathan down the corridor.

'Wish I did. She seem pissed off or am I just being paranoid?' He stopped and turned to Maggie. 'Have you done something I need to be aware of?'

'No!' *The bloody cheek.* Maggie wasn't sure if Nathan was being serious or joking, but there was no time to ask as the pair arrived at their DI's office.

Nathan tapped on the door.

'Come in,' DI Rutherford growled.

Maggie stepped in behind Nathan and the pair stood in front of Rutherford's desk waiting to see what she next barked their way.

'Have a seat.' DI Rutherford's tone had softened as she pointed at the chairs. 'You're going to need one after you hear what I've got to tell you.'

Maggie sat and looked between Nathan and DI Rutherford. The silence was deafening.

'Bear with me. I'm not exactly sure where to begin – it's a highly sensitive situation.' DI Rutherford took a sip of water. 'Argh. I'll just come out with it and, Maggie, the reason I'm including you in this conversation before I speak to the team, is because we've all worked with DCI Hastings the longest, so I wanted you to be prepared, okay?'

Maggie looked at Nathan before returning her attention back to Rutherford – it must be something big.

'We believe that DCI Hastings, his wife, and his daughter have been abducted. Two officers attended his home early this morning after he failed to show up for work or answer any calls for the last few days. The officers knocked on the door and when there was no answer, despite the DCI's car being in the drive, they walked around the property. At the back of the house, they noticed a broken window and the back door was found to be insecure. They called it in and were advised to proceed into the house. Upon entering the property, they noticed some drops of blood on the floor and shouted out to the family. When they got no answer, they grew concerned about the safety of the DCI and his family. They proceeded through the rooms and happened across a large pool of blood in Hastings's home office … they then called for backup.' DI Rutherford paused, no doubt to let everything sink in.

Maggie rested her hand. She had been taking notes as Rutherford spoke and her hand felt like it was on fire.

'Furniture in the living room was in disarray. More blood was seen on the carpet. The officers searched the whole property and the DCI and his family were not there. Mrs Hastings's purse was found, along with the DCI's mobile phone, but their daughter's mobile phone was missing. We're trying to locate that now.' Rutherford rubbed her forehead. 'It's not looking good … okay, any questions?'

Maggie never handled news of this kind well. Her heart was racing but her head immediately jumped into work mode. Before Nathan could open his mouth, Maggie jumped straight in. 'Has there been any contact from the kidnappers, any ransom demands made?'

'Nothing. Nathan? Your thoughts?' The DI turned to him and waited.

'I'm a little lost for words, guv. I mean.' He took a breath and held it. 'I'm actually still trying to process all of this. I take it we're waiting for the forensics on the blood?'

'Yes, they are still processing the scene, and although Dr Blake has been made aware that we need the information urgently, she won't have anything for a little while at least – even with everything being expedited. We're hoping that the drops of blood on the back entrance window is from the perpetrator, rather than residual splatter from the Hastings family.' Rutherford rested her hands on the desk.

The enormity of the situation sank in.

'I know you have a murder investigation ongoing, but this will need equal priority and we'll have to figure out how best to manage that.' She looked at Nathan.

'We'll manage, ma'am.' Nathan twisted the wedding band on his finger. Maggie looked at him and cocked her head. She wondered if he had some sort of secret plan she wasn't aware of, as they struggled enough as it was without the addition of another serious case on their workload – especially one that really should be with the Misper Unit.

'Forgive me, guv, but wouldn't it be better to have a separate team investigating the possible abduction? We are thin enough on the ground as is and as you've said, this isn't an actual murder investigation ...' She looked at Nathan for some sort of backup which didn't seem forthcoming. After overhearing rumblings about her own and the team's involvement in the Living Doll Killer case, in which the killer had targeted Dr Moloney, Maggie worried that they may be too close to DCI Hastings to remain completely objective. She normally wouldn't be bothered by this, but she had worked with DCI Hastings since starting in the MOCD over ten years ago and her fear about what could have happened had her wanting to be as far away from the case as possible.

'Ah yes. Let me just wave my magic wand and conjure up another team, shall I?' DI Rutherford rolled her eyes. 'Where is this other team you speak of going to come from?'

Maggie felt her face flush. 'Perhaps the field team … or the Misper Unit would be more appropriate.'

'I think you've said enough on the subject. We don't have another team, and this is our DCI who has gone missing. We'll have to divide the time between the two cases. At the moment, we don't really know what has happened with the Hastings family, so until we do, we're stuck with the resources that are available. If …' The DI coughed. '*When* more information becomes available, I'll speak to whoever they get around to putting in charge and see what we can get – given it's a police officer, I suspect they will be able to support us.'

Rutherford was right. With a high-ranking officer missing, it was likely that all stops would be pulled and the resources they required to ensure a swift result would be forthcoming.

Maggie excused herself and left DI Rutherford and DS Wright to iron out the details. She needed to be out of that room, as her head was pounding.

What had happened to DCI Hastings and his family?

Chapter Fifteen

An hour had passed since Maggie had left the guv and Nathan. In that time, Kat had spoken to the two security guards and found out that one had been ill – food poisoning – and she'd be in to leave the details of her visit to A&E. The other guard, it turned out, had found a job somewhere else. He emailed over the details, which Bethany checked and confirmed to be true. So that cleared up those questions.

Meanwhile, Maggie had followed up on her earlier email to Markston Police Station and spoke with PC Pete Reynolds. Pete had been new to the DAHU when Maggie was temporarily seconded to the unit and now found himself splitting his time between the Neighbourhood Policing Team (NPT) and the DAHU.

'Thanks for getting back to me so quickly. Can you tell me anything about the street robberies that have been occurring?' Maggie grabbed a pen to jot down any details.

'Yeah, though not sure it will be helpful. We had a spate of street robberies a few months back. Random youths held at knife point and robbed of mobile phones and anything else of value that could be carried there and then. We caught the little shits a few weeks back. Sorry.'

'Well at least you caught them. To be honest, I wasn't fully convinced of the robbery angle, but at least I can tell the team that your fellas hadn't moved over our way. We might just have a new crew … Anyway, take care.' She updated the system and would park the information for now.

Everyone was gathering their things and heading to the incident room. Maggie followed suit.

She sat next to Kat and tapped her pen on the table – the silence was making her conjure up sinister thoughts of what had actually happened to the Hastings family. It could all be something innocent – maybe he just needed time away, fed up with things. He may be their DCI but they all felt that way from time to time. But something told her that wasn't the case, and although Maggie was still reeling from the bombshell that Rutherford had dropped earlier, she needed to bury those feelings for the time being. She didn't want the rest of the team to wonder if Rutherford and Nathan had been playing favourites, so she'd act like she was hearing the news for the first time if Rutherford shared it here today.

Recalling the guv's behaviour before, Maggie accepted that her boss blew hot and cold with her at the best of times, but when she was stressed, Maggie often felt the repercussions of her frustration. She tried not to take it personally and had to control herself on more than one occasion from telling her boss to just fuck right off, though she suspected many felt the same about her. What she liked about her team, despite the ranks, was that everyone had the opportunity to speak their minds. Maggie wondered if there was something else going on behind the scenes with Rutherford that she wasn't aware of. She was disrupted from her thoughts when the guv and Nathan walked in and stood in front of the room.

'I know you're all busy, but we have another ... erm, situation and it has to be dealt with sensitively ...' DI Rutherford paused and Maggie's initial annoyance at her soon softened. The guv's face said it all. This situation would just add to the stress that Rutherford was already feeling.

'In a nutshell, DCI Hastings and his family are missing under suspicious circumstances.' There was a noticeable intake of breath from her colleagues in the room.

Kat tapped Maggie's arm and whispered: 'What the fuck? Did you know about this?'

Maggie feigned surprise and raised a finger to her lips, pointing back to the front of the room. She ignored the fact that Kat continued to stare at her.

'I'll tell you what we know so far before Nathan goes over the details of your current murder investigation. Let me get through this without any interruptions and then feel free to ask what you need to – though I'm not sure I'll be able to give any definitive answers.'

The team nodded and whispered amongst each other.

'Can I have your full attention, please?' DI Rutherford waited as the last few mumbles subsided. Maggie listened as Rutherford relayed the same details to the rest of the team that she had learned earlier.

'This needs to be kept within these four walls for the time being. I thought it was important for you all to be aware. I'll hand you over to Nathan now, but I can't stress this enough – if you do have any information that you think may be helpful in finding the Hastings or you hear anything while you're out making your rounds in the community, make sure you inform me immediately.' Rutherford handed the floor to Nathan and left as quickly as she had arrived.

'I know that was a lot to take in but let's switch the focus to our current murder investigation and look at what we have so far: We've had formal confirmation that our victim is Tim Griffiths, aged eighteen years. Maggie and Kat have been tasked to speak with his parents and will update us on anything significant from that as soon as the information is available. The hammer that was found beside Tim, Dr Blake has confirmed this is the murder weapon after matching the injuries. We're awaiting the results from the trace evidence on the hammer itself. It looks like Tim may have fought with his attacker. He had swollen and scraped knuckles, so we're hopeful that forensics will find something that may identify our killer. Bethany is trawling through CCTV – maybe that will bring some further news by the end of the day.'

Maggie waved to get Nathan's attention. 'Can I have a word?' Nathan nodded and Maggie waited as the room began to clear.

'Would it be possible for me to stop by the Hastings's home once finished with the Griffiths?'

'Why?' Nathan was gathering his notes.

'I'd just like to see the scene as is. You know what I'm like.'

He scratched his chin. 'Okay – but make sure you don't rush your time with the Griffiths to get over there. Am I clear?'

'Got it. Thanks.'

Maggie waved Kat over. 'Let's grab the address from Bethany and head over to speak to Tim's parents.'

Chapter Sixteen

Lucy was desperate to speak with Mark at the DAHU to see if he could find out any more information on Ronnie, but in order to do that, she would need more details. She knew that this was a fragile time for the young woman, so had to be careful. Ronnie had let her know that she was thinking about going out into the town and Lucy thought that was a good sign, so now might be the right time.

When Lucy had gone upstairs, Ronnie was not in her room or anywhere else on that floor. Lucy returned downstairs and went through each of the rooms until she finally caught sight of Ronnie walking the perimeter of the back gardens. Every now and again, Ronnie peered into the windows of the outbuildings which would later be the residential space for any male victims referred to the haven. She had on a pair of dark sunglasses and a thick, long sleeve jumper much larger than her actual size. She must have brought these items with her in that satchel she had arrived with. Lucy cringed. Ronnie's wardrobe was familiar to her, as it was how Lucy would dress after a particularly harsh beating from Patrick. Eyes covered, arms covered, oversized clothes – to hide the bruises and avoid tight clothing chafing any wounds.

Lucy opened the back door and called out. Ronnie stopped and for a moment Lucy thought that she might have heard her as the young woman had said that she had partial hearing with her aids in, but that thought was short-lived when she didn't respond. Lucy realized that she would need to go over to her, so she pulled on the boots she left by the back door and walked over the damp grass to speak to Ronnie.

Tapping her on the shoulder, Lucy wasn't surprised when the girl jumped. 'Sorry. I called out to you, but obviously your hearing aids must be turned down, as you didn't hear me.' Lucy smiled. 'I wondered if we could have a quick chat before you go into town?' When Ronnie agreed, Lucy turned and gestured for the woman to follow her back into the kitchen.

They sat on the small couch in the spacious kitchen, and Lucy watched as Ronnie took out her mobile phone – she had one of those text-to-speech apps that she had been using to communicate.

'You're looking much better today. How do you feel?' Lucy crossed her legs.

Ronnie began to type. *'Okay. I feel like I need to get out though. I took the residents' phone and spare set of keys you left for me. I hope that's okay? Vicki gave me information on the buses, and I thought I might pop into town.'*

'Of course. You're not a prisoner here.' The woman looked down and Lucy realized her choice of words was probably not the greatest. 'Sorry. Sometimes I put my foot in my mouth. As long as you feel ready to go out, I think that's great. How are your injuries?' Ronnie had a large cut on her arm which the paramedics had treated but advised Lucy to keep an eye on it so that it didn't get infected.

Ronnie began typing and when she had finished, she stared ahead as Lucy listened.

'Still sore, but I'm using the antibiotic cream. I know you want me to talk about what happened, but I don't feel ready to do that just yet. You'll only go digging and then he'll find me. He did that before when I went to the police. I will tell you that I'm not from Staffordshire, but someone at the last refuge I was at mentioned seeing you talk about this place after you had been released. I knew you'd understand, and she gave me the details. Don't ask about her either, as I won't grass her up.'

Ronnie was getting agitated. Lucy saw her eyes well up and she began tugging on her sleeves.

'Okay, hun. I want you to trust that my only interest is to protect you and keep you safe. When you're ready, I'm here for you and I'll keep reminding you of that. I know how hard it can be to open up to others. How about you go and get ready – I could drop you into town if you want?'

Ronnie shook her head. Lucy understood that she would still want her independence. She then put her phone in her bag and her demeanour changed; her shoulders loosened, and she looked relieved.

'The code for the gate is on the phone – under S.A.F.E, okay. I'm making a roast dinner for later so keep your appetite.' Lucy winked. She reached into her pocket and pulled out a bus scratch card which would let Ronnie travel around the local area for the day. The Police and Crime Commissioner had provided these to the refuge when Lucy had applied for some funding. 'You can use this all day. Follow me.' Lucy walked to the office and opened the safe.

'Here's a bit of spending money if you want a coffee or something.'

Ronnie pulled away, shaking her head.

'It's okay. Think of it as an emergency fund. You don't have to use it, but I'd hate for you not to take it and then feel stuck.' She held the ten pound note out, and Ronnie took it and placed it in her back pocket.

Lucy watched her leave. She felt nervous for Ronnie, though if what Ronnie said was true, she was far enough away from her abuser to not be worried at this stage. Problem was, Lucy wasn't sure what she believed at the moment.

Chapter Seventeen

Maggie stared out the window and collected her thoughts as Kat drove towards Tim Griffiths's home. Visiting a victim's home was one part of the job she hated, as emotions were understandably high, and she had to admit that sometimes she struggled to get the right words out – seeking the facts while remaining sympathetic when it came to how she asked questions. Not intentional but it did happen. Nathan had confirmed that a Family Liaison Officer (FLO) had been assigned to the family and would be waiting for them when they arrived. As they pulled up to the Millwood Estate, Kat shuddered.

'What's the matter?' Maggie turned to face her colleague.

'I grew up around here and it's not the best place to live. Drugs, alcohol, little shits with big mouths. Brings back bad memories.'

The detective frowned. 'But you turned out okay, so it can't be all that bad – well, minus that mouth of yours that is.' Maggie nudged Kat's arm and winked.

'Cheeky cow!' Kat laughed. 'Which block of flats did Tim live in then?'

Maggie pointed to the one on the far right. 'Ford House. Third floor. Flat 308.'

'Can I suggest we take the stairs instead of the lift? If my memory serves me correctly, the lifts were always covered in piss or puke. The stairs might not be much better, but at least we're not stuck in a small space.'

'Sounds like a plan to me.'

They exited the vehicle. There was a small gang of youths – both male and female – in the distance and Maggie could hear them snorting like pigs. She noticed that Kat was about to shout out to them but raised her hand. 'Leave it. They might steer clear of our car if we don't antagonize them.'

Kat mumbled something under her breath, probably starting with a fuck and ending with little shits if Maggie had to guess. They radioed in to base to let Bethany know they were about to enter the building and, once inside, Maggie pushed the buzzer for Flat 308.

A gruff voice called out: *'Who is it?'*

'DC Jamieson and DC Everett. We're here to speak with Mr and Mrs Griffiths.'

The door buzzed, there was a popping sound, and Kat pulled it open. Maggie followed her to the stairwell, and the smell of urine hit their nostrils instantly. As they proceeded up the stairs, Maggie tried not to breathe in through her nose. Kat was right, the stairs weren't much better than the lift, with needles on the landing and a putrid smell that stung her eyes.

'For fucksake.' Kat gagged and used her sleeve to cover her mouth. Maggie did the same and followed Kat up the stairs.

A man in cut-off jogging bottoms and a stained white shirt

stood in the hallway outside Flat 308 and gestured to Maggie and Kat. 'Your mate's inside. You'll have to 'scuse the mess. The cleaners are off today.' He moved aside to allow the officers in.

'Are you Mr Griffiths?' Maggie looked at the man.

'Sure am. Name's Jack and my missus is Eileen. She's through there.' He pointed towards an open door. Maggie noticed the FLO in the kitchen area and waved. She'd speak to her once they were done.

Maggie led the way into the living room. Jack wasn't lying about it being a mess, but given the news the couple had received about their son, she could understand why cleaning was not the highest priority on their list of things to do.

'Would you mind if we had a seat and asked you a few questions?' Maggie smiled, but it felt wrong.

The woman looked up briefly and nodded. Her eyes were red and glassy. Maggie wondered how much of the interview she would be able to take part in.

'Thank you both. First, we're sorry for your loss and that we have to ask you questions at such a difficult time, but the sooner we do this part, the quicker we'll be able to catch whoever did this to your son.' Maggie waited to see if they responded, but Tim's parents just stared at her.

'Do either of you know if Tim had any trouble in the neighbourhood or with someone in particular recently?' Maggie watched as Kat prepared to note down their answers.

'He was always messing about, but no one had a bad word to say about our boy. Kindest heart. Probably too trusting if anything. Some of the arseholes around here took advantage of his generosity.' Mrs Griffiths reached for a tissue and dabbed her eyes.

'Could you explain what you mean by that?' Maggie leaned forwards; something was digging into her back and she didn't want to make it too obvious.

'Getting him to run their errands. Drugs – couldn't be anythin' else. When he', she pointed at Mr Griffiths, —'found out, he went round and had words. It soon stopped. Or at least we thought it had.' The woman reached across her husband and picked up a glass containing clear liquid. It could easily be mistaken for a glass of water, but Maggie suspected it was something of an alcoholic nature from the slight slur in Mrs Griffiths's response.

'Did Tim have anyone in particular he hung about with that we could speak to?' Maggie suspected they wouldn't get much out of this pair and it may be better to speak to his friends. How forthcoming they'd be was a different matter.

'He was attending a few college courses at South Staffordshire Academy but not sure who he hung about with there. He kept that side to himself – think he was embarrassed of where he come from,' Mr Griffiths offered. 'You could try the group of kids who are in the courtyard out front. Tim hung about with them sometimes. They liked the fact that an older kid took an interest in them. Don't you have any idea of who done this? I mean, what sicko smashes a boy's head in? If I find the person before you do, God …' Mrs Griffiths squeezed his knee, and he didn't finish the sentence.

'We understand your frustration, but we'll do everything we can to find out who did this to your son. Would you mind if my colleague and I took a look around his bedroom?' Maggie stood. She couldn't bear sitting on the chair any longer and when she glanced behind her, she realized she had been sitting on a pile of clothes with hangers still in them.

'What for? Your mates already done that – took his computer too. When will we get that back?' Mr Griffiths's leg shook. Maggie didn't want to agitate him further if she could help it.

'We want to get a feel for your son, really. His personality, likes, dislikes – see if anything was overlooked ... that sort of thing,' Kat offered. Maggie knew Kat was saying that to placate the couple, as she had no doubt that forensics would have picked up anything of relevance, but it often helped them understand the victim's background and get into their heads.

'Fine. It's the first door on the left. If you don't mind, I'd rather not be a part of whatever you're doing. I can't even go into Tim's room at the moment.' He rubbed his chin. 'Just too bloody much.' A tear rolled down his face and he turned away.

'We appreciate that. Thank you both. We'll just do that now and pop in here before we leave, in case you think of anything else.'

'Sure – do what you need to do.' Mr Griffiths turned the volume of the television up and stared at the screen. Maggie doubted he was taking in or even interested in the programme that was on; it was just a distraction so that he didn't have to deal with his son's murder.

The FLO returned to the room with a tray full of mugs and some biscuits. She placed them on the table and sat in the seat Maggie had just sat in. Unlike Maggie though, she pushed the clothes back so that the wire hangers wouldn't poke her in the back.

Maggie followed Kat down the hall.

'Bloody hell. I feel for those people but,' Kat looked over her shoulder, Maggie assumed to make sure the parents weren't in earshot, 'Mrs G is off her face and Mr G looks like a ticking time bomb.'

They opened the door to the room that Tim's father had directed them to. 'Let's not make assumptions about either parent at the moment. They'll be struggling with all the questions and people they are having to deal with while trying to come to terms with their grief.' Maggie had said that aloud just as much for her own benefit as Kat's. She recalled when she started out as a detective herself, she had often made assumptions which turned out to be wrong. Experience would see that Kat understood this, but while she worked in the MOCD, Maggie would make sure she helped her any way she could.

Maggie looked around Tim Griffiths's room. Typical of a young male – a few sports posters on the wall, clothes balled up on the floor, a TV and PlayStation were on the dresser, along with the usual grooming products Maggie expected to see. Maggie walked over to the closet and opened the door. More clothes on the floor, with very few items hung up. A pair of dress shoes that looked hardly worn. There was a full-length mirror on the inside of the closet door and, in the corner, a picture of Tim with a girl. 'Hey. Come look at this,' Maggie called Kat over.

'So, he had a girlfriend?' The picture only showed the back of the girl. Auburn hair hung past her shoulders and stopped just before her waistline. She wore a sweat top and a pair of cropped jeans. Black trainers adorned her feet.

'Is it me, or does it look like she purposely turned her face away from the camera? The parents didn't mention a girlfriend. In fact, the way they spoke of him, it sounded like he didn't have very many friends his own age. Maybe we'll get more from the college – we're due to speak to someone there tomorrow.' Maggie looked at the picture closely before taking it off the mirror. 'We'll ask if we can take this with us. Maybe this mystery girl is a student too.'

'Are we going back to the office now?' Kat looked at her watch. 'Only my stomach is telling me it's about lunch time and I'm not sure it's going to shut up.' Maggie laughed when Kat's stomach rumbled.

'We'll stop at the Greggs in the services on our way.' Maggie left the room and headed back to Mr and Mrs Griffiths.

When she popped her head in the living room, the couple hadn't moved. 'We're going to go now, but before we do, we found this picture on the mirror in Tim's room. Do either of you know who this young woman is?' Maggie walked over and held the picture out. Mrs Griffiths looked briefly and shook her head. Mr Griffiths took the picture from Maggie's hand and examined it more closely.

'No idea who she is. He never mentioned any lady friends. No girls have been here. Maybe she's from the college?' He handed the picture back to Maggie.

'Yes, we wondered that. Would you mind if we took this photo to ask when we go to his college? I'll make sure to keep it safe and bring it back as soon as I can.'

Mr Griffiths nodded. 'We don't have many pictures of Tim … please get it back to us.'

Maggie nodded, waved goodbye to the FLO and they left the parents to their grief.

It must be heartbreaking for a parent to say goodbye to their only child.

Chapter Eighteen

Before heading back to the station, Maggie asked Kat to drive over to DCI Hastings's house and gave her the directions.

'Does Nathan know about this?' Maggie thought she heard an edge in Kat's question. She couldn't expect Kat would want to be involved in doing anything outside of their remit after having just joined the team as a detective.

'Don't worry. I cleared it with him before we left.' Maggie winked and Kat's shoulders loosened. 'If you ever feel uncomfortable about doing anything though, just say the word.'

'Sorry, I don't mean to be such a by-the-book kinda person because I know sometimes you have to do things out of the ordinary to get results – well, not illegal of course but … I don't want you to think I wouldn't go above and beyond for the team.'

'No explanation needed. You need to do what feels right for you and question anything that doesn't. I respect that more than I would someone who felt that way and then ran to the boss telling tales. Anyway, I know how much you give to the job.' Maggie paused. 'Looks like we're here.'

Kat parked up and when they got out of the car, Maggie looked around and noticed that although the houses were scattered throughout the street, they were detached and there was a noticeable distance between them. A few of the houses also had high security walls or bunches of thick trees which shrouded them from street view. Hastings also had trees and it would be difficult to see anything from the road, though probably not impossible from the one house directly across the street. She parked that thought for the moment.

'Let's see what the scene can tell us.'

Maggie and Kat signed in with the crime scene manager, kitted up and headed in the front door.

Maggie looked at all the scene markers that the forensic officers had placed in the front room. The markers often painted a picture to determine when an individual died. Maggie cursed inwardly – no one has died … that they knew of. She needed to stop the negative thoughts and let the scene tell her what happened.

Kat walked off, leaving Maggie to focus on the room. The first marker was right inside the door at the uncollected mail and few newspapers that littered the floor. A quick glance told her that the post on the top was delivered on Friday, so she surmised that the earliest date the family could have been targeted was Thursday night; the other post was neatly placed on a rack below a mirror. The hall lights and a lamp in the front room was on. She stopped one of the forensics officers. 'Were the lights on when you arrived?'

He nodded.

Maggie also noticed that the coat rack was full. She recognized DCI Hastings's jacket from his comings and goings into the office. From this, she surmised that he and probably the rest of his family didn't go willingly – with the cool nights, they surely would have taken their coats.

Maggie kept on the stepping plates and walked towards the back of the house, through the dining area, and into the kitchen. A few dishes were left on the counter and the food was crusted over.

Maggie noted that the team would need to speak with the field officers to find out when the neighbours last saw DCI Hastings, his wife, and his daughter. It also just dawned on her that there weren't many, if any, photos of the family around the parts of the house she had seen, although this wasn't necessarily strange, as she herself only had one picture of her own family on a shelf in her office space. She remembered at an office party how proud Hastings was of his family – he almost pressed the issue so much that Maggie wished he had shut up at the time. Maybe the neighbours could shed some light. They might have noticed a change in the family's normal routines or habits, a strange vehicle in the neighbourhood. Anything that might give the police a clue as to what had happened in the house – it was like a murder scene without any bodies.

Maggie looked at her watch. It was getting late; they had spent longer at the scene than she had anticipated.

Maggie headed through the hall towards the upstairs, careful not to disrupt anyone or anything. She had clocked the broken window in the kitchen that DI Rutherford had mentioned and blood droplets in the living area and kitchen floor.

Kat called out: 'Maggie, I think there's something you'll want to see up here.'

She climbed the stairs and saw Kat standing in the doorway at the end of the landing. 'Look at this.' Kat stepped aside to let Maggie into the room. It was Hastings's home office.

'Where am I looking?' But she didn't need to wait for a reply, as the large pool of blood over on the far side of the room caught her eye. 'What the fuck?'

'That's exactly what I said. But look where it's located. Something is missing from that area.' Kat pointed at the floor. 'See how the blood seems to ... and excuse the pun ... bleed out right here. There must have been something against the wall.'

Maggie nodded. 'You're right. Someone was bleeding heavily. The DCI's office, it may well have been him.' She glanced at the floor. 'Something feels off though – no splatter anywhere else.'

'There's a few things that have been knocked over too – sign of a struggle.' Kat shuddered. 'I have a bad feeling about all of this.'

'Me too, Kat. Me too. Did you come across anything else noteworthy?'

'Most of the bedrooms look undisturbed. The beds were made, and nothing seems out of place. Though in the master bedroom it looks like a jewellery box was rifled through. Not sure how we'll tell if anything was stolen.'

'What a mess, eh? It's getting late. Let's wrap it up now and if you drop me off at the train station, I'll make my way from there. I'll text Nathan and let him know we'll be going to Tim's college tomorrow first thing, so can you pop round mine at around 8:15 and we can go from there.'

'Sounds like a plan.'

During the car ride to the train station, Kat was talking a mile a minute and Maggie had to stifle a laugh. She certainly was keen, but Maggie was grateful when she got on the train and it was dead silent. She used the time to go through everything from today and be ready for what tomorrow would bring.

Chapter Nineteen

The next morning, Maggie stood outside her house waiting for Kat to pick her up. She rubbed her eyes, having only had a few hours' sleep, as her brain took longer than normal to shut itself down. It was spitting rain now and she hoped Kat arrived soon, as she didn't want to have to dig through her bag, find her keys, and go back inside to get a brolly. A red car turned the corner and raced towards her, pulling up sharply. Maggie got in the car and mumbled, 'You're late,' as she buckled her seatbelt.

'I know. Sorry. The power in my building went out, my alarm didn't go off, and then I couldn't find my keys. At least nothing else should happen today, as they say bad luck comes in threes, right?' Kat pulled away from the kerb and headed towards the college.

'I bloody hope so. Things have become more complicated now and the sooner we figure out what's happened to Hastings and his family the better. It's all such a mess now.' Maggie felt her phone buzz in her pocket. She looked at the screen. 'Fuck.' Instead of answering the call, she sent it straight to answerphone.

'Guess that wasn't work?' Kat smiled, and Maggie's shoulders tightened. She should have just answered it, as Kat wasn't one to leave things alone.

'No, but I have no doubt it was about work. It was Julie Noble.' Maggie put her phone back in her pocket and a ping let her know there was a message waiting.

'The reporter from the *Stafford Gazette*? Why's she calling your personal phone?' Kat raised a brow.

Shit. Maggie hadn't clocked that before she had answered Kat's previous question and she wasn't going to lie ... But she didn't have to tell her the whole truth. 'Julie and I are ... I want to say friends but more like, we're friendly. For the moment, I'm doing my best to tolerate her, as she was a big help in the Living Doll case.' She hoped Kat would leave it at that.

'Gotcha. She's pretty persistent though – like a dog with a bone. If she has any inkling as to what is going on, you can bet your arse she'll be calling again.'

Maggie pursed her lips. Kat was right – but there was no way that Julie could know anything about the Hastings's situation, unless she really did have a contact in the police feeding her information.

'I think we should speak to the Head Teacher – actually, I think they call themselves Chief Executive Principals now – in the first instance and see if he or she is able to point us in the right direction. If Tim Griffiths was a troublemaker, they may know of him and who he associates with. If not, we can see if they will allow us to talk to a few of the students.' Maggie looked out the window. 'I wonder if the girl in the photo attends the college? It's weird that no one else has come forward about him, even to say they found it odd that they hadn't heard from him.' This idea had been playing on Maggie's mind. Usually in murder investigations, especially when it was reported on the news, the police were inundated with calls from members of the public offering their theories, or telling them they saw the victim, whether it was true or not. But there had been nothing in this case so far.

Kat pulled into the college car park. The massive building was surrounded by trees and a large expanse of greenery. Maggie picked her bag off the footwell and waited until Kat pulled into a space before she unbuckled the seatbelt and got out of the car. There were a few doors to choose from, but Kat pointed to the side of the building.

'That looks like the main entrance.' Maggie waited as Kat grabbed a notebook from the back seat of her car and the pair proceeded.

When they arrived in the reception area, Maggie identified herself and Kat and asked to speak to the Chief Executive Principal. They were told by the receptionist that the principal wasn't in, but she would see if the Deputy Chief Executive, Mr Dodd, was available. Maggie looked around while they waited.

Fifteen minutes had passed, and Maggie was getting annoyed – she'd had only one cup of coffee that morning. She'd need another soon or she might get snappy. Just as she was about to ring the bell on the counter, the door to their right opened and a nervous-looking man gestured for them to come through.

'So sorry for the delay. I wanted to get some information

together for you so I didn't have to keep you waiting and ended up keeping you waiting.' He jammed his hands in his pockets. 'If you'd just like to follow me to my office. Would either of you like some water or perhaps a coffee?' His eyes flitted between Maggie and Kat.

'I'd love a black coffee if you're making one.' Kat brushed passed Mr Dodd.

'I'll have a coffee too. Skim milk, no sugar, or black if you don't have that.' The offer was music to her ears.

Mr Dodd nodded and asked the receptionist to get the drinks, adding a tea to the order. 'Please, have a seat. I guess you're here about young Tim Griffiths. Nasty business that. Do you know who's responsible?'

Maggie shook her head. 'We'd like to know how Tim got on in college. Was he liked? Did he do well?' Maggie tapped Kat's knee and asked if she could jot down some notes. Kat had been distracted by the photos on the wall. She returned her attention to the room, ready to take down the details.

'Tim was never brought to my attention.' Mr Dodd cleared his throat. 'I looked through his records and spoke to some of his teachers after getting the call yesterday. They described him as quiet and said he got by in his classes. He wasn't a genius by any means, but he was passing. I got the impression he was a loner of sorts.' Mr Dodd closed the book in front of him.

Maggie took out the photo and placed it on the table. 'Do you recognize anyone in this picture?'

Mr Dodd pulled out a pair of glasses from his pocket and picked up the picture. 'Well, the boy looks like Tim; I saw pictures of him on the news.' He paused. 'I'm sorry. I don't know who the young lady with him is. Is she a student here?'

Before Maggie could respond, the receptionist came in and

placed the tray of drinks on the table. Maggie held out her hand to Mr Dodd and he passed her the photo back. 'Before you go, I wondered if you could help us identify who the people in this picture are?' She handed the photo to the woman.

The receptionist's lips turned down. 'That's Tim Griffiths.' She shot a glance at Mr Dodd before continuing. 'And I think the girl with him is Olivia – I'd recognize her hair anywhere. Those lovely red locks of hers. She was always in and out of here for one thing or another. I don't like to gossip, but … if I had to hazard a guess, I think Tim had a crush on her and she definitely used that to her advantage. They were like polar opposites, but he'd always try and take the blame for things that we're pretty sure she was responsible for. Don't you recognize her?' She passed the picture back to Mr Dodd. He looked again and shifted in his seat.

'Now that you say it, yes … yes I think you're right. It is Olivia, isn't it?' He examined the photo again. 'Yes, definitely her.' He placed the photo on the table and pushed it towards Maggie.

'Do you have a last name for Olivia?'

'Uh, yeah but I thought you might know her. Her father's a police officer at your station, I believe. That's Olivia Hastings.'

Chapter Twenty

Maggie stood. 'Can you excuse me for just a moment? I just need to make a call. My colleague will take some details from you about Olivia Hastings if you can gather that together for her?' She signalled to Kat, who nodded.

Out in the reception area, Maggie found a quiet spot in a corner and dialled Nathan's number.

'How are you getting on?' Nathan didn't even bother with a greeting; his voice had an edge to it, and she wouldn't waste his time.

'You could say that. We found a picture at the Griffiths's house yesterday. It was Tim and a young girl, with her back to the camera.'

'Yeah and …?' His shortness momentarily caught her off guard.

'Uh – we've had two members of staff advise that they believe the girl in the photo is Olivia Hastings.' Maggie paused to let the news sink in.

'Fuuuuuuck. DI Rutherford is going to go ballistic. Okay.

Okay. Okay. See if anyone else can verify that. I'll have Bethany continue to track down any of Hastings's relatives, though it's not looking good on that front. When his house was being searched, there didn't seem to be any contacts with family members and Rutherford said she recalls him mentioning he was estranged from them so … Shit! Shit! Shit! This is …' Nathan didn't finish the sentence.

'I know.' Maggie ran her hand through her hair. Once the media got a hold of this … 'When's the press conference?'

'Tomorrow morning. Finish up there as quick as you can, we've a lot on today – I'll see you when you get back.'

'Okay, boss.' Maggie ended the call and was heading back towards the deputy's office when a young man who had been sitting in the opposite corner of the room approached her.

'Are you the police?' He tugged at one of his sleeves.

'Yes. Can I help you with something?'

'You here 'bout Tim? Heard he was murdered. It was all over the news.'

'Did you know him?' Maggie wondered if the student would be able to shed some light on Olivia.

'Nah. I mean I seen him here a few times and at some parties, but he wasn't really one to mix with the crowd, you know what I mean? Liked to be on his own, except for Liv. He didn't mind her company at all.' A sly grin formed on his face.

'Liv? Do you mean Olivia Hastings?'

He shrugged his shoulders. 'I guess so. Don't know her last name, just that she was called Liv. Fiery, like that hair of hers. She was a bit of a weirdo but harmless. It was her eyes – she'd stare at you for ages. Guess they weren't bothered about talking to each other though, y'know what I mean?' Another grin adorned his face. Maggie would forgive his assumptions because most teenage boys assumed that if a girl and boy were friends, they must be doing more than swapping anecdotes.

'When was the last time you saw Olivia? Can you remember?'

'Nah. Coulda been a few days ago, or maybe weeks. She's in a few of my classes but seemed to be off a lot. She was pretty smart; probably thought she didn't need to attend classes.'

Maggie noted all the information down and took the young man's details. She reached into her pocket and took out a card. 'If you remember anything else, or if you see or hear from Olivia, give me a call on this number.'

The boy shrugged, took the card and shoved it in his back pocket. 'Is Liv in trouble?'

'No. Not at all. It's just important that I speak with her – so tell her to get in touch if you do hear anything, okay? Tell your friends the same. Can you do that?'

He puffed his chest out. 'Course.' There was a swagger to his walk as he returned to the chair he came from. He was clearly enjoying the bit of gossip he thought he was privilege to, and Maggie had no doubt it would be spread across the campus as soon as he left the office. That's exactly what she needed to happen.

Maggie walked into Mr Dodd's office as Kat was closing her notebook.

'DC Jamieson, I've just given your colleague all the information I could at this time.' He stood and looked as if he was ready to escort them out of the building.

'One more thing.' Maggie stopped him. 'I was just speaking to a young man out there.' She pointed to the reception area. 'He suggested that Olivia may have some attendance issues. Could you tell us anything about that?'

A strange look came over his face. 'Uh. Well, her records indicate she was a little ... troubled. I really can't go into too much detail without her parent's permission but yes – we've had to speak to Mr and Mrs Hastings a few times about Olivia's behaviour and attendance. I'm afraid that's all I can say about that ... Now I really must get on with things. I'll show you out now if that's okay?'

'For now. We'll need to see all the information you have on her at some point, but we'll get a warrant and be back for that. Thanks for your time. If Olivia does appear here or gets in contact, please make sure to be in touch immediately. Would you have any objections to us talking to a few of the students before we go?' Maggie eyed him, knowing what his answer would be before he opened his mouth.

Mr Dodd became flustered and sputtered out his words. 'I think I'd need to speak with my manager first. I'm sure the students' parents wouldn't be too happy if you just questioned their children without their consent.'

'You do realize that this is a murder investigation, right?' Maggie clenched her fists at her side. This guy went from being fully cooperative to shifty as fuck and she didn't like it one bit. 'Is there something you're afraid to share with us? If we find out that you've been hiding something, you could be facing some serious charges.'

'How dare you! That's enough now. I'd like you both to leave the premises immediately. I've been more than helpful and as I said, I can't say any more without speaking to the Chief Executive Principal and the parents.' Mr Dodd gestured towards the door. 'Now if you will follow me, please.'

Maggie looked at Kat and moved aside so that Mr Dodd could pass. They followed him out of the college and walked over to Kat's car. Maggie looked over her shoulder and saw him watching them, making sure they left as he instructed.

'What the fuck is his problem?' Kat took her key fob from her pocket and unlocked the car doors.

'I've no idea what I said to get his back up. How was he before I came back into the room?' Maggie opened the passenger door, dropped her bag in the footwell and eased into the car seat.

'Fine. He didn't offer much more than what he said when you came back, but he was pleasant enough. He did say that Olivia has been missing classes, had become slightly withdrawn and had one or two outbursts – her teachers were worried that something was going on at home, but when they asked her about it, she immediately clammed up. The college invited Hastings and his wife in, but the DCI only came once and his wife made excuses the other times, promising to talk to Olivia and apologising for any disruptions.'

Kat backed out of the parking space and narrowly missed scraping the car beside her. 'Can't these wankers learn to park properly? Fucksake.'

Maggie shook her head but kept her mouth closed about Kat's driving. 'Something strange has been going on and the more we find out, the more I wonder if Tim's death and the Hastings's disappearance are connected. Can't be just a coincidence that Tim and Olivia were friends.'

'Yeah. I was thinking the same.' Kat stopped at the end of the driveaway. 'Where to now?'

'Nathan wants us back at the office.'

Kat signalled left and they headed back to Stafford Police Station in silence. Maggie didn't have a good feeling about any of this.

Back at the station, Maggie relayed everything they had learned at the college, while Kat got the coffees in. Maggie hadn't had a chance to drink hers at the college and was gasping. Nathan was nowhere to be seen, so Maggie started updating the system with the information they had gathered. Something about the deputy's behaviour also concerned her and she made a note to get more of his details so she could follow up.

Her desk phone's sharp ringing made her jump and she snapped out of her thoughts. Looking at her watch, she hadn't realized the day had gone by so fast.

'Hello?'

'Good – you're back. I tried your mobile, but it went straight to answerphone. Can you come up to Hastings's office, please?'

Maggie let her colleagues know where she'd be and took the stairs up to their DCI's office with speed.

Nathan was standing by the DCI's desk and papers were strewn on the floor. 'How'd you get on at the college?'

'We'll have to get a warrant if we want to know anything else about Olivia Hastings. What's going on here?' Maggie sat down and Nathan handed her a piece of paper. Her eyes scanned the sheet and widened. 'Adopted? Where did you find this?'

'It's why I called you in here. We got permission to search the office – hoping for something that may explain Hastings's sudden disappearance ... hence the mess. We found a small safe in the bottom drawer of that cabinet.' He pointed to the locker on his left. 'When we eventually got it open – those papers as well as a lot of other personal information mainly relating to Olivia. I don't know why he kept it here, but it looks like that young woman had a very troubled background.'

'Would it be worth contacting Social Services? I know someone who might be able to help.'

'Yes, but it's late now. No one will be there. We can start on that avenue tomorrow. Press conference is at 10am. Be ready, it's going to be a very long day.'

Chapter Twenty-One

Maggie had not been sleeping well and she had only meant to close her eyes for a few minutes when she got home, pulling the blanket off the back of the couch and lying back. With no real leads on the Griffiths case and not knowing where DCI Hastings was, everything seemed to be at a stalemate.

She sat up, stretched her legs, and rubbed her eyes. Scrappy lay curled up on the cushion at the opposite end. She reached across and stroked him as she thought about what she needed to do.

Maggie could really use Kate's expertise on the case for added insight. They had been discussing snippets of what was currently happening over calls, but Maggie felt like the investigation was going in circles. The consultant post with the MOCD was still proceeding, as DI Rutherford had assured her that the funding had been granted and set aside, but Maggie knew this would not be indefinitely and worried that Kate would not be ready before the funding was allocated elsewhere.

'Fuck it.' Maggie threw the blanket off her and momentarily felt bad when Scrappy gave her the evil eye, but he settled back in his sleeping position soon enough.

'Sorry, Scraps, things to do, people to talk to.'

Maggie got up and went to her desk, where her laptop sat open, and returned to the living room. She sat on the chair this time, to avoid any grumbles from Scrappy, plus it gave her a nice view out of the window. Maggie turned on the TV for some background noise as she logged into her laptop. She bit her lip as she typed out the email, hoping that it would be received as it was meant and hit send. She set the laptop on the coffee table and ran her fingers through her hair.

With her brother away, the house was quieter than usual. Maggie had lived most of her life on her own, but she'd grown accustomed to Andy's company and, although she would never admit it to him, she'd miss him when he decided to find his own place. Her phone buzzed.

'Hello?'

'Hi Maggie! I got your email.'

'Hey! How have you been?'

'Fine. Better than fine, actually. Everything is falling into place.'

'Ah – great, I guess.' Maggie hoped she hid her disappointment. 'No plans on returning here any time soon?'

'Well, I was about to say that I missed work. I miss my colleagues. I even miss you a little bit.'

Maggie smiled. 'Phew.' She laughed. 'I'm not going to lie – I'm glad to hear that, but you obviously don't want to come back too soon. You'd have a lot to sort out; a new place for one thing. Of course, you could always stay here until you found somewhere and—'

'Hang on! I didn't say I was ready to come back yet. I was offered a position at the National University of Ireland Galway to teach psychology. I'm a little torn if I am honest.'

'Oh, right.' Maggie's shoulders slumped. She wanted to tell Kate why a better option would be her position with the police but knew that would only be for selfish reasons.

'You've gone quiet. Is everything okay?'

'I'm fine. That sounds like an interesting offer.'

'You're fooling no one, Jamieson! I haven't accepted anything yet, but I've at least got that option. Thanks for not harassing me to come back – I know you've probably been wrestling with yourself on that. I have my parents in my ear every five minutes about taking the lecturing position. They don't want me to go back to consulting with the police, even though I explained that the stalking had happened long before I even joined you lot.' Kate sighed. 'But you know parents. I will always be the little girl they need to protect. Anyway, I was surprised it took you so long to ask me about work. I've been following the news over there and see you have another murder case. A young man, right?'

'I didn't want to pressure you, so feel free to tell me to fuck off if you need to. I'm just stumped and thought maybe if we chatted, some of the cobwebs might clear.'

'It's late now and you sound tired – I just wanted to touch base to let you know that I'm still here and willing – if you ever had any work matters you need to discuss. When you have more information to hand, we'll chat again. I'll make sure I'm free.'

'Sounds like a plan. But only if you're sure. On top of the murder investigation there's something else going on – it's quite a sensitive case. I'll explain why when we chat next – and if it gets too much you can just—'

'Maggie. I wouldn't have offered if I wasn't ready. Just get everything together and text me the details. Speak soon.' Kate ended the call.

Maggie couldn't help the smile forming on her face. She already felt the invisible grip around her neck loosen. She was looking forward to bouncing ideas off Kate – if anyone could offer objective insight, it was her.

She yawned and when she noticed the time, she ignored her stomach grumbles and headed up to bed.

Chapter Twenty-Two

Lucy opened the door and a big smile formed on her face. 'Come in. What a nice surprise – I wasn't expecting you until later.' She moved out of the way and pointed to the living room. 'Can I get you a coffee or anything?'

'I thought I'd come by now, before work and see if you've had any luck with your … guest. A coffee would be great.' PC Mark Fielding walked into the communal lounge and sat. She had given him the code for the gate, as he would be referring men and women to the haven once the refuge's doors had officially opened and, in some cases, may escort people to the premises. Lucy held up two fingers indicating that she wouldn't be long. The coffee was already brewing, and she wanted to ask him something.

Returning with two large mugs, Lucy sat opposite. 'Nothing more – other than her name is Ronnie, and she said she's from outside the area. She also hinted that this is repeat behaviour and she's been involved with a refuge in the past, but she's keeping everything else a secret so far. I was going to ask if maybe you'd speak to her? She can hear partially with her aids in but also relies on lip-reading. She still won't tell me her last name or anything about what happened and refuses to go to the hospital, though she did let me know that she wasn't sexually assaulted, so I guess that's something. The large gash on her arm is healing well with no signs of infection, thankfully. The other cuts and bruises are fading too. I'm nearly one hundred per cent sure that her assault is domestic related.' She rubbed her arms.

Lucy was concerned. Without knowing the history of the young woman, she didn't feel comfortable opening the refuge doors and allowing new referrals as she had planned prior to Ronnie showing up. If someone was after this woman, she didn't want to place anyone else at risk. Vicki had contacted all the agencies they would be working with to let them know about the delay. Lucy's thoughts had drifted, and Mark's voice returned her to the room and conversation.

'I can definitely try. Do you think she'd be willing to talk with me? Wouldn't Sharon be a better bet?' Sharon Bairden was the Independent Domestic Violence Advisor (IDVA) linked to the DAHU and a good friend. After Lucy's own experience, Sharon had proved a good friend and ally.

'Sharon's away at the minute but I've left her a message. She was due to pop around before she left, but with Ronnie turning up the way she did, I just thought if you could get something from her you may be able to check against the records in the DAHU or other police areas. She can't have travelled from too far away. She may already be known in the system – or at least her abuser might.' A floorboard creaked and Lucy looked through the doorway. 'We'll soon find out.' She gestured for Ronnie to come through.

The woman walked into the room and stopped dead when she saw Mark. Lucy waved to get her attention. 'It's okay, Ronnie. This is PC Mark Fielding, but you can call him Mark. He's a friend. Do you think it would be okay if he asked you a few questions?'

Ronnie looked at Lucy and then back at Mark. She nodded slowly, and Lucy pointed to the big leather chair. 'Have a sit there and I'll get you a cup of tea.' Lucy wasn't sure whether she should leave them alone, but Mark was trained in working with both victims and perpetrators of domestic abuse, so wouldn't push Ronnie into talking without Lucy present.

She returned to the room five minutes later and placed the cup of tea on the side table. 'Would you like me to stay?'

The young woman nodded, and Lucy sat back down across from Mark. 'Okay. I'll just be here if you need me.'

'Why don't we start off with the easy stuff? You take your time and if you want to answer, great, but if not, that's fine too. If you don't understand what I'm asking, signal to me – hold your index finger up.' Mark showed her before continuing. 'If I am talking too fast, just put your hand up as if you're telling me to stop … like this.' Mark held his hand up, palm facing them. 'Does that work for you?'

Ronnie nodded and took her mobile phone out of her pocket. She started typing something and then looked at them – a robotic voice said, *'Thank you.'*

Lucy smiled. She forgot to mention to Mark that Ronnie used a text-to-voice app to communicate. Ronnie smiled back at her and seemed to relax in Mark's company.

Mark was everything that Patrick, her ex, wasn't. Kind, caring, patient, and decent. She hoped that he'd be able to find out more from the woman. Someone could be missing her –

her parents, a sibling, maybe even a child. Lucy sat back in the chair and drank her coffee while Mark continued.

'Can you tell us your last name?'

Ronnie typed in her phone and held it out. *'I don't want to.'*

'Okay. Is that because you are afraid of someone finding out?'

Ronnie nodded.

'Can you tell us who that is?'

Lucy looked at Mark with wide eyes. Ronnie had already said she wouldn't disclose the name, so why was he pushing her? It seemed out of character.

Ronnie shook her head and tucked her legs underneath her. She looked visibly upset to Lucy.

'Mark, maybe this isn't such a good idea.' Lucy frowned. She didn't want Ronnie to feel pressured and close up completely.

'Do you want to stop?' Mark spoke slowly.

The woman nodded and held out her phone.

'I'm sorry.'

She stood, took her tea, and walked to the window where she turned her back to the pair and looked out.

'It's too soon, Mark. Sorry, I shouldn't have asked you to do this. Maybe she's uncomfortable because you're a man? Have you had any luck with the Misper Unit?' Lucy had asked Mark to speak to Missing Persons before he dropped around, to see if anyone had reported the young woman missing.

'Nothing so far, but I asked them to call me and gave them a description from what you had told me that first night, to see if anyone matching Ronnie's description was reported. Now that we have a first name, that might narrow things down a bit.' Mark leaned back and rubbed his eyes.

'Are you okay? You don't look too well.' Lucy frowned.

'I just feel a bit dizzy. The joys of diabetes. Do you have any juice – a small glass should do.' Sweat formed on his brow.

'Uh yeah. I'll be back in a moment.' Lucy was in and out of the kitchen as fast as she could, passing Mark the glass and looking over him like a worried mother. 'Are you sure you're okay? Where's all your kit?'

'My travel cooler is in the boot of my car.' The colour returned to Mark's face.

'Well what good is it in there? Shouldn't you have it closer to hand when you're driving?'

'I usually do, but I just threw everything in the boot on my way here.' Mark pointed to the woman. 'Do you think she's going to be okay? My presence seems to be upsetting her – whether that's because I am a police officer, a man, or both.' Lucy could tell he was uncomfortable talking about his diabetes with her, as he swiftly tried to change the subject.

'She'll be fine. I'll make sure of it. Thanks for stopping by. Will you be okay going now? You are more than welcome to wait until you are feeling a bit better. There's no rush.'

Mark looked at his watch. 'I have to get back to the station anyway. Just gimme a shout if she tells you anything more. I'll try and check in with you later.'

Lucy walked him to the door, and Mark squeezed her hand on the way out. 'See you later.'

She smiled. 'Be careful – pull over if you need to,' she called after him and he waved back before she closed the door.

Ronnie was sitting down in the big chair again. She stared blankly, and Lucy knew that she wasn't going to get all the answers she needed to find out this woman's identity. But that wasn't going to stop her from trying.

Chapter Twenty-Three

'Grab your coat, Maggie, you're with me,' Nathan called out from his office before returning to whoever he had on the phone.

Maggie had been inputting her information on the system; she looked at Bethany and shrugged. Kat had been sent out to an allotment that was owned by DCI Hastings when she had arrived in to work, so it was just Maggie and Bethany in the office today. She grabbed her coat off the back of her chair and waited outside Nathan's door. Once he hung up on whoever he'd been speaking to, he motioned for her to come into his office.

'What's happening?' She was just about to sit down when the look on Nathan's face told her that it would be a waste of time.

'That,' he pointed to the phone, 'was a call about the allotment I sent Kat to this morning.'

Maggie didn't interrupt.

'They found a body and believe it could be Mrs Hastings. Dr Blake is on her way there. I asked Kat to speak to anyone on site and do some door-to-door enquiries in the surrounding area. DI Rutherford is there as the SIO – she wants us to attend immediately. We'll have to postpone the press conference ...'

'What the hell is going on!?' Maggie struggled to believe that their DCI would be a part of what had happened, but in situations like this, she knew that usually a close family member was involved. She shook the thought away – the DCI was missing, and Maggie needed to focus her attention on that instead of thinking the worst.

Nathan grabbed his keys and Maggie followed him to his car. 'Off the record, what do you make of all this?' She turned to Nathan, hoping he may have some logical explanation that would make her own thoughts seem ridiculous.

He shrugged as he reversed out of the car park. 'At the moment, it's not looking good. DI Rutherford shared some things with me in confidence and when you take that information and put it together with where we are heading now,' he paused to let the information sink in, 'it presents like Hastings had some sort of breakdown and his family is in danger.' Nathan's forehead creased as he focused on the road.

'What did Rutherford tell you?' Maggie understood that Nathan and Rutherford would have information not available to the whole team immediately, but it didn't mean she wouldn't ask him to share. If the details would paint a picture to explain what they were heading to, she thought the team needed to know everything.

'I can't say at the minute. I'm sorry, I probably shouldn't have even said that much. I'm sure the guv has her reasons for keeping this information back and will share it when the time is right. Just a heads-up, another small team may be coming in to join us *if* Hastings is involved in any of this. Before you get all territorial, just remember we'll need the help. It's not because we aren't capable.' His brows furrowed. 'And before you throw a strop, I'm warning you not to push me on this.'

'Fine.' She huffed. 'I hope for all our sakes that keeping important details to yourselves doesn't impact on the investigation negatively then.' The last point was a little out of order but sometimes Maggie couldn't help herself – and she knew she wasn't wrong. Every bit of information could be key to moving a case forward and she wouldn't apologize for challenging her superiors, as they would do the same if the tables were turned.

'Like I said, Rutherford will tell us all in due course, if need be. Right, that's the allotment on the left. You jump out here and get suited, signed in, and I'll meet you in there. Just got to find somewhere to park.'

The street was lined with cars and there was no way to drive right in. Maggie jumped out and made her way over to the forensics van. She grabbed a forensics suit and put it on. The crime scene manager was just beyond the fence and she signed in before heading towards the cordoned off area.

There was a shed with its double doors open. Maggie stepped underneath the cordon and greeted DI Rutherford.

'Where's Nathan?' Rutherford's response was curt.

'Just parking the car, guv. What's happened here?' Maggie looked past her boss at Dr Blake, who was examining the victim.

'Although we still need a formal ID, I'm pretty certain that's DCI Hastings's wife, Sophia. I met her a few times at different events. She's been beaten pretty badly. I'll let Dr Blake fill you in while I go and speak to Nathan.' DI Rutherford waved and Maggie looked over her shoulder as Nathan approached.

'Okay. Thanks.' Stepping into the shed, Maggie looked around. There was a small worktable along the right side with various tools on it. The usual pots and soil were underneath the table and neatly stacked along the wall. A small summer table and chairs were set up on the left side of the room with a double-seater couch against the back wall. It was like a home away from home. It must be where Mrs Hastings would escape to when she needed a bit of peace and quiet. There was a definite feminine touch to the set up. The victim was posed awkwardly on the double seater, and Maggie waited while Dr Blake did her thing.

'Is that you, Maggie?' Dr Blake called out without even turning around.

'Yep. How'd you know?'

'I recognize the smell of that ghastly shampoo you use. Are you just going to stand there, or would you like to know what I found so far?'

Maggie brushed by Charlie, the forensic assistant, and stood beside Dr Blake. 'What do we know so far then?' She was tempted to add her own snark into the mix, but that wouldn't help with what they were dealing with.

'Female. I'd estimate she's between fifty-five and sixty-five years old. Feet bound tightly – the skin beneath has been broken. Looks like some sort of garden wire was used to tie the hands as well. See the cuts? She must have tried to wriggle out of these, but the more she tried, the deeper the wire cut into the skin. If I had to guess, I'd say she was killed shortly after we discovered Hastings and his family were missing – though I can't be more specific than that. She was badly beaten before those garden shears were rammed forcefully into her neck. There are multiple stab wounds on her chest and stomach, but these look superficial. Don't quote me on that though – the post-mortem will tell us more.' Dr Blake leaned forwards and gently prised open the victim's mouth. 'If you look closely, you'll see there is something pushed into her throat. Once I get her back to the lab, I'll have more information for you. That's it, any questions?'

Maggie leaned in and looked in the victim's mouth. It looked like a ball of paper had been shoved in. She stood back. 'Do you think this is where she was killed? Or was she placed here after death?'

'Given the blood soaked into this couch, I'd say she was probably brought here alive and then killed.' She pointed to the floor. 'You see that dirt swirled about from the entrance to here? I think it's possible that she walked in on her own. She may have fought against it – or there were two people with her. If there's nothing else, I'm going to head back to the lab while my team finish up.'

She removed her gloves. 'Make sure you bag her hands and feet, Charlie.'

Dr Blake stood and looked at Maggie. 'So, is there anything else?'

'Uh … No. Thanks for that.' The crime scene investigators were documenting and processing the scene for fingerprints and trace evidence. 'Do you mind if I shadow some of your team?' Maggie queried Dr Blake before she exited the shed.

'Knock yourself out – but please don't get in their way. I know what you can be like.'

Maggie rolled her eyes as she turned and chose one of the

forensics team to follow. She avoided Charlie after the awkwardness from the last case they worked on together, plus he was busy following Dr Blake's last instructions. Small mercies.

Maggie took out her notebook so she could jot down the pertinent points. Reports from other agencies were useful but you often didn't get a full sense of what occurred at a crime scene unless you had those key elements – the who, what, when, why, and how. The essence of those aspects was often missing and could only be experienced first-hand.

The crime scene officers would be recording a scene description that included the weather, location type and condition, major structures, identification of transient and conditional evidence – especially points of entry, containers holding evidence of recent activities (ashtrays, trash cans, et cetera), clothing, furniture, and weapons present, so she didn't need to note any of that down. What she did note down was the damp feel to the room – how the victim must have been terrified despite being in a place she often came to for comfort.

They'd also record the victim description. The position of the body, lividity, wounds, clothing, jewellery, and whether identification was present or absent. In this case, they were all pretty confident that the murdered woman was Sophia Hastings; however, this still would need to be confirmed by the lab.

When Maggie looked at the body once more, she noticed the blood pooling on the furniture and splashes on the wall in all directions. It seemed like a frenzied attack. Personal. She noted her thoughts down.

Maggie observed the scene was being photographed and from that, the police would be getting a true and accurate pictorial record of the death scene and physical evidence present. The scene and body were photographed before anything was moved or removed.

Maggie turned and headed out of the shed to where her superiors were huddled talking amongst themselves. As Maggie approached, the pair stopped talking.

'What's the big secret?' Maggie smiled.

'What have you found?' Nathan's tone made it clear to Maggie that this was a conversation she would not be a part of.

'Dr Blake thinks the victim was killed shortly after being abducted, based on the premise that it is Sophia Hastings, of course, but everything seems to suggest it is. Looks like the murder was committed here, rather than at the house. It was pretty brutal, Nathan. She was beaten, stabbed repeatedly in the torso, and finally stabbed in the neck. There was something personal about this – I can feel it.'

'That mirrors my exact thoughts.' DI Rutherford looked to the sky. 'What the hell is going on and where are you, Hastings?!' She shook her hands.

Maggie knew that was a rhetorical question, so waited before she asked a few questions of her own. 'What motivation would DCI Hastings have for abducting and killing his wife?'

'I was just filling Nathan in on some information that has come to light. I'll save the majority of details that I can share for our briefing, as I really don't want to have to keep saying this – just the thought of it chills me, but there were some call outs to DCI Hastings's home of a … sensitive nature. Recently he'd been behaving oddly – not around for meetings, missing work – arrghh – why didn't I dig deeper? I thought he just wanted out of the police. He's not far off retirement age, so was pissing about in the hopes of a handshake and shove out the door.' She crossed her arms.

'Are you saying there's a history of domestic abuse in the household?' Maggie hoped she had jumped to the wrong conclusion.

'It's a possibility, yes.' DI Rutherford looked at the ground before shaking her head and turning to Nathan. 'I am going to head back to the office. I'll see you pair there and we'll all meet up at 4pm.'

Maggie and Nathan watched as DI Rutherford walked out of the allotment. 'I'm really worried about her.' Nathan turned and faced Maggie. 'She has a lot of pressure from the higher-ups about this – anyway, I've said too much as it is.'

Before Maggie could ask Nathan anything further, there was a shout from one of the Forensic Investigation Officers (FIOs). 'Over here.' He waved. 'I've found something.'

Maggie and Nathan ran over to the FIO and bent over to see what he was pointing at. 'Shit. Is that what I think it is?' Maggie squinted.

'Bloody hell.' Nathan straightened up and ran his fingers through his hair.

On the ground, stuck in the damp grass, was a driving licence with the picture of DCI Hastings staring out at them. Nathan thanked the FIO, who then bagged the item.

'Let's head back. I'd rather be the one to break the news to the guv.' Nathan turned on his heel and Maggie followed him back to the car.

Inside the vehicle, Maggie stared out the window as Nathan pulled away and headed back towards Stafford Police Station. The idea that DCI Hastings could be responsible for the murder of his wife played on Maggie's mind. Although she didn't know the personal side to him as well as their DI did, the few interactions she'd had with him had never made her believe that he was someone to be concerned about. What secrets did they need to uncover? There was a bigger question though. Maggie bit her lip.

If he *is* responsible for this murder, where is his daughter?

Chapter Twenty-Four

When they arrived back at the office, Nathan made an immediate beeline for DI Rutherford's office and once inside, shut the door. Maggie thought she heard a frustrated scream when she was walking down the corridor towards her desk.

'Hey, Bethany. Any news from Kat?' Maggie greeted her colleague.

'She radioed in about ten minutes ago to say she was heading back. What happened out there? Kat was swearing a lot – was it bad?'

Maggie nodded.

'We're having a briefing at 4pm and although we still need to wait for formal ID, we're pretty sure the victim is DCI Hastings's wife. It was a pretty bad scene.' Maggie shuddered.

'That explains all the banging I could hear from down the hall earlier – DI Rutherford was there?'

'Yep.' Before she could continue, her mobile rang. Maggie

looked at the screen and groaned. 'Hold that thought, Bethany. I need to take this.'

Maggie went into the staff kitchen for some privacy before hitting connect. 'Hi. I told you I can't take personal calls at work.'

'Calm yourself. This is work related. I've heard a body has been found at Cotton House allotment. That true?' Julie Noble queried.

'You're speaking to the wrong person. You need to call the Comms Department. All press queries go through there.' Maggie sighed.

'Aw c'mon. Give a gal a break, will ya? Just cough if there was a body at the allotment and cough twice if it's linked to the first murder. I'll owe you.'

The last sentence was said in a sing-song tone and Maggie couldn't help but smile. Regardless of any personal feelings that danced around in her head from time to time about the reporter, she wouldn't compromise a case just to appease her.

'Sorry. If that's all you've called about, you've wasted your time. I've really got to go and suggest you speak to Comms. I won't change my mind.' Maggie was stern in her response and hoped Julie got the message. Ever since they had started meeting each other outside of work from time to time, Maggie couldn't help but worry about the crossover between home and work, so much so that she hadn't shared anything about Julie Noble with anyone on the team yet. She knew that at some point soon she might need to disclose, but as things stood – other than a coffee or meal with a friend – she thought she had a little time to play with.

'Fine. Can I just say one more thing?'

'As long as it is not about the case, go ahead.' Maggie leaned against the wall.

'I kinda like it when you get angry. Catch you later, Mags.'

Julie ended the call, and Maggie laughed to herself.

She pocketed her phone and returned to the open-plan office. She had a puzzle to solve and all thoughts of Julie Noble needed to be put in the back of her head.

Chapter Twenty-Five

Two officers from the weekend had arrived at the haven to follow up on the situation with Ronnie. Lucy surmised that they would need to either progress a case forward or close it down, noting no charges from the victim was forthcoming. Lucy showed them into the communal living room where Ronnie was wrapped in a blanket and staring straight ahead. Although fading a little bit now, her bruised and battered face told a story in itself. Not only had Lucy witnessed similar injuries when reading the Crown Prosecution Service (CPS) papers for pre-sentence reports (PSRs), she'd also seen them in the mirror too many times after Patrick had let loose on her.

'If it's okay with you – and Ronnie – I think it would be good for me to stay while you speak with her?' Lucy looked at both the officers.

'As long as Ronnie is fine with it, then so are we,' the officer said out of Ronnie's earshot. 'How did she end up here? I tried looking up the details of this place online, but it wasn't easy – looks like you require agency referrals.'

'Actually, she mentioned that she had been in a women's refuge on previous occasions and someone there had mentioned this place to her, giving her the details. It's not the correct process, so I have some work to do on that front, but …' Lucy shrugged. 'Why don't I go over and let Ronnie know what's happening as I am sure you have a busy day ahead?' The officers moved aside and let Lucy go through and speak to Ronnie.

Lucy sat next to Ronnie and caught her attention. 'There are two police officers here who just want to chat to you about the incident. It might help you to tell them what you can. The more they know now, the more they will be able to take action or at least ensure your future safety. I said I'd sit with you through the interview if that was okay?'

Ronnie nodded at Lucy. Still not verbalising much other than through the app on her phone, Lucy felt protective of the young woman and questioned whether talking to Ronnie right now would be of any use – after all, she hadn't opened up to Mark. Her own experience made her fear that if the officers pushed too hard, they may trigger flashbacks to the night she arrived. If Ronnie wasn't going to press charges, the police would move on, but she was still clearly in distress and could be for some time. Lucy waved the officers over. The female officer took the lead.

'Hi, Ronnie, how are you today? We'd like to get some details from you about your injuries. Are you able to tell us anything more about the night in question and whether you wish to press any charges?'

Lucy felt the woman stiffen beside her. She began to shake

her head and whimper. Lucy reached out to touch her hand, but the woman flinched. She wouldn't look at the officers and began rocking back and forth, tears streaming down her face.

Lucy looked at the officers. 'Sorry, it looks like you've had a wasted trip. She's distressed and this will all still be very fresh in her head.' Lucy couldn't help the disappointment in her voice, as it looked like the police would be able to close the matter sooner with Ronnie being uncooperative. It wasn't unusual. Even when women did come forward, they'd often retract statements – fortunately, even if this did happen the police could still bring a case forward, but they needed a perp. Lucy doubted they would get one today – if ever.

One of the officers leaned in and whispered something to the other. Directing the conversation back to Ronnie, she spoke. 'How about I leave my card here and Lucy can call us when or if you change your mind? Would that be okay, miss?' The officer waited for a sign, but when there was none from Ronnie, the pair stood up.

Lucy walked with them to the door and gave the officer credit for trying.

'Sorry, I had hoped that having had a few days, Ronnie might be more willing to let you know who did this to her. I'll see if I can get anything more out of her. She refused any medical treatment, though with her permission I took a few pictures of the injuries that I could see. I'm feeling less certain now that she's going to want to pursue any criminal charges against whoever did this to her.' Lucy shrugged. 'Sometimes we just have to accept that.'

'You used to work at the DAHU, didn't you?' one of the officers asked.

Lucy nodded.

'I thought I recognized you when we first arrived. Could you email those pictures over to the unit and we can add them to our information? I know we took photos when this was first called in, but the more we have, the better. Without any details of an address or perpetrator, we're kind of stuck here. Who knows what the situation is? I mean she could have assaulted her attacker in retaliation. Might be why she is so reluctant to pursue this. I'll check out if there have been any call outs or assaults reported with other areas. That's about all we can do for now.' He smiled.

'I get it.' She could tell the officers were as disappointed as she was; it wouldn't be the first or last time they came across a victim of domestic abuse who didn't wish to pursue the matter. 'I agree that there may be more to this situation and she's worried about what trouble she may get into.' Lucy exhaled. 'We've seen it happen so often, right? Thanks again for coming out. I'll be in touch.' Lucy waved the officers off, opened the gate and once she saw the officers leaving the premises, shut the front door behind her. She took a moment, leaning against the door.

Lucy sent a quick text to Sharon, asking her to hold off on visiting until she came back to her and a final note to enjoy her holiday. She'd catch her up with everything when she was back at work. The reply came back quickly, and Lucy smiled as Sharon expressed concern but also complete understanding. They worked in an area in the criminal justice system where things could happen at the last minute and where trust in colleagues was paramount. She placed her mobile back in her pocket and locked the door before returning to the living room.

The woman was asleep on the couch. She looked so small and vulnerable. If Lucy had to guess, she figured Ronnie must be in her early twenties. When the police had been asking their questions, Ronnie had rubbed her arms and Lucy caught a glimpse of some scratches and old scars, confirming her earlier suspicions about self-harming.

Lucy decided to let her rest for a while and closed the door to the communal living room over. She went to her office and turned on her laptop – the secure one that Probation provided for her agency work on reports. She logged in and attached her phone to the laptop so she could upload the photos of the woman. Once the pictures had uploaded, she wrote out an email to Mark at the DAHU. She explained the situation, gave the officers' names who attended and advised that if she learned anything new, she would forward it on. She knew that Mark couldn't share specific details with her now that she no longer worked with the DAHU, but attached a copy of her referral form and asked if he could refer the young woman to her haven so everything would be above board. She instructed him to leave the unknown areas blank and they could be completed once they knew more.

She sat back in her chair and once again the same question popped in her mind.

What the hell happened to Ronnie and what was preventing her from pressing charges?

Chapter Twenty-Six

Within the open-plan office, word travels fast and Maggie had heard that they had some more information from the forensics team. An update was imminent, so she waited as patiently as possible, though she wasn't known for her patience. Gathering her notebook and pen, she walked towards the incident room and sat near the front so she could get a good look at everything that had been collected so far. The board in front of her was riddled with lines, pictures, and notes – she closed her eyes and mentally attempted to restore some order to the chaos, but it was difficult.

'I'll make this as short as possible.' DI Rutherford spoke as she walked towards the evidence boards. 'New information has come in which puts an interesting but somewhat concerning spin on things.'

Maggie leaned forwards in her chair, pen poised, ready to capture whatever details were to follow.

'I've recently been given access to information that confirms there have been previous call outs to DCI Hastings's home, relating to accusations of physical violence towards his wife and daughter.'

'What the fuck?' Kat blurted out.

'It's somewhat … controversial. When his wife was spoken to, she denied all claims, but his daughter, Olivia, was adamant that her father had been abusive towards them on more than one occasion. Seems that because there were no physical injuries to corroborate what was being said, the information was recorded, logged, and then only accessible to the superintendent and above. Hence why we are only receiving this information now.' Rutherford blushed. Maggie could see she wasn't comfortable with the decisions made by her superiors.

Maggie recalled conversations she'd had with Lucy about no further action being taken on domestic abuse cases in the past. If there had been no blood or bruising, one person would be removed from the situation and no further action taken. It was shocking, but fortunately with better training and an understanding that physical abuse may not show injuries until a later time, this sort of thing rarely happened any more. At least that's what they were being told.

'So, are we saying that DCI Hastings is now definitely a person of interest in the abduction of his daughter and murder of his wife?' Maggie had to ask this aloud, as she could see the question was on her colleagues' faces but no one was verbalising it.

'Yes. I think that is a fair assumption to make. We need to speak with him but … we can't rule out that there is something else going on and that Hastings is a victim himself.' Rutherford clearly was reluctant to move on from thinking of Hastings as a possible victim and Maggie agreed.

'What would you like us to do now?' Nathan pulled at his collar. Maggie immediately knew that the whole situation was now escalating, and the team would be in turmoil at the possibility that a detective chief inspector – their DCI – was now someone who they needed to track down … for murder.

'We'll be releasing an embargoed press release to relevant newspapers that will go out to the public as soon as we get the go-ahead. We're working on the wording now. What we don't need is to scare Hastings away if he is responsible or cause his abductors, should that be the case, to do something foolish. The last thing we want is two more bodies on our hands – though the amount of blood in Hastings's home suggests there may already be another body we've yet to find. We're trying to gather as much information as possible about the family, their history, and a timeline in the days leading up to the abduction.' DI Rutherford rubbed her temple. 'In the meantime, I need you all working around the clock to manage the murders and work with the Misper Unit in terms of the possible abduction angle – we'll see how forthcoming they are with sharing information.'

'So, they are still being treated as two separate investigations? Well, three actually.' Maggie groaned. She hardly slept as it was; the pressure of two murder investigations as well as liaising with another team about the abductions would be draining.

'For the time being, though it's likely that we will have to re-examine things shortly. I'm still waiting for news on additional support from outside the area. Nathan will be more on the operational side also …' DI Rutherford mouthed 'sorry' to him, but he shrugged his shoulders. Nathan never minded getting stuck into a case and Maggie knew he enjoyed the investigative side more than the managerial.

'Maggie and Nathan, can I see you in my office after this? The rest of you should know what needs doing – so unless you want me to spoon-feed it to you, let's get a move on.' She clapped her hands as she walked out of the room.

'Shit just got real.' Kat leaned over as she gathered her things.

'It sure did. I'll catch you later.'

Maggie led the way to Rutherford's office and took a deep breath before she stepped inside. She had no idea what to expect, but she also knew that whatever it was, it wouldn't be good.

Chapter Twenty-Seven

DI Rutherford was pacing her office when Maggie and Nathan joined her. She had never seen her boss in such a state over a case – even at the most stressful times in her career, Rutherford had always managed to keep calm and, in turn, run a seamless investigation. They'd had sensitive cases before, but this was clearly much more than that to their boss.

'I realize that I'm coming down hard on the team, but the longer this goes on, the worse my mood is going to get I'm afraid. The reason I called you both in is because I'd like you to attend the post-mortem of Sophia Hastings. I spoke to Dr Blake and she's expecting you there in an hour. Clear your schedules; Nathan, delegate what you can and get over to the HQ. I want to know exactly what happened and whether Dr Blake can add any insight. Okay?'

'Absolutely, guv.' Nathan turned to Maggie. 'Give me fifteen minutes to sort things out and we'll go.'

Maggie nodded.

'That's all. Report back to me when you're done.'

The pair left the room and Nathan rushed ahead. Maggie gathered her things and while she was shutting down her computer, Nathan came bounding out of his office.

'You ready?'

Staffordshire Police HQ was only a twenty-minute drive if traffic was clear, so when Nathan and Maggie arrived, they had enough time to sign in and make their way to the purpose-built forensics lab that had been built on site. Dr Blake was waiting for them at the door.

'Well, isn't this nice. Partners in crime back together again. I'll let you in to the observation room. If you have any questions, there's an intercom on the wall, but please don't interrupt me unless it is absolutely necessary.'

The sarkiness in her tone didn't go unnoticed by Maggie.

There was a large microphone suspended from the ceiling, although Maggie could also see a handheld device. 'For the benefit of DS Nathan Wright and his colleague, DC Maggie Jamieson, who are observing today, I'd like to reiterate some of the initial findings when the victim, Sophia Hastings, arrived at the lab. Estimated window of death is approximately but not limited to six days before she was discovered.'

Maggie turned and whispered to Nathan: 'Hang on. So does that mean she was murdered before Tim Griffiths?'

Nathan pointed at her notepad while staring ahead. She understood his message – write it down, ask me later. Dr Blake was circling the table as she spoke; most of the descriptions went completely over Maggie's head.

'The hands and fingernails have traces of blood and

possibly skin.' Dr Blake paused momentarily and looked in Maggie and Nathan's direction. Neither said anything. Although Maggie didn't completely understand everything that had been said, she noted down the possible defensive wounds and the fact that Mrs Hastings may have left marks on her attacker.

Dr Blake continued. 'The deceased was found in an upright position with ...' She stopped as she counted the wounds on the torso. 'Eight stab wounds covering the chest and stomach area. One deep laceration to the neck.' Dr Blake bent down, and it looked to Maggie like she was checking the depth of the wound. She motioned to her assistant. 'Can we turn her over, please?' Dr Blake placed her recorder down as they turned the body. Picking up her recording device again, she carried on. 'The heels of the feet have some sort of gravel and sand embedded. There are also scratches present.'

The forensic assistant held out a small container in which Dr Blake deposited whatever had been embedded in Sophia Hastings's heels.

'Some scratches on the mid-back as well as shoulders.' The pathologist stopped the tape again and looked directly at Nathan and Maggie.

'I can't be sure, but given the marks on the back, shoulders, and heels, I think she was dragged or carried by two people. If it had been one person, if she had been dragged by the arms, her heels would have scuff marks, but nothing would appear on the back and shoulders and vice versa if she had been dragged by her heels.'

Maggie pressed the intercom. 'Could it have been that one person first dragged her by the feet but then switched when the body became too heavy and dragged her by the arms?' If two people had been involved, that could mean that Hastings was not responsible for the murder or that he had someone working with him. Maggie dismissed the second premise as unlikely, especially if this was some sort of murder-suicide to avoid prosecution. But it would support the abduction theory. Maggie was trying to consider as many angles as possible, but it was hard to know what to think.

'Yes, that could be a possibility, though I would have expected deeper marks if this was done by one person.' Dr Blake continued with her examination. 'Bruising on the wrists and left elbow.' She placed the recorder down and started feeling Mrs Hastings's head. 'No contusions on the head. Okay, let's turn her over again and open her up.' Dr Blake motioned to her colleagues.

While the forensic assistants were cutting her open, Dr Blake went over to the wall where X-ray film viewers were and switched on the light. Placing the X-rays up on the board, she began to speak. 'There are small fractures on the left index finger and right wrist. Calcium deposits indicate these injuries have healed over and are approximately two years old.'

Maggie scribbled in her notebook – *check if these are consistent with the DV call outs*. Dr Blake placed another X-ray up – they looked to be the ribcage.

'More fractures – two to be exact. Left side.' Maggie watched as Dr Blake turned around, noticing the body was ready for her. She placed the recorder on a small table beside where she stood and began to speak. Maggie wondered how much of this side of things she would be able to grasp.

Dr Blake turned to Nathan and Maggie. 'No head injuries, external or internal, present.'

She then went on to explain that other than the bones she

had highlighted in her discussion on X-rays, the skeletal system was unremarkable and within normal limits. Dr Blake paused then and picked up a large set of tweezers. She carefully separated the lips and reached in to pull out the rolled-up ball of paper.

Maggie got as close to the glass screen as possible and watched as the pathologist unravelled the paper.

'Well, this is interesting. Five dots. Quite similar to the ones found drawn on Tim Griffiths's body. I don't think this is a coincidence, do you, detectives?' She held it up for them to see before passing the paper over to the assistant, who bagged it. Maggie noted down the configuration.

The post-mortem continued as Dr Blake discussed the heart and other internal organs. Maggie's mind, however, was stuck on what had been found shoved in Mrs Hastings's mouth.

When Dr Blake reached the genital system part of her examination, she confirmed that there was no evidence that the victim had ever given birth. Maggie now wondered whether adoption was the only option that Mrs Hastings had. Not that it was important in terms of who she was, but Maggie had known friends and relatives whose marriages were under a lot of strain due to fertility issues. Could there have been a deep-seated resentment about this?

Blood samples were also taken and sent for toxicological analysis. As bad as it sounded, Maggie hoped that Mrs Hastings had been drugged, as the number of wounds indicated it was more than probable she'd suffered a painful and tortuous experience.

Dr Blake turned to the detectives. 'Sorry. I hope that was clear. I got caught up in my world and forgot I had an audience. I'm now just going to summarize the injuries and whether they contributed to the cause of death.'

Dr Blake began recording the details of her findings in an almost list-like manner. This time she also used the handheld recording device. The pathologist looked at the pair again before describing the stab wounds – eight in total covering the chest and lower abdominal area. Each wound was deep, with some described as fatal and others nonfatal; however, it was the wound to the neck which severed the carotid artery and death would have followed shortly after.

Dr Blake recorded other defensive injuries, including wounds on the palm and base of both hands. These appeared to have been inflicted before the fatal stab injuries.

Maggie looked at Nathan. His brows furrowed. 'What an awful ordeal to have had to endure.' He couldn't tear his eyes away from the victim as he spoke.

'I couldn't even imagine the fear she must have felt, especially if …' Maggie couldn't finish the sentence, but Nathan nodded his understanding.

Dr Blake concluded by saying that, overall, most of the wounds suggested a single-edged blade, although a double-edged blade could not be excluded. The neck wound was caused by sharp, handheld garden shears which were found on the body. 'I can't give you an exact time of death, but I think I can say with some certainty that Mrs Hastings was killed on the Friday – following her abduction, which you believe occurred some time on Thursday night or the early hours of Friday morning. Immediate cause of death: exsanguination due to multiple stab wounds on the torso and neck. Manner of death: homicide.' Dr Blake then said something to her assistant and walked over to the detectives. Removing and then discarding her gloves, she opened the door and came into the observation room.

'Hope that helped somewhat. I'll get a more formal report over once we have the tests back and I'll send over the paper with the dots.' She indicated the exit and they followed her out.

'Thanks for letting us observe. It was ... useful.' Nathan coughed. They headed to the car.

'What do you think about the marks on the paper stuffed in her mouth?' Maggie sat in the passenger side of the car.

'It's a message, but what it means I have no clue. What are you thinking? Your face has done that scrunchy-up thing it does when you are putting pieces together.'

'It's probably nothing.' Maggie paused before turning to Nathan. 'If the marks on the paper are significant, it could mean that Sophia was killed before Tim – if the dots are decreasing and not increasing, that is – and maybe their murders are linked. But what reasons would Hastings have, if he did do this, to kill Tim?'

'That's what we'll need to find out.'

Nathan put the car in gear and headed back to the station.

Chapter Twenty-Eight

When they arrived back at the office, Maggie shared her experience of the post-mortem viewing with Kat and Bethany. She laughed inwardly at the difference between the two – Kat very keen to hear the specific details while Bethany cringed before turning around and focusing on her computer monitor.

Once finished, she returned to her task at hand. Maggie stared at her computer screen after inputting the markings into Google and seeing things such as a dice and morse code pop up as possibilities. Nothing was jumping out at her and her frustration grew. She threw her pen down.

'Hey! This might be something,' Bethany shouted across the room.

Maggie pushed her chair out and walked over to Bethany's desk. 'What are you looking at?' A newspaper article was displayed on the screen.

'You asked me to do some digging on old cases and I came

across this article. Do you remember the case? It was before my time.'

'Oi! How old do you think I am?' Maggie placed her hands on her hips. 'It's before my time too, you cheeky cow.' A sideways smile formed on her face. 'That's a recent article though, so you'll have to spell it out for me, as my psychic abilities seem to have fizzled in my old age.' Maggie squinted at the small print on the screen. She rubbed her eyes and realized she may have to bite the bullet and get tested for glasses.

Bethany laughed. 'Okay. This guy, Craig Nolan, was given a life sentence for a string of robberies and a murder. It looks like he was suspected of or connected to another string of murders, but no evidence for those – organized crime maybe?'

'How is this connected to Tim's murder or Sophia's?' Maggie scanned the screen looking for a commonality, but nothing jumped out.

Bethany scrolled down the article a bit further and Maggie continued to read. 'It seems DCI Hastings, who was a DS at the time, was the one who put this guy away.' Bethany pointed and highlighted the section on her monitor.

Maggie leaned in closer. 'Hmmm. Has this guy made some recent threats?' Maggie had often come across offenders who openly threatened officers involved in their case – Bill Raven immediately came to mind, but these generally panned out to nothing. Just words shouted in anger.

Bethany closed the article and pulled up some statements. 'Once I saw the article, I pulled these up. This guy made some pretty vicious threats towards DCI Hastings – basically saying that Hastings stitched him up and he would get his own back one day.'

'Shit – that article says he was released. Do we know when?' Maggie tapped the screen and Bethany pulled up the article.

'No date listed here. But it was a high-profile case, and he was interviewed by …' Bethany scrolled down the screen to the end of the interview, 'Julie Noble. Isn't she your mate at the *Stafford Gazette*?'

'Fucksake. I should have known she'd be involved somehow. Good spot, Bethany. Can you email me over everything you have? I'm going to contact Probation and see what they can tell me.' Maggie returned to her desk and called Markston Probation Office, where she learned that Sarah Hardy was Nolan's supervising officer but was unavailable to speak with her.

Maggie ended the call and tapped her fingers on her desk. She knew she'd need to speak to Nathan to find out how much she could share with Sarah. She looked over into his office and saw he was on the phone. His forehead was creased, and his free hand was waving about. She didn't envy whoever was on the other end of the line. Maggie felt a bit sorry for him then; he had taken the temporary DS role because he thought it would be less risky and less stressful. He had told her that his wife wanted to start a family and have him at home more. But lately it seemed like the police station was more of a home and he looked to have aged about ten years. She wouldn't tell him that though, not yet.

While she waited for him to get off the phone, Maggie waded through the statements that Bethany had sent over. Craig Nolan was not someone to be messed with by all accounts. He had form dating back twenty years and the recent photo showed he had kept himself very active in the prison gym. He was pure muscle from head to toe and covered in what looked like a mix of professional and prison tattoos. Maggie could only hope that he wasn't involved in the DCI's disappearance, as she feared Hastings would not come out on the better side in a fight. Though it could be what took the DCI off their persons of interest list.

Fuck it. She went over and knocked on Nathan's door. This couldn't wait.

Chapter Twenty-Nine

Maggie stood in the doorway; Nathan looked up and waved for her to come over. She sat and he finished his conversation, placing the handset down.

'Sorry to interrupt you but Bethany may have just found something worth pursuing. Just wanted to get your thoughts on it.' Nathan didn't need to know that Maggie had already tried to speak to Probation in the first instance.

'What's that then?'

Maggie had his full attention.

'Bethany came across a news article – an old case of DCI Hastings's. Looks like the guy was involved with organized crime – lots of robberies and he was put away for life but must have cooperated or cut a deal, as he had a short tariff. After ten years in prison, parole was granted and he's been released on life licence.'

Nathan held up his hand. 'The short version, Maggie.'

'Sorry. Reading between the lines, it looks like he wasn't too happy and made accusations that DCI Hastings fitted him up. He's only been out a few months. What if all this is revenge? Kidnap the Hastings family and – without sounding horrible – this guy, or maybe he got someone else to do it, is murdering Hastings's family, possibly setting him up the way he feels *he* was stitched up.' Maggie took a breath.

'Hang on a minute. Don't you think that's a bit far-fetched? Why would this guy risk going back to prison, especially if he felt Hastings set him up? I don't think we can jump to those sorts of conclusions without solid evidence.'

'I agree. That's why I'd like to talk to his Probation Officer – it's Sarah Hardy. See if he's been behaving strangely or maybe let something slip in supervision. We could bring him in for questioning.'

'Back up. What are you going to pull him in for questioning on? A random comment he said over ten years ago when he was angry? Or a throwaway comment to Probation? You'd need more than that, and we'd have to clear anything with Rutherford in the first instance. Once all the information we have hits the news, there will be a media frenzy and this guy has already spoken to the papers. There's protocol to follow.'

'But what if …?'

'But nothing. Stay away from this until we know more. If you go and raise suspicions before we have any reason to, you could screw up the whole case.'

'Fine.' Maggie huffed. 'Shouldn't we liaise with Probation anyway, to see if they have any other potentially risky cases?'

'Of course. Just make sure that you don't mention anything about Hastings's possible involvement at this time.'

Maggie stood. 'No problem.'

Maggie wouldn't mention Hastings's possible involvement, but Nathan hadn't said that she couldn't mention Hastings at all.

Chapter Thirty

Maggie picked up her mobile and walked down the hall in search of an empty office. Nathan made it clear that she shouldn't be sharing any information with other agencies yet, but she could always ask for forgiveness if this blew up in her face. This wouldn't be the first time she acted on a hunch.

There was a free office at the end of the corridor and Maggie closed the door behind her. She sat facing the door, dialled Probation and tapped the table to the music from the other end of the line as she waited for Sarah to pick up.

'Sarah Hardy speaking. How can I help?'

'Thanks for taking my call. I can't risk anyone overhearing our conversation at this stage, and I trust you'll keep whatever we speak of in confidence for the time being.' Maggie waited for a reply.

Sarah sighed down the line.

'Sounds serious. Am I going to get into trouble for any of this?'

'Honest answer? I've no clue. So, if you want to just forget we even started, no harm done, and we can wait for the official request. I totally understand, but I want to stress that people's lives may be at stake.'

Sarah paused. Maggie realized she was placing Sarah in an awkward position but felt she had no choice. Waiting could mean another victim and Maggie didn't want that on her conscience.

'Shit, Maggie. I'll hear you out and we take it from there.'

Maggie could hear Sarah's keyboard clacking in the background.

'What I'm about to tell you is highly sensitive and confidential. If any of this information is leaked, my arse will be on the line ... I could lose my job.' Maggie bit her lip. 'So, promise me that what we discuss goes no further.' Might be a bit dramatic, but she needed to get her point across.

'Shit! Shit! Shit! That's a lot of pressure.'

'Listen. We don't have a lot of time. I'll keep your name out of it for the time being. And if it comes to nothing, then there is no need for me to share your involvement at all. This will all hit the news at some point and at that stage, we'd be looking to speak to the agencies any way. I just need a bit of information for now.'

'I know you wouldn't be asking me if it wasn't paramount but fucksake, why does trouble seem to follow you?'

Maggie ignored the comment. Sarah wasn't wrong though. 'I need to know what you can tell me about Craig Nolan.'

There was more silence and clacking of a keyboard.

'Why do you need to know about him?'

'Are you okay?' There was something in Sarah's voice that made Maggie wonder if there was more to Sarah's nervousness. Had she hit a nerve?

'I'm fine. You just caught me off guard. That guy is a complete

dickhead. So far up his own arse and … never mind. What do you need to know?'

'I was going to ask how he was presenting in supervision with you, but your reaction has said it all.'

Sarah's voice cracked.

'Yeah, he's a bloody pain. His attendance is fine, but he tries to turn his sessions around every time he's here and thinks he has an audience. Never gives a straight answer and has this tone … like he's threatening you without actually threatening you – do you know what I mean?'

'Hmmm. Does he ever talk about his arrest and conviction? I know you do some work on that in your sessions from what I can recall when I worked in the DAHU, but I'd be interested to know if *he* actually brings it up?'

'It's all he fucking talks about. How he was stitched up. How the police have it out for him. How karma is going to get every officer who fucked him over. He was pretty pissed off with one in particular. Hang on …'

Maggie could hear Sarah typing on her keyboard.

'DS Hastings. Says he is the reason he ended up in prison.'

'Fuck. I was hoping you wouldn't say that.' Maggie rubbed her temples.

'I take it that's significant?'

Maggie wondered how much information she should share and, in the end, realized she had probably said too much already, so offered up enough without revealing everything – if Sarah understood the seriousness, she may be willing to share more information than she had in the first place. 'It's *DCI* Hastings now and his family is missing. I think there is more to the story and Mr Nolan may be the key to some answers.'

'Oh fuck. I don't think I want to know any more, Maggie.'

Sarah's breathing quickened down the line. *'Do you have any evidence that Craig is involved? I mean, should I be thinking of recalling him?'*

'Nothing yet. That's why I wanted to talk to you first. If Craig still has bad feelings towards Hastings, maybe he has something to do with the disappearance of the family.'

'Well, I can't just leave this now. I'm really sorry, Maggie, I am going to have to speak to my manager.'

'Just give me a bit more time. I still need to speak things through with DS Wright. Please, Sarah. We don't want to alert Craig and have him do something to Hastings or his family if he is involved.'

'This really is unfair. You've really put me in a situation I would have rather avoided.'

'I know and I'm sorry, but I couldn't think of any other way. I'm going to speak to Nathan as soon as I can and get the official ball rolling. I just have to convince him and Rutherford that Craig is a person of interest.'

'Fine. But make it quick. I'll be seeing him soon – what the hell should I say?'

'Just ask him about his latest offence and jot down anything that may be significant in terms of Hastings. He needs to say it himself though, no prompting from you. I promise I'll come back to you ASAP.'

Sarah ended the call, and Maggie hoped she hadn't overstepped the mark. She'd go and speak to Nathan – she had just about convinced herself that he wouldn't have an issue with having Probation involved if Craig Nolan was the perpetrator. After all, it took the heat off the DCI and that couldn't be seen as a bad thing.

Chapter Thirty-One

A loud crash coming from DI Rutherford's office caused Maggie to jump out of her chair. When Nathan came bounding out of his office, Maggie chased after him towards the location of the boom.

Maggie stood in the doorway as Nathan entered DI Rutherford's office. A printer lay battered on the floor, pieces of the machine scattered on the carpet, and DI Rutherford was pacing around the room, cursing in between the moments she stopped to kick the already broken machine.

'Are you okay, guv?' Nathan stood between the DI and the printer. Maggie wasn't sure if he was more concerned about DI Rutherford causing herself injury or the DI causing further damage to the printer, making it irreparable and adding a further cost to their already depleted budget. She had overheard him telling someone that the department's money was tight so they would have to watch every penny when it came to securing additional resources.

'Obviously I'm not okay, Nathan. Christ, I'm attacking a

printer.' She leaned over to catch her breath. 'Right. Get everyone together in the briefing room. I need a minute to calm down.' Rutherford took a deep breath and stared at Maggie and Nathan. 'I'm fine. Go ... now.'

Maggie didn't need telling twice. Nathan shifted his head towards the door. 'Gather the team. I'm just going to hang back and make sure she really is okay. See you in five.' He returned to DI Rutherford's office, and Maggie headed to the team's open-plan space. She held her hands up when Kat and Bethany fired questions at her simultaneously.

'DI Rutherford wants us all in the briefing room now. I don't know why, but after seeing what she did to her printer, I think we need to be prepared.' Maggie picked up the notepad off her desk and strode to the briefing room, grabbing a seat at the front.

Kat plonked down beside her and leaned in. 'Fucking hell – it's all going off, isn't it?'

Before Maggie could respond, DI Rutherford stomped into the room, with Nathan trailing close behind. He took a seat across from Maggie. The look he gave her told her all she needed to know. She braced herself for what would follow.

'We've got a situation here, people. I've just had the results back from the hammer that was found beside Tim's body.' DI Rutherford rubbed her forehead. 'Partial prints were found on the handle and – they definitely belonged to DCI Hastings. But that's not all, folks, the blood in his office – all Olivia Hastings.' She rubbed her hands together. 'If you recall the crime scene photos – that was a lot of blood.'

The room rumbled with various expletives, gasps, and heads shaking.

'I haven't finished. Hair strands matching Hastings were

also found on Tim's clothing and, the final nail in the coffin … skin cells which were a direct DNA match to DCI Hastings, Sophia Hastings, and Olivia Hastings were found underneath Tim's fingernails.' DI Rutherford poured herself a glass of water from the jug in front of her and took a large gulp of water before continuing. 'I know we were unsure about adding Hastings as a person of interest, as none of us really wanted to believe that was the case. However, we now have definitive evidence, and I can confirm that at this very moment, DCI Hastings is no longer being considered a victim of abduction. He's now a direct POI in Tim's murder, Sophia's abduction, and the abduction of his daughter, Olivia. In terms of Sophia Hastings's murder, we don't have all the physical evidence to connect him to that – yet. So, we'll keep an open mind but given the situation … there has to be a reasonable explanation for all this. I should add that Dr Blake advised the prints on the hammer were disturbed, so that means that Hastings wasn't necessarily the last person to hold the hammer, or he wore gloves when he committed the assault. We're still waiting for information on the blood and skin cells found under Sophia Hastings's nails.'

'Holy shitballs! This is huuuuuge. We're going to have to tell the press all this now, right?' Kat blurted out what everyone else appeared to be thinking.

DI Rutherford looked at Nathan before responding. Her face drained of colour. 'Nathan and I will be meeting with the Comms Department after this – but we'd like to go over everything again, so we're not caught off guard.'

'Something doesn't feel right about any of this, ma'am. I had a bad feeling at Tim's crime scene – I mean who steals a mobile phone but leaves the murder weapon that could identify them? How do we know that Hastings isn't being set up? Or Tim killed Sophia and Olivia and Hastings was acting in self-defence?' Maggie frowned, immediately wondering if the probation case – Craig Nolan – could actually be involved in turning the tables on the man he believed had set him up.

'We don't. We won't know for sure until we locate and question him – but the evidence strongly supports his involvement. Who is to say that he was disturbed and then couldn't go back for the hammer?' She threw her hands up in the air. 'There are too many ifs. Hastings has been acting strangely for the last few months and more noticeably in the last few weeks. I should have talked to him or told someone.' DI Rutherford seemed to be talking more to herself than the room. 'I just want to reiterate that if anyone feels uncomfortable working on this case with this new information, now is the time to let me know; otherwise, we need to forget thinking of DCI Hastings as our boss and treat him the same way we'd treat any other person of interest, okay?' She sat down.

'We couldn't have known any of this would happen despite his recent behaviour. Like you said, until we speak to him, we won't know anything for sure. Let's look at what we do know.' Nathan stood and looked around the room. Maggie was pleased to see how Nathan jumped in to take charge when he saw Rutherford was struggling with the possibility that DCI Hastings had been hiding a dark secret for so long.

'Nothing from CCTV, but I'm waiting for the information from ANPR.' Bethany looked through her notes. 'I found some articles which were interesting. I passed them over to Maggie.'

Maggie sank in her chair. She wished Bethany had left that last bit out of the conversation, as Nathan had given her instructions not to pursue it, so instead of focusing on it, Maggie shifted the conversation. 'When we spoke to the college, we learned that Olivia Hastings was friendly with Tim Griffiths. So, there's a link there, although whether Tim was known to the rest of the family is unknown. We're assuming, based on confirmation from some of the staff and a student, the girl with her back to the camera in the picture is Olivia and this is why no one has come forward when we asked about information relating to Tim. The girl in the photo – Olivia – had already been taken.'

'So, what does that tell us in terms of Hastings?' Maggie could see that Nathan was trying to piece everything together.

'Maybe Tim walked in on something. Threatened Hastings and then he felt that Tim had to be … erm … taken care of.' Bethany didn't sound too convinced despite it being her suggestion.

'Hmmm. So why would Hastings want to obliterate his family – what's the motive? Financial? To hide that he was abusing them? And how the hell did he think he would get away with it?' Nathan turned to the evidence board.

'You've already highlighted a few reasons – money is always a good motive but if the abuse was about to come to light, maybe Tim confronted him? I don't know. I really can't see him doing something like this, unless he had some sort of breakdown, lashed out, and then panicked? Or …' Maggie stopped and wondered whether she should add another option to the floor.

DI Rutherford stood. 'Or what, Maggie?'

She noticed Nathan's eyes widen and he shook his head, but she had to say something. 'Or someone else is setting him up.'

'Why would someone do that?' Maggie could see a glisten of hope in the DI's eyes. Anything that might take the onus from their boss would be a welcome avenue to explore, so Maggie explained despite the look of anger on Nathan's face. 'There's a licence case, managed by Sarah Hardy, who swore revenge on Hastings, as he believed that he was set up for murder.'

There was a murmur in the room.

'And why am I only hearing about this now?' Rutherford looked at Nathan and then Maggie.

'I only just found out and was in the process of arranging to speak to Probation – just had to clear it with Nathan.'

Rutherford looked at her watch. 'Make it a priority for tomorrow then, okay?'

Looks like it was time she paid Probation a visit.

Chapter Thirty-Two

Sarah tapped the pen against her lip as she read over last week's supervision session with Craig Nolan. The conversation with Maggie had thrown her even though she had her own suspicions about Craig's behaviour. Maggie had asked her to explore his offences further to see if she could garner any information about his current attitude towards DCI Hastings. Sarah didn't like being used in this manner by the police. However, once Maggie had raised the concerns, Sarah just couldn't get them out of her head. Probation was always being vilified in the newspapers when a serious further offence was committed, even though the right steps were taken. Sometimes the procedures they had to follow limited what they could do.

Craig was due in for supervision shortly. He was on a life licence for a handful of robberies and murder, but until the last few years of his sentence, he had always protested his innocence. Sarah had been doubtful of his sudden change of tune and noted this in his parole report; however, the parole board saw fit to give him an opportunity and released him despite Sarah's reservations. It was her job now to manage him in the community and he wasn't always open to working with her. The desk on her phone rang. It was reception. Sarah glanced up at the clock on the wall. She answered the call. 'He's early. Can you ask him to take a seat and I'll be there in five minutes?'

Sarah gathered everything she needed before heading to reception. 'Hi, Craig. Would you like to come through?'

Sarah held the door open as he walked towards her. Once inside, she led him to the high-risk interview room. She'd be asking him about his offences and if he kicked off, she wanted to be sure she had followed protocol and could easily escape if things got heated.

She swiped her card against the security panel and let him in the room. 'Take a seat.' She pointed across from her. Sarah sat nearest the door and gently brushed her fingers across the underside of the desk to check which side the panic alarm was on in case she needed it. 'So how are you today?'

'Same as always. What do you care?' he growled.

'Are we going to start like this? No need for the attitude.' Starting him off in a bad mood wouldn't get her the information she needed, so she changed tactic. 'How about we just get stuck in then?' After going through her initial check-in list, Sarah eased into the session with an outline of what they would be discussing. 'Today we're going to revisit your previous convictions and I'd like you to tell me how the *old you* differs from the *new you* sitting across from me now.'

He scoffed. 'Why do we have to go over the same shit time and again? And where the fuck do you get those sessions from – you do see how patronising that bullshit sounds right? All the information you need is in my records. You've been my officer long enough to know how I feel about this.'

Sarah held up her hand. 'And you've been sat across from me enough times to know that this is what we need to do. If you don't like the wording, change the narrative – no need to get so defensive.' Sometimes it was like going in circles with the offenders she supervised. Craig was a classic example. When he needed or wanted something he would work with Sarah; she thought his patronising comment was rich considering he did it all the time, as if she couldn't see *his* manipulative behaviour. She also found it interesting that if she wanted to do any sort of offence-focused work with him, he did everything he could to waste time and avoid the topic. Sarah would persist though. She wouldn't let him be in control of the session. She pushed him again with the same question.

'Fine. Where do you want to start? My juvie record? Well, I could give you the sob story about my father being a prick, more interested in drugs and beating my mum or maybe we can start from when drugs took over my life and I started robbing banks? Got myself in with the wrong crowd. What's your preference?' He leaned back in his chair and crossed his arms.

'How about we start with your latest offence? It's your heftiest sentence and I'd like to explore how you went from everything you just described to ending up in prison for murder.'

He slammed his fists on the table, and Sarah jumped.

'I fucking told you, I didn't have anything to do with that murder. I held my hands up to the robbery, didn't I? But the police stitched me up. Fucking pigs.'

'I warned you before about your behaviour in sessions. Not

acceptable. So, take a moment and calm down. Once you've done that, you can tell me more about why you feel you were stitched up by the police – but watch your temper.' Sarah sat in silence and waited.

Craig stared at her through slitted eyes. He started ranting about how the police had always wanted him off their patch, particularly Hastings, who was a DS at the time. 'That fucker wanted to make a name for himself, didn't he? Needed some big case to get himself up the ladder and he didn't give a shit who he stepped on to get it. I heard he's a goddamn DCI now. Bet he fucked over a few other people to get that gig, as he definitely didn't have the brain cells.'

'You keep spouting off about this Hastings guy stitching you up, but let's look at it from another angle. What did he allegedly do? Why didn't you lodge a formal complaint at the time?'

'I'll tell you exactly what he fucking well did. He took a knife from my flat, covered it in Jimmie's blood, and planted it on the scene. Bish bash bosh – I get done for fucking murder. I mean, don't get me wrong, Jimmie was a fucking dildo and would've ended up dead at someone's doing, but it wasn't me. Oh, and then the receipt I had which fucking proved I was somewhere else … miles away … at the time they say I stabbed that fucker, ends up disappearing – Poof! Gone just like that. Seems it never got logged into evidence they say. I mean, what a fucking shambles.' He shook his head, and Sarah struggled to tell whether this was part of the act or whether he genuinely believed what he was saying.

'You never answered my second question. Why didn't you lodge a complaint or appeal your sentence?'

'What would be the point in that? A bunch of paperwork

that would be ignored by the police – or lost like that receipt. Pffft. Probably all in on it together. I did appeal – all turned down, so if I wanted any chance of getting out, I had to say I did it, didn't I?'

'How do you feel about DCI Hastings now?' Sarah stopped taking notes to watch for any changes in his behaviour or body language with her full attention.

'How do you think I feel?' he replied through gritted teeth. 'That arsehole took away over ten years of my life. The judge must have questioned something in the flimsy evidence the CPS presented, as he gave me a decent tariff – it could have been twenty-five years or more. Meanwhile, my girlfriend left me, my kids don't speak to me, and I can't get any sort of legit job to pay for a decent flat, so have to live in a shithole because no one wants to give a murderer a chance.' He leaned forwards in his chair and almost whispered. 'But karma's a real nasty bitch and I'm sure he'll get what he deserves.'

Sarah could see by his mannerism that he meant every word he said. 'You seem quite confident about that, Craig. What exactly do you think he deserves?'

'Exactly what I said. Serve that fucker right if he ended up in prison for something he didn't do, wouldn't it?'

That made Sarah sit up straight and listen. Could Maggie have been right? Was DCI Hastings being set up by the man who sat in front of her? 'Do you want to expand on that further?'

'Huh? What more's there to say? He'll get what's coming to him for sure. I just hope I'm still around to see it happen.'

That could be taken any number of ways and Sarah knew she'd have to share the information with Maggie, as it was obvious that Craig still felt persecuted and victimized. He hadn't exactly threatened DCI Hastings directly, but the tone of his voice made it clear to Sarah that this was something he had been thinking about, was *still* thinking about. He would've had plenty of time in prison to put together a plan. Could he be involved in DCI Hastings's and his family's abduction? At this point, Sarah wasn't prepared to rule it out. She needed to speak to her manager.

'Okay, Craig. Is there anything you need to tell me or wish to discuss before we end this session?'

'Nope.' He looked around the room, avoiding eye contact.

Sarah pulled out an appointment slip and noted down the details for his next appointment. 'I'll show you out then. Don't forget your keyworker appointment later today.' She tried to remain as calm as possible.

'I won't. See you next week.' He snatched the piece of paper from her hand.

Sarah stood by the door and watched him leave.

Fuck. If Maggie was right, and he was involved, a whole shitstorm was going to come her way. She didn't need this right now. She had enough problems of her own.

Sarah shook her arms out to release the tension she was feeling. Time to speak to her manager.

Chapter Thirty-Three

Sarah ignored the looks from her colleagues as she stomped back to her desk and threw her notebook down. She sat down in her chair, ran all the options through her head. If she went to Andrew Bourne, her manager, he'd wonder why Sarah now believed Craig's risk had escalated and would no doubt point out that the information she received from the police had somehow got under her skin and was in fact the reason for her concern, rather than any solid evidence.

Has Craig threatened anyone directly? No.

Has he committed a further offence? Not to her knowledge.

Is there a real escalation of risk? No, but there's potentially a risk of serious harm given his feelings of persecution.

Can he safely be managed in the community at this time? Yes.

Fuck.

The discussion with Maggie had seeped its way into her head. Craig Nolan had always expressed anger towards his conviction, so what evidence did she have that anything had changed now? None – that's what. No grounds for recall.

There's no way she could discuss this with her manager, as he'd just go through everything she had and tell her to come back when the police had charged him.

Yet – something still niggled at her. She picked up the phone and dialled.

'DC Maggie Jamieson. How can I help?'

'It's Sarah. I need to speak with you,' she whispered down the phone.

'Hello? Sorry can you speak up? I can't hear you.'

'It's Sarah. I need to speak to you about …' She looked around the office, but no one was paying attention to her. 'Craig Nolan. Do you have time today?'

The line went quiet. Sarah figured Maggie was checking her diary for the day.

'Yeah, I was going to call you anyway. I've shifted a few things around and can meet you in about an hour. Should I come down to Markston?'

'No!' She said that louder than she had wanted to. 'Sorry, uh no. I have a home visit to do this afternoon, so I'll figure something out and come to you.'

Sarah hung up the phone before she changed her mind. She rubbed her eyes. If she was wrong, she could risk a disciplinary or worse. But what if she was right and did nothing?

Sarah logged into her computer and printed off the home visit paperwork she had prepared for this afternoon's visit. The offender was a drug user, so Sarah would say she was dropping by the Drug and Alcohol services first to speak to her keyworker. The Home Visit Risk Assessment was already signed off by her manager, so she just needed to cover the other bases.

Sarah shrugged on her jacket, put her notebook in her bag, and let reception know her whereabouts.

'I'll ring when I arrive.'

The receptionist barely glanced up as Sarah left the paperwork on the desk.

She got into her car and prayed she was making the right decision.

Chapter Thirty-Four

Maggie had a knot in the pit of her stomach after that earlier phone call from Sarah. She had spent the last hour gathering the information she would need. This could be a major break in the case and move suspicion away from DCI Hastings. Before they could even think about bringing Craig Nolan in for questioning, she needed as much information as possible.

Her desk phone rang.

'We have a Sarah Hardy from Probation here to see you.'

'Thanks, I'm on my way.'

Kat looked up from her keyboard. 'Do you need me to come with?' Maggie smiled at Kat's eagerness to be involved.

'Nah. Just Probation. Won't be long.' Maggie hoped that her hunch was right so that Nathan would have no reason to tear her a new one.

'Okay.' Kat returned to whatever she was working on, while Maggie rustled through a filing cabinet and took out a file before she went down to meet Sarah. She made her way down to the reception area and opened the door.

'Come through. We'll use this interview room. I grabbed the information we have on Mr Nolan, hence the file.' She held it up before placing it on the table. 'Are you okay? You look a little pale.'

Sarah followed Maggie into the room and sat before speaking. 'Nothing feels right about any of this. I was going through things on the drive over and really don't want to get mixed up in a witch hunt. This could be my job on the line you know.'

Maggie nodded. 'I know and I'm sorry I placed doubts in your head, but I wouldn't have asked if I didn't think it was important. I don't want to keep you any longer than necessary, so what have you got?'

Sarah ran through her notes from her supervision session with Craig. 'He was really angry about Hastings, as you suspected – but like I told you before, he's never made a secret of that. What did concern me was the karma bit at the end. It wasn't a threat, but I got a bad vibe as he said it.'

'If that's the feeling you got, you're probably not wrong. It doesn't bode well. Do you think he has it in him to commit a murder in order to frame Hastings? Leaving aside any personal feelings and just looking at everything objectively, like a colleague came to you and asked your advice once they presented everything we have discussed, what does your gut tell you?'

'He's adamant that he never committed the murder in the first place. Has anyone investigated his complaint about being set up? Maybe that's what you need to do first – then if that fits, you might be able to add him to your persons of interest list or cross him off completely. I don't think I want to be involved in this any more until something solid comes up.'

Maggie looked at Sarah and couldn't believe her unwillingness to share further details. 'Is something else going on? I can't help but think you are avoiding the possibility because it calls into question your own work with him, but I can assure you we're not here to blame any person or agency. This is a murder inquiry, and we don't want to waste any time pursuing false leads.'

'Back off, Maggie. If you had anything on Craig, you would have arrested him by now. I can't recall him on a hunch – you know that.' Sarah's hands shook. 'Sorry. I don't mean to snap but the implications if Craig is involved … I guess I am a little off lately. Just some crap at home, nothing I can't work out, but that doesn't change what I said.'

'Fair enough. Can I ask just one more thing before you go?' Maggie took out her notebook and found the page she needed. She turned the notebook towards Sarah and showed her the pictures of the dot arrangements which had been found on both their victims. 'Do these mean anything to you?'

Sarah pulled the notebook towards her to get a better look. 'Yeah. I know what that one is.' She pointed to the image of the five dots – the one that had been rammed down Sophia Hastings's throat.

'What is it?' Maggie hoped she wasn't going to say something obvious, like dice.

'A prison tattoo. Quite a few gang members have them. See, the outer four dots represent the prison walls and the inner dot, the prisoner. Usually found on the hand or the neck. Why?'

'Do you know anyone on your books who has one?'

Maggie had thought of the gang culture when she had first seen the images and this confirmed it.

'Well, yeah. Craig Nolan has one on his neck. Is that significant?'

Maggie gathered up her file and stood. She needed to speak to Nathan and DI Rutherford. 'It might be very significant. Don't say anything to alert Craig Nolan that we were asking about him.' Maggie held the door open for Sarah. 'And thank you. This has been very helpful.'

After letting Sarah out, Maggie raced up the stairs. They may have just found their primary suspect and she wanted to let the team know so they could arrange to bring him in for questioning.

Chapter Thirty-Five

Without stopping to catch her breath, Maggie barged into Nathan's office. 'I know what the dots mean!'

Maggie walked around the room, burning off the excited energy the new information brought to the case.

'What are you on about? What dots?' Nathan's brow furrowed.

She stopped. 'The ones found on the piece of paper rammed into Sophia Hastings's throat. They're from a fairly common prison tattoo – often associated with gang members but not exclusive to them. What I don't know is what the one on Tim means. Unless the killer is removing a dot for each victim? In which case they have already murdered two people, Sophia being the first and that leaves three more victims: Hastings, his daughter and … who?'

'Whoa. You're rambling now. Take a moment and then explain to me how you found this out?' Nathan leaned forwards.

'I was speaking to Probation … Sarah, she supervises Craig

Nolan. He has the tattoo, Nathan! We need to bring him in now and search his property. He might be holding DCI Hastings, his daughter, and potentially someone else … we need to action this before it's too late.'

Maggie could see Nathan was going over everything she had just said. His eyes were searching the walls the way they always did when his mind was racing through details. 'Do we know of anyone else who may be acting with Nolan?'

'We can figure that out later, if we need to. He might not have got that far ahead yet. Can I go and bring him in for questioning?' Maggie was already halfway out the door.

'Take Kat with you. I'll get a warrant arranged so we can search his property.'

Maggie gave him the thumbs-up and called out to Kat. 'I need you to come with. We finally may be on to something!'

After finding Craig Nolan at his property, he'd been cautioned and brought into Stafford Police Station for questioning. This would allow for his property to be searched without any aggro from him. Everyone now knew how he felt about the police.

Kat turned on the recording device and explained the purpose for the interview. A duty solicitor sat quietly beside her client, pen in hand; she looked ready to pounce and Maggie suspected that Mr Nolan had told her all about his theory of being framed.

'I've been interviewed by the police before; I know the score.' He stretched his hands behind his head. 'What's this all about?'

Maggie had to be careful. She didn't want to alert him to

the fact that DCI Hastings and his family had been abducted, in case he wasn't involved, so she started talking about Tim Griffiths's murder.

'Do you watch the news, Mr Nolan?'

'Sometimes.'

'Have you seen that a young man was murdered on Castle Bank Industrial Estate? We're looking for any leads in that case that might help us find his killer.'

'I saw that. What's it got to do with me?' He looked at his solicitor.

'Did you know Tim Griffiths?'

'No. Should I?'

Maggie could see she was going to struggle to get more than a few words out of him, so she tried a different angle. 'That's an interesting tattoo you have on your neck. Can you tell me about it?'

'Which one, detective?' He pointed to an angel. 'This one is for my mother; God rest her soul.' Then he pointed to the five dots. 'This one I got when I went into prison for the first time. I must have been about fifteen, maybe sixteen. Prison walls. The dot in the middle is supposed to be me.'

'Were you part of any gangs back then?'

'I guess I was – though I didn't really think of it as being in a gang. I was a lackey really – ran some drugs. Beat up a few people. Small-time stuff but worked my way up until I branched out on my own. Why split my earnings, right? Why are you asking me all these questions about my tattoos?'

Maggie ignored him when Kat passed her a note. She read it and then looked at Craig Nolan. 'Do you still have any contact with your old associates? Maybe have some grudges that need to be resolved?'

'If I had any grudges, I wouldn't rely on those dipshits to sort it for me.' Craig's solicitor leaned in and whispered in his ear. She must have warned him about being careful what he said, as he turned to Maggie and carried on. 'I don't know what you think you have on me, but whatever it is, you're wrong. I'm on a life licence now – I'm not going to risk my freedom for some stupid grudge. I'm getting too old for that shit.'

Maggie rubbed her chin. 'Can you tell us your whereabouts for last Thursday and Friday?'

'Probably the same as I do every single day since getting released – Probation have had me on useless courses which take up most of my bleeding days and has done for weeks now – ask my PO, she'll tell you. Supposed to help me get a legit job … and chilling at home in the evenings.'

'Can anyone vouch for your whereabouts in the evenings?'

A sly smile crept upon his face and Maggie had a feeling she wasn't going to like what she heard.

'Yeah. REMS can confirm I was home all night.'

Maggie looked at Kat who shrugged her shoulders. 'Who's Rems?'

He moved his leg out from under the table and pulled his trousers up. Maggie saw the electronic tag – REMS – Ratcliffe Electronic Monitoring Services. 'I'm on curfew. Can't go out between 7pm and 7am every night for another two months. Whatever you think you have me for … I'm telling you, you're wrong.'

Maggie tried to hide the sarcasm in her voice. 'This was always just a friendly conversation, Mr Nolan. We'll have to check with your Probation Officer that there were no curfew violations, of course.'

He stood. 'Of course. Am I free to go now?'

'Yes. We may be in touch again.' Maggie slumped in the chair as she waited for Craig and the duty solicitor to leave the room.

'Fuckity fuck. I thought we might have had him there for a minute.' Kat started to gather her things.

'Me too.' She smacked her hands on the table. 'How did I miss the curfew?'

'Didn't Sarah mention it to you at all?'

'No. But I never asked about his licence conditions or the timings and I wasn't specific about why we needed to speak to Craig. I fucked up.'

'Well, we don't know that for sure. He could have been outside the curfew boundary, and he'd have to sign in for any courses. Get Sarah to send you over any violations he's had.'

'Yeah, I will do. Right, guess I'd better fill Nathan in – I'll leave it to him to tell the guv.'

Kat's face scrunched. 'That won't be a fun conversation.'

'That's why I am glad he's DS and I'm not. I'll catch up with you when I know more.'

Maggie took her time returning to the office, trying to think of the best way to let Nathan know that they were back to where they had started.

But even if Craig was on curfew, it didn't mean he wasn't involved.

Chapter Thirty-Six

Maggie walked into Nathan's office with her tail between her legs. She had been too sure that Craig Nolan was someone they should focus on, mainly because she hated the idea that one of her colleagues could be a cold-blooded murderer.

Nathan looked up from what he had been reading on his desk. 'Shit. I take it you didn't get the answers you wanted. Tell me what happened.' He gestured for her to sit and Maggie obliged.

She put on her best poker face and explained the information she did have before trying to change the topic. 'I still have to do some further checks with Sarah, so it doesn't mean he's in the clear, but then another thought came to mind. Do we know anything more about Olivia Hastings's birth parents?' Maggie braced herself, hoping Nathan didn't see through her and get pissed off.

Nathan clasped his hands in front of himself before responding. 'Have you been able to speak with Social Care?

There was nothing in Hastings's paperwork that we stumbled across, but Social Care should be able to give us more about Olivia's background. Might be an idea to see if her birth parents had been in contact recently.'

'I'll get onto that now.' The sooner she left his office the better. Even if she believed she was good at hiding some things, Nathan was also good at reading her.

Maggie returned to her desk, dialled Social Care, and asked for Claire Knight.

While she was on hold, Maggie typed out a quick email to Sarah to find out about any breach relating to attendance on the course and curfew violations. She was pretty sure that Probation could share that information if there were ongoing concerns, but she'd be ready to get Nathan or DI Rutherford involved should it be required. The Senior Probation Officer, Andrew Bourne, at Markston Probation was usually agreeable, so she didn't foresee any problems. Her next step would be to get Craig Nolan's alibi verified. She had known cases where violations had been recorded and no action from Probation or the Electronic Monitoring Services (EMS) had been taken, so the sooner they had those details, the quicker they could decide on their next move.

'Claire Knight speaking. How can I help you?'

'Hey, Claire, it's Maggie from Stafford Police here. Do you have a few minutes to talk?'

'Sure. What can I do for you?'

'We have a highly sensitive case here at the moment and what I need to find out is whether you have any information on the birth parents of an Olivia Hastings. She was adopted at the age of five and we have reason to believe that she had a pretty bad childhood – so is likely known to your agency.' Maggie gave Claire the date of birth for Olivia.

'Well, she could have been known to us, but if there were no ongoing concerns, her case would have been closed and the records destroyed six years after her last contact with us. She'll be what, nineteen or so now?'

'Dammit. Yeah, nineteen. If I email you over what I have, would you be able to look into it? Even if you could find out who her birth parents are. Is that possible?'

'It might be a longshot but if I do find out who her birth parents are, Data Protection would prevent me from sharing that information without consent, as Olivia would be an adult now. However, if she is potentially at risk of harm from her birth parents …' Claire paused. *'Leave it with me. We may have to get a bit creative but if you can assure me that someone may be at risk of serious harm, I can see what I can find out for you.'*

'Olivia and her adoptive father may be at risk. That I can assure you of. Anything you can find out would be fantastic. If you need anything from me, just let me know. Thanks, Claire.' Maggie terminated the call. She hoped that the social worker would be able to find the information they needed. If the records had already been destroyed though, they'd be back to square one.

While Maggie was updating the system, she felt a tap on her shoulder and turned around to see Nathan standing behind her.

'Do you have a minute?' He pointed towards his office. 'I just want to have a quick word. Finish what you're doing and pop in.'

She watched him walk away and scratched her head. All sorts of things ran through her mind: maybe he already knew about the curfew? She looked over at Kat but shook the thought out of her head. Kat wouldn't say anything when she knew Maggie was going to already. Maggie was aware that she could piss people off at times, but she couldn't think of anything recently that would warrant a conversation with the boss.

She closed down the browser on her screen, logged out of her computer, and went to face the music. She tapped gently on the door.

'What's up, boss?' She sat across from him and crossed her arms. 'Did you already hear about the curfew then? I was just going to tell you after I updated my notes.'

'No need to be defensive.' He pointed at her crossed arms and smiled. 'I really just wanted to check in and see how you're doing. I realize we haven't had much time for supervision, so I thought it was a good time to catch up. But why don't you tell me about the curfew you're on about? Does this have to do with Craig Nolan?'

Maggie nodded. 'I emailed Sarah and asked her to send over any violation details, but she did confirm his attendance on his course and with Craig's tag, he couldn't have been out during the times in question. He seemed pretty confident when I told him I'd be checking. Looks like we're back to square one.'

Nathan's lips pursed. 'And you didn't tell me this before because … never mind.' He held up his hands. 'We have the IT guys checking Nolan's phone records, so we'll see if maybe anyone else was involved with him, old associates who owe him a favour. I don't think we're ready to rule him out just yet.'

Maggie sat up straight and relief washed over her. 'I was a little worried there for a minute. I was expecting to get told off

– I guess I'm so used to it that I come to expect it when you call me into your office out of the blue.' She smiled awkwardly. 'Everything else is fine with me. Well, obviously this case is getting on my nerves – I'm frustrated at the lack of progress we're making, but it's not like we all aren't working our arses off.'

'Yeah. But that's not what I'm talking about.' He raised his eyebrow.

'Are you referring to Kate? No problems there either. I chat to her weekly and send her a picture of Salem every day – she'd kill me if I didn't. I've grown quite fond of him myself. Not sure if I want to give him back.' She forced a smile, realising she was waffling and hoped Nathan wouldn't see through her act.

He sat back in his chair. 'Have you forgotten who you're speaking to? Before all this …' He waved his hands around the room. 'I was your partner, your friend. I can read you like a book and I know that what happened with Kate really affected you. Talk to me.'

Maggie sighed. 'Shit. I forgot how well you could read me. Is this one of those tick box exercises you need to complete?' She took a deep breath. 'Fine – you win. No, it hasn't been easy. I feel incredibly guilty about what happened to Kate and I really miss working with her. We just bounce off each other – she helped me see things I may have otherwise missed, you know, beyond the evidence. Like this curfew bullshit. I should have asked for more details.' Her leg shook. 'Of course, I also feel so guilty about Kate. Did I fuck up there too, Nathan? Could I have stopped what happened?' Maggie had been a good detective prior to working with Kate, but having someone outside of the police to work with made her question things more.

'I knew you'd feel this way. There was nothing you could've done. We were dealing with a cunning killer who would stop at nothing to get what he wanted. Has Kate ever said she blames you?'

'That's just it. She doesn't. But that doesn't stop me feeling that way. I guess I was just having a crisis of confidence. I'll get over it. Thanks though. It's good to know I can still talk to you like before despite having to answer to you now. I miss having a partner.'

'If you need to talk about it or anything at any time, let me know. If I can't help, I am sure I can find someone who can.' He tapped his pen against his mouth like he was thinking about what he was going to say next. 'I'm glad you said that about a partner, as I want to pair you up with Kat.' He paused. 'Would you have a problem with that?'

'No. Why would I have a problem?' Maggie shifted in her seat.

'You've been working on your own or with Kate for the last few cases, so I thought you might feel like I was dumping a newbie on you.'

'I've worked with Kat in the DAHU. She's a good officer. I know her mouth is lethal, but she actually has a really good rapport with the offenders she worked with at the DAHU and this shows in her investigating and interviewing of suspects. I promise not to come across as a know-it-all if that's what you're worried about.' Maggie crossed her heart and smiled.

'I was more worried about your methods. You can be quite insulated, and I don't mean that as a criticism. You see things in that brain of yours we don't immediately pick up on – I guess what I am asking is to keep that in mind and maybe talk things through with Kat. Take her under your wing – you've got over ten years' experience as a detective. Kat is more than competent but I'm sure she'll appreciate some guidance.'

Maggie blushed. 'I'd be happy to. With your temporary promotion and the uncertainty as to whether Kate is coming back or not, well it would be nice to have someone to work things through with.'

'Great. I'll be honest, I was a bit worried you might fight me on this.' He wiped his brow jokingly. 'I have something else to tell you as well. Between us for the time being.'

Maggie leaned forwards. 'Oooh. Gossip? Or something more serious?'

'I've interviewed for this post on a permanent basis. There were three other candidates, and I wasn't sure I would get it, so I kept it to myself … but … I've been appointed the permanent DS of the MOCD as of yesterday.'

Maggie jumped out of her chair and ran over to Nathan. She wrapped her arms around him and squealed. 'That's fantastic news! Congrats, boss. I'm absolutely thrilled for you.' She stood back. 'When will you tell the rest of the team? Finally, some good news!'

Nathan laughed. 'I'll tell them when all this is over. I think we'll all be up for some celebrating then. Maybe Rutherford will even join us.'

'Already brown-nosing the brass, eh, Wright? You'll go far.' She poked him in the arm.

'Bugger off! Is there anything you want to talk to me about?'

'Nothing I can think of. Are we done then?'

Nathan nodded. 'Can you ask Kat to come in and see me? I'd better break the bad news to her.'

Maggie stood to go. 'Bad news?'

'Yeah, that she's now stuck with you as a partner.'

Maggie stuck her tongue out. 'Glad to see you haven't lost your bad sense of humour, boss. I'll let her know.'

Maggie left Nathan's office and called out to Kat. 'Nathan wants to see you. Brace yourself, you might not like what he has to say.'

Chapter Thirty-Seven

Lucy looked at Ronnie rocking in the chair in the corner. There was a void in her eyes. One that Lucy recognized. 'Would you like something hot to drink?' She could see the woman was shaking but when no immediate response was forthcoming, Lucy walked towards her and gently touched her arm. She leaned over and asked again. 'Would you like a hot drink?' Ronnie stared at Lucy's lips and nodded.

Lucy went into the kitchen and flashbacks shot into her head as the kettle boiled. The fear. The pain. Wanting to scream. She knew that triggers could come at any time but being around Ronnie released more memories than she cared for. Lucy heard a click and the signal that the water had boiled brought her back into the room, into the reality that she had a young woman in her living room who had possibly escaped an abusive partner. She had to ground herself and remember that it wasn't about her, though she still had her own triggers to deal with or she'd be of no use to anyone who came to the haven.

She walked back into the room and stopped dead in her tracks. Ronnie was smiling. Staring straight out the window, but definitely smiling. It would be all the emotions escaping – Lucy recalled her own experiences: laughing at inappropriate times, making jokes during serious situations. It was a way to deflect what she had really been feeling at the time. Lucy sat opposite and put the mug on the table. 'Here you go, sweetheart. You know how I told you that I'd been in an abusive relationship? One thing I've realized is that I wished I had confided in people sooner. I'm not saying that you need to right now, but sometimes getting it all out helps.'

The vacant stare out the window persisted but the smile disappeared. Lucy couldn't figure out if the woman before her had issues with her hearing aids, maybe they were faulty, or she was so lost in whatever had just happened that she was coming in and out of focus. She leaned across and tapped Ronnie's knee, repeating what she had just said.

Ronnie's eyes widened. She shook her head. Mouthing the words: 'No. No. No.'

'Okay. Don't worry. I know exactly how you feel. Well, I know how I felt in similar circumstances …' Had she pushed her too far?

Ronnie seemed to relax back into the chair. Lucy wondered if sharing some of her story might help but also feared that if she unlocked those memories now, her own nightmares might return. She had made a vow when she opened the haven that she would be as honest as possible with those who came to her for help. Her own counsellor had suggested it may help but reminded her that she didn't have to. But if her experience as a Probation Officer taught her anything, it was that people often opened up more if they knew that someone else had gone through the same thing. This was why a lot of the keyworkers and mentors in the Drug and Alcohol services were recovering addicts themselves.

Lucy bit the bullet. 'I want to reassure you that you'll be safe here. Just like the name implies – my purpose here is to keep you safe, accepted, free, and empowered – S.A.F.E. You call the shots here, okay? If you want to stay, you can. But I can't force you to. I lived with my abuser for far too many years but deciding to leave was the hardest decision I ever made.' Lucy took a deep breath before continuing. 'Everything was wonderful at first – isn't it always?' She smirked. 'But when he started to physically, emotionally, sexually, and financially abuse me – it was too late. He had spent two years worming his way into my head. Taking away my power and I let him.' Lucy looked at Ronnie. A tear streamed down her face and Lucy just wanted to lean across and hug her. She could see the familiarity and pain on the woman's face. 'I won't go into all the details, but as you can see, I did break free. I found my voice again and I want to help you find yours if you'll let me.'

Ronnie's eyes fluttered. She looked exhausted. The rain battered down on the window behind her and for Lucy it sounded like a million tears for all those lost voices who had yet to escape their abusers. She snapped out of her thoughts. 'I do have a room made up if you'd like to stay a while longer. Until you figure out what you want to do? The couch can't be that comfortable. I only stayed on it a day and my neck was done in.'

Ronnie's head dipped.

'If there's anything else you need, just let me know. You know where my room is, and the office. If I'm not in one, I'm usually in the other. Never worry that you're bothering me –

I'm here to help in any way I can and, of course, come and go as you please. You've a key and we can set up some benefits until you find your feet. I also have some funding available, like an emergency loan. We can work out all the details later.' Lucy stood and held out her hand. 'Come. I'll show you the room and you can settle properly. We can talk more whenever.'

A shaking hand cupped Lucy's and the pair walked up the stairs. Lucy stopped at the top of the landing and turned to the woman. 'That's your room there, if you want it.' She pointed to the first door on the left. 'I think I mentioned before, but in case I haven't, there's a kettle and everything you'll need for a hot drink. A small TV. All the details for WIFI – kind of like a hotel.' She smiled. 'And just down there is the communal bathroom. I haven't officially opened the haven yet, so there are no other residents expected; no need to worry about bumping into a stranger in the night. I'll be right downstairs if you need me.' Lucy waited until the woman closed her door before returning to the communal living room.

She sat on the couch and pulled the blanket that lay across the back over her. She hadn't realized the emotions she would feel at sharing space with people with similar experiences to hers, hadn't realized how it would affect her when they would one day come through that door. The emotions flooded over her like a tsunami and she felt like she was drowning. The tears came then, and her body shook as she let the memories invade her head. She would never be free of the memories, though they may fade with time.

She was fighting to keep her eyes open even though it was only the afternoon. A short nap wouldn't do any harm; she didn't have to be anywhere later. The minutes passed and as each memory came and went, she grew more tired. Patrick's face. Shell's face. Rory's face and little Siobhan. She had made her peace with most, but Siobhan still wouldn't speak with her. She understood and when she visited Rory last, he told her that Siobhan had asked about her again. Small steps.

Closing her eyes, Lucy let sleep take over. She was stronger than she gave herself credit for. She needed all that strength now more than ever. There was a woman upstairs who was counting on her and she wouldn't let her down.

Chapter Thirty-Eight

Kat walked out of Nathan's office with a sideways smile. 'That wasn't so bad at all.'

'Can you be ready in five?' Maggie slipped on her coat and grabbed her phone, placing it in her pocket as she waited for Kat. She had an idea and wanted to follow through before anything else popped up.

'Hell yeah. I can't wait to see how you piece things together. Should I bring anything?' Maggie watched as Kat searched around her desk for a pad. Maggie wasn't the neatest of people, but Kat's desk was like a typhoon had come through the office.

She shrugged. 'Up to you. I'm going to want your insight too though. Having another pair of eyes can really add to an investigation and don't be afraid to speak up either. I do know that I'm not always right …' Maggie coughed. 'Mostly.'

Kat burst out laughing. 'I'll drive'

Traffic had been a nightmare and it took the pair over an hour to reach the first scene, where Tim Griffiths was found. Maggie got out of the car first and stretched her legs. She tapped on the roof and looked in. 'How do you want to do this? Start from where the body was found or go to where we believe the assault was initiated?' Re-examining a scene a few days later could bring a fresh perspective and allow the police to pick up other clues they may have missed the first time around.

Kat unbuckled her belt and grabbed her notebook. 'I'd like to start from the assault site and work our way forward ... if that's okay?' Kat got out of the car.

'Sounds good. How about you tell me what you see as we make our way there?' Maggie walked ahead, as she was more familiar with the crime scene. Even though the tape and markers had been removed already, she could see them all in her head and pointed out any relevant areas to Kat as she took in the scene.

'The statements say that this was a local spot for kids to gather and drink.' Kat's eyes were scanning the woods as they entered.

'That's right. Younger teenagers and some sixth form college kids, who I'm assuming supplied the alcohol. The crime scene was littered with bottles of that white cider shit, rubbish, and a few piles of vomit.'

'Fuck. You mean Frosty Jacks? Do they still make that shit? May as well drink embalming fluid. It stinks like glue. Can you imagine what it does to their insides? I remember those days.'

Maggie laughed. 'I do too ... well mostly, though having arrested and dealt with a lot of alcoholics who drink up to nine litres of that shit a day ... really puts you off hard-core drinking. Why do you think that's relevant?'

'Just wondered if the Griffiths's lad was at the party and maybe lured away.'

'Hmmm. Good point and certainly a possibility, though Dr Blake didn't mention anything about his blood alcohol level. If he had been drinking, she'd have mentioned it. We haven't located all the kids who attended the party and, those that did, either can't remember the night let alone who was there or are just not saying a word.'

Maggie continued through the woods, stepping over the broken branches which littered the makeshift pathway. About fifty metres in from where the body was found, Maggie stopped. 'Here's where we think Tim was first struck. Blood was found—' A small flower memorial had been laid out and Maggie bent down to look at the cards that were attached. 'Might be worth noting down these names.'

Kat bent down and made note while looking around the ground. 'So, he was struck on the back of the head once and fell here.' Kat stood back and took in the scene. 'Then he dragged himself out to the edge of the woods, down there – where it lines up with the clearing?'

'Yes. That's the theory based on everything we know.' Maggie stared into the distance and then turned and looked behind her. The trees were more overgrown the deeper into the woods you went. If there had been a party happening, chances are no one would have been able to see very far. It was a struggle for Maggie during the daylight. What a gloomy place to take your last breath.

'The killer must have watched Tim drag himself and then struck him on the front when he turned to – what? Look at the killer? Call out for help? Whatever the case – this is where he bled out and died. What I don't get is why didn't anyone notice him when the party had ended? Even if none of them drove, and let's face it, a few fuckmuppets would have driven, the nearest bus stop is through the car park.' A line etched between Kat's brows.

'Exactly, but if you look down there ...' Maggie pointed behind her. 'It's hard to get a clear view. Given what we know now, we have Hastings's prints on the hammer; teenagers surely would have noticed an adult amongst them. That's not something they'd likely forget, even if Hastings tried to blend in – you've seen him, he'd still stick out like a sore thumb.' DCI Hastings was over six feet tall and quite a wide build – he appeared to keep himself in shape, probably from his rugby training, which he still managed to take part in now and again according to some of his colleagues.

'Yeah, with the storm and overcast weather, it was pretty dark, and that area is poorly lit, so maybe they just thought Tim was passed out drunk and didn't notice the hammer? I know people who trip over things and don't even remember what they saw. The security guard was the one who found him and even he thought he was drunk.'

Maggie nodded and bit her lip. 'What if Hastings – and for the sake of argument let's assume it was Hastings – knelt over Tim to give him the final blow, then when he heard people coming, he dropped the hammer and pretended he was helping a drunk friend, obscuring his face so he couldn't be identified. The security guard didn't come across Tim until much later; by then the killer was long gone. He would have had to have had a vehicle, right? CCTV didn't pick up his car in this car park. The camera didn't show as far as the crime scene, but there is another way out of the woods through there.' Maggie pointed to her right and started walking. 'Keep your eyes open – I'm sure this area was searched but you never know.'

Maggie and Kat walked for nearly fifteen minutes before the woods ended and a small side street was visible.

'There.' Kat motioned to the left. 'That camera may have picked up something. We can ask Bethany to check it, if it's not already on her radar.'

'This road leads out to Kirkland Drive. So not much help really.' Maggie took out her phone and opened Google Maps. 'If I put in Hastings's address …' She entered the details. 'It's about half an hour away by car in that direction.' She pointed. 'But something about this whole scenario doesn't sit well with me.'

'I know what you mean. He's a cop. Why would he leave evidence he knows we would link to him and then abduct his family and disappear? Unless …'

Maggie felt a shiver down her spine. She didn't want to say the words, but she knew it was what Kat was thinking. 'Unless he wasn't planning to ever come back.'

Chapter Thirty-Nine

Neither Kat nor Maggie spoke as they made their way back through the woods and over to the pool car. Maggie knew that everyone was trying to come up with different scenarios to explain evidence that normally would have them nailing their perpetrator. 'Let's go over Mrs Hastings's crime scene. I'm not sure forensics have completed their work on site, but I can talk you through what I saw, even if it's from a distance.'

'I can see how revisiting the scenes can add value to the investigation when you're stumped. It's not too far from here if I remember correctly.' When they got in the car, Kat punched the address into the GPS and reversed out of the car park.

'Any regrets about going for detective now?' Maggie looked over at Kat, noting the grin on her face.

'Fuck no. I didn't think I'd be working on such a big case so early on. I actually thought I'd be desk bound for a bit; but this will be great experience.' She shifted the car into gear.

'Just make sure you don't burn yourself out. It's so easy to forget to shut off in our downtime. I'm guilty of that. But if I can offer any advice, I'd say that when you're clocked off, at home … forget about the case or you will find yourself exhausted and wondering why you have no friends other than your work colleagues.' Maggie laughed at the irony; she needed to follow her own advice.

'I hear ya. I've seen it happen and been guilty of it myself from time to time too. Think we all have.'

Kat indicated right and found a parking spot directly across from the allotment. The pair got out of the car and Kat followed as Maggie led the way to the second crime scene.

As they reached the shed, Maggie stopped. 'I want you to look at the scene as if it was your first time seeing it. Forget all you know so far, forget the crime scene photos. We've been working on the premise that Sophia Hastings was taken here forcibly. Probably not long after the Hastings's home was ransacked. See the drag marks on the floor? There has been some mention of two people carrying out this attack.' Maggie waited to hear what Kat would conclude.

'Hastings's family home wasn't the primary murder scene.' Kat was in the zone, and Maggie smiled.

'It is where it all started, but it isn't where any of the murders occurred. No doubt about that. Sophia was definitely in the family house, as the neighbours had said they had seen her the night before and no one could remember seeing her leave the following day. Some blood droplets also suggest a scuffle took place, but my feeling is that the scene at the house looked staged.'

'Like Hastings was trying to make it look like someone else was involved?'

'Or someone else was trying to make it look like Hastings

was involved.' There was still some activity with the forensic officers happening in the shed. 'Looks like they are still collecting evidence, so we'll just stand out here. Can you see that couch clearly from where you are standing?'

Kat nodded. The dark blood stains were hard to miss.

'Let's visualise this as if it is real time. Crime scene photos only give us a snapshot. That's where Mrs Hastings was discovered. She had numerous stab wounds to her body and a pair of garden shears protruding from her neck ... here.' Maggie indicated where the wound appeared on their victim.

'Christ. A personal attack? Revenge maybe? Multiple wounds to the body are often done in a frenzy when the victim is known to the perpetrator.' Kat studied the crime scene.

'Yes. But why stage her body in the shed? It's like the killer wanted her to be found.' Maggie went on to explain that the shed door was wide open, with Mrs Hastings in full view of anyone who came into the allotment.

'If we look at it from the perspective that someone is framing Hastings, maybe it was them mocking him – they took his wife, killed her, and then dumped her body somewhere they knew he would look or where they knew the police would look.'

'Hmmm. And if it was Hastings, maybe once he calmed down and realized what he'd done, he didn't want his wife to be left somewhere where she couldn't be found?'

'That works too. Fuck this is bad either way you look at it. Mind if I have a smoke?' Kat fidgeted with her lighter.

'Go ahead. Have a think about anything else we should be considering. Just stand back there so we don't contaminate the scene.'

Kat raised her brow at Maggie and instantly Maggie

realized she didn't need to say that – although she may be a rookie detective, Kat was an experienced police officer. 'Sorry. Force of habit.'

Maggie watched the forensics team as they worked. They were wrapping things up, ready to release the scene after all the evidence had been collected. That little niggle that had been poking her since they found Tim Griffiths was back again. She just couldn't see any motive behind DCI Hastings abducting and murdering his family or the youth. DI Rutherford had told them of a few concerning happenings involving domestic abuse accusations, but even they seemed off – but Maggie couldn't figure out what it was about them that bothered her.

She started walking through the allotment, keeping clear of the remaining forensics team as they worked. The lighting here was poor, so it would be easy to come at night and place the body. The area was fenced in and you needed a key to get on the actual allotment. She carried on along the outer perimeter when she spotted something. 'What the fuck?' Maggie immediately radioed Kat. 'Finish that fag and come to the back of the allotment. Follow the path along the left side.'

'Roger that.'

Maggie took out her mobile phone and took a few quick pictures.

'What's up?' Kat looked where Maggie pointed. 'Oh shit. Do you think that's how the killer entered?'

There was a large hole in the fence. Enough for a body to fit through.

'We'll find out. I'm going to get forensics over here. Can you stay there and make sure no one contaminates the scene further?'

Maggie turned and headed back towards the area where the forensics team looked to be finishing up. She approached one of the officers and gestured for them to follow her. 'Wondered if you guys had the chance to look at the fence along the far back? Only I was just walking around and noticed a big hole there. Could be how the killer got in.'

'We were just packing up – got everything we need from here, as far as I'm aware. You said at the back? I would've thought we'd have cordoned that off and collected what we needed.' He pulled out a notebook and flipped through some pages. 'Looks like nothing was processed there. The thick bushes were noted but no fence or hole. I'll come have a look.'

Maggie turned on her heels and the forensic officer followed behind. She stopped by Kat. 'Just there.'

The forensic officer walked through the grass to the fence and bent down. He had to force the bushes open, and this made Maggie wonder how one person and a dead weight would be able to do it.

'I can't say anything specific about the cut, but I'll check it out.' He rubbed his forehead. 'Can you stay there, and I'll get my equipment and collect some samples?'

Maggie nodded and turned to face Kat. 'Dr Blake had recorded scratches on Sophia's back and heels when Nathan and I attended the post-mortem. Could be where the body was dragged through this area – out of sight of the main entrance.' She rubbed her hands together. 'We'll get Bethany to check the CCTV from over there. What street is that?' Maggie took out her phone and opened Google Maps. 'Long Street – can you note that down?'

The officer returned. 'I've just spoken to a few of my colleagues and they confirmed that a thorough search was done when we first arrived, but with the thick brush, the hole could easily have been missed. You'll have to speak to the officers on duty to see if they noticed anything overnight. Either way, someone will get an arse kicking for this.'

Maggie smiled. 'Hmmm! Just glad it won't be me for a change. Thanks again. Let's hope it's nothing but kids messing about.'

She turned to Kat. 'Let's head back. We can chat through what we found today and see if our theories match.'

Chapter Forty

Maggie tapped her foot and stood over Bethany as she waited for Kat to pass the details they collected to their colleague. She knew it was a longshot, but once Bethany interrogated the CCTV around the backstreets of the allotment, Maggie hoped even a glimmer of new information may assist in moving the investigation forward.

'What did you find then?' A tired voice called out.

They all turned to find a haggard-looking DI Rutherford in the doorway.

'Are you okay?' Maggie walked towards her and as she got closer, she thought she could smell alcohol on the DI's breath. 'How about we go back to your office and I'll update you.' Maggie expected her boss would follow and breathed a sigh of relief when she saw her out of the corner of her eye.

In the DI's office, Maggie sat down and crossed her legs. 'Do you want to talk about what's going on?'

'No. Not really. Tell me about the case, instead.' DI

Rutherford shuffled some papers on her desk. Maggie's concern grew.

'Guv, you're in no state to discuss the investigation. I could smell the alcohol on your breath and if you don't mind me saying, you're looking pretty rough. It's late now anyway. Why don't you go home?' Even though Rutherford was her senior, she would never forgive herself if someone else came across the guv in this state.

The guv's head hung low. 'Shit. I'm never like this. I'll be the talk of the station.' She put her head in her hands.

'No, you won't. This is a difficult case and with everything going on, I'm sure the pressure from above is immense. What can I do to help?' Maggie had never known Rutherford to be like this or have alcohol on her breath no matter how tough an investigation was. Something more than the case had to be on her mind.

'I can't burden you with my personal stuff, Maggie. It's not professional. This investigation needs to be priority but …' She burst into tears. Maggie rushed around the desk and draped her arms over DI Rutherford's shoulders.

'Abigail. It's okay to share your problems. You don't have to carry whatever it is on your own. It can be between us. But if you keep things bottled up, you'll be no good to anyone.' Maggie reached across and grabbed a tissue, handing it to her boss. She rarely called the guv by her first name, not because it wasn't a done thing, but the team had always referred to her as DI Rutherford or guv; this time, though, she felt a more personal touch was needed.

'My divorce is a mess, okay. My ex is making ridiculous claims and it looks like he'll take me for everything I've got. Then I heard a rumour about the DCI coming in to cover for

Hastings while all this is going on … and well, it's just too much. This morning I woke up and just wanted to go back to bed, shut the world out and cry. Instead, I had a large drink for courage – just the one, I swear, jumped on the bus and hours later, made a fool out of myself in front of my team. What's wrong with me?'

'You're human, we've all had days like that. Look, Nathan can hold the fort until tomorrow – go home. Get some rest and come back fresh and focused tomorrow. If there are any emergencies, we know how to get hold of you.' Maggie started to walk out of the office when DI Rutherford called out.

'Thanks. I appreciate your discretion. Let Nathan know I'll ring him when I get home and explain things. Just tell him that I wasn't feeling well or something.' DI Rutherford stood and ran her fingers through her hair. 'Any emergencies or developments, let me know.'

'Will do, guv.' Maggie returned to the open-plan office and stopped in Nathan's office. 'Do you have a minute?'

'Sure. What is it?'

Maggie closed the door and sat. 'The guv's not feeling well. She'll call you when she gets home and wants to be informed if there are any new developments. Speaking of which, when Kat and I went to the allotment we noticed a large hole in the fence at the back. Easily missed the first time around because of the overgrowth, but a person could definitely fit through. Kat's asked Bethany to look at the streets behind the allotment – the killer could have parked on any one of them and dragged the body to the Hastings's shed.'

'Could they have done that without being spotted? If my memory is correct, there are quite a few houses on those side streets.'

'I guess it depends on timing. But Bethany has a good eye, so if anyone can find a car, a clue, anything – it will be her.' On that note, Maggie returned to her desk. The day was getting on and there wasn't much for her to do. She logged off her computer and picked up her bag.

Maggie's phone bleeped and she smiled when she read the message.

'That's me done for today. I'll see you both tomorrow.' Maggie gathered her things, waved to her colleagues, and headed home.

Chapter Forty-One

With the pressure of the case, Maggie needed a break, so when she received a text from Julie Noble just before she left work, to go out for dinner and a film, she accepted. Her brother was always nagging her to put herself first and it would be a good thing to do something for herself for a change.

Maggie looked at herself in the mirror for the hundredth time. Was her hair right? Too much make-up? Too little make-up? She held up a frilly blouse, usually kept for special occasions, against the black V-neck sweater she had on.

Fuck sake. She threw the blouse on her bed. She had no idea why she was making such a big deal or why her stomach felt like a million pins were poking her. The nerves were kicking in and if she spent any more time overanalysing things, she feared she would cancel altogether. This was one of the reasons she enjoyed just staying home. Leggings, a T-shirt, and her hair in a bun – heaven. Julie's text had been casual – no expectations – yet Maggie all of a sudden felt self-conscious and angsty. Like a bloody teenager getting ready for a first date.

Fuck it. Jeans, black sweater, and boots – her leather jacket to finish the outfit. That's it. No fuss. She mussed her hair, deciding to leave it down but pocketing a pony band in case it started to annoy her. She looked on her dresser for her favourite perfume – Olympéa by Paco Rabanne – and spritzed a few times on her wrists, neck, and sweater before heading downstairs.

'Well, what do we have here?' Her brother whistled. She hadn't seen him when she stopped at the bottom of the stairs to put on her boots.

She gave him the finger. 'Just meeting a friend for dinner and a movie.'

'Wait … did I hear right?' He pretended to stumble backwards as if he had been punched in the stomach. 'You're actually going on a date?' He clapped.

'Bugger off. It's just two friends meeting – not a date, okay? I feel enough pressure as is without thinking I have to impress someone.' She bent down and put on her boots, hoping her brother would leave it at that.

'Well, whatever it is, enjoy yourself. Nothing wrong with having a bit of fun. I guess I better find myself a girlfriend soon.'

'Huh?' She looked up.

'You know … so we can double date.' He winked.

Maggie picked up the soft cat toy from the foot of the stairs and threw it at Andy. When it hit him, he grabbed his chest as if he had been shot.

'Ow. No need for violence. If I'd known that bagging yourself a girlfriend was going to make you so moody, I would have stayed on holiday a little longer.' He turned and as he walked back towards the kitchen called out: 'Don't behave!'

Maggie smiled as she walked out the door. She'd decided to drive to the restaurant – with a murder inquiry hanging over them, she didn't want to risk having a drink and then being called in to work if any new developments came her way.

Maggie had arrived earlier than planned at the restaurant and she was surprised to see Julie Noble already seated. She walked over to the table, removed her jacket, and hung it on the back of her chair before sitting. 'I thought I'd be the first one here.' She smiled.

'To be fair, I thought you would be too! I've not been here before, so figured I'd leave home earlier in case of traffic or parking – but there weren't any problems. Nice place.' Julie tucked a lock of hair behind her ear.

Maggie looked around. 'It is. This is my first time here too. Bethany – do you know her? She works with me at …'

'Yeah, the small one, right?'

'Don't let her hear you say that; she'd rip you a new one. She mentioned she'd been here a few times, so I thought it would be worth checking out.' Maggie shifted in her seat. She hated small talk but preferred not to get into anything serious with the journalist, as she was never sure what her intentions were.

The waiter arrived, placed a menu in front of them, and asked what they wanted to drink.

'Sparkling water with lemon for me, please.' Maggie noticed Julie's eyebrow rise at her choice.

'I'll have the same.' Julie fiddled with the cutlery on the table.

The waiter nodded and said he would return shortly with their drinks, ready to take their order.

'Not drinking then?' Julie snapped her napkin and placed it in her lap.

'Not tonight. Just in case I have to go.' Maggie regretted her choice of words instantly when she saw the look on Julie's face. 'I mean for work, of course.'

Julie laughed. 'Makes sense. Let's get our order in and then you can tell me all about yourself.' Julie's lip curled in a smile as she picked up the menu.

Once the waiter had brought their drinks and taken their order, Julie wasted no time in asking the questions she wanted answers to. Even in her downtime, she made it sound like she was interviewing rather than just having a chat.

Was this what people thought of her when she was speaking to them?

'Tell me about your family. I know you live with your brother, but not much more beyond that. Any other siblings?'

'No, just me and Andy. I'm the oldest. My parents live in Glasgow – it's where my father is from. Once he retired, he wanted to move back to where he grew up. Mum and he love it there. I try and visit once a year and they come down here to visit their friends too. In fact, they were due to come down when all the Raven shit was happening, but I put them off because of Kate moving in.' Maggie noticed Julie's lip twitch. 'What is it? Don't you like Kate?'

Julie shrugged. 'I don't really know her. But you like her, don't you and I'm talking about more than friends.'

Maggie's eyes widened.

'Why do you look so surprised? Was it supposed to be a secret or something?'

Maggie wasn't sure how to respond to the question. 'Erm. Well … Kate is straight, so we're just friends.'

A smiled formed on Julie's lips. 'That's good to know. I hate to think I'd have any competition for your attention.'

Maggie blushed.

'So will your parents be down soon now that Kate's left?'

'I haven't really spoken to them about a visit, but I guess I should. I think maybe once this investigation is over, and as long as nothing else comes up, they probably will be down – but I have to tell them about Andy first.' Maggie bit her lip.

'What about him?'

Maggie told Julie about her brother's gambling addiction, borrowing money from their parents and the friction caused over the years. The meal had arrived, and Julie listened intently as she ate. Maggie had yet to let her parents know that Andy was living with her, was attending Gamblers Anonymous in Birmingham when he needed to and that she had paid off his last debts, in return for him doing up her house while working at the factory.

'It's his last chance really. He knows if he fucks up again, I won't be helping him.'

'Harsh but fair.' Julie stuffed a spoonful of pasta into her mouth.

After dinner, the pair went to watch a film at a small theatre that had been due to close down but the locals had petitioned to keep open. It didn't play any of the blockbusters, but it was a good atmosphere and Maggie enjoyed herself – she even enjoyed Julie's company. At the end of the evening, they said their goodbyes and parted. Friendly. In fact, Maggie felt a little disappointed. She guessed a part of her had maybe hoped that they would have made plans for another evening. The Julie outside of work was a person that Maggie could see herself getting on with.

Maybe it was best they just leave it as is …

Chapter Forty-Two

When the team met for the morning briefing, Bethany had some updates she wanted to share. Nathan welcomed the team before handing the floor over.

'I've searched the bank and phone records of the Hastings family and it looks like £800 was withdrawn in total from three separate cash machines. The card has a daily withdrawal limit of £300 so this happened over a few days. However, none of them had working CCTV but we did manage to get this image. Unfortunately, the quality is very poor and the person – who could be anyone really – is wearing a cap, so we can't even get a good look at the face. We were also able to triangulate the location of the daughter's missing mobile and field officers located it dumped in a bin not far from the Hastings's home. It's with the digital forensics team now.'

'Is there any way to uh … tidy up the image? Or get an image from another angle?' Maggie squinted to see if she could define any of the features to no avail.

'I tried. No luck. I also tracked the sat nav in Hastings's car and the coordinates indicate that the car was used to go to the allotment but was then returned to the family home. After some digging, I learned that Sophia Hastings had a small runaround vehicle – a VW Golf – but that hasn't been located yet.'

'What about Tim Griffiths's crime scene? Was Hastings's car there?' Maggie hoped the answer would be no, as it could just be a coincidence that the car went to the allotment.

'Yes. The backstreet you and Kat mentioned to me, the one that leads into the woods, is where it was parked. One of the houses on the street has a security camera, grainy images, but the car was seen with at least two passengers, but maybe more. It was really hard to tell.'

'Are you saying Tim Griffiths possibly got in the car with Hastings? Maybe he'd offered Tim a lift home? They fought after Tim confronted him about what he knew and then he needed to take care of it,' Kat piped in.

'Well, we know Sophia was killed before Tim, so you might be on to something. Maybe Tim didn't know about Sophia but came around to visit Olivia and witnessed something. Can you tell anything more about the passengers in the car?' Maggie leaned forwards and strained her eyes to see if the images gave any details away.

Bethany enlarged the image on the screen, but it was too dark and once again, the camera quality was poor. 'I'm afraid not. We tried various things, but this is as clear as it gets.' Bethany then pulled out some papers. 'We have all their phone records and are working through these at the moment. So far, nothing unusual except with Tim Griffiths's records. There are repeated calls from an unknown number. I'm thinking it may be a burner phone, but we're still waiting on more information.'

'All the calls from that number – what is the time frame?' Maggie was curious as to why all the other numbers could be accounted for.

Was Tim involved?

'Starts the week before Hastings and his family went missing.'

'That seems a bit odd, doesn't it? If Hastings is to be taken seriously as a suspect, do we really believe he's likely to get someone else involved in his plan? How would that benefit him other than to get him caught?' Maggie tapped her pen on the table.

'No, you're right. We know Tim was often used by some of the older drug dealers on his estate to deliver for them. It's more than likely this is what those phone calls are about. Scrolling through Tim's phone records show there is a history of similar … bursts of calls all from various unknown numbers and spanning a short period before silence again. But we'll dig a bit deeper and see if anything else can be uncovered.'

'Excellent work, Bethany. Anyone else have anything to add?' Nathan eyed the room.

'Just one more thing to throw onto the con list …' Maggie pointed at the sheet listing the pros and cons of Hastings as a person of interest. 'The blood found on the back window at Hastings's was Tim Griffiths's. Tim's not the killer, but he could have seen what was happening to Olivia and her family and broke in to try and stop it. The killer forced him into Hastings's car, drove him to the area where we found his body and then returned to the Hastings's home to finish what he had started. This would explain the car trips, as that never made sense to me and that perhaps there was more than one person involved – the organized crime link – payback – Craig Nolan ... all seems to fit more than Hastings himself.' Maggie waited as Nathan stood back and looked at what he had just noted on the sheet.

'I see what you're saying but it's a bit tenuous at best, don't you think? We'll leave it up there for now – we may be able to make stronger links later. Anyone else?' Nathan turned back to face the team. 'No? Let's start crossing some things off the boards so we can whittle the information down and identify a suspect. I think we're close. Any day now we'll find that missing link and be able to blow the case wide open.'

Maggie hoped Nathan was right. The team were deflated – long nights, no solid leads – morale down – they needed to catch a break.

While they waited for more information, Maggie spent the majority of her day chasing up the curfew company, cross-referencing the prison tattoos – which was proving to be a very tedious job – and chasing up Social Care.

While waiting on hold, she recalled a conversation she'd had with her brother about how funny she found it that a large majority of the public believed that everything in a murder investigation was so exciting and moved quickly because of the way that it was portrayed in movies and TV – however a big part of her job focused on calls, computer work, research, and reports. She wished it was the opposite!

She hadn't heard from Lucy in a while, so during a short break, she sent her a text, to see if she could find out any more information about whatever had happened a few days ago. Lucy must have had her hands full, as she hadn't responded.

By the end of the day, Maggie's eyes were sore and a headache was looming – she couldn't wait to get home and relax.

Chapter Forty-Three

Maggie was more than relieved to finally arrive home that evening. After her routine of feeding Scrappy and Salem and throwing together a quick sandwich, Maggie changed out of her work clothes and into her pjs, headed to her little office area and opened her laptop. Salem meowed as he strutted out of the kitchen and joined her, looping around Maggie's legs. She scratched his head and laughed. 'How did you know I'd be calling your mum? She'll be so happy to see you.' Maggie picked him up and placed him on her lap. He wasn't as nervous as he had been when he first arrived and was quite independent.

She clicked on the Skype app. After two rings, Kate answered.

'Wow! You look better every time I see you. Ireland is definitely treating you well.' Maggie was genuinely pleased to see the smile on Kate's face.

'Ah sure, when you're at home, all everyone wants to do is feed you and smother you with attention. Especially when you've been

away from it all so long. Like a novelty. It's grand, most of the time, but can get quite tiresome. I do feel much better, if I'm honest. Distancing myself has done me the world of good.'

Just then, Salem jumped up on the table and headbutted the laptop.

'I think someone misses you.' Maggie laughed but as she tried to pick him up, he smacked her hand away with his paw.

'Aww Salem! Hope you're being a good boy.'

Maggie noticed Kate's eyes welling up.

'He's been an excellent guest. Even Scrappy's getting used to having him here … sort of.' Maggie used caution as she picked him up and placed him on the floor.

'Well, he'd better not make himself too much at home. I'll be wanting him back you know.' Kate tilted her head and raised a brow.

'Don't worry, I'm sure he can't wait to see you again and be glad to get his own space back. I don't want to keep you too long, so why don't I tell you what we have so far, and you can jump in at any time if something stands out to you?' Maggie didn't want to ask the question that had been on the tip of her tongue: *When are you coming back, Kate?* Talking about the case would be a welcome distraction and Maggie thought she saw a touch of relief in Kate's eyes.

'Fire away!'

'First victim, Tim Griffiths, just shy of his nineteenth birthday, was found on Castle Bank Industrial Estate …' Maggie went on to relay everything they knew about Griffiths and the crime scene.

'The murder weapon was left behind. Hmmm. Either the killer was startled and accidentally left the weapon, or it was left on purpose, maybe to taunt the police?'

'What I'm about to tell you next is of the strictest confidence. I know I can trust you to keep it to yourself, but I have to say it anyway.'

Kate leaned into the computer as if Maggie was going to whisper in her ear.

'Okay. I'll keep it to myself.'

'Fingerprints on the hammer were identified as DCI Hastings's. Skin under the victim's nails was also identified as Hastings's.' Maggie heard Kate gasp.

'Oh shit. What relationship did your DCI have with the victim?'

'No direct relationship that we can find at the minute. Hastings's daughter, Olivia, was friends with Tim, maybe even a girlfriend. But Tim's parents didn't know about her, so I'm assuming Olivia's parents didn't know about Tim. Do you think it was revenge or maybe he caught this kid doing something?'

'What did your gut tell you at the scene? Talk me through it.'

'Kat and I returned to the scene once forensics had released it. Someone from Hastings's home, using his car, we assume it was Tim as the CCTV was too grainy to make out faces, drove to the site.' Maggie paused and found a piece of paper. 'On the victim's face were four dots – like this.' She held the paper up to the screen and let Kate take the image in before she continued. 'We now believe those dots bear a similarity to a prison tattoo – but not the full tattoo. Maggie drew an image once again and held it up to the screen – the full five dots. 'This is what we believe the full image looks like and, coincidentally, this image was found on Sophia Hastings's body.'

'Sophia was murdered first and the killer is leaving their mark. Clever. If it's a prison tattoo, sounds like revenge could be the motive – I assume that you've found someone who may hold Hastings

responsible for something? If not, that is definitely an avenue you need to explore.'

'Yes. A lifer who was released a few months ago has always pleaded his innocence on the murder charge that Hastings brought against him. Claims our DCI – who was DS at the time – planted evidence in order to get himself a promotion.'

'And was Hastings promoted after that case?'

Maggie looked down and fiddled with her notes before looking up at Kate again. 'Yes. Something else you should know though – he has a pretty strong alibi ... he's tagged. We're waiting to see if there are any violations – the bloody EMS is taking ages to come back to us, but Sarah says that's common.' Maggie tapped her pen on the table. 'He'd need to have quite a few violations spanning over days, though, for all the evidence to fit.'

'Well, if he has links to organized crime, why couldn't he have someone else involved – helping him? They usually work in groups – have someone else do their dirty work.'

'He could. We just haven't found anything yet to suggest he does. Phone records are clean. He doesn't have a car, so ANPR and sat nav tracking came up with nothing. But we do have someone else in the frame.'

'Other than Hastings you mean?'

'Yes. A Mr Dodd. He's the Deputy Chief Exec at the college where Hastings's daughter attends.'

'And how does he fit in?'

'Some allegations were made about inappropriate behaviour towards Tim Griffiths. Hastings is on the board and he apparently had words with this guy, but no charges were ever made. There were previous allegations made against him – also found to have no substance. But if Hastings threatened him or he felt threatened, he could have snapped and sought revenge.'

'Seems unlikely though, don't you think? I mean maybe attacking Hastings, I could see that – but why Tim? Because he was the accuser? What purpose did it serve to kill Mrs Hastings? To prove what he could do? Hurt Hastings? And how does Olivia fit?'

'You're asking all the questions I asked myself.'

'What answers did you come up with?'

Maggie liked the way Kate challenged her rather than pointing out the answers – she made Maggie work for it.

'That so far, the two most likely suspects are the lifer and …'

'Hastings himself. I know you all probably don't want to hear it, but with his knowledge and even the fact that you're all second-guessing it could be him, I think he is the stronger contender from what you've said.'

'I was afraid you were going to say that. Thanks for talking everything through.' Maggie looked at the time. 'Best we call it a night and I'll come back to you if I think of anything else. You've given me a lot of food for thought.'

Maggie closed her laptop and made sure Scrappy was in before making a herbal tea. She'd need to shut her brain down if she had any chance of sleeping tonight – easier said than done.

Chapter Forty-Four

There was a buzz in the main MOCD office when Maggie arrived. Kat and Nathan were standing around Bethany's desk and they looked like they were watching a video. Maggie dropped her bag and immediately joined the group.

'What am I missing?' She squeezed in between Nathan and Kat.

'Bethany thinks they found Sophia Hastings's car on CCTV.' Kat was jumping from foot to foot – Maggie thought she was either really excited or she needed the loo.

Maggie squinted to see if she could identify the passengers in the car. 'Pretty dark. Is that two or three people in the car?'

Bethany turned and looked up at Maggie. 'I wish the government would invest in the cameras they have. The quality is pretty shit. There are definitely two people in the car – possible a third – just like before. See that shadow in the passenger side back seat? To me, it looks like DCI Hastings is driving, but I can't be sure. That's why I called them over.'

'You're right. It does look like Hastings. Where are they heading?' Maggie looked at the street sign but could only make out the last few letters, which was no help.

'ANPR and CCTV track the car as far as Compton Lane, but that's where we lose it. There are quite a few back roads out that way, some going out of Staffordshire, but if they left the area, the car would have been picked up on the cameras there. Looks like the vehicle is still in the county, but who knows where.' Bethany shrugged.

'Great work, Bethany – I know you've spent hours on these recordings. I'll let DI Rutherford know and we'll liaise with the Road Policing Units and field team to see if they have any spare bodies and ask that they keep their eyes peeled. Can you ping me over the make, model, and year of the car and I'll make sure to pass it on? Maggie, can you chase up those curfew violations with Probation – what's taking them so long?' Nathan called over his shoulder as he jogged back to his office.

'Will do.' Maggie returned to her desk, booted up her computer and while she waited for the machine to get going, dialled Probation.

'Markston Probation. How can I help you?'

'It's DC Maggie Jamieson from Stafford Police. Any chance Sarah Hardy is free?'

'I'll just check for you. Hold the line.'

Maggie drummed her fingers on the desk as she listened to the music down the other end of the phone. A moment later Sarah answered.

'Sarah speaking.'

'Hi! It's Maggie. I've been tasked with following up on Craig Nolan's curfew violations. Any updates?'

'Let me check – I haven't had a moment to go through my emails.'

Maggie waited while Sarah clicked her way through the emails. When Sarah came back on the line, her voice told Maggie that it was not promising.

'Sorry. Nothing back yet. I have contacted them again, explaining the urgency, but I'm afraid they can take ages to respond.'

'Would it help if I contact them do you think?'

'No offence, Maggie – but it wouldn't make a difference. However, if you want to have a crack at it, I'll forward you the details. They may ask for more information before they share details with you, so I'm happy for you to let them know you are working with me and the possibility of recall due to breach matters. That way, you won't need to go into specifics about the offence. I can deal with all that should we proceed to recall.'

'You're a star, Sarah. I'll get onto that. Has there been anything else of interest? Is Craig still attending his appointments?'

'He is. The only other interesting thing is that he mentioned in a recent call that he's heard that it was a rival gang member who planted the evidence that got him convicted. It's still being investigated through the Guns and Gangs Unit. Apparently, someone grassed in exchanged for lesser charges. I can't believe he was actually right about being set up – I thought he was just bullshitting! He's still angry at Hastings but he's speaking to a solicitor now about what action he can take. Thinks he's going to get a huge payout if his conviction is overturned.'

'Wow! That's some news and he's not wrong. I've heard of massive compensation payouts for things that aren't even as serious. I'll let you know if I get anywhere with the curfew.'

They ended the call, and Maggie immediately started to write an email out to the tagging company. Craig Nolan shouldn't get his hopes up about that compensation if they can prove that he was out during the times the murders were committed, and Maggie didn't envy the person who had to tell him that. He wasn't off the hook that easy.

Chapter Forty-Five

Maggie was exhausted after spending the day arguing with the tagging company for any information on curfew violations for Craig Nolan. They just wouldn't play ball and didn't take too kindly to Maggie getting Nathan involved. She hated days where she was stuck on her computer, but it was a necessary evil. She left work wanting to spend the evening on her couch, flicking through the TV or reading a book. Anything that would take her brain away from the case for a short while, but she was her own worst enemy and knew she'd probably end up thinking about the case regardless.

A knock at her door stopped her from feeding the cats. 'Sorry, guys. Let me get rid of whoever that is and then I'll sort out your dinner.' Scrappy let out an anguished meow and Maggie laughed at his dramatics as she headed down the hall towards the front door.

When she opened the door, she rolled her eyes. Julie Noble stood with a bottle of rosé in one hand and from the smell that danced up Maggie's nostrils, an Indian takeaway in the other.

'Wondered if you'd like to help me with these?' Julie held up the items in her hands.

'Haven't you heard of calling? How did you even know I would be home?' Maggie stood firm in the doorway. She didn't know whether she was annoyed or curious at the spontaneous visit, but still thought it was pretty cheeky of the journalist to just show up.

'I called your office and was told you left about an hour ago. I did the maths and guessed you'd be home by now. This food is getting cold and I'm starving – are you going to let me in or what?'

Maggie shrugged her shoulders and stepped aside to let Julie in.

'You adding stalker to your CV?' She knew that even if she had closed the door in her face, Julie would have stood there – she wasn't one to take no for an answer. 'The kitchen is straight ahead. I need to feed the cats first, then we can eat. And thanks – I hadn't even thought about what I would make for myself, it smells good.'

Maggie followed Julie into the kitchen and grabbed some cat food before the felines went into attack mode. Scrappy rubbed up against Julie's leg and Maggie laughed as Julie jumped back.

'Not an animal person then? That doesn't bode well.' She placed the bowls of food on the floor.

'I don't actually mind animals, but they usually don't like me. I thought that orange one may be getting ready to scratch me, and I wasn't about to give him the chance.'

'He's only interested in that.' Maggie pointed at the takeaway bag. 'You interrupted me feeding them – you're lucky you didn't get a scratch. Why don't you take those through to the dining room and I'll bring through everything when I'm finished here?' Maggie pointed through the doorway. She watched Julie and felt her face flush as Julie looked back and smiled.

'Nice view, eh?' Julie gave a wiggle.

Maggie ignored her and unlocked the cat flap for Scrappy. Once he had finished, he jumped through and Maggie locked it behind him. Salem would be a little while longer and then saunter up to the spare bedroom, which he had taken over since Kate had left.

She grabbed some plates, cutlery, and wine glasses and joined Julie in the dining room. Julie had been eyeing Maggie's desk and shelves in her office area. She put down the picture of Maggie's parents.

'So why are you really here? Not to borrow a book, I take it.' When Julie turned around to face her, Maggie handed her the plates and opened the wine, pouring each of them a generous glass before sitting down across from Julie.

'Can't a friend just pop round to chat?' Julie plated up the naan bread, rice, and chicken balti and passed it back to Maggie.

'Well, if we were close friends, I'd say of course, but we're not exactly BFFs, are we?' Maggie took a sip of wine.

'Fine. Shall we just cut the bullshit then? I'm not one to faff about and we've been doing this little to and fro for far longer than I usually allow. I fancy you, okay. I'm pretty sure that despite your snarky comments and the huge wall you manage to put up whenever I'm in the room, that you fancy me too. That's not conceit either. I did just catch you checking me out five minutes ago. So here I am. We've had some enjoyable evenings and I'm hoping for some more. Is that a crime?'

Maggie nearly choked on the forkful of food she had just shovelled in her mouth. She coughed and took a sip of her wine. She didn't know how to respond to that. 'Erm. Okay. What more do you want to know?' She shifted the balti around on her plate, unable to look Julie in the eye.

'Maybe we can go a bit deeper than the weather? I know a bit about your family, but how do they feel about you being bisexual? Do you have any interesting hobbies or is your life all work? Do you want to kiss me as much as I want to kiss you?' Julie raised a brow.

'Christ. You don't beat around the bush, do you?'

'I'm too old for games, Maggie. If I'm interested in someone, I flirt a bit, gauge the response, and then lay all my cards on the table. I spent a long time living a lie. Life is too short to waste dancing around and creating issues when there needn't be any.'

Maggie toyed with a lock of hair. Julie had a point; she'd done enough dancing around people to last a lifetime. 'Fair enough. My father is not very comfortable with same-sex relationships. I've not come out to either of my parents, as I guess … I don't want to disappoint them. My brother knows, Nathan knows, and Kate knows, and I am sure some of my colleagues suspect. When my folks, or anyone for that matter, ask me when I'll be getting married or having children, I avoid the subject.' Maggie was waiting for Julie's head shake but instead, her mobile pinged.

Saved by the bell.

She took it out of her pocket and read the message. 'My brother. He's out tonight and will be staying at a friend's, so I don't need to worry about saving him any dinner. Good thing I didn't bother then.' Maggie saw the smile creep across Julie's face but carried on.

'I'm a little embarrassed to say that outside of work, I don't have many hobbies. I like reading, going to the movies, hiking now and again … Fuck, I sound like one of those lame dating adverts.' Maggie blushed. Why did she always feel like a teenager when it came to dating? She could kick herself.

Julie laughed. 'No, you don't. Are both your parents Scottish? I've always wanted to go there. Never had the opportunity yet.'

Maggie shifted in her seat. 'My dad is Scottish. My mother's Irish. Andy and I were born in Staffordshire though – my parents ended up here when they got married. So, what about you?' Maggie scooped up another forkful of food so she wouldn't have to speak about herself some more. It was easier for her to hear about others than it was to open up about herself. She'd always been that way.

'What you see is what you get really. I hate exercise. I also like going to the movies, but no sappy shit – action thrillers or a good slasher movie are my thing. I've been single for far too long to remember – work has been my mistress as they say.' She took a sip of wine.

'What about relationships?'

Maggie thought she saw Julie's eyes glisten.

Has something upset her?

Maggie felt the heat rise up her neck.

'Not for a while.'

She looked at Julie's plate. 'You finished? I'll clear these up.' Maggie stood and took the plates into the kitchen. She rinsed the dishes and placed them in the dishwasher.

Why do I feel so awkward?

This was new territory for Maggie. She had experimented with women in her younger years, but all her relationships had been with men. She was stalling for time.

Biscuits. I'll put out some biscuits.

Maggie opened the cupboard and took out the chocolate Hobnobs she had been saving. She put a few on a plate and headed back to the dining room. Julie was gone.

'In here. I thought we'd be more comfortable on the couch. I hope that's okay?' Julie patted the seat beside her.

'Of course.' Maggie walked through to the living room and placed the biscuits on the table. 'In case you wanted something to nibble on.' She sat in the chair opposite Julie.

'I can think of something I'd much prefer to nibble on, but we'll play things your way. You can sit beside me, you know; I won't bite … Unless you want me to, of course.' Julie crossed her legs.

'Does everything have to be an innuendo with you? No wonder you've been single for a few years,' Maggie snapped and immediately regretted it when she saw Julie's shoulders tense. 'Sorry. That was out of order. Do you want to watch a film or something?'

Julie looked at her watch. 'Okay.'

'Do you need to be somewhere else?'

'No. I was just trying to see how late it would be when the movie finished. It's a school night for you after all. What do you want to watch?'

Maggie turned on the TV and put Netflix on. She stood and handed the remote to Julie. 'You choose. I'm just going to let Scrappy back in.' Maggie went to the back door and called out for Scrappy. Five minutes later he appeared from the bushes and sauntered into the house. Ignoring Maggie, he licked his paws and then trotted upstairs.

When she returned to the living room, Julie once again patted the couch. 'Please. I promise to behave.'

Maggie relented and sat beside Julie. As they watched the film, she gave her sideways glances. Even in her casual clothes, Julie looked gorgeous. Maggie hated to admit that they were probably more alike than she cared for. They drank wine and watched the film, laughing and enjoying each other's company. The film had ended, and Julie turned to her. The wine made Maggie feel a little more courageous and she leaned forwards. Julie had been right earlier – Maggie did want to kiss her.

'Whoa. Slow down.' Julie moved back and held a hand up.

'Oh God. I'm sorry. I thought this is what we both wanted?' Maggie rubbed the back of her neck, feeling the heat and hoping her embarrassment was not written all over her face.

'I do. But can I just put my wine down, that way I can do this …' Julie reached across and cupped Maggie's face. She looked into her eyes before leaning forwards and brushing her lips against Maggie's. They kissed passionately – tongues probing and hands exploring.

'You're shaking.' Julie stopped and looked in her eyes. 'Are you okay?'

Maggie nodded and stood. Something clicked right after she kissed Julie. She reached over and, holding out her hand, she led Julie to the front door.

'Well, I wasn't expecting that.'

'I know. I'm sorry – I just realized that right now is not the time to be starting something. It's not fair on you and I know I wouldn't be able to give you my full attention, but I'd still like to remain friends. Maybe sometime in the future if you're still single and interested, we can pursue something more … but now is not the time.'

Julie stroked Maggie's cheek. 'Okay. But don't wait too long. It may be too late.' And with that she walked out the door.

Maggie stood in the hall for a few minutes. The realization of what just happened sinking in. The funny thing was, as soon as Maggie and Julie kissed, it was like a spark went off. But not a romantic spark, that was there, of course, but it was at that moment that Maggie realized she didn't mind being on her own. She wasn't in the right place for a relationship, and it actually had nothing to do with her choice of partner. She also realized that she'd have to make some more time just to do normal things – coming home and working of an evening all the time wasn't healthy.

Maggie yawned. She tidied up before heading to bed and, despite feeling comfortable with her decision, she couldn't help but wonder if she had made a mistake.

Chapter Forty-Six

Maggie rolled over and reached across the bed. All she felt was an empty space and when she opened her eyes, she once again queried whether she was relieved or upset that she had let Julie leave last night. There were so many reasons that a relationship wouldn't work with the reporter but none that couldn't be talked about and worked around. Julie and Maggie were like chalk and cheese most times, but also quite similar. Maggie enjoyed their banter even when it annoyed her.

What have I done?

Had she made a mistake?

Reflecting on the evening before, she had wanted the kiss to happen; in fact, she smiled when she realized she had been the one to initiate it, so she had no regrets. Confusion washed over her. *Fucksakes, Maggie. Pull up your big girl pants – the case has to come first.* Of course the case had to come first.

She flopped over the other way and felt around for her phone. Her alarm was set for 6am and it was only 5:30. She returned to her thoughts about the evening before and smiled. Despite the way it ended, it was just what she needed, and they did leave it on good terms. Julie seemed fine when she left. When she was ready for something more, at least she now had paved the way …

Then she remembered why her alarm was set.

The press conference.

Maggie tensed. What if Julie wasn't discreet? The last thing she needed was to have her personal life talked about in the office. When she sat up, there was a dull throb in her head. She groaned and threw the blankets off her legs.

Maggie glanced around the room. Where was Scrappy? She looked at the door and noticed it was closed. She must have shut it behind her when she came up to bed. The cats would not be happy.

The pulsating in her head increased when she stood up; she rubbed her temples. She didn't think she had had that much wine, but she was probably dehydrated. She opened the door, grabbed her mobile and was greeted with two meows in perfect sync.

'Okay. Okay. A little quieter please.' Maggie nudged the pair out of the way with her toes and walked to the bathroom. She opened the cabinet and found the ibuprofen. Filling a glass from the tap, she threw the pills in her mouth and washed them down with the cold water. Her eyes were bloodshot – she'd need to think about late nights when she had work the next day, as she looked like she had been on a bender. She was glad she had some time to straighten herself up and could kick herself for being so reckless when she knew how important today would be.

Maggie headed downstairs and fed the cats. Her phone beeped.

Who the hell would be texting at this time?

A smile crept over her face.

I'm not sorry for anything that happened last night. I had a great time. Just for the record though, I'm going to tell people that I put the brakes on things. I have a reputation to keep, you know. ;) Anyway, I guess I'll see you later at the press conference. Looking forward to it in fact. Speak later. X Jules.

Maggie put the kettle on and scooped a spoonful of coffee into a mug.

She opened her iPad and browsed Facebook. She hardly went on the social media site but now and again she'd check in to see what her friends were up to. It was mainly pictures of their partners, children, or exotic holidays – they had a life. Maggie's timeline was filled with Scrappy and now a few pictures of Salem. She had a friend request. It was from Julie Noble and when Maggie looked at her profile picture, her breath caught. Julie's profile picture was stunning and as much as the reporter could frustrate her at work, she was drawn to her personality as much as her looks – if not more. Julie was bold, sassy, and not afraid to speak her mind. But underneath it all, Maggie saw something else – and it made her want to know more about the journalist. The way Julie was when she glossed over her past relationships made Maggie wonder what secret she was keeping close to her chest.

In a different time, Maggie may have pursued more than friendship, but she realized that she was looking for something to fill a void she thought she had in her life. But there was no void. Maggie realized she had been putting pressure on herself, thinking she needed to be in a relationship when, actually, she was okay on her own. Her family was part of the problem. Only Andy knew who she really was and accepted her for that. Her parents were not so understanding and because of this, Maggie had spent a lot of her adult years living a lie.

Maggie gulped down the now lukewarm coffee and after rinsing the cup, went upstairs to have a shower. The hot water released the tension that had been building up – though a cold shower would have been more appropriate. She rinsed the shampoo from her hair.

After getting dressed, she checked that Salem was in the spare room before going downstairs to let Scrappy out. He didn't look impressed that she had made him wait. She gave his head a rub. 'Sorry Scraps.' She locked the cat flap behind him. She left Andy a note to make sure he unlocked the flap for Scrappy when he got in.

Maggie put on her coat, grabbed her bag, and headed to the train station. Today could turn out to be very interesting for many reasons.

Chapter Forty-Seven

The MOCD office was busy when Maggie arrived, with the team in early, prepping for the press conference later that day. Maggie wasn't looking forward to what the press would be asking once they learned more details about how DCI Hastings was missing and now wanted for questioning.

Nathan had left a Post-it note on Maggie's desk asking her to go to the briefing room as soon as she arrived. She threw her coat over her chair, dropped her bag into her bottom drawer, and made her way down the hall. Nathan and DI Rutherford looked like they were deep in conversation. Maggie tapped on the door and Nathan waved her to come in.

'Thanks for getting here so early. We just want to get your thoughts on a few things before the team join us in a bit.' DI Rutherford's voice was shaky and the creases around her face spoke volumes. She looked like she hadn't slept in days. Maggie liked the fact that although she was a DC, Rutherford had always sought out her opinion on cases – Maggie knew her boss still wanted her to take up a DS role, as she had passed the exam at the same time that Nathan had, but management was just not her thing. Having one less pressure in her life was appreciated and the reason why she was always straight to the point with her senior officers. It was a mutual respect.

'How are you today, guv? You look exhausted.' Maggie rested a hand on her hip.

'You're not looking too great yourself. Late night?'

Maggie's eyes widened. She hadn't expected her boss to snap at her.

'Sorry. That was uncalled for. Please, take a seat and let's start again.'

Maggie pulled a chair out beside Nathan and looked at the evidence board. The picture of DCI Hastings with SUSPECT written in red underneath stuck out like a sore thumb. She still couldn't get her head around the fact that he was possibly involved in all this and that he had moved from being a person of interest to a viable suspect despite the other people who could easily fit the bill too.

Nathan turned to her. 'Could you use that brain of yours and go over the day we found Timothy's body at the industrial site? Talk us through everything.'

Maggie felt like everyone had gone over this a million times but appreciated that her colleagues wanted to make sure that they had not missed the tiniest shred of evidence that could clear Hastings, especially before the press conference. One of the things they valued was her ability to visualize a scene as if she was there at the time – it could be a burden at times, as she relived cases in her mind even after they had resolved them.

'Sure.' Maggie closed her eyes and began to recount the details to her colleagues. They listened intently as she spoke.

'Tim was lying face down on the grass, halfway between the edge of the forest and the grassy field …' Maggie paused, squeezing her eyes tighter to focus her thoughts. 'I still can't get the hammer out of my head … When I first saw it, I thought it was odd. Something is off … I know that Dr Blake said Hastings's prints were on it, but she also mentioned that the forensics team noticed a hammer missing from the toolbox in the shed – it could easily have been planted. The killer wearing gloves so that the only prints on it were the DCI's …' A thought came to her just then. 'I'd be interested to know from Dr Blake how tall she thinks the killer is.' Maggie opened her eyes.

'What difference will that make? I know you don't want DCI Hastings to be involved in this, but at the moment it's hard to rule him out.' DI Rutherford leaned back in her chair.

'My gut tells me we are wasting time focusing on Hastings as our prime suspect. He may well be involved – maybe he argued with Tim about his relationship with Olivia? Maybe they fought. But can you really see him following our victim into the woods, creeping up on him, and then hitting him over the head … twice? After allegedly driving him there? Can you see him standing there, watching Timothy drag his body to the edge of the forest and bleed out without feeling remorse or calling for an ambulance? Picking up the mobile phone and dropping the murder weapon beside a dying teenager? That's just not Hastings – he was so involved in helping people – the person we're looking for is more concerned about themselves rather than others. But even if we did accept all that, he's a police officer. He'd have known that would be too easy for us to trace.'

'That may be true, but it would explain why he is missing

right now. We don't know what happened between the family prior to their disappearance – an argument that ended up in murder is also a possibility. We still haven't found Olivia; with the amount of her blood found at their home, she's unlikely to be alive and there's also the question of how her mobile phone was found down the road from the family home. Although most of the information had been deleted, the messages found are concerning. Was she asking for help or covering her tracks? Mrs Hastings's car is still missing. He could be planning his next move as we speak.' Nathan rubbed his chin.

'Yeah, those messages are a mystery but the tech team don't seem to be able to find anything else. So frustrating. What about the markings on the victim's bodies – the dots? You think Hastings is trying to get us to look at Craig Nolan? He would have had to have been planning all this from before Nolan was even released on parole. It just doesn't make sense – but I guess it could be another theory …' Maggie tapped her pen on the table. 'How are you going to play this with the press?'

'That's kind of why I wanted you here … Nathan will explain in more detail.' DI Rutherford turned to Nathan and nudged his arm. A movement Maggie didn't miss, no matter how subtle her boss thought she was being.

'First, don't make any assumptions or jump to any conclusions. I'd like you to listen to what we have to say first and take a few moments before responding.' Nathan's eyes pleaded with Maggie.

'Why do I have the feeling that I'm not going to like whatever it is?' Maggie crossed her arms.

'I'm just going to come out with it. We're going to be vague with the press. We're going to push the missing persons

/abduction angle and ask for people to come forward. Bethany hasn't had any luck locating any relatives – well, she did locate an aunt, but she refused to speak to us and now isn't answering her phone.'

'Okaaaaay. I still don't see how I fit in with this.' Maggie clasped her hands together and waited for the hammer to fall.

'We know that you and Julie Noble don't have the most amicable relationship, but we'd like you to speak with her and see if she can do a special report on DCI Hastings – pushing the abduction angle. The Police and Crime Commissioner is offering a reward for any information that leads to finding the family – well Hastings and Olivia. But we have to be careful and not spook Hastings. If he is responsible for all this, we don't want him freaking out and harming someone else.'

Maggie felt herself blushing and tugged at her collar. 'I'm not sure that's a great idea and I can't really see how it's going to help.'

Rutherford looked directly at her. 'Our thinking is that if the public learn Hastings, a police officer, is a murder suspect – one of our own – well how do you think they are going to react? We need you to be a buffer between the public and the press. Julie Noble has a lot of clout both in the community and at the *Stafford Gazette*. She's instinctive. Make sure she doesn't find out all the facts – steer her if you need to.'

Maggie stood and paced the room. 'I don't like it. You know what she's like. She'll immediately suspect something if all of a sudden I'm willing to work with her or if I start feeding her information. She's too clever and even if she did buy what I was saying, she'd twist it for her own purposes. Don't underestimate what she's capable of.'

'You're clever too. Don't underestimate *your* ability to do this. We wouldn't ask you if we didn't think you could. You don't have to be best friends. Play the antagonistic part if you prefer, just monitor what she knows … and what she shares with the community.' Nathan wiped his brow.

DI Rutherford stood. 'I'll leave you two to work out the details. I have to go over a few things with the Comms Department before the press arrive.' Before she walked out the door, she stopped and turned, looking directly at Maggie. 'Don't let us down, Maggie. We're counting on you.'

'Christ. No pressure then? Nathan, this really isn't a good idea.' Maggie's foot shook under the table. She didn't want to have to tell him about Julie. Not yet. She didn't know where they stood after last night and moving from the professional to personal, it could be interpreted as a conflict of interest on all levels. 'Fuck.' She ran her fingers through her hair and took a deep breath before she spoke again. 'Can I trust you to keep something between us? Just for the time being? I'm speaking to you as my friend, not my boss.'

'What have you done?' Nathan crossed his arms.

'I haven't *done* anything … well … it would be nothing but now it might be something – shit. Okay, between us, right?' Maggie was flustered and her words were getting tied up in knots.

Nathan sighed. 'Spit it out, Jamieson.'

Maggie sighed. 'I've been out … socially with Julie a few times and well … last night, we kissed.'

Nathan's eyes widened and he ran his fingers through his hair. 'Oh! I'm not exactly sure what to say.' He rubbed his neck and Maggie could have sworn he was blushing.

'You're acting like I was a virgin and just told you I finally popped my cherry.' She laughed awkwardly, intending to break the tension but perhaps adding to it more.

'Well, I guess I'm not surprised but jeez … I suppose I didn't think you'd pursue anything with her; she's a bit … full on and I know how you struggle to open up with people.' He leaned forwards and Maggie moved back.

'Do you see why what you're asking is really difficult? We kind of left it that we'd focus on a friendship first, as I've no time for anything else, regardless of how I feel.'

'Damn. You actually like her; it's written all over your face! I just thought you pair were flirting a bit before, but damn … this does change things. I think for the time being, it's best you forget about attending the press conference. Let me think more about this.'

Relief washed over her. 'You see the problem then.' Maggie sat back in the chair and crossed her legs. 'Thanks for understanding.'

She hoped Nathan didn't share the information with DI Rutherford. He may be her friend, but he was also her boss.

Did I do the right thing?

Time would tell.

Chapter Forty-Eight

When she left the conference room, she didn't know how she felt. She trusted Nathan would take her feelings into account and weigh the options, but she knew that no matter what she felt, she could be put in a position where her personal and professional life might collide one day – and she hoped it was not any time soon. She went downstairs to catch up with the field team; she wasn't expecting to bump into Julie. It was almost like the journalist was waiting for her.

'You freaked out about what happened last night?' Julie stood with her hands on her hips, and Maggie immediately felt defensive.

'No … well … no. Why would I?' Maggie looked away.

'Exactly. We're two consenting adults. It doesn't have to mean any more than that. It was only a kiss. Why complicate by overanalysing one evening?'

Maggie tried to smile but inside she felt all sorts of uncertainty. Julie was absolutely right, so why did she immediately start to worry about what her colleagues might think? Not about her being bisexual, she knew they wouldn't give a rat's arse about that. More about the professional side of things – that she was *sleeping with the enemy,* even if that wasn't actually the case. If the news got hold of any privileged information, she'd be the first person the finger was pointed at. She didn't need that kind of grief.

'What are you thinking? You look miles away.' Julie reached across to touch her hand, but Maggie pulled it away.

'Look, it's not ...' Maggie's eyes dipped to the floor.

Julie held her hand up. 'Stop right there. Please, for the love of God don't give me that *it's not you it's me* bullshit. I don't need an explanation. You're uncomfortable or ashamed, whatever.'

'Don't pretend you know what's going on in my head. That's not how I feel at all. It's a bit more complicated than that. I'm a police officer. You're a journalist. We're in the middle of a murder investigation. Think about that for a moment. What do you suppose people are going to be thinking if you happen across some information that you shouldn't be privy to?'

'Ah.' Julie smirked. 'So, you're going down that route.' Her lips twisted. 'Well, maybe you're not giving your colleagues enough credit. Or me for that matter. I have my own sources and since when did the finger ever point at you when I reported something?'

'Well ... that was before this ...' Maggie's hand waved between the pair of them. 'Work is stressful enough without having to explain my personal situation.'

'Why does anyone have to know at all? We could keep it between ourselves. It's early days, Jamieson. We're not getting married, just two people who want to get to know each other better. Isn't that what friends do? Where's the crime in that? It's a wonder you have any friends at all.'

Maggie stayed silent. Julie was right, and she wanted to follow her logic, but if anything did develop between the pair, she'd eventually have to disclose it to her seniors formally. *Would they even care?* She shook her head ... she'd made up her mind.

'There you go again. Off in your own thoughts.' Julie's arm slackened. 'I'm going to leave you alone now. You have a think about all this ...' Julie exaggerated looking around, leaned over, and kissed Maggie on her cheek. 'But mark my words, Jamieson, you'll be back.' She waved her hands up and down her body. 'How could you resist this!' Julie winked and walked towards the conference room.

Maggie watched her leave. A smile crept up on her face. The journalist wasn't wrong – but it still didn't sway her view. At least the experience showed her that one day, when she was ready to pursue a relationship, she didn't need to fear rejection. A change was on the horizon, she just didn't know what that change would be. Yet ...

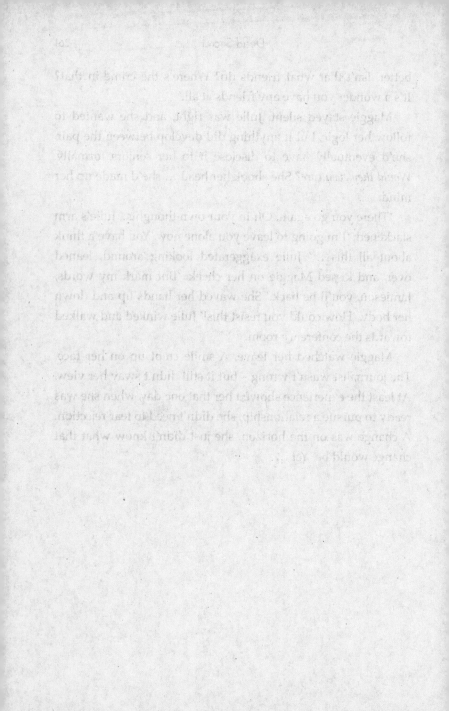

Chapter Forty-Nine

Lucy watched Ronnie out of the window as she walked laps around the front area of the property. Lucy loved the expanse – a large field out back, trees surrounding the property like an overgrown evergreen fence, and a massive front lawn hidden by shrubbery and a wrought-iron fence. When she had happened upon the property, she'd known it would be perfect.

Although it had been a tough time, Lucy was relieved to find that Ronnie was slowly trusting her and was pleased when she had asked Lucy if she could speak to Mark about the situation that had brought her to the refuge.

Lucy heard a car approaching, looked out the window and recognized it as it pulled up to the gate. She watched and smiled to herself as Mark got out and punched in the security code. Her heart raced as she saw him waiting for the large metal gate to open. Lucy walked to the door and opened it as Mark pulled into a parking space. Ronnie had stopped when she saw the car and waved over to Lucy. Lucy waved back and

Mark turned to look over his shoulder. Ronnie's head was down so she didn't see Mark wave and he shrugged as he walked towards Lucy. Mark squeezed Lucy's hand and greeted her with a smile that made her stomach flutter.

On her way around, Ronnie had stopped when she reached Mark's car, pulling her mobile out of her pocket and Lucy watched her type. She held the phone out:

'Will I make some tea?'

'That'd be great. I'll just have a word with Mark first and then you two can talk in the room I showed you earlier, okay?'

Ronnie nodded and typed: *'I'll just do one more lap and then be in.'*

Lucy gave her a thumbs-up and returned inside with Mark close behind her. She led him to the communal living room and, once he was inside, she closed the door behind them.

'Why do you think Ronnie has changed her mind now and wants to speak with the police?' Mark sat facing the window and Lucy noticed the frown as his eyes followed Ronnie's movements around the yard.

Lucy sat beside him and tapped his leg to get his attention. 'Why do you say it like that?'

'Like what?' Mark turned and faced her.

'With suspicion.'

'Well don't you find it strange? Asking to speak only to me? Just seems so out of the blue. Are you sure that what she has told you is legit?'

'Not at all. Something traumatic has happened to her – for God knows how long, she's been keeping it inside, living with it on a daily basis. She's not trusted anyone before – so it's only natural that she would err on the side of caution. There's no rhyme or reason behind when a person is ready – no time limit

– and who even knows what she'll actually disclose to you; but it's a start and rather than questioning that, we need her to feel that it's okay to talk whenever she is ready to, okay?' Lucy hoped Mark could hear the disappointment in her voice. He knew all about her abusive relationship with her ex-husband and how Lucy had kept it secret for years, lying to family, friends, and even her colleagues in the Probation service.

Mark shook his head. 'You're right. I'm so sorry, ignore me. I'm moody today and naturally suspicious when I really should know better.' Mark shifted on the spot. 'Will you be sitting in with us?'

'No. I've told her the session would be recorded and I'll watch from the office. I've also told her that she's under no obligation to speak if she feels uncomfortable. She can share as much or as little as she wishes, and she can stop the meeting at any time.' Lucy noticed a bead of sweat on Mark's brow. 'You don't look well at all. Are you sure you're okay?' She reached across him and took a tissue from the box on the side table, handing it to Mark.

'Yeah. I've been feeling a bit off the last few days but nothing I can't handle. Must be a virus or something.' He used the tissue to wipe the sweat away.

Lucy shuffled away from him. 'Ugh. You could have warned me.' She smiled to make sure he knew she was joking – she didn't want to have to deal with him misunderstanding her intention.

'Shall we make a start then? I'll see if Ronnie is in.' As the pair stood, there was a knock on the lounge door. Lucy opened it and Ronnie stood with a tray of drinks. Lucy stepped aside so Ronnie could pass; Ronnie handed Mark a mug, placed Lucy's tea on the table, and held her own, along with the tray.

'Why don't you leave the tray there and I'll take care of it while you and Mark have your chat? Let's get you two sorted.'

Lucy walked down the hall and pushed open the door to one of the interview rooms. She had wanted a less formal space in the house, so this room was filled with four comfortable chairs and a small coffee table in the middle. 'If you want to get settled, I'll go into the office – you'll see when I've started recording because a red light will appear in that corner.' Lucy looked up and pointed to the camera just above the door. 'Did you understand what I said?' She looked at Ronnie, who nodded. 'Okay. Remember what I told you – you can stop the conversation at any time.' She put her hand on Ronnie's shoulder and gave it a gentle squeeze.

Lucy turned and left the room; the door was on a hydraulic hinge and closed behind her with a swoosh. She went back to the lounge, collected her tea and the tray, which she left in the kitchen before she went to her office, and observed the interview.

Lucy observed Mark explaining things to Ronnie – what to expect, reassuring her that if she felt awkward or uncomfortable, they could move on to another question or stop altogether. He explained that he'd begin with some easy questions and then move on to the night in question, but Ronnie should feel free to be herself and not worry about what her revelations would lead to, as they would do all they could to protect her. He took a sip of his tea and then took out his notebook.

'Do you have any brothers or sisters?'

Ronnie typed into her phone. *'One sister.'*

'Do you talk to your sister a lot?'

'I wasn't allowed.'

'Are you married?'

'No.'

'Do you have a partner?'

'Yes.'

'Boyfriend or girlfriend?'

Ronnie paused at this before answering. *'Boyfriend.'*

'Does he …' Mark coughed. 'Excuse me one sec …' He took a large gulp of tea before continuing. 'Does he stop you from talking to your friends and family?' Lucy thought it sounded like Mark was slurring slightly. She watched as he pulled on his collar.

'Yes.'

'How long have you been deaf?' Mark's head was down when he said this, and Lucy frowned. *What was he playing at?*

Ronnie had been about to type something but stopped and Mark looked up at her. 'Sorry, do you need me to repeat the question?'

'What do you think?'

A flash of anger crossed Ronnie's face as she pointed at the hearing aids. Lucy's phone rang and she turned away to answer it. When she turned back to the screen, Mark was slumped over in his chair and Ronnie was crying and waving at the camera.

'Oh my god!' Lucy pushed the chair back and raced into the interview room.

Mark was sweating and his breathing seemed laboured. Lucy looked at Ronnie and shouted, 'What happened?' She tried to get him into a sitting position, but he kept slumping over.

Ronnie backed away into the corner. She was crying. Lucy dialled 999 on her mobile. Her hands were shaking.

When the call handler answered, Lucy explained to him that Mark was diabetic and was currently unconscious. He seemed to be having trouble breathing and was sweating profusely. Lucy didn't hear the next question, as Mark started convulsing.

'Oh God. You need to get here quick. Please!' she pleaded down the phone.

'The ambulance will be with you shortly. Please stay on the line.'

Lucy dropped the phone as she moved the table and chairs out of the way. Mark had fallen to the floor and she placed him in the recovery position. She heard the sirens and turned to Ronnie. 'Go and unlock the front gates.' Ronnie stared at her. 'Ronnie … I need to stay here. Open the gates now!'

Ronnie ran out of the room as Lucy whispered to Mark. 'Please be okay. I need you to be okay.' Tears streamed down her face. Minutes passed and finally the paramedics were in the room. Lucy stood back and watched as they stabilized and placed Mark on the gurney. 'Can I go with you?'

'Sure.'

She followed them out to the ambulance. Ronnie was standing outside – dazed.

'I'm going to the hospital. Lock the gates behind us. I'll call Vicki and ask her if she can come around.'

There was no reaction from Ronnie, but all Lucy could really think about was making sure that Mark didn't die.

Chapter Fifty

Maggie had spent the day following up on minor leads that the field team had been passing to them since the investigations had started. Calls and messages from members of the public purporting to have seen or heard something, but so far, none of them had panned out. On one of the messages, an officer had written 'psychopath' and then crossed it out and added 'sociopath'. There was nothing else on the paper. Maggie had her own thoughts but knew who would be better placed to clarify things, and before she left the office, Maggie messaged Kate to set up another Skype call.

Saying goodbye to her colleagues, Maggie packed up and headed to the train station.

Once inside the door, Maggie kicked off her shoes and fed the animals before making herself a sandwich and cup of tea. She'd eat while she chatted with Kate; otherwise, she probably wouldn't eat at all. She headed to her office space in the dining room and sat down, not even bothering to change.

'Thanks for agreeing to this at such short notice. I know I shouldn't be bothering you, so feel free to tell me to bugger off if you want.'

'Not a bother at all. So, what exactly were you wanting to know? I have about an hour before my parents call for me. We're on a relative round.'

Maggie raised a brow. 'Relative round?'

'Yes. Where we go and see every relative within a 20-mile radius and fill up on tea and cakes.'

Maggie laughed. 'Okay. Let's get to it. Your parents hate me enough as it is. I had a curious note left on my desk and basically, I wanted to know your thoughts on whether the person committing these killings is a sociopath or a psychopath. I have my own thoughts, but I think the team would benefit from your expertise on the subject.'

'This is why labels are so dangerous and I'm surprised that you of all people are quick to jump on that bandwagon.'

Kate's head tilted to the left, almost goading Maggie in a playful way to try and get out of the situation with her beliefs intact.

'Oh, low blow, Doc.' Maggie smiled and raised her hands in defeat. 'But I'm not afraid to admit when I'm wrong. I think we'd have a better chance of catching the killer if we knew more about what is going on in their head.'

'In the clinical sense, there's really no difference between a sociopath and a psychopath. Both are often used when describing people with Antisocial Personality Disorder. However …' She raised a finger for dramatic effect. *'A psychopath can also describe a person who's physically violent or puts others in danger.'*

'Yeah – that's what is confusing me. With both being dangerous and capable of murder ... well it is more of a challenge to get things right.' Maggie rested her chin on her hand.

'Well, yes – but there are small differences. Sociopaths can be dangerous; they are often consumed by their need to be in control – for power. They have absolutely no feelings of guilt or remorse. But contrary to popular misconceptions, they're not inherently evil, and some are highly productive members of society. In fact, you probably work with a few yourself.'

Maggie looked up at the ceiling. She probably could name a few sociopaths if she tried hard enough and laughed inwardly when she began to wonder if she herself could be one. 'I hear you.' She shook her head – she needed more, though, to ensure her own thoughts were on course. As if reading her mind, Kate continued with her explanation.

'Breaking it down even further then, in my experience, a sociopath is generally a person who might find that within their lifetime, they'll have committed minor crimes that don't cause serious harm or distress. But a psychopath will have been described by people close to them or a therapist as someone who's physically violent or puts others in danger. Both also fall under the characterizations of Antisocial Personality Disorder and those in the field of psychiatry will have differing views. For me, a psychopath is the more dangerous one. They are often narcissistic and selfish over a long period of time and simply don't give a shit.'

Kate tugged her ear.

'We all can have a selfish streak though. I guess if we recognize when we're selfish, and adapt our behaviour, that's what would distinguish us from being a sociopath. But a psychopath wouldn't care at all and just carry on with that behaviour – do whatever it takes to get what they want? Is that what you're saying?' Maggie took a sip of her tea. She was beginning to see things in a different light and realized that it was probably a psychopath they were dealing with in the murders. Did DCI Hastings fit that profile?

'Impressive! Have you been taking some psychology courses while I've been over here – you're not planning on switching careers, are you? I'm still after that consulting job if it's available.' Kate laughed.

Maggie shook her head. 'Don't worry, I prefer my job – I'd rather keep out of the minds of these people – it's bad enough having the little glimpses I do have. I don't know how you do it on a daily basis.'

'Hang on a minute.' Kate stood and walked away, returning with her large sheets of paper. She tacked the blank pieces up on the wall behind her. *'Can you hear me okay still?'*

Maggie nodded.

'Looking at the similarities between the two, these are the key traits that sociopaths and psychopaths share, and this is just off the top of my head so there could be more, okay?'

She held a green marker in her hand and began to write on the paper:

- *A disregard for laws and social practices*
- *A disregard for the rights of others*
- *A failure to feel remorse or guilt*
- *A tendency to display violent or aggressive behaviour*

'So, while I am writing these down, have a think about your persons of interests and where any or all of them may fit … I'll break down characteristics for sociopaths first …'

She carried on making notes and reading them aloud as she wrote:

- *Make it clear they do not care how others feel*
- *Behave in hot-headed and impulsive ways*
- *Prone to fits of anger and rage*
- *Recognize what they are doing but rationalize their behaviour*
- *Cannot maintain a regular work and family life*
- *Can form emotional attachments, but it is difficult*

'And now we can look at psychopaths a little more closely.'

She picked out a red marker and began writing.

- *Pretend to care*
- *Display cold-hearted behaviour*
- *Fail to recognize other people's distress*
- *Have relationships that are shallow and fake*
- *Maintain a normal life as a cover for criminal activity*
- *Fail to form genuine emotional attachments*
- *May love people in their own way*

'Many in the field suggest that sociopathy is more likely the product of childhood trauma and physical or emotional abuse and this is because sociopathy appears to be learned rather than innate; sociopaths are capable of empathy in certain circumstances and with certain individuals, but not others. So, I guess you could say that psychopathy is rarer than sociopathy and is considered to be the most dangerous of antisocial personality disorders. Not surprisingly, many serial killers have been labelled as unremorseful psychopaths. Do you watch that programme Killing Eve*?'*

'Yes. I love Villanelle!' Maggie exclaimed.

'Well, Villanelle would be classed as a psychopath – she uses people as a means to an end, lies easily, and has absolutely no remorse for her actions.'

'You should have said that at the start, would have saved you writing all that other stuff down.' Maggie burst out laughing as Kate crinkled her nose.

'Cheeky cow! I can take some pics of these and send them over to you. Your colleagues might appreciate my efforts.'

'That would be awesome. You know I was only pulling your leg, right? One quick question and then I promise to let you get off. The news is throwing around the serial killer label, but that niggles at me and I can't explain why. Any thoughts?'

'I guess, from the public's point of view, there is someone murdering people, but with only two victims – I wouldn't be so quick to jump on the serial killer bandwagon. From what you've told me so far, there seems to be a personal connection – even with Tim Griffiths. Don't ask me why, but I'd bet my career that he's connected to the victims and the killer. You just have to find out how.'

Maggie could hear Kate's mother calling out to her in the background. 'On that bombshell, you've given me a lot of food for thought. Thanks. I'm sure the team will be grateful for your input.'

Kate waved to the screen as Maggie ended the video call. Maggie leaned back in her chair and stretched her arms. Was Tim Griffiths the key to solving the murders and abduction? Maggie wasn't so sure, but a good night's sleep might put everything in perspective.

Chapter Fifty-One

Maggie had arrived at the office early in the hopes of getting her head around all the information Kate had provided her with last night. To her surprise, everyone else seemed to have had the early start idea too. She waved at Kat and Bethany before sitting down and booting up her computer.

Once she had logged in, Maggie opened up the Word document where she was putting together some notes on the case; she was planning to share this information with the team when she worked out all the kinks. An email pinged and was marked as URGENT. When she opened and read it, she looked over at her colleagues. 'Anyone know what the email is about?'

Kat and Bethany shrugged simultaneously. DI Rutherford had called a briefing at short notice. 'Hey!' she called into Nathan's office. 'Have you seen the email from the guv?' Even Nathan looked confused and the shrugging of his shoulders confirmed he was also none the wiser. Part of her wondered if they'd be in for a bollocking because they were no further ahead in identifying any viable suspects or locating their missing DCI and his daughter. Maggie stood and followed her colleagues down the hall to the incident room.

DI Rutherford walked to the front of the room with a man following close behind her. She stood talking to the mystery man as the remainder of the team found their seats. He looked like he was a throwback from the TV series *Life on Mars*. Triangular, bushy sideburns covered his face, and his sandy brown hair was almost feathered. He was handsome for his age and Maggie smiled to herself as she thought that all he needed was a long camel-coloured coat and he could almost pass as Gene Hunt – the foul-mouthed, crass DCI from the TV series. Maggie hoped his attitude didn't match the dress sense – outdated.

'Thank you all for coming at such short notice. I'd like to introduce you to DCI Aidan Meechan. He'll be stepping in temporarily to oversee the investigation and cover while DCI Hastings is ... erm ... missing.'

DCI Meechan touched the DI on the arm before speaking. Maggie thought she saw an awkwardness between the two. 'Thank you, Abigail. I'll take it from here.' Rutherford stepped away and took a seat across from Maggie. She was rubbing her hands as the new DCI continued to talk to the team.

'I want to assure you all that I haven't made any judgements on how the investigation has been run so far or on the possibilities, okay? I'm not here to step on any toes, but I am here to make sure that we have all the resources available to us to make sure we get this case closed as quickly and efficiently as possible. I'm a hands-on DCI and I also expect my whole team to be hands on. Whatever targets we've been set, will get met, if we're all doing our job. It's as simple as that. We need manpower and we do have that – only problem has been that some people have been tied up with meetings, spreadsheets, and other shit that can either wait, or be worked on in other ways. What am I proposing?' The DCI looked around the room and stopped at DI Rutherford. 'Your DI will work closely with myself as well as with DS Nathan Wright. They will be more actively involved in working with you all.'

There were murmurs around the room. It wasn't because Nathan and DI Rutherford weren't involved in cases, it was because they were more focused on the strategy while the rest of the team worked the operational side. How most police teams worked. Maggie wasn't opposed to the new DCI's way of working, as she knew Nathan missed being a full part of the investigation, but he'd still have the managerial side of things to juggle and the long hours he was already putting in would become much longer.

'What I need from you all is to make sure the lines of communication are open and free flowing.' He turned and looked at Maggie and she shifted in her seat. 'No one here is more important, more senior or knows more than anyone else – understand?' He paused. 'DI Rutherford has brought me up to date on the case, so this is what I want to happen ...' He pulled a piece of paper out of his pocket. 'PC Bethany Lambert.'

Bethany held up her hand.

'You'll collate the timelines and CCTV footage and pass these on to myself and DI Rutherford. We'll be looking deeper into Hastings's movements in the time running up to his disappearance. We'll also be looking deeper into his background. Have we missed something? If we have, this is the time we need to find it.' He looked at his paper again.

'DS Nathan Wright and DC Maggie Jamieson.' Maggie and

Nathan held up their hands. 'You two will be re-interviewing Craig Nolan. I read the previous interview – I think you need to push harder. Something about this guy doesn't feel right. Find out what that is. Curfews can be unreliable.' Another look at his paper.

'PC Lambert and DC Kat Everett.'

Kat raised her hand.

'I'd like you to go back to the college and speak to that Mr Dodd again. Why is this guy being so evasive? Is there more in his background that we haven't uncovered? What's he hiding?' He folded the paper and returned it to his front pocket. 'Someone knows something – maybe they don't realize the significance. Maybe they are deliberately trying to cover something up. Maybe they are involved. The field officers will continue to screen calls, speak to witnesses that come forward, and make sure we have all the up-to-date information as it comes in. I want everything recorded as it happens or immediately afterwards. The sooner you do it, the more accurate it will be and the less likely your methods can be called into question. If that means coming back to the station after your shift has ended – you do that. Last thing, I'm toying with the idea of doing a reconstruction, like *Crimewatch*. May jog some memories. We'll leave that in our back pocket for now. I don't want this case taken off us because the public or our colleagues lose confidence in our decisions. At the moment, the evidence against Hastings is quite damning – but it also leaves room for doubt. Right then, unless you have any questions, I suggest we all get a move on and solve these murders before we have another body to deal with.' DCI Meechan didn't even wait for a response from the team before walking out of the room.

Maggie turned to Nathan. 'Well, that was interesting. What do you make of this guy?' But Nathan was distracted. He was looking at DI Rutherford; she was rubbing her eyes. 'Nathan? Did you hear what I said?' Maggie waved her hand in front of his face.

'Sorry. Fuck, this is going to be interesting and maybe a bit awkward.' Nathan turned to Maggie. 'Do you not know who DCI Meechan is?'

'No. Should I?'

'He's Rutherford's first ex-husband and it wasn't exactly an amicable split.'

'Oh Jesus. No wonder she looks stressed.'

'And I have to work with her.' He took a deep breath. 'Okay, best get to it. I hear Meechan is a decent boss, but he can be something else behind the scenes.' Nathan stood and walked over to Rutherford.

'Great.' Maggie sighed. She knew her thoughts wouldn't be welcome at the moment, but DCI Meechan made a lot of sense and having a fresh pair of eyes might just be what they all needed right now.

Chapter Fifty-Two

Back at her desk, Maggie was debating whether now was the time she should disclose what she and Kate had been discussing, when one of the field officers from downstairs walked over and handed her a message. Maggie read the message and headed directly to Nathan's office.

'Something just came in. Looks like while the forensics team were searching the allotment shed, they came across a diary. They believe it belonged to Sophia Hastings and are just running some tests on it now.' Maggie handed the note to Nathan and watched him read it.

'Why was this given to you? Have they sent over any copies of the diary yet?' Nathan handed the piece of paper back to Maggie.

'No idea and I've not received anything more that I'm aware of. Do you want me to call them and find out? I wasn't sure if it was something you'd rather follow up first yourself?'

'I'll give Dr Blake a call now. Do me favour and let Rutherford know. I'm just going to pop outside after this; some fresh air would do me good. Banging headache.' He rubbed his temple.

'Sure thing, boss.' Maggie left Nathan to it and walked down the hallway to Rutherford's office. The door was open, so she tapped on the frame and waited for DI Rutherford to look up from her computer before speaking.

'Just wanted to let you know we had a call come in about some possible evidence. Nathan's just contacting the forensics team and we'll update everyone when we know more.'

DI Rutherford waved her hand and Maggie realized that was about all the response she was going to get from the guv. She bumped into Nathan as she headed back to her desk. 'Guv seems distracted.'

'She has a lot going on.' Nathan was vague but Maggie understood. He wasn't one to gossip despite their friendship.

'Well, she definitely looks like she's on the edge. Big murder case with her boss as a suspect, ex-hubby coming in to oversee the investigation, currently going through what I heard is quite a messy divorce. Really feel for her and definitely makes you realize she's bloody resilient to be in charge of such a highly sensitive case while dealing with all that shit in her personal life.' Maggie had heard rumours within the office but made no judgements.

Nathan's eyes widened and one side of his lip curled. 'Did you actually just compliment the guv? I've asked Dr Blake to send you what she has, by the way. Distribute it amongst the team if there's anything of relevance.'

'Bugger off.' She tapped his shoulder. 'If you tell her, I may have to kill you. Will do.' They ended the conversation there and Maggie returned to her desk. She looked out the window and wondered if taking the first step to working on her own personal life outside of work might be to get to know Rutherford a bit better, but she also didn't want to cross any boundaries. The thought went as quickly as it came when Maggie heard her phone buzz. A text from Dr Blake.

Sending over some pages to you now. It's a fairly large file so might take a while. Happy reading. Fiona

Chapter Fifty-Three

Maggie tapped her pen on the desk while she waited for Dr Blake's email. She seemed to still be in the pathologist's bad books and couldn't figure out how she would or if she could make things right between them again.

She was so engrossed in her thoughts, she hadn't heard Nathan creep up behind her. 'Penny for your thoughts.'

Maggie jumped. 'You don't want to know what darkness brews in this head of mine.' She tapped her head with the pen.

'You're probably right. What are you waiting for?'

'Email from Dr Blake.' As if on cue, her computer pinged and she opened up the email. A brief message from the pathologist with several attachments. 'Pull up a seat, we can look through these together if you want.'

'Wish I could. I've got to go and speak to the Comms Department. You make a start and I'll join you when I'm finished.'

Maggie waved and her focus immediately returned to the screen. Nothing really caught her attention from the first few pages. But then she noted that Sophia Hastings had started to record dates. No pattern evident – they seemed random but left an impression that Maggie couldn't ignore. As she scrolled through, a passage caught her eye:

Sick of lying to Dr Ross. She's probably already guessed anyway. Another broken rib. The pain is unbearable. Police were called and I had to lie again. Something needs to be done. I can't take this any more.

Shit! Maybe the dates she had seen earlier related to police call outs? 'Bethany, do you have a minute?'

'Sure, what do you need?'

'This might be a long shot, but can you check these dates against any call outs to DCI Hastings's home?' Maggie scribbled the dates on a piece of paper and passed it to her colleague.

'Will do.'

Maggie returned to the journal pages.

Still happening. I had to call in sick or they'd see the bruises and question me again. Why won't he do something about it?

Maggie's stomach tightened. Was DCI Hastings hiding a darker side? She knew that despite the public's general perception, domestic abuse wasn't limited to those of a lower socio-economic background, as Lucy – a Probation Officer – had been a victim and she herself had come across a few people from various backgrounds: teachers, fellow officers, judges as both victims and perpetrators.

'Maggie – you might want to come over and check these out,' Bethany called across the room.

Maggie wanted to keep reading but tore herself away from her own screen and headed to Bethany's desk. She looked over her colleague's shoulder. Five call outs recorded but no further action taken. The records were limited and although onscreen it looked like more information had been recorded, neither Bethany nor Maggie could access the details.

'Well, I wasn't expecting that!' Maggie bit her nail. 'DI Rutherford had sort of hinted at this, but these calls seem to come from the daughter and no visible injuries have been recorded. I think I'd better speak to Nathan. Thanks.'

Maggie caught Nathan sneaking back into his office. His meeting with the Comms Department had been quick and he didn't look very happy.

Bethany closed the call out list down and returned to trawling the CCTV evidence. Maggie stopped at her desk and logged out of her computer before knocking on Nathan's door.

'Do you have a minute?'

Nathan waved her in. 'What's up?'

'It's not looking good for Hastings, that's for sure. The wife's journal has random passages, talking about injuries, being afraid and then dates on various pages. When Bethany looked up the dates, they seem to correspond to police call outs that their daughter, Olivia, made. But no further action was taken, and no injuries were recorded by the police. Has Rutherford said anything to you?'

Nathan shifted in his seat and cleared his throat. 'It's definitely … unusual. Have a seat, this might take a little while.'

Maggie sat and waited for Nathan to continue.

'The team will be told all this anyway; it's why I had to meet with the Comms Department earlier, as we have now reached a point where we need to give the press something before they start making things up themselves.'

Maggie knew all about that from the Raven case.

'But for the time being, keep this between us, okay?'

'Of course. Should I be worried?'

'There *have* been previous call outs in the last two years to DCI Hastings's property. Olivia has called the police claiming that DCI Hastings has assaulted her and her mother on a few occasions. However, when the police went to the property, Mrs Hastings did not support those claims and declined to press any charges. Olivia refused to speak to the police at all but did show cuts on her arm; her mother advised these were self-inflicted. Apparently, the daughter has a quite … traumatic background and has been prone to making false allegations in the past.'

'Well, looks like all those decisions might come back and bite the police on the arse. I know from working in the DAHU that it can take up to seven years of abuse before a victim gets up the courage to call the police – and if the perp is a police officer? Jeez. Was he given preferential treatment because of his position in the force, Nathan? Because if he was, that's going to open a whole other investigation surely? I'm kind of glad I left the DAHU now – even though it was probably out of their remit, I'm sure they are going to get some flak for this.'

'I know. It's a huge mess and we're sort of in damage control mode. We've had no luck getting hold of relatives who may be able to shed some light on the situation; seems that the Hastings closed themselves off.'

'Many domestic abusers cut off family and friends. I

remember Lucy telling me that Patrick did that to her. Where do we go from here?'

'I believe DCI Meechan is going to be sharing the new strategy for dealing with Tim's murder, Mrs Hastings's murder, and Olivia's abduction. I think we are going to have to assume that she may be the next victim. We're going to appeal to the public again for any information on sightings of DCI Hastings. We'll give them as much information as we can without compromising the case. But some of the evidence in Tim's case just doesn't add up, so although Hastings is certainly looking good for it, we're not going to rule out others at this time.'

'Thanks for the update. I'm going to go back and finish reading the notes Dr Blake sent me and see if anything else comes to light. I can share that in the briefing later.' Maggie stood. 'I really hope we find something else.'

'Me too, we don't need any more shit on our doorstep.'

Chapter Fifty-Four

Maggie shook her head. After scanning through the documents sent from forensics, the evidence against DCI Hastings was damning – she couldn't see anything other than his involvement in the murder of his wife and disappearance of his daughter. What was also curious was Sophia Hastings's references to their daughter's mental health deteriorating and wondering whether this was hereditary or not. Nathan tapped her shoulder.

'You ready?'

Maggie logged out and followed Nathan to the briefing. She sat beside Kat, who was writing something down in her notepad. She tried to see what it was before Kat looked up at her.

'Just trying to tie up some of the loose ends in my head. I figured if I wrote them out, I'd have a better chance of picking up on something, but none of this case makes sense … well, except that Hastings is guilty as hell.' A few officers turned her way and frowned. 'Oops. Maybe I need to keep my mouth shut.'

'Always feel free to share an opinion, but comments like that will need backing up. You might get some answers in a minute.' Maggie pointed at DCI Meechan who walked into the room with confidence.

'Right folks. I'm not going to sugar coat anything today. DI Rutherford and I have just spoken to Comms and there will be a press release sent out later today, so we wanted to let you all know what's happening and look at where we go from here.' DCI Meechan walked to the whiteboard, removed the picture of DCI Hastings and placed him on a separate board, circling the picture with a red marker and writing – 'Suspect'. 'Let's stop dancing around the possibility and face the fact that we can no longer treat the case as a family abduction. Instead, DCI Hastings is wanted for questioning in the murder of Sophia Hastings, the abduction and possible murder of Olivia Hastings, and the murder of Tim Griffiths, based on the evidence we have so far. However,' he turned and faced the room, 'I'd like to investigate Tim's murder independently of the family's murder. Yes, the evidence connects Hastings to Tim's murder, but it's not definitive. The connection to Tim is thin – I'm just wary of accepting any scenarios without something more solid to back them up. Maggie, I understand you've had a quick look at Sophia Hastings's journal. What have you learned?'

Maggie opened her notebook. 'I first came across some random dates scattered throughout the journal. When Bethany did some digging, we learned that most of these dates coincided with police call outs to the property – domestic disputes it seems – though no charges were brought against the DCI and no detailed account of what was actually said was recorded. I'm assuming, until I am told otherwise, that once the officers learned it was a fellow officer, the matters seemed to disappear – though they still remain on record.' Maggie paused to let that information sink in. She could see the look of disbelief on her colleagues' faces; however, some nodded as if they agreed that was the right thing to do. As if being a police officer should let DCI Hastings have a free pass to commit a serious crime. 'I then came across vague entries from Sophia Hastings which alluded to physical and emotional abuse, and although DCI Hastings wasn't named as the perpetrator, the entries, coupled with the call outs, leads me to conclude that she was being abused by Hastings. Interestingly – it wasn't Mrs Hastings who called the police, it was their daughter. Mrs Hastings never pressed any charges and she didn't support her daughter's claim that Hastings was abusive to them both. That's pretty much it. I still need to read the journal in full once forensics have finished with it.'

'Thanks, Maggie. So that leads us perfectly into sharing a bit of background to the police call outs and hopefully ease any concerns about a police cover-up. DI Rutherford and I had been looking into Hastings's background and there is evidence to suggest that Olivia was making malicious calls due to a history of mental health issues. Olivia was adopted by the Hastings when she was five years old. She herself came from a very abusive background, but we can't get any details on the birth parents at the moment because the records are sealed. We did find out that Olivia is emotionally disturbed and goes through periods where she is very difficult to control – so much so that up until a few weeks before this all happened,

DCI Hastings had disclosed to his seniors that he was looking at having Olivia sectioned for long-term psychiatric care.'

'I guess killing them was easier,' Kat mumbled.

'What was that, PC Everett? Comments like that aren't helpful. I know that I've just come onboard, but I'll have no problem removing you from the case. That goes for everyone. We have to be objective and follow the evidence. Am I clear?'

'Yes, sir. Sorry.' Kat sank in her chair, and Maggie felt sorry for her. She had a similar thought in her head but was working hard at keeping thoughts like that to herself, or at least only sharing them with people who would know what she meant.

She nudged Kat's shoulder and whispered: 'We've all been there before, it's a learning curve and quite different from the DAHU. You'll be okay …'

DCI Meechan stopped talking. 'Oh, I'm sorry DC Jamieson – would you like to take over the briefing?' He stepped aside and actioned for her to come forward.

'Apologies, sir. I won't interrupt again.' Maggie could feel her neck redden. No wonder DI Rutherford divorced this bastard. Her initial feelings about the DCI were fading.

'Like I said earlier, what I'd like to do is run these investigations separately. Kat and Bethany, I want you to focus on Tim's case – go back and speak with the Dodd fellow at the college – DCI Hastings was actively involved on the college board. So once the news goes out, we might get more people willing to talk to us. Students who knew him – maybe he told them something and it only makes sense to them now? Nathan and Maggie, I'd like you to focus on Sophia Hastings's murder – try and get the family we have spoken to, to share more. I have a feeling that Sophia's relatives may be more forthcoming now that this is a murder investigation. She volunteered somewhere, might be an idea to find more out about that and speak to her colleagues. I know we were told that she didn't work, but it looks like she spent a bit of time outside the home. DI Rutherford and I are working with Missing Persons, as it frees up some resources and also that's all Olivia is at the moment – we have no evidence to suggest she has come to any harm yet.'

DI Rutherford interrupted. 'Before any of you start questioning this strategy amongst yourselves, although they are being worked as separate cases, we'll all still meet and brief each other on progress – we can then map out where things cross over and ensure that all available resources are allocated accordingly.'

She turned to DCI Meechan. 'Is that everything, as I'm sure the team would like to make a start before the day ends.'

Maggie couldn't tell from DI Rutherford's tone whether she was being sarcastic or serious but smiled inwardly anyway. DCI Meechan closed down the briefing and the rest of them finished their notes before packing up and returning to their desks.

Has DCI Meechan just made this case more complicated than it needs to be?

Chapter Fifty-Five

When Maggie arrived home from work that evening, all she could think about were the journal entries. Something just didn't sit right with her. She pulled out her phone and texted her brother to see what time he would be in; she didn't really feel like cooking and although he never expected her to cook for him, it had become a habit between the pair of them. Whoever got in first would make the meal while the other did the dishes. She preferred the dishes if she was honest: she wasn't the best cook.

Working till 2am so nothing for me. A. X

Well, that solved one of her problems; she decided she'd see if she could work out the other one.

You up for a Skype chat this evening? I have a bit of a puzzle I'd love your help on – but no pressure if you want to avoid work stuff at the moment. X

While she waited for a response, Maggie went to the kitchen to feed the cats. She opened the tin of food and laughed when she heard the patter of feet coming down the stairs. 'Both of you napping during the day? Lazy kitties. Here you go.' She left the bowls on the floor and made herself some soup, with a few slices of bread. The crusty kind which soaked up the soup perfectly.

Maggie went to the dining room table, placed bowl and plate of bread down and began to set up her laptop on the table. Even if Kate wasn't available this evening, Maggie knew she wouldn't be able to relax until she tried to work out some of the minor niggles gnawing at her brain.

Maggie had recalled that DCI Hastings had appeared in a few newspaper articles which included his family. She wondered if there would be any information about Sophia Hastings in the articles. Maggie had considered contacting Julie Noble to see if she could find out for her, but quickly shook the thought out of her head, as Julie would ask more questions than Maggie was prepared to answer. It was still too soon. Thankfully, Nathan and Rutherford had dropped the idea of using her to feed Julie information about the case – but she knew the door would now be open for this to happen in the future. She'd cross that bridge when she came to it.

She opened up her browser and began her search. Five articles popped up and she went through each one meticulously. The first three talked about Hastings's policing initiatives and contributions he had made to the community. The final two were more interesting: one mentioned his daughter but seemed to quickly move on – the picture had only DCI Hastings and his wife and there was an odd look on Mrs Hastings's face. Maggie scrolled to the bottom of the article and noted the journalist's name. He would be someone that she and Nathan should speak to; even though the article was nearly a year old, the journalist may remember something to help with their enquiries. It was the final article that was a gold mine of information. It hinted at the awkwardness felt, probed a bit about Olivia Hastings but didn't seem to get too far and mentioned that Sophia Hastings was a regular volunteer at the local hospice. When Maggie scrolled to the bottom of the page, she wasn't surprised to see that Julie Noble had written the article.

She resisted the urge to call the journalist, knowing what Julie would read into things and she didn't want to have to go through their usual battle of 'tell me' and 'you know I can't' before both of them ended up frustrated and annoyed with the other. DCI Meechan had asked her to go and speak to Sophia's colleagues at the hospice, and if nothing came of that, she'd think of a way to get the information out of Julie without raising her suspicions.

It was getting late and Kate still hadn't responded. Time to pack up for the night and look at things from a fresh perspective in the morning.

Chapter Fifty-Six

Maggie had to drag herself into the office that morning and a big yawn escaped from her lips. Sleep was not something she was getting much of lately, but she knew she wasn't the only one going home for a few hours to catch some shut-eye before having to return to the office. Maggie looked up from her screen to see Bethany and Kat walking with purpose out of the office and down the corridor. They looked like they were heading downstairs to the interview suites.

Maggie turned her chair and called through Nathan's doorway: 'What are those pair up to?'

Nathan looked at his watch. 'Shit! I didn't realize the time. They've asked that guy from the college to come in for further questioning and I'd like you to go and observe if—'

'What? They don't need babysitting. Anyway, the room will be cramped if I join them. Dodd didn't take too kindly to me the first time around and might clam up if all of us are bombarding him with questions.' Maggie frowned.

'You really need to stop jumping to conclusions before you

speak. Had you let me finish,' he smiled, 'I was going to say that I want you to watch him on the video monitor. See if you and that brain of yours can spot any tells – does a certain question affect him? Does he pause when the answer should come easily? That sort of thing. It's easy to miss these things when you are directly involved in the questioning, and with the stakes so high in this investigation, we can't afford to miss out on anything.'

'But—' Maggie wasn't given the opportunity to finish.

'But nothing. Get down there. Hopefully, we can either charge him or rule him out of further enquiries.'

Maggie picked up her notebook. Only a few interview suites had video cameras installed and were used where there were concerns about violence when being interviewed. The monitors were located in a room just off of the enquiry desk. If anything kicked off, the alarm was raised and officers responded in a matter of seconds.

Maggie walked into the office and was led to an area set out for her to observe. She sat and placed the headphones on so she wasn't disturbed by her surroundings.

Mr Dodd had his solicitor present, and Maggie watched as Bethany cautioned him and explained the purpose of the meeting before diving right in with her questions.

'You're married, Mr Dodd, is that right?' Bethany was easing him in, and Maggie noticed his shoulders relax.

'Well, yes. What's that got to do with anything?' He looked to his solicitor, who shrugged.

'Good marriage? No problems?' Bethany persevered.

'We're fine. Yes. I thought I was here to help with your enquiries, and I don't see what business it is of yours how well my wife and I do or don't get on,' he huffed.

'You're relatively new at South Staffordshire Academy, aren't you?' Bethany looked down at her notes. 'Says here, just over a year. Where were you before that?'

'Down south. At another college. I'm sure you must already have this information – are these questions going anywhere?'

'Why did you leave your last teaching position?' A smile crept on Bethany's face. She'd have to work on that if she didn't want to give her game away.

Mr Dodd's eyes widened, and he turned to his solicitor. 'Can they ask me these questions?' There was a whine in his voice. Bethany had unnerved him. 'What does my previous employment have to do with Tim?'

Bethany shuffled through some paperwork and pulled out a piece of paper which she passed to Mr Dodd and his solicitor, allowing them a moment to read the contents. 'Do you recognize this?'

Mr Dodd paled, and Maggie noticed his fist clench under the table. She zoomed the camera in on his face.

'Lies! All lies!' His solicitor touched his arm. 'Get off me.' He shrugged the hand away. 'What games are you playing, PC Lambert? Why don't you just get straight to the point?'

Kat interjected. 'For the benefit of the tape, PC Lambert has just shown Mr Dodd and his solicitor an email that was sent to the Chief Executive of the college from Tim Griffiths, stating that Mr Dodd had touched him inappropriately.'

'This is outrageous!' Mr Dodd's face grew red. 'The matter was dropped. All fabricated. Haven't we been through all this already?'

'Well, that's not strictly true, is it? You were spoken to by DCI David Hastings, who cautioned you, as it seems there were other students who backed Mr Griffiths's claims. Surely your solicitor explained to you that by accepting a caution, you were admitting your guilt?' Bethany leaned back.

'What? No, that wasn't explained to me. I spoke to DCI Hastings – he's on the board. Everyone agreed it would be the best way to resolve the situation. I didn't have a solicitor at the time. I was told I didn't need one. Had I known what I was agreeing to, I never would have signed that!'

Maggie hadn't realized that Mr Dodd was also a board member, but she guessed it came with his position at the college.

'Surely a man of your intelligence would have dug deeper and found out? How are you allowed to continue working at the college?'

He blushed. 'I was told that if I agreed to the caution, I could work the remainder of the year as long I handed in my resignation and only had contact with students in the presence of another. That was my suggestion, by the way, to avoid any further false claims. The college said they would give me a reference. Now you're telling me my life is ruined.'

'What about all those students who made allegations? Do you think their lives weren't ruined?' Kat eyed him, daring him to say something more.

His head dropped into his hands and his shoulders shook. The solicitor jumped in. 'Do you have any more questions for my client? As you can see, he is clearly distressed and wasn't expecting his past to be dragged up. We'll need a moment.'

Kat reached over and turned off the recording. 'Interview suspended. We'll be back in fifteen minutes.' They left the room. Maggie muted the sound as per protocol but continued to watch the body language of Mr Dodd and his solicitor. His hands were flying everywhere, and his eyes bulged. He had not been expecting the questions that were thrown at him.

Kat and Bethany joined her.

'He's one pissed off fella, eh?' Kat motioned to the monitor.

'Yes. A little too pissed off, don't you think?' Maggie tapped her pen on the table. 'Might be worth finding out exactly how DCI Hastings cautioned Mr Dodd. If he made it seem like nothing, that could well be motive for revenge … even murder, wouldn't you say?'

Chapter Fifty-Seven

With their strategy discussed and agreed, Kat and Bethany returned to interview Mr Dodd. He stared straight ahead as Kat resumed the interrogation.

'Have you had some time to think things through?' Kat leaned forwards.

He inserted his finger inside his collar and shifted it about. 'Yes. My solicitor has advised I should proceed with no comment, but I haven't done anything wrong.' Maggie could have sworn she saw his eyes glisten.

'How about I tell you what we think happened? It might jog your memory.' Kat opened her notes. 'You said that DCI Hastings gave you a warning, which actually turned out to be a caution and that you didn't understand what you had agreed to at the time. Is that correct?'

'That's exactly what happened. I met him here, at the police station, and we discussed the situation. I explained exactly what happened. That young man – Tim – claimed I touched him inappropriately, but it was all an innocent matter. There had been some trouble between him and a group of lads. I spoke to them all in my office on a one-to-one basis. Tim was very upset. I just squeezed his shoulder … like a reassurance … there was nothing inappropriate about it. But then he sent that email, egged on by Olivia Hastings, accusing me of leering at him as I did it. Okay, I shouldn't have touched his shoulder, but for God's sake, this could ruin my career.'

'DCI Hastings would have verbalized the caution, explained it in detail to make sure you understood the meaning before you signed anything. Are you saying that never happened, as we can go through the records to find that out easily?' Kat waited for the response, and Maggie noticed Mr Dodd's shoulders tighten.

'I don't know, okay? I can't remember exactly. I was shocked at the time, but your boss said it was nothing to worry about. I believed him. Why would he lie to me?'

'And then when you found out, you got angry? Confronted Tim Griffiths and things went too far? Where did you get the hammer from?'

'What are you talking about? What hammer?'

'The hammer used to bash Tim's skull in. Did you follow him to the woods after college? Confront him? Things got a bit heated and when he tried to run away you hit him? Then you realized he wasn't dead, watched him drag himself to safety before delivering the final blow? When you heard the other people in the woods, you ran off, dropping the hammer as you fled? Is that what happened?'

'Oh my god, no! What is going on here? Stop this now!' He looked at his solicitor.

'Back up, DC Everett. Do you have any evidence to support

this ridiculous story you have concocted?' the solicitor challenged.

'We're just talking through a theory – which seems to have upset your client. What's he hiding?'

'I'm advising my client not to respond to your ludicrous theories. We'd like to hear about the evidence before we proceed.' Maggie noted the confidence in Mr Dodd's solicitor.

'On the day in question, your secretary said that you left the college in an agitated state. Mobile phone records indicate numerous calls to DCI Hastings's mobile. What did you speak about?'

'We had a school board meeting. I spoke to David ... er ... your DCI frequently – surely you saw that on my phone records? Sometimes he would pick me up. I don't recall being agitated but there could be a dozen reasons for that. Maybe I was late for something. Maybe I just had a bad day. Why are you doing this to me? I haven't done anything wrong!' His fists thumped on the table and Maggie couldn't help but think that he was genuinely upset at being accused. Could they have misread the situation?

The solicitor jumped in. 'Look. You either charge my client here and now or we are walking. You've got nothing and what you do have is inaccurate. You're trying to make fit a situation that is just plain false. Meanwhile the real killer is out there and laughing in your faces. What's it going to be?'

The solicitor was right, and Maggie knew that they'd have to end the interview at this point, and as she watched Mr Dodd closely, he genuinely appeared to be shocked by everything he had learned today.

'We may have more questions for you, so please don't make

any plans to leave the area, Mr Dodd. Interview terminated.' Kat reached across and turned off the recording device.

'Just as I thought. Really officers – before bringing my client in again, you'd better make sure you have some solid evidence. Look at him.' She pointed to her client. 'He's an emotional wreck because of what you've just put him through. Come on, we're leaving.' The solicitor and Mr Dodd were escorted out of the station, and Maggie waited for Kat and Bethany.

'Well, that was a bloody mess. I was sure he was going to break then.' Kat shook her head. 'Everything seemed to fit – he could have been wearing gloves when he handled the hammer, like Dr Blake had said was possible. Maybe he picked it up when he went around the Hastings's place. I was sure he was going to confess.'

Maggie saw the frustrations in her colleagues' faces. 'It was a good theory and just because we didn't have enough to charge him now, doesn't mean we won't find it later if he is guilty. He still could be connected to the murder of Tim – the timings of the complaint, then caution and murder are too coincidental, and I don't like that. But …'

'Most of the evidence points at someone else, doesn't it?' Bethany folded her arms.

'Yes. I know we're being told to investigate the murders and abduction separately, but I still feel the connection is too strong to point to more than one killer. And right now – we need to rule out who *didn't* do it, so we can narrow down our persons of interest. What I suggest you both do is see if Mr Dodd had any other contact outside of college with Sophia and Olivia. Maybe he knew about the abuse? I think we need to keep a close eye on him – if he is involved, he could lead us to where Hastings and his daughter are being held.'

When they returned to their office, Maggie told Nathan what she had observed and suggested that someone watch Mr Dodd's movements over the next few days. Nathan agreed to get a field officer on it so as not to tie up their own resources. He didn't seem as convinced as the rest of them were and the more Maggie thought about it, the more she doubted it herself.

Better safe than sorry though.

'You free now?'

Maggie nodded.

'Follow me. The press is here, and DCI Meechan is going to talk about Hastings.'

Although she wasn't too keen on bumping into Julie Noble, this was one press conference she didn't want to miss.

'Hang on while I grab the popcorn.'

Chapter Fifty-Eight

Maggie stood at the back of the room alongside Nathan as they waited for the press conference to begin. She could see Julie Noble looking around the room and didn't want to get into a conversation, so avoided eye contact as best she could. Maggie could openly challenge some of the scariest individuals, but when it came to dealing with her own emotions or anything personal, sometimes things were best left unsaid was her motto. It may seem childish to some, but when something has been ingrained in your head for as long as you can remember, it's easier to just push it aside to deal with another day. Even when that other day never seems to come. She had her father to thank for that.

'What are you doing?' Nathan nudged her over. 'If you get any closer to me, people will start talking.'

Maggie forced a laugh – her thoughts still on Julie. It would save her giving him a load of bullshit as an explanation. 'Nothing, just trying to get the best view. It's DCI Meechan's first press conference on the case – it could go either way and I don't want to miss a word.'

'Good point. You really should've brought the popcorn.' He winked.

DI Rutherford stood next to Meechan, her face not giving away anything other than confidence. Maggie admired her ability to put on a strong front when Maggie knew Rutherford had her own demons at the moment. As much as she herself believed she did that, too, subconsciously Maggie knew sometimes the lines got blurred.

The room got quiet as DCI Meechan tapped the microphone – Maggie sniggered to herself, picturing the DCI saying 'testing … testing …' and maybe bursting into some random song that would really throw the crowd of stone-faced journalists off kilter. He didn't, of course. But it would have been funny if he had. Her focus returned to the room.

'Thank you all for coming at such short notice. I'd appreciate if you let me speak first and there will be time for a few questions afterwards. I'm DCI Aidan Meechan and I've been temporarily seconded to Stafford Police from Coventry. I'd like to put a stop to some of the rumours that have been on the news as of late because frankly it's upsetting family members of the victims, unnecessarily scaring the public, and largely untrue. We're working hard to identify and arrest the person or persons responsible for the murders of Tim Griffiths and Sophia Hastings. At present, DCI David Hastings and his daughter, Olivia, are missing persons and we're working closely with the Missing Persons Unit to ensure that all information is transparent, shared, and as accurate as possible. We're also working several lines of enquiry at this time and hope to draw a close to the investigations as swiftly as possible. There's absolutely no evidence to suggest that a serial killer is roaming the streets of Stafford, so we'd appreciate if those ridiculous claims are quashed now. Do you have any questions?'

Julie Noble stood. 'I do. What's your response to the accusation that there is a cover-up happening in Stafford Police? Were you brought in to sweep everything under the carpet?'

'I'd say people need to get their facts straight – especially those reporting the news. Next question.'

'Hang on. You didn't answer my question at all. My sources tell me that DCI Hastings is a person of interest in the murder of Tim, his own wife, and the abduction and possible murder of his daughter. I thought you said you wanted to be transparent – or was that just to placate us?'

'What's your name?' DCI Meechan tapped his foot. His patience looked to be growing thinner by the minute.

'Julie Noble from the *Stafford Gazette*.'

'Well Julie from the *Stafford Gazette*, let me make one thing clear. I don't do cover-ups. If a member of this team was found to be corrupt, behaving inappropriately, or abusing their position, they would be dealt with the same way anyone else would be – and if that resulted in a criminal conviction, so be it. I am all about accountability. Next question.'

Maggie wasn't surprised to see Julie Noble still standing – though her gob hanging open was a new one. Maggie knew she wouldn't give up that easily and felt a little torn if she was being honest. She admired Julie's tenacity for the most part, but also felt sorry for DCI Meechan having been placed in this situation in the first place. The higher-ups were more than happy to throw him to the wolves, as long as nothing bounced back on them. He would need to be careful – especially if Julie found out anything from her sources, as she'd print it first and apologize later.

'I wasn't finished. Why did you say suspects in your statement? Aren't you looking for one killer, and what efforts have been made to bring DCI Hastings in for questioning?'

'Miss Noble. Stop trying to hog the limelight and let some of your colleagues ask a question. I said suspects because we have nothing definitive to say that we are looking for one person – unless one of your sources has shared that detail with you and you care to pass it on? As for your second question – DCI Hastings is currently a missing person. Had you been paying attention earlier you would have caught that. I think I made it pretty clear. Unless you can reveal his location, he can't be brought in for anything until he is found. Anyone else have anything to ask?' DCI Meechan scanned the room and waited while the crowd murmured. 'Okay then, any further questions can be directed to the Comms Department.' He nodded at DI Rutherford and she followed him out of the room.

'Well, that was interesting,' Nathan whispered. 'Looks like Julie was put in her place and by the look on her face, she's not too happy.'

'I'm actually speechless. I don't know whether to cheer him or hide away. He gets straight to the point though, doesn't he? I thought they were going to appeal to the public about Hastings though?'

'They've obviously thought twice about it.' Nathan shrugged.

Maggie turned, about to leave the room when she felt someone tap her shoulder. She knew exactly who it would be and wasn't in the mood for a chat, so carried on walking. Nathan followed alongside her.

'Hey, Maggie! Can I have a word?' Julie shouted after her.

'Fuck. Can't she take a hint?' Maggie mumbled under her breath and then stopped.

'You two have a tiff or something? Look, I've got to get back upstairs and if you don't want to be in Meechan's firing line, I suggest you make your conversation quick. You don't want people to think you are siding with the enemy, do you?' He laughed at his own joke. Maggie didn't. She'd get him back for that one.

Maggie was about to protest when Julie pulled her aside. 'Why did you ignore me back there?'

'I'm really busy, Julie. You heard DCI Meechan – anyway, I'm a DC in this case, what could I possibly tell you? We've got a lot of plates to juggle at the moment and I can't stand around to chat with you. Did you want something important?' Maggie could see the look of hurt in her eyes and for a moment, regret washed over her.

'Forget it. Look, I don't know the full extent of your daddy issues, but unless you start being true to yourself, those labels you say that don't matter will always be a noose around your neck. You're not sixteen any more so who the fuck cares? This isn't about us, it's about the case – so grow a pair. Never let anyone tell you who you are. You tell them.' Julie turned and followed the rest of the journalists out of the building while Maggie stood and let what Julie had said sink in.

She hated when Julie was right.

Chapter Fifty-Nine

With Vicki in the hostel for the day, Lucy felt comfortable to go back to her agency work at Probation after agreeing to write a pre-sentence report. She checked the panic alarms and cameras and popped her head into the communal living room to say goodbye to Ronnie. Lucy had been worried about the young woman recently, as after the incident with Mark, she had become further withdrawn. Then there had been some vandalism to the gates of the haven, and Lucy couldn't be sure whether Ronnie's abuser had found her or whether it was just a random act. She had reported it, but the police had no leads and there had been no further incidents.

Lucy tried to reassure Ronnie that Mark would be okay, even if she wasn't sure herself – but that didn't seem to help any. Ronnie would go off the property for hours and, although she didn't need to check in, with everything that had happened, it worried Lucy.

'If you need me for anything, let Vicki know – she has my

number. It's a nice day out – if you wanted to go into the garden and read ...' Lucy wasn't expecting an answer. Ronnie looked up for a moment and then went back to whatever she was looking at on her mobile phone.

Before she left, she texted Maggie a quick update on Mark, as she had been brief when she informed her about the situation. She let Maggie know that if she wanted updates, DI Calleja at the DAHU was regularly checking in with Mark's family and the hospital.

Markston Probation Office was busy when she arrived. Lucy greeted the reception staff and let herself in to the main office with her swipe card. There was a buzz of voices in the room, officers speaking with clients or on the phone. She smiled. As much as she loved her work in Probation, she was also glad she only had to come into the office occasionally. She found a free desk and set up her encrypted laptop. Lucy looked around while she waited for her laptop to start up. Sarah Hardy was sitting in the corner, head down and writing some notes.

Lucy called out, 'Hey stranger! I'm going to grab a drink; do you want anything?'

When Sarah looked up, Lucy immediately noticed the dark circles under her eyes. She walked over to Sarah's desk. 'Oh hun. Are you okay?'

'I'm fine, thanks. I'll have a water though. I feel a headache coming on. Nothing to worry about.' Sarah's face said the complete opposite.

Lucy crouched down beside the desk and talked softly. 'Are you sure everything is okay? Is it a case you're working on?'

Even though they were colleagues, if there was a specific case troubling her, Lucy understood that Sarah may not be able to talk about it and that would rest heavy on her.

'I never could hide anything from you, could I? Come with me.' Sarah motioned for Lucy to follow her to the quiet area. Andrew Bourne wasn't in his office, and officers used the room as a private meeting area when available. Lucy sat as Sarah closed the door.

'It's Justin. He's been acting really strange and working odd hours. I'm really worried about him. He's become really distant and snaps at me when I ask him what is going on. I don't know what to do.' Sarah's eyes glistened; she was fighting back the tears.

'Maybe he has a new client who's demanding his time?' Lucy didn't know much about Justin's work – he had his own office space in Stafford town centre and Lucy thought he did something with insurance, but she didn't know for sure and she felt ashamed that she had never asked her friend more about what was happening at home lately. Especially as Sarah had been a huge support to her when she was dealing with her own stuff.

'Maybe. I just can't help but think he is hiding something from me. I went to the bank the other day and I don't know what possessed me to check, but I asked about our joint savings account – Justin has taken out a large amount of money.'

'What did he say when you asked him about it?'

'He snapped at me and told me it must be a bank error. He said he would sort it out himself, but the money is still missing. I don't know what to think. On top of all this, I have a case where the police think one of my clients may be involved in some serious offences and are pushing for a recall, but Andrew won't sign it off. I just don't need all this shit right now.'

'I may not be able to help you with Justin, but can you talk about the case? If I can help take that burden off you, it would be one less thing to worry about; but if Andrew won't sign off the recall, there's really not much you can do. Do you think there's a risk to the public?'

'If my guy is involved, yes there is – but it's a bit more complicated than that. I can't really say anything more, though, as it's a pretty high-profile case.' She put her head in her hands. 'Arggh. It's all so stressful.'

'I hate to see you like this, what can I do?' Lucy knew the answer, but she wanted her friend to know that she was there for her. 'Maybe you should talk to Andrew again about the case? Tell him how it's making you feel.'

'It's a mess. Stafford Police even had their superintendent call me to try and pressure for a recall. She wasn't too happy when I asked her why they haven't arrested the guy if he is such a risk. Tried to intimidate me, using her position which kind of made me laugh, as I don't work for the police.' Sarah shrugged. 'I guess I could talk to Andrew – see if he can tell them to back off while we figure everything out. I bet they wouldn't be pushing so hard if one of their own wasn't involved.' Sarah suddenly stopped and her hand covered her mouth.

'Is this about the murders on TV? Wasn't that DCI Hastings's wife murdered?' Lucy didn't want to push her friend, but if it meant she could share the burden, she would.

'You can't say anything outside of this room. I'll get the sack for sure, but yes. I'm supervising someone who had previously threatened to get Hastings back – he claims that he was set up by him. Not long after he was released, Hastings's family went missing and now his wife and a friend of his daughter's has ended up dead. But then new information came to light about who really set him up and he's on a curfew … and … It's a bloody mess.' Sarah was waffling. 'Anyway, enough about me. How's Mark doing? I heard something happened at your place.'

'That case does sound a mess, but it sounds like recall is not the way forward. As for Mark, word travels fast. They think it has something to do with his diabetes, but he's still not conscious, so they are running further tests. It was awful at the time. I was really afraid we'd lose him.' Lucy tried to hold back her emotions.

'Jesus. I hope he's okay soon. At least you got him to the hospital in time; it's the best place for him. So much shit happening at the moment, eh?' Sarah reached out and squeezed Lucy's arm.

'For everyone.'

A knock on the door stopped the conversation. Sarah looked relieved that Lucy wasn't going to steer the conversation back to her problems. The receptionist popped her head in the door.

'Sorry to interrupt you both. Lucy, your PSR appointment is here. Just a heads-up, I thought I smelled alcohol on him, so you might want to see him in one of the high-risk interview rooms. He seemed a little agitated.'

'Thanks. I'll be right out.' Lucy stood. 'Don't keep everything bottled up, okay? You know how to reach me if you need to talk.'

Poor Sarah. Lucy felt so helpless and guilty that she couldn't do more for her friend. She hoped she took her advice and reached out if she needed it. Lucy knew too well what happens when you keep things hidden for too long.

Sarah was gone by the time Lucy had finished for the day, so when she arrived back home, she texted her friend and reiterated that if she ever needed to talk, she could call her at any time. Sarah responded with a 'thanks' and that's all Lucy could do for the time being. She'd try and make more of an effort to catch up with Sarah over the next little while.

Ronnie was tucked away in her room, and Lucy was shattered. An early night, drama free, was exactly what she needed.

Chapter Sixty

On the train into work that morning, Maggie fidgeted in the seat – her legs were restless and her thoughts unfocused. She rubbed her hands together. She had spent the night tossing and turning, going over the last conversation she had had with Julie Noble. She was torn and when she woke, had decided that she needed to approach the subject with Nathan but worried about how he would react. He knew most of the story: Maggie and Julie had a turbulent relationship professionally, but she wanted to make it clear to him that she would never cross or blur any boundaries when it came to her job – his joke the other day made her think he wasn't convinced of that. Journalists were not favourites amongst the police in her force.

Stafford train station approached and a bead of sweat formed on her brow. She wiped it away – *everything would be fine.*

Maggie walked the fifteen minutes to the police station at a snail's pace. Normally she was geared up for work, but with everything up in the air – the case, her personal life – she had to drag herself in. *If I don't say anything about it, it never happened, right?* Denial was not an easy pill to swallow.

'Hey guys!' She waved at Kat and Bethany before looking behind her to see if Nathan was in his office. 'Have you seen him yet?' She hoped he had a meeting or was busy dealing with something else.

'He was just there five minutes ago.' Bethany turned in her chair. 'Maybe he's with Rutherford. She stormed in here about half an hour ago. I wouldn't want to be on the receiving end of whatever has pissed her off today. Seems to be a regular occurrence lately.'

'Thanks for the heads-up.' Maggie took off her coat and placed it over her chair. Opening the drawer in the cabinet beneath her desk, she placed her bag inside and sat down.

'What's up with you?' Kat called across the room. 'You're looking a little pale. You're not ill, are you?' Kat held up her fingers in the sign of the cross and laughed.

Maggie shook her head. 'Nope. I'm fine. Just need to speak to Nathan.' She started up her computer.

Kat pointed to the doorway.

'Did you need to see me, Maggie?' Nathan stood behind her.

'Uh. Yeah. Do you have five minutes?'

'Sure. Come through.'

Maggie stood and tugged on her blouse; taking a deep breath, she followed Nathan into his office.

'Have a seat. You're looking a bit off this morning.'

Nathan sat across from Maggie and frowned.

'I'm fine. I just have something to speak to you about and, for once, I'm not exactly sure how to say it.'

'It's me, just spit it out,' Nathan reassured her.

Maggie took a deep breath. 'Okay, well it's kind of a weird one. I feel I need to disclose something but I'm also looking for a bit of advice.'

Nathan's phone rang. 'Hang on two secs. I need to take this.' He held his hand up. 'Hello, DS Nathan Wright speaking. What? How the hell did she get that information? Okay. Yep. I'll do what I can.' He slammed the phone down. 'Shit!'

'What is it?'

'That bloody reporter, Julie Noble, is at it again. She's just done a story on Hastings – questioning how his team is involved in the case and whether we're part of a cover-up relating to the wrongful conviction of Craig friggin Nolan. Fucking hell. What is it with that woman?'

Maggie was silent.

'Well, you're taking this rather calmly. I expected I'd have to scrape you off the walls – I mean isn't this the kind of shit that put you off her in the first place?' Nathan eyed Maggie, waiting for an answer, and she wasn't sure what she would say.

'Uh, I guess I'm in shock? What exactly has she said and where did she get the information?' Maggie wracked her brains trying to think if she ever let anything slip in their conversations.

'I don't know the details yet. Look, I've got about five minutes before I have to go and speak to Rutherford about this mess. What was it you wanted to say?'

There was no way Maggie could tell Nathan anything now. She bit her lip. 'It's nothing, it can keep. Go and get this mess sorted. I'll catch up with you later.' She stood.

'If you're sure. Bet you're glad you called a halt to things with her now, eh?' He looked at his watch. 'I really do need to get a grasp of this. The last thing we need is that reporter feeding false facts to the public … again.' He ran his fingers through his hair.

'Go. It's fine, really.' Maggie returned to her desk and pull out her mobile phone. Finding the number, she texted.

WE NEED TO TALK … call me ASAP.

Chapter Sixty-One

Maggie wasn't surprised that Julie Noble was taking her time to get back to her. But she could wait. Meanwhile, she'd focus her energy on speaking to Sophia Hastings's fellow volunteers at the hospice; she also had an appointment to meet with Claire Knight.

Kat accompanied her – dressed in black trousers, a blouse, and boots. Not the T-shirt- and jeans-wearing officer Maggie had known at the DAHU. There was also something else … 'Where's the sweary Kat? You seem a bit subdued.'

Kat's eyes widened. 'I thought I should probably tone it down, being the newbie and all. You know, ease my way in before I let the foul mouth loose.'

'I've already told people what you're like, and now it seems like I was lying.' Maggie tried to keep a serious face but couldn't. 'You can be yourself. There's a time and a place for everything, you're right – but you don't have to change who you are.'

'Thank fuck for that. It's been a struggle.' Kat burst out

laughing. 'This hospice we're heading to, what are we hoping to find out?'

It was a legitimate question, and one Maggie wasn't sure how to answer. 'We need to know whether Sophia shared what was going on in her home life. The family had secrets, that much is apparent after reading through the journal we found. But even that is vague.'

Kat pulled into the driveway and parked. The hospice was a large, converted bungalow. The landscape out front was well groomed, with a few benches where those residents who were up to it could sit and enjoy the fresh air. The gravel crunched beneath their feet as they walked to the front door. Maggie knocked and a middle-aged woman answered.

'You must be the police. Come in. We have tea and coffee brewed if you'd like a cup.' The woman ushered them inside.

'That would be nice, thank you.' They followed the woman through the hallway and into a living room area. Two other women sat sipping tea and acknowledged the pair when they were introduced.

'Thank you for agreeing to speak with us. We just have a few questions which we hope you can answer.' The ladies whispered amongst themselves before turning to Maggie and Kat. It seemed the one who answered the door was designated the mouthpiece.

'We'll do whatever we can to help. We were all very shocked to learn of Sophia's … death. Horrible. Do you know who's responsible?'

'We can't really say, but our hope is that you all may be able to offer some insight.'

More murmurs between the women. They seemed excited

at the prospect that they might be able to help the police bring Sophia's murderer to justice.

'Were any of you particularly close to Mrs Hastings?'

Heads shook. 'I can't say any of us were.' The women looked at each other before their spokesperson continued. 'Sophia was a kind soul but very quiet. We knew her husband was a police officer, and her daughter was a bit of a handful, I think, but when she was here, she just smiled and got on with things. Even when she looked low, she'd paste on a smile and help with the garden or teach some of our residents how to knit.' The woman's eyes glistened. 'It's just so sad.'

'Did she ever have any injuries that she couldn't explain? Or were any of you suspicious of anything happening in her home life?'

All three women leaned forwards as if some good gossip was coming their way.

'No. Should we have?' Again the looks amongst each other. 'Their daughter came by once, very upset, but Sophia calmed her down and sent her away. Apparently, the girl had got into an argument with her father. But that was the only time we really had a glimpse into her life. They adopted that child, you know. She was from a broken home and quite … dramatic, shall we say. Sophia told us that underneath it all, their daughter was just looking for love and that's what her and her husband would give her. Have you found them yet?'

'We haven't.' These women couldn't offer anything more than the police already knew or suspected.

'Sorry to interrupt, but you said that Sophia never had any unexplained injuries when she came here. Were there ever times that she was due to volunteer but called to say she was unwell?' Kat's experience in the Domestic Abuse and

Homicide Unit gave her the knowledge of particular questions that may add more insight to the situation.

'Oh yes. She generally volunteered three days a week. There have been times where she has cancelled coming in, and she was always very apologetic. She hated to let us down. Why is that important?'

'It may not be, just useful to know. Had this increased in frequency recently or was it random?' Kat started noting down some points which she would no doubt share with the team later.

'Now that you mention it – it had increased over the last year or two. I only noticed as she was even more quiet when she did return. Often just coming in, doing her work, and going home. Less social, if that makes sense.'

'It does, thank you.' Kat looked at Maggie. She was done with her questions.

Maggie stood. 'Thank you for the tea and your time. If we think of anything else, we may be in touch but if any of you think of anything else that you think may be significant, please feel free to call us.' Maggie handed the woman her card.

When they got outside, Maggie was keen to hear Kat's thoughts. 'Great questions. You were thinking that things have got worse in the last few years, weren't you?'

'Yes. I remembered something Lucy had told us after it all came out about Patrick. She said she'd often use her annual leave or call in sick if she had injuries she wanted to hide.'

'I think our suspicions about the Hastings's home life is spot on. Behind closed doors, that family was something other than everyone believed they were. Let's see if Claire can tell us more about the daughter.'

Chapter Sixty-Two

The offices for Staffordshire's Social Care were in the town centre. They decided to park the car back at the police station and walk to the building. On arrival they signed in at reception and waited for Claire Knight.

When Claire had called Maggie and invited her over to talk, Maggie'd been more than intrigued about what information she had to share on DCI Hastings's daughter, Olivia. Meechan and Rutherford had been cagey when releasing the details, but Maggie's gut told her there was more to the story, and she couldn't understand why her seniors seemed keen on keeping the rest of the team in the dark.

At the reception desk, Maggie caught her breath before speaking to the older woman behind the plastic screen and realized that once this case was over, she would spend some of her time outside of work getting herself back into shape. Those stairs shouldn't have left her breathless.

'Hi. My name is DC Jamieson, and this is my colleague DC Everett. We're here to see Claire Knight. She's expecting us.'

The woman smiled and pointed to the seats directly behind Maggie. 'If you'd like to take a seat, I'll let Mrs Knight know you're here.'

Maggie sat down and pulled out her mobile phone. One missed call and a message. She opened the message and rolled her eyes.

What's with the attitude? What have I done now? X Jules

Maggie didn't have time to deal with Julie now, but at least she had finally come back to her. With Kat trying to read over her shoulder not so discreetly, Maggie decided she would get back to the journalist when she was on her own. She put her phone back in her pocket, and the door to her right buzzed. They were greeted by a very serious-looking Claire Knight.

'Sorry for making you wait. I just had to deal with a situation first. Come through.' Claire held the door open as Maggie and Kat passed through and waited. They followed Claire to a small room that had a two-seater couch and a small table and chairs. There were some children's toys piled in the corner. They sat in the comfortable area rather than the more formal interview-style setup.

'How lovely to see you both, despite the circumstances.' Claire wasn't going to be the first to offer information, and Maggie smiled. 'What can I do for you both?'

'We're hoping you can help us with some clarity on Olivia Hastings. Did you have a chance to look at the information I sent over?'

Claire bit her lip before answering. 'I did. Unfortunately, I don't think I am going to be of much help. Olivia's adoption records are sealed and her records with us have been closed and archived. Normally we would destroy records after six years of a case being closed, if there had been no other issues. But Olivia's appeared to have been kept and archived due to the abuse she suffered at the hands of her birth parents.'

'Can you tell us anything about her birth parents? Did they know who adopted their child? Were there other children?'

'You're placing me in an awkward position. I honestly don't know too much, but I do know that her birth father is in prison. I don't know where her birth mother is, and I don't know whether they knew who adopted Olivia – though I suspect they would have been told something.'

'Is there any way for us to get hold of more information without having to wait bloody ages to get them?'

'Sorry, Kat, with GDPR and everything else, it's hard enough for us to get the records for legitimate queries, let alone anything for someone who's now an adult.' Claire leaned forwards. 'But I can tell you that Olivia did request access to her records when she was sixteen, if that helps.'

'And was she granted that?' Maggie wondered what prompted her to want that information.

'I believe she was. But other than you two today and that request from Olivia herself, there's been nothing – not even a letter from her birth parents to pass on when she was old enough.'

Realising that without jumping through all the red tape they would get nothing, Maggie thanked Claire. It was getting late; a quick stop at the police station to update the records, sign out, and then home.

Chapter Sixty-Three

After work Maggie had thought about what she could do to relax more and get in shape. She wanted to record a list of activities, maybe outside of her comfort zone, and she'd begin researching them. 'Have you seen my voice recorder?' Maggie looked around her makeshift office and waited for Andy to respond. Her father had built her an oak desk when she was in university, and Maggie had set it up in the dining room. It was more of an office space than an office, but Maggie liked it.

'No idea what you are talking about,' Andy shouted from the kitchen.

'You know – my digital recorder. I'm sure I left it on my desk here.' Maggie was removing books and papers from the side shelves when her sleeve caught on something on the underside of the shelf. She bent down and tried to unhook it. 'What the hell is this?' She tugged the small object and cursed herself for ever trusting Julie Noble. In her hand she held a small recording device. No wonder Julie knew things about the case. She had obviously been listening in on her conversations with Kate. 'That fucking sneaky bitch.'

'What's got your knickers in a twist?' Andy wandered into the dining room, and Maggie held up the small recording device. 'Is that a bug, like in the movies?'

'That's exactly what it is, and I know who stuck it there.' Maggie didn't wait for her brother to respond. She raced upstairs and grabbed her mobile from the bedside table. Her hands shook as she scrolled through to find the journalist's number. She hit connect and tried to control her breathing.

'Hey Maggie! What's up?'

'You mean you don't already know? I knew you were sneaky, but this is pretty low even for you. What do you have to say for yourself? Is that why you've been making the move on me – playing with my feelings?' A flash of her father's face popped into her mind. He'd love this – would probably say it proved his point. Her anger grew.

'Whoa. You need to calm down. What the hell are you talking about?'

'The listening device you planted on my desk. I found it. Are you watching me too? I wondered how you knew so much about the case, but you were obviously listening in on the conversations I was having with Kate. Bloody unbelievable.'

'I have no idea what you found, but I can assure you, it wasn't me who planted it there. I thought you knew me better than that.'

'So did I. Well, at least I know now that you will stop at nothing to get a story. I really thought we had overcome a massive hurdle – your little show of popping around my house unannounced all makes sense now.'

'You need to stop right there before you say something you're going to regret. I told you before, I have a source and you know that I

can't reveal that source. But here is something I can tell you – even I don't know who the bloody source is, okay! They just email or phone shit in. All I can say is that the person contacting me is male. If I had any idea that someone planted something in your house, I would have let you know. And you're the one who told me to stay away; as much as I know you'd like to think you're irresistible, I'm not going to make an arse out of myself and have you keep pushing me away.'

'Do you really expect me to believe that? You never asked where your source got the information? The only person who knew I was speaking to Kate was you – in fact, if I recall correctly, you encouraged it. How would anyone know I spoke about the case at home?' Maggie took a deep breath; she believed Julie was being evasive – telling a half-truth – and wanted to unleash her fury on the journalist, but there was something about her tone that made her hold back. 'How long have you been receiving these alleged emails and calls then?' Julie's answer could salvage what little friendship they had forged.

'Not long after that kid, Tim, was killed.'

'And you kept that to yourself? Can you at least share what they said? Are you still getting calls and emails?'

'One question at a time. Yes, of course I kept it to myself. You know I can't reveal my sources. No matter what happened between us, that will never change. You can't play it both ways and expect me to accept work is separate from personal if you aren't going to, can you? If people can't trust me to share their information anonymously, they'll never send me anything. You know what was said anyway – I reported it all on the news. And yes, my source is still in contact – though I suspect that will stop now once they realize that you've found their device.'

'What's that supposed to mean? You do know I have no

choice but to report this to my DS. Like you, I have my own reputation to protect.' Maggie sighed. Everything had become so complicated.

'Wait! Can't you use this to your advantage? And open your eyes, Maggie. Won't you get in trouble anyway – Kate is not consulting with the police; she's in Ireland, on leave. So, don't throw this back on me to protect your Irish rose. Any conversations you are having with her should be at work and recorded, shouldn't they?'

'Well … yes. But I don't see how I can't share this with Nathan. If he finds out some other way, it will be more trouble on my doorstep.' Maggie could've kicked herself and she hated that Julie was right.

'I guess. But …'

'You're not going to change my mind on this. I'll just have to deal with the consequences. I know what you're trying to do.' Maggie's stubborn streak prevented her from thanking the journalist, so she reverted to what she knew best.

'And what exactly is that then?'

'Manipulate me into keeping the device so you can use it to *your* advantage. Anyway, like you said, they know I know now … no way of getting around that. Look, I've got to go – I need to think about my next move.'

'Fine. I'll call you in a few days when you've calmed down … we can discuss us then … maybe go for a walk or to the pub?'

'We'll see.' Maggie's mind was racing. She knew Julie wasn't at fault; but trouble seemed to follow her, and Maggie couldn't deal with the aftermath. There were too many complications. 'I'll ring you when I can.'

'I won't hold my breath.'

Julie Noble ended the call before Maggie could say anything further.

Maggie wandered back downstairs, holding the device with her fingertips in one hand and her phone in the other. She couldn't decide whether she should let Nathan know now or wait until she saw him tomorrow. Seeing her bag in the hallway, she dug around and found an empty plastic bag. She chucked the device inside, placed it in her bag, and headed to the couch.

Andy was watching a movie and it would be just the thing she needed to distract her.

'Everything okay?' He paused the film.

'It will be. Catch me up on what's been happening.'

Chapter Sixty-Four

Maggie didn't stop at her desk when she arrived at Stafford Police Station; instead, she headed straight for Nathan's office.

'Morning! What's up? You look like you're about to explode.'

Maggie sat and took a few deep breaths before sharing her news. He'd be pissed off and she wanted to be sure she had all her answers at the ready for when he unleashed. 'I've something to tell you and you're not going to like it.'

'What have you done now?' He crossed his arms. That should be Nathan's catchphrase. When it came to Maggie, he seemed to be saying it a lot.

'I came across a recording device in my home last night. It was on the bookshelf over my desk.' Maggie watched his face. Stone cold. Since becoming a DS he had become a master at disguising his feelings. Maggie didn't like it. 'You remember how you wondered how Julie Noble was getting her information?'

Nathan leaned forwards. 'Please don't say what I think you're going to say.'

'Someone placed a listening device in my house … they shared details from the cases with Julie Noble.'

Nathan's face creased. 'But why would you be talking to yourself about cases at home? You've totally lost me.'

'I've been speaking with Kate about the cases. She's been helping me with profiles and looking at the persons of interest.'

Nathan pushed his chair out, leant over and rested his head in his hands. He slowly raised his head. 'Fucksake, Maggie. That's highly confidential information. What the hell were you thinking?' She watched him stand and pace the room.

Maggie knew she had put him in a difficult position. If he reported her to DI Rutherford or DCI Meechan, not only could she be disciplined and removed from the case, she was facing a possible suspension. If he didn't report her and it got out, he'd look like he was playing favourites and could face a warning at best or a demotion if they really wanted to nail him.

'I'm sorry. In hindsight and given the circumstances now, I know that it was wrong – but it's not like Kate is just anyone. She'll be working with us when she returns. To be fair, Julie hasn't reported a lot of what Kate and I spoke about, so that has to mean something.'

'Yeah, it means she could be saving it for a massive story – dammit, Maggie! You could … no … you should have done all that here in the office.' His voice was raised but not so much that their colleagues would overhear. At least he seemed to be weighing his options rather than racing to throw her to the wolves. Nathan sat back down and pulled his chair in. 'I know we're all encouraged to think outside the box and use our initiative, but you should have run it all by me first. Where is the device now?'

Maggie lifted up her bag. 'In here.'

'I think we may be able to rectify this. But first, I need you to promise me that any further conversations you have with Kate are done on police premises and recorded on our system with the investigation information as every conversation should be. Next, get that device logged into evidence – have them check for prints. Do you still have outside cameras on your property?'

'No. Once Kate left, they were removed.'

'Damn. We'll get forensics over to your house – though it's unlikely we'll find anything of interest with you and your brother contaminating the scene. Did Julie say who had been sending her the info? We don't even know how long it has been there or when it was placed.'

Maggie shook her head. She'd only been out of the house a few evenings when her brother was away or working. It could have been any one of those times. She shuddered at the thought that someone could even have entered her home while she was sleeping. 'Julie claims it was an anonymous source and she wouldn't reveal it to me anyway.'

'Okay – go do what I asked and come back to me in an hour or so. I think I might be able to salvage this situation and keep your job in the process.'

Maggie got up. She could see the disappointment etched on Nathan's face. 'Thanks, boss. If it's any consolation, I really am sorry. I never meant for any of this to happen.'

He waved his hand. 'Don't go thanking me yet.'

Chapter Sixty-Five

Maggie headed downstairs to the field team offices and explained the situation. She was led into an interview room and smiled at the young PC who sat across from her. 'I know that it's unlikely that anything will come about it, but someone was in my home and planted a listening device. In all honesty, I never even noticed that someone had broken in, so not sure what you are likely to pick up.'

'You said you thought that the device was planted shortly after the murder of Tim Griffiths, which you are currently investigating? Why's that?'

'It correlates with information that was passed to the press and reported on. I know I'm being really vague – but I do have to be careful at the minute because of the ongoing investigation. What my DS would like is for forensics to go around and check whether prints or evidence of a break-in can be found.'

'We can certainly get that organized. Will you be around tonight?'

'I'll make sure to be home. I brought the recording device into work and my colleague has had it logged into evidence. By the time I realized that it was related to a possible break-in, I had already handled it.'

'I'll note that down. Is there anything else you can think of that we may need to be aware of?'

'Could all information be passed to DS Nathan Wright in the MOCD?'

'I'm sure that can be arranged. We'll get the Neighbourhood Policing Team out to you – I can't give you an exact time frame but if you're home after six, that should be fine.'

Maggie thanked the officer and returned to her desk upstairs. Nathan had suggested that, for the time being, she spend the day logging information and going through what they had so far. Maggie thought it was more about keeping an eye on her to make sure there were no other fuck ups while he handled what they discussed. As much as it frustrated her, she did what she was asked for a change. The day dragged.

A half an hour after Maggie had arrived home, there was a knock on the door. She'd wanted to have a look around herself but refrained, as she feared she could compromise any evidence that the police may locate.

She made her way to the front door and welcomed the officers. 'I'll keep out of your way and stay in the living room, if you need me for anything.'

'That would be helpful, DC Jamieson.' The officer brushed passed her.

'Please, call me Maggie. No need for formalities – I'm off the clock.'

'Ah, okay. Can you just point us in the right direction, and we'll make a start?'

Maggie pointed down the hallway. 'If you go straight through there, that takes you to the kitchen. There's a back door which leads out onto the garden. At the bottom of the garden there's a gate which backs out onto a ravine of sorts. There are woods and paths back there. The kitchen also connects to the dining room where my office space is. It's nearly an open-plan setting. The device was on the second shelf of the bookcase.'

'That's great. Okay, we'll make a start now and holler if we need you.'

Maggie waited by the door as the officer and forensics team entered. She closed the door after them and went into the living room. Nathan hadn't come back to her about the Kate situation. She could tell that he would have to be creative in his explanation and hoped that he would be able to smooth things over with Rutherford and Meechan. She hadn't made her mind up about the DCI yet. After finding out that he was DI Rutherford's ex-husband, Maggie had asked around to see what people had thought of him. She had received a mixed bag of gossip. She hadn't always seen eye to eye with her own DI, but underneath it all, she knew that Abigail Rutherford was fair and protective of her team, but she couldn't say the same about Meechan if the rumours were to be believed. Fellow officers had told her that he was a man out for himself – and looking to progress his way through the ranks by whatever means possible. She also learned that he had apparently started the relationship with DI Rutherford to give him a boost up the ladder and was fast tracked through the ranks. Once he had achieved DI status, the couple separated and divorced shortly after.

She rubbed her hands repeatedly. If DCI Meechan had plans to go higher in the force, she might have to get used to sitting on her couch. Maggie picked up her mobile and scrolled down her contacts. She had left the office while Nathan was still in with their bosses and was growing impatient. If it had been bad news, surely Nathan would have called to give her a heads-up – after all, they were not only colleagues, they had been friends for years. She typed out a brief text and just as she was about to press send, someone from the kitchen called out to her.

'We found something – you might want to come in here, Maggie!'

Chapter Sixty-Six

Maggie dropped her phone on the couch and raced into the kitchen. One of the forensic officers was standing by the back door and waved her over. 'See here. Looks like the lock was jimmied. This is quite an old make and easy to break into. You might want to look at replacing it with something more secure.'

Maggie bent down and looked at the scratch marks on the outside door. 'You're right. Damn. I meant to change the locks after some trouble awhile back, but instead, my brother just changed and secured the gate at the back. Was that tampered with too?'

'No, there was an old crate back there which we're going to take to the lab and examine further, but if I were to guess, I think they used that to hop over the fence. You should consider getting motion lights in the back as well, since that backs out onto a ravine.'

'Mmmm. Yeah. Another thing I had considered but never acted on.' She rolled her eyes – security 101 was biting her in her arse. 'I guess I just became too complacent ... Anything else you can tell me?'

'We've got a few prints; your brother will have to supply his, as yours will be on file. We'll rule those out and then see what we're left with. We'll know more when we test everything. Without a timeline we might struggle, though, so don't get your hopes up.'

Maggie left them to finish what they were doing and returned to the living room, where she picked up her phone and dialled Andy's number. It went straight to voicemail. 'Hey. Could you do me a favour and pick up a secure lock for the back door? Looks like we had a break-in, and we'll need to change the lock. Also, see if you can find any of those motion detector lights for outdoors. I'll tell you more when you get back, but you'll have to pop into the police station and get your prints taken tomorrow – so they can rule you out.'

She placed her phone on the table and lay back. Clearly whoever had broken into her house had not done so to steal anything, as nothing was missing. The goal seemed to have been leaving the listening device. She called out to the forensic officer closest to her and motioned her over.

'Have you found any other devices? Might be worth doing a sweep for those,' she whispered and immediately felt awkward when she saw the officer's eyes roll.

'That's being looked into as we speak.' The woman turned and carried on dusting the bookshelf.

Maggie's mobile buzzed beside her. Looking at the screen, her hands shook as she swiped to answer the call. 'I hope this isn't bad news.'

'I'm just checking in – has anything come to light at yours?' Nathan's voice sounded upbeat, so perhaps Maggie was

overreacting, and he had managed to smooth things over. She relayed the information she knew.

'They won't know any more than that until the results come back, but if it wasn't Julie who placed the device – and regardless of what she said, I still haven't ruled her out – then who could it be? The killer? Seems a bit over the top to bug my house on the hope that I would disclose information, doesn't it? They would know everything and could pass it on without using me as a source.'

'It does. Maybe someone following the case, wanting to make a name for themselves?' Nathan offered.

'I guess that's a possibility too. So … er … what happened with the guv and Meechan?' Maggie knew if she didn't ask, she wouldn't get any sleep tonight wondering.

'For now – everything's fine. But I have to go over a few things with you when you're in. Don't ask for any more than that, as I'm shattered. I just wanted to make sure everything was okay at your place.'

'Thanks. I've asked Andy to bring back some things to secure my house – so at least if the person tries again, it will be tougher for them.'

'Good. Okay. I've got to go now. See you tomorrow.'

The call ended and Maggie sighed. She thought back to the conversation and guessed that some measures would be put in place to make sure that from here on in, she followed procedure – she knew the rules were there for a reason, but she was known to get creative in her career and still get results. She had always been given some leeway because her conviction rate was excellent. However, this could also put Kate's career with the MOCD in jeopardy upon her return, and it was one thing to screw up her own opportunities, but she wouldn't mess with another's.

She had arranged to speak to Kate this evening about the case, but with everything that was going on she called her instead.

'I thought we were speaking later. Everything okay?'

'It is and it isn't.' Maggie took a deep breath. 'I've had a bit of a bollocking and there have been some new developments so, for now, I can't contact you about work stuff outside of office hours. I have a meeting tomorrow morning, but after that, I'll call you and fill you in on everything. Sorry to be so vague, but I've been warned—'

'Well, that's so un-Maggie – since when do you worry about following the rules?' Kate laughed but there was a slight edge to her words.

'You're right. But this could affect other people and their futures ... including yours ... so I've no choice at the minute. Promise to bring you up to speed tomorrow.'

'Ah, okay. How about early afternoon? About 1pm if you're done with your meeting. I've a few things to take care of here tomorrow morning myself – does that work?'

'Perfect. If anything changes, I'll let you know.'

The pair chatted for a few minutes before saying their goodbyes. Something in Kate's voice caught Maggie's attention but she couldn't place her finger on it. Was it excitement? Maggie knew that Kate didn't like to be pressured, so she would tell her when the time was right. Those might be the errands she had to do.

Maggie all of a sudden felt anxious. What if Kate took the uni job offered in Ireland and wasn't coming back? As if he knew that Maggie had been speaking about Kate, Salem trotted down the stairs and sat at Maggie's feet. She leaned over and petted his head.

'Hey you. Are you hungry? Where's your partner in crime?' Salem meowed. 'Still outside then?' She laughed and stood up, Salem following closely at her feet.

'Would I be able to feed this guy or do you need to do anything else?' The forensic team looked like they were packing up.

'All done here. We'll see ourselves out and keep you updated.'

'Thanks.' Maggie reached up and grabbed two bowls. When she started opening the cat food, Scrappy burst through the flap and skidded across the floor – nearly knocking Salem over. 'Careful, Scraps. One day Salem might shove you back.' She laughed as she dished out the food and placed it on the floor.

What a night. Tomorrow could be just as trying. She had wanted to wait for her brother to return, but her eyelids were heavy and she eventually gave in. She left Andy a note about where to go to have his prints taken. Her bed called and she wasn't about to ignore the pull.

Chapter Sixty-Seven

'I'm going into Stafford to visit Mark in the hospital.' Lucy was gathering her things together and would leave a note for Vicki, who was coming by to work on the backlogged referrals they had been receiving since the decision to push back the opening of the haven had been made.

Ronnie took out her phone and began to type. *'Can I tag along?'*

Lucy was surprised that Ronnie would want to, but the company would be welcome. Stafford County Hospital was a forty-minute drive and Lucy hated driving alone. Patrick used to drive her everywhere – when he managed to stay sober. Driving alone always made her dwell on her past.

'If you're sure?'

Ronnie nodded and waited while Lucy grabbed her bag and threw on a light jacket. 'Do you need to bring a coat? I can lend you one.' Lucy noticed the bulge in Ronnie's bag.

Ronnie opened her satchel and pulled out a hoodie, catching a few items that nearly fell out and stuffing them back in her bag. Lucy didn't recognize the top – it must be one that Ronnie brought with her.

'Ready?' Lucy grabbed the gate fob, locked the doors behind her, and Ronnie followed her out to the car.

Ronnie placed her satchel in the footwell and held it tightly by the strap. Lucy guessed it must bring her some kind of comfort, as she was rarely without it.

Lucy shot glances at Ronnie as they drove to the hospital. She had wanted to talk but Ronnie was fixated on the fields, closing her eyes now and again, and Lucy was sure she caught her smiling as they passed one of the old, abandoned farms.

Lucy reached over and turned on the radio – not too loud – as she noticed Ronnie fidget with her hearing aids. When they arrived at the hospital, she found a parking space as close to the doors as possible. A habit of hers since she had taken up driving again.

Inside the hospital, Lucy and Ronnie took the lift to the third floor. Mark was still drifting in and out of consciousness; although he had stabilized after he collapsed at Lucy's place, the doctors were still concerned about how it had happened and the after-effects that were still problematic. Tests were ongoing and Lucy hoped he would be his usual self in a few days, as he seemed to be on the mend.

'You don't have to come in with me if you don't want to. I wouldn't want to trigger any memories linked to the day. I know you're still affected even if you won't admit it. See over there?' Lucy pointed to the waiting area. 'You can sit there if you'd prefer and here …' She reached into her bag and pulled out a handful of change. 'Grab a coffee. I won't be too long. The toilets are just over there if you need them.'

Ronnie took the change and mouthed *'Thank you'* before

heading to the waiting area. Lucy watched and waited before going into Mark's room.

'Hey you!' She plastered a smile on her face, even though Mark's eyes were closed. She tried to keep her voice as upbeat as possible despite feeling quite the opposite when she saw how fragile Mark looked lying there. 'Just wanted to pop in and see how you are. Everyone has been asking about you – Maggie, Sarah, Vicki, Kat – the usual suspects. You know Vicki has a soft spot for you and even Sharon sounded a little concerned when I rang her – so you had better get well soon with all these ladies wanting your attention.' She felt her voice quiver; she was getting emotional and her mobile ringing was a welcome escape.

Shit, I forgot to turn this off, I'll take it outside ... Lucy left Mark's room and walked towards the lifts. She glanced at the waiting area and saw Ronnie glued to her phone.

'Hello? Everything okay?' It was Vicki, and she knew Lucy wouldn't want to be disturbed when she was at the hospital, so it must be something important.

'Is Ronnie with you?'

'Yes, she just ...' Lucy turned to look but Ronnie was no longer sitting where she had last seen her. 'Oh – she must have gone to the toilets. Why, what's up?'

'I was tidying up and I know you told me not to bother, but I thought it would be a nice surprise and—'

The loud beeps emanating from Mark's room and the nurses running in distracted her. 'Sorry, Vicki – I need to go. Something is happening with Mark.' Lucy ended the call and ran towards Mark's room. They wouldn't let her back in, but she stood on her tiptoes and glanced over the team working on Mark. 'What's happening? I was just in there and he was fine.'

Lucy noticed a pillow on the floor and some dark, black markings on the hand that lay limply down the side of the bed. She mentally made note so she could ask about them later.

'What the hell is going on?' Lucy tapped the woman just inside the door on the shoulder.

'I'm sorry. We can't say at the moment.' The nurse inclined her head.

Lucy watched as the doctors worked on Mark. She needed to find Ronnie – but she didn't want to go anywhere until she found out what had happened. Minutes later, police officers arrived on the floor and were speaking to the nurses. She noticed one of them point to her and then they headed her way.

What the hell was going on?

Chapter Sixty-Eight

'There's been a match on those prints from your house – Joe Clayton – mean anything to you?' Nathan waited while Maggie tried to place the name.

'Nothing – what's his history?'

'Long-time drug user, burglary, robbery, theft – all acquisitive to support his habit, I guess. Previous organized crime connections but he was small-time – probably cut loose when his habit became too risky to have him involved.'

'Has he been arrested?'

'They're just going out now. DCI Meechan sent one of his sidekicks.' Nathan's nostril's flared. It was clear to Maggie that he didn't take too kindly to being pushed aside. No one on the team had raised any issues with investigating the case when they had been asked, so why outsiders had to come in now and try to take over was beyond their understanding.

'Why? I get that I couldn't be involved but—'

'The other print was matched to someone else, that's why.'

Maggie waited for Nathan to explain when it finally dawned on her. 'No way. Are you saying what I think you're saying?'

'Hastings's print. It was a match. And we're assuming he didn't pay you any social calls in the last few weeks.' Nathan's radio crackled and he leaned over to his shoulder and listened. Maggie caught a few of the words.

'Needles … eye … dead … severed finger …'

'What the hell! C'mon let's go!' Maggie stood and grabbed her coat. Nathan grabbed her arm.

'You're not going anywhere. You're the victim in this case, no matter what else is happening in terms of our own investigation. Kat …' Nathan gestured for her to join them. 'Head over to Oldbury Road. The guy who broke into Maggie's house has been found dead. One of Meechan's people is already there. I'll let him know you're on your way.' Nathan wrote out the address and handed it to Kat. 'Update me as soon as you can.'

Kat took the piece of paper and Maggie caught her eye before she left. Kat nodded her understanding. She knew exactly what was wanted.

'I guess I'll carry on cross-referencing the prison tatts with anyone connected to Hastings. So far, no luck other than Craig Nolan and a few of his crew, but there could be thousands.'

'Keep digging,' Nathan instructed.

Maggie returned to her desk, took out her mobile phone and texted Kat.

Let me know when you arrive.

Be my eyes – tell me what you see. Between us of course ;)

She was placing Kat in a difficult position, but she knew Kat wouldn't have an issue telling her to fuck off if she felt Maggie was crossing any boundaries that she was not comfortable crossing herself. She waited for a reply.

Twenty-five minutes later and her mobile rang.

'You inside?'

'You've got some fucking cheek, Maggie. But yeah, I'm in. Looks like Dr Blake is finishing up and they're bagging the body.'

'What can you see?'

'He's got a needle in his eye and one in each arm. There is drug paraphernalia everywhere – the place is a dump – surprised the stench in here didn't kill him first. Smells like a shithole. Hang on …' Maggie could hear Kat mumbling to someone.

'Sorry. Dr Blake said this guy had two dots – just below his eye. They also found a severed thumb – looks like he was trying to hide it from someone – it was rammed in a small box and shoved deep in the back, underneath the sink. Fucking disgusting.'

'How were the two dots placed? Can you take a pic and send it to me?' Maggie waited while Kat took a photo. Her phone pinged and she opened the message.

'Thanks for that. Why two dots? Who is number three? Hastings wouldn't cut off his own thumb and then go looking for it – that doesn't make any sense. Wonder if the vic knows Craig Nolan.' Maggie was thinking out loud. It often helped her piece things together. 'Whoever did this left their signature and wanted us to know it was them.'

'We don't know who the severed thumb belongs to, but Dr Blake said she would get it processed as quick as possible.'

'It has to be Hastings's. The thumb print found in my house was his, along with Joe Clayton's – so who sent Joe to my house and why did they want him to speak to Julie Noble?'

'Have you spoken to her?'

'Not yet. I'll do that now. I'll speak to you when you get back.'

Chapter Sixty-Nine

Maggie ended the call with Kat and scrolled through her numbers, hitting connect when she found Julie Noble.

'I knew you'd come crawling back, though I didn't expect to hear from you for a while.'

'Not a social call. Can we talk off the record, please?'

'Depends on what it's about.'

Maggie clenched her teeth. 'I'm not saying anything more until you tell me that it won't go any further. If I tell you that I'll speak to the Comms Department and my bosses to make sure that you get to break the story – if there is one – will you help?'

'I love that you think you have so much influence, but fine. Off the record. What do you have?'

'Your source – the one we spoke about. What were you giving him in exchange?'

'Money. What does anyone ever want in these situations? Fifty to a hundred pounds depending on what I got. I'd drop it in the bin on

the corner of Ridland Hill and Kingstone. I was told to place the money in a McDonald's bag and drop it in the bin. Very cloak and dagger. I watched him collect it once – he was a drug addict for sure – in a rush when he collected the money. I haven't heard from him since you found the device. Why are you asking me this?'

'Wait – you knew who he was? You lied when you said he was an anon source – even after you knew I had been burgled?' Maggie swallowed.

'Would you have told me? Come on, Maggie. Neither of us would risk our career for the other. If I thought anyone would come to any harm, I probably would have told you.'

'You're fucking unbelievable,' Maggie snorted. 'Someone did come to harm. Never mind. Enough of this back-and-forth shit. None of this conversation makes it to the news, okay? I'll confirm when you can release some details – we should know soon enough, as Dr Blake is pushing the results through.'

'Really? Must have something to do with your big murder enquiry – not an accidental overdose – Interesting. Gotta go.'

'Wait. Julie? Hello?' Maggie looked at the screen, and Julie had hung up on her. She hoped Julie kept her word and didn't spread this all over the news just yet. But she wouldn't hold her breath.

They were getting closer. Maggie could feel it in her bones. She hoped that the conference call with Kate shortly would put everything into perspective.

Chapter Seventy

Maggie had set up the equipment in the briefing room after DI Rutherford agreed to have Kate give the team an update on the victimology information she had collated via a conference call. Once everyone was seated, she began the call.

When Kate appeared, there were a few waves in the room and from Kate herself.

'So lovely to see you all. I'm not going to waste any time here, as I know time is of the essence. I just wanted to share some of my thoughts on your persons of interest and on victimology. If you're ready, I'll just make a start?'

'Thanks, Dr Moloney. Whenever you're ready,' DCI Meechan acknowledged.

'I've had a brief update on the latest discovery, so have quickly thrown together my views on victimology in this case, which I will talk you through now and let you draw your own conclusions.'

Maggie noted that she had her points already written on

those big white sheets of paper she seemed to always have to hand and tacked up on the wall behind her.

'I put the victims in the order they were found – though we know Mark is a bit of an anomaly; I'll expand on that shortly. So, we have: Tim, Sophia, Mark, the recent murder – Joe I believe his name was and you'll see I have added DCI Hastings and his daughter Olivia on the end. I'll explain why in a moment. Each murder or attempted murder victim has the dots, which you have said started out similar to a common prison tattoo often found on gang or members of organized crime syndicates.'

'Wait. Mark? DAHU Mark? How is he involved in this? He's not dead too, is he?' Maggie covered her mouth with her hand.

'Ah sorry. I thought you'd have all been informed by now. An attempt was made on Mark's life earlier today. Someone tried to suffocate him. He's okay – but three dots …' Kate stepped aside and pointed at the board, *'like this, were discovered on his hand.'*

Maggie jotted down the picture.

'Sorry, I didn't mean to shout but you caught me off guard. So, Mark survived – was that deliberate do you think?'

'No. I think the killer had been interrupted rather than any desire to let Mark live – he was meant to be the third victim – the killer either knows of a connection between all these people that we don't, or Mark knew something. His situation was improving each day – it was only a matter of time before he could reveal what he knew.'

'What was Mark working on when he collapsed?' Maggie wracked her brains to try and remember if Lucy had mentioned anything in their conversations.

'I may be able to answer that.' All eyes turned to Kat. 'I was speaking to a few people at the DAHU and they had nothing significant going on. Mark was helping Lucy with a domestic abuse case that ended up on her doorstep. Around the time we found Tim, in fact.'

'Thanks, Kat.'

Maggie watched as Kate noted the information on her big whiteboard.

'Looking at your persons of interest, the Deputy Chief Exec at the college, Mr Dodd.' Kate picked up a red marker and crossed him off the board. *'I think you can rule him out. Even if he had confronted Hastings about the caution, what's his motive for everyone else? Also, from the information you passed on to me, doesn't he have an alibi for one of the murders?'*

The team had learned that he had been out of town when Sophia Hastings was killed. A family emergency took him to Manchester, and when they looked at the timings, there was no way he could have made it back in time to murder Tim. The motivation wasn't there. The timeline didn't fit.

'Then there is that lifer – Craig Nolan. Now he definitely has a motive to harm Hastings, abduct his family, torture him by killing people and making it look like Hastings was responsible – payback for his own persecution complex. He thinks Hastings set him up for murder and now it is payback.

'But he couldn't have done any of them, as even his curfew violations show that he was not out of his house for more than fifteen minutes at a time. And someone else is being looked at for planting evidence. Damn.'

Maggie watched as Kate crossed him of the list.

'Now this isn't an exact science. I'm giving you my opinion based on everything I have learned about the case. I think your perpetrator is aged between twenty and forty years. Your killer is controlling the narrative. Feeling powerful. If we look at the meaning behind the prison tattoo – and I think it is certainly inspired by the tattoo – the

person values their freedom. They are telling you they will not be caged. Each dot representing a bar. Each kill removes one of those bars. I believe the markings came as an afterthought – they had some victims identified but others who were just circumstance. The person you seek is potentially hiding in plain sight.'

'So that leaves …' Maggie was about to share her thoughts when Kate held up her hands.

'Hold that thought and let me finish. Human behaviour is context driven. We're all capable of abnormal behaviour, it just depends on what the drive to behave a certain way is. Compulsion for risk versus control. Find that drive, you'll find your killer. Which leaves us with Hastings.'

Kate circled his name.

'And his daughter, Olivia.'

Kate circled her name.

'I can see why the evidence points to DCI Hastings, but I'm worried that he's either dead or will be soon.' She crossed his name off the list.

'Bloody hell, Kate. That means … she isn't a victim – she's the perp. We need to find Olivia Hastings.' Maggie jolted upright.

'That's right – find her, and I believe you'll have your killer.'

The silence in the room was overwhelming.

Chapter Seventy-One

Ah – dear, sweet Olivia – the girl with so much potential. I looked at her. Remembered her as that little girl rescued from those monsters she called mummy and daddy. Scars – physical at least – still covered her body from her time with them: faded burn marks from the cigarettes, her arms and legs the ashtray. Aching bones from the breaks. Accident prone, that's what her parents had told Social Services at first, and those dumbass professionals believed them. No one took in the emotional scars from everything else that was forced on her. Some people shouldn't have children.

She stared back at me. Is that fear in those eyes?

My heart pounded. I knew why I was doing this. It was for her, always for her. People whispered behind her back ... *she needs help, aren't you worried about what she'll become ... a drug user, a drop-out, a danger to those who have cared about her?*

What the hell did they know? I was never worried though.

All grown up now, but I can still see that frightened little girl inside her if I look deep enough. Wide-eyed, trembling but never wanting to be touched. She'd fight any form of love towards her. Lashing out. Of course she would, because love meant pain. What was love anyway except one person having control over another?

The weak side.

I pulled out the baton I had in my bag. Looked once more at the lost innocence of Olivia and then hit the face that stared back at me.

The mirror shattered.

Time to finish this once and for all.

Chapter Seventy-Two

When Lucy arrived back at the house after the police had spoken to her, she was worried. Someone had tried to kill Mark and then Ronnie had run off and wasn't answering her phone. The haven door was open. *Fuck. What if it was Ronnie's boyfriend? Had he finally found her?*

'Vicki? Are you still here?' She looked in the living room, kitchen, and office before going upstairs. At the top of the landing, she found Vicki on the floor. Lucy raced over to her and felt for a pulse. 'Oh my god! Vicki, it's okay. I'm here now. I'm going to call an ambulance.' As she spoke to the call handler and gave the information, she looked up and saw the bathroom mirror was shattered.

What the hell?

Vicki was coming around.

'Hey. Don't move. An ambulance is on the way.'

'R-r-r-onnie.' Vicki tried to speak but ended up in a coughing fit. 'Ow.' She raised her hand to her head.

'Don't move, hun. What about Ronnie? Are you saying she did this to you?'

Vicki nodded and struggled to reach into her pocket. She pulled out a driver's licence and handed it to Lucy. Lucy looked at the picture. The girl in the photo had longer hair and it was a different colour, but the face was the same. This was definitely Ronnie. But the name on the licence said 'Olivia Hastings'.

'Fuck. Fuck!' Lucy needed to call Maggie. She heard the ambulance pull up. 'Will you be okay here if I go and let them in?'

'Yes.' Vicki lay still on the ground.

Lucy took off her jacket and lay it under Vicki's head before she ran down the stairs, opened the door, and pressed the fob to open the security gates. She greeted the paramedics, telling them that Vicki was upstairs.

'I think she was hit on the head. I found her on the floor when I came in. She couldn't have been there long. I just need to make a call.'

Lucy dialled Maggie's number.

'Hey. I heard about Mark, is he okay?'

'Yeah, he's fine. Maggie, listen to me – Olivia Hastings was here.'

'What? How do you know Olivia?'

'The woman I told you about. The one who collapsed at my doorway? She called herself Ronnie, but we've just found a driver's licence with her name and a picture. I mean, she disguised herself but it's her. It's Olivia. She can't be too far from here. She attacked Vicki, probably to get away.' Lucy leaned up against the wall.

'Shit! Is Vicki okay? Stay there, lock the doors. I'm on my way, Lucy. If she comes back do not let her in.'

Lucy hung up the phone. She had wanted to go to the hospital with Vicki, but Maggie had asked her to wait at the house. Her heart was racing.

How did she not know?

Lucy had brought her to the hospital. It was her fault Mark nearly died. She hoped Maggie caught her in time and no one else was harmed. She'd never forgive herself.

Chapter Seventy-Three

After filling Nathan in on her conversation with Lucy, Kat and Maggie raced towards Lucy's refuge.

'Fucking hell! All this time and that little bitch was right under our noses. Kate was right. She was hiding in plain sight.'

Maggie was staring out the window when something caught her eye. 'Hang on. Stop the car!'

'What the fuck?' Kat looked around.

'Someone is running through those fields. Short dark hair – she looks like the description Lucy gave. Stop the bloody car!'

Kat did as she was told and they jumped out, running towards the figure in the distance.

'Hey! Stop, police!' Maggie shouted. Kat was ahead of her and gaining on the woman.

Olivia Hastings looked over her shoulder and appeared as if she was slowing down; just as Kat was on her heels, she bolted again.

'Fuck!' Maggie watched as she ran.

Kat kept up the pace with Olivia.

'Keep going, you nearly have her. I'm going to cut across here,' Maggie called after her.

Maggie turned left and ran up the hill. She thought she would be able cut Olivia off or at least slow her down. As she reached the top and was about to jump forwards, Kat launched herself on the woman and dragged her to the ground.

Olivia wasn't going down without a fight. Kat took a punch to the eye and the jaw and fell back. Olivia scrabbled to get up and Maggie saw her reach into her back pocket. She wouldn't risk a weapon being pulled and Maggie took out her baton and caught Olivia behind the knees. Olivia fell face first to the ground but kicked out and caught Maggie in the knee. Maggie fell to the ground. Olivia pushed herself up and took off again.

Where the hell did she get her energy from?

Maggie struggled to get up. The pain in her knee stopped her momentarily. She looked back at Kat. 'Are you okay?'

'I'm fine – give me a minute and I'll be right behind you. Go! She's getting away.'

Maggie wasted no time and although her knee hindered her, she ran after Olivia. She was closing in. Olivia was slowing down; she must have used up the adrenaline that had kept her one step ahead.

'You won't get away. You may as well stop now,' Maggie shouted after her.

Olivia turned and Maggie noticed the uneven ground ahead.

The woman stumbled and that was Maggie's chance. She used every ounce of energy she had. Her legs were on fire. She leapt on Olivia's back, knocking her to the ground. Maggie straddled the woman, pinning her arms down with her knees.

'Olivia Hastings, I'm arresting you for the murders of

Sophia Hastings, Timothy Griffiths, and Joe Clayton and the attempted murder of Mark Fielding and Vicki Wilkinson.'

Kat had finally caught up and passed Maggie a pair of cuffs. They hauled Olivia back to the car.

'Where's your father?'

Olivia turned to Maggie and smirked. 'You're the detective. Figure it out, bitch.'

Chapter Seventy-Four

The young woman's ice-cold eyes stared back at Maggie. She had never seen someone as void of emotion as the woman before her. She shivered as Nathan cautioned Olivia and started the recording.

Olivia leaned forwards, arms stretching across the table, and whispered: 'So what do you want to know? How I did it? Every-little-detail? The cries for help. The blood? Each thrust of the blade. Each blow of the hammer?' She used her fingertips to slowly push herself back and smiled. A sneer more than a smile. 'Just tell me. I'll gladly let you know.' She began to hum as she closed her eyes. Rocking back and forth in her chair.

A chill crept over Maggie and she turned to face Nathan.

He nodded.

'Where's your father?'

'No. No. No. No. NO! That's not how this is going to play out!' She slammed her hands on the table.

'Okay. Tell us about Tim then, Olivia.'

'Why so formal? We're all family, aren't we? That's what

my *Dad* …' She spat the word 'dad' out like it left a bad taste in her mouth. 'That's what he used to say all the time. His colleagues were his family – he'd do anything for them … but nothing,' she slammed her fists on the table again, 'nothing for me.' She rubbed her hands on her trousers. 'So, Tim is where you want to start then. You sure? I can go even further back. You know – don't you want to know why it all started? Isn't there some sort of protocol? A lead up – why did I do this? My *motivation*.' The corner of her mouth raised. She was taunting them.

Maggie didn't want to push too hard or she could just shut down completely. Though Kate had said Olivia would want to talk, take pleasure in sharing her story because she felt she had earned the right to do what she did … and she didn't care. She'd have no feelings or remorse. She was a psychopath through and through.

Maggie and Nathan waited. They wouldn't fill the silence. A technique they learned many years ago for interviewing – though Maggie suspected that even if they had tried to fill the awkward silence, it wouldn't have made a difference.

'They won't get the best of me now, will they?' Olivia looked at Nathan and then at Maggie. 'Well? Will they?' She slammed her hands on the table, and the PC standing by the door moved forwards. Maggie held up her hand. Olivia had no intention of harming Maggie or Nathan. From everything they knew so far, Olivia had done everything she had set out to do.

'Have you finished? Or is there more to this show before you start telling us about Tim?' Maggie was getting tired, and Kate had advised her to pull Olivia back if she was going off on a tangent. She might not like it, but she wouldn't want the police to lose interest either.

'Fine. Tim served a purpose. I met him in college. A loner. People pleaser. And I knew he fancied me. Once I had played up to his emotions, I had him wrapped around my finger. I told him my father was planning on sending me away. Locking me up in an institution. Poor, poor Tim. That scared him. I knew it would. I watched how he got so upset, the tears and then the anger.' Olivia looked up, her hands waving as if she was moving something across the ceiling. 'It wasn't hard to copy him. Emotions are ridiculous, don't you think?' She looked at Maggie. Was she hoping for a reaction?

Maggie started tapping her pen, and a darkness formed in the girl's eyes as she shot a look at the pen and then back at Maggie's face.

Maggie didn't stop until Nathan reached across and put his hand over hers.

Olivia looked at Nathan. 'Ah. You have to control that one, don't you?'

'Can we please get back to Tim, Miss Hastings?' Nathan sighed.

They were playing Olivia just like Kate had suggested. If Olivia associated Nathan with her father and Maggie with herself, she may open up quicker. In some respects, Maggie could relate to Olivia – she too had a father who wouldn't see her for who she was. Would never accept her. But never in a million years did Maggie ever think of killing him or wish he was dead. That is what set them apart. Maggie's thoughts returned to the task at hand. She wasn't hopeful, though. Olivia was too clever for these tactics. She had probably come across them from other agencies throughout her life.

'It took a lot longer to convince Tim than I had anticipated. He kept changing his mind. He was worried that he would end up in prison for life and we would never see each other.' Her voice was flat. As if she was reading a script rather than retelling what led to the heinous acts she committed. 'Once I convinced him that we could … we *would* get away with it, he was in. You see, I couldn't do it on my own. I needed him to help knock out my father and tie him up while we got my mother to the allotment to kill her.'

'Why did you kill your mother?' Maggie wondered where the hatred came from.

'I knew it would hurt David – your precious DCI. He loved her. Protected her. And she protected him. If only she had backed up my claims of abuse to the police. He could have taken the fall. He would've got a slap on the wrist. But no. Always by the fucking book.' She drummed her fingers on the table. 'We popped some GHB in the water we gave them when we tied them up at my house – I did the same in Mark's tea. You see, Mark suspected something and thought he was clever. He had to be stopped – and even though he was never part of my original plan, it worked out so well with the markings I left too. Who knew?' She laughed a deep, piercing sound. 'But I digress. When it was dark, we drove mommy dearest to the allotment and well … you saw what happened there. Dropped the car back at the house and drove Mum's car to where Dad is now … Wonder if he's still alive? … He wasn't doing so well the last time I saw him. I chopped off his thumb, you know – needed to leave that print in your house, DC Jamieson. Looked pretty infected when I last saw him.' She paused. 'Wait! This question answer bullshit isn't working for me.' Olivia stood. 'I need you to see what I saw – the whole picture. The main players … Let me start again.' And then her voice changed, and Maggie and Nathan listened as she recapped every murder from the beginning ... her story.

It was then that Maggie knew Olivia wasn't a serial killer – she had killed for the thrill, to get revenge, and to prove to her father she was everything he worried she would grow up to be – a cold, calculated killer.

Chapter Seventy-Five

The tea had arrived, and they watched as Olivia paced the room before sitting down and recounting the events that had led her to where she was now. A strange smile washed over her face and then she began.

Maggie looked at Nathan and he raised a finger to his lips. They didn't want to disturb the flow. Olivia was confessing everything without being prompted.

'I can still hear the shrill scream when I think back to Sophia's death. If I had any feelings towards her left, I may have even regretted killing her. Luckily, I don't.

'Sophia initially put up a fight – hands flailing, trying to hide. *"Come out, come out wherever you are,"* I sang as I walked around the house.

'I needed Tim to be involved for my plans to work. I promised him that I would protect him; he'd be deemed a hero in the public's eye, because I lied and told him he would be the one to find and save her. What … a … muppet.

'When I met Tim a few hours before the deed was to be

done, I handed him a balaclava and told him that when he saw the car in the driveway, he needed to wait an hour and then come through the back door. I'd leave it open for him and then we'd make it look like a break-in after the fact. He did what he was told. Always eager to please – dumb fuck that he was.

'When Tim had finally joined the party, we tied Sophia to a chair in the living room, taped her mouth over and I bent down and whispered in her ear, explaining what would happen, and if she did what we asked, she'd be let go. She was quiet at first. Compliant. I guess she thought everything would be okay if she did what she was told. She learned well over the years to keep her mouth shut. That was her downfall.

'We had a few things to take care of in the house before we could go. I told Tim exactly what I needed him to do and stood looking out the window as he followed each instruction meticulously. Oh … I forgot to tell you about the blood! You found it, right? In the house. My blood. Now that hurt like a mutha fucking bitch. Here let me show you.'

Olivia rolled up her sleeve and unravelled a cotton bandage on her arm.

'You'd be surprised how much comes out of a cut like that. Took nearly forty minutes for me to stop it. But it was worth it … Did you buy it?' Olivia didn't wait for a reply.

'Back to Mum. When Tim had finished placing the chest in the car, I returned to Sophia and tears fell as I told her that we'd be going for a short ride. When we untied her hands, she struggled for a bit and I held the knife to her throat. "One word and you can say goodbye to this *loving* family of yours." Her face tensed and I smiled. "Scratch her face!" I bellowed at Tim. I wanted to laugh as he hesitated – until he saw my eyes. His feeble hands shook as he reached over and drew his nails across her cheek.

'After that, she didn't need much convincing to get into the car, and I drove to the allotment – wearing my Dad's clothes. She thought I didn't know she went there to escape. Escape what? SHE had it good the ungrateful bitch! After parking up on the backstreet behind the allotment, where I knew there were no cameras – did my homework you see – Tim and I took hold of her arms and marched her to the fence. I handed Tim a pair of wire cutters from my backpack and told him to make a hole big enough for us to get through. The fucker had the nerve to ask me why we didn't just use the front entrance. "You have the code," he moaned. I smacked the back of his head. "DO IT!" He didn't need asking twice. Once the hole was big enough, Tim pushed through first while I held on to Sophia. She went through willingly – well, a knife in the back would convince anyone, wouldn't it?

'Once we were in the shed, the fun started. I pushed her on the couch and as I ripped the tape from her mouth, I whispered, "One word and I will make this as painful as possible." She whimpered. "Why are you doing this to me? I've never done anything to you." Suffice to say I lost it then. I stabbed her multiple times. It was like cutting meat – jab after jab. Deep enough to hurt but not deep enough to kill. Yet.

'Tim stood by the door, turning his face away from what I was doing. I think the little bitch even cried a bit. Though that could have been Sophia; it was hard to tell, as I focused on my task at hand. I was in the moment and loving every second of it.

'"Hand me the garden shears!" He passed them over, and I stood back and looked at her sitting there. Wrists bound.

Ankles tied together. She was slumped over, struggling to breathe. I pulled her head back by her hair. "Are you sorry you ever met me now?" Her eyes widened. I wonder if she was thinking about how to answer that question. Maybe she thought if she said no, I might stop what I was doing and she'd have a chance to live? But she must have found some courage. Her chance to defy me now in front of her. She had accepted her fate and I almost had second thoughts … almost. She nodded and then I plunged the garden shears into her neck and … have you ever danced in the rain? I've always wanted to – I imagined dancing as the blood sprayed around me. Was this what happiness felt like?'

Maggie listened intently. Olivia was not well – Hastings was right about seeking professional help.

'Then it was time to go. I told Tim to meet me in the woods behind Castle Bank Industrial Estate and make sure he stayed out of sight. I was putting my trust in Tim – he could have easily gone to the police despite it implicating him. But I knew deep down, he wouldn't. He belonged to me now. I had one more thing to take care of back at the house and then there would be no turning back. I wondered if Tim knew what would be happening when I met up with him. I bet he was running through everything in his mind. Hoping that because he had done so well – not protested too much and did what he was told – maybe I would spare him. Or did he realize and accept his fate the same way Sophia did?

'Would anyone miss Tim? Would he fight back? Would he even be at the designated meeting place we had spoken about when I planned this?

'We already know how that story ended. Don't we?'

Chapter Seventy-Six

'Poor Tim. He really didn't take much convincing. Thought he'd be helping – and he did – but he wouldn't be around to bask in that glory.' She blew on the steam coming from the mug of tea before taking a sip.

'It wasn't difficult to convince him to meet up in the woods. He would have done anything if he thought it would gain him more friends. He just wanted to be liked and when the seed was planted, he followed like a lost puppy. After we spoke, Tim looked confused. At first, I wondered if he was piecing everything together. I didn't need to be worried; he wasn't that clever.

'But then came the questions. For the sake of all the fucks. The whine in Tim's voice was annoying as he fired question after question. What did he know about anything anyway?

'A spark in Tim's eye – when I saw it, I knew he understood. At first, he tried to play me – like he was on my side. He wasn't a good actor and when I had called him on it, he didn't like it. He said he wasn't going to go along with it –

despite all the promises he had made. After everything we'd already done. Was he really that stupid? He was in it as much as I was, except the police would know of his involvement … they'd never believe him. "You'll never get away with it." Oh that sulking bastard voice of his.

'We fought then – and everything began to fall right back into place. You see, I needed to look like a battered woman; otherwise Lucy would never let me stay, and I had to stay close by. It couldn't be any other way.

'Poor Tim. Punches connecting with flesh. Blood oozing from already swollen lips and open cuts. "Harder you pussy! Harder!" I shouted at him and laughed when I saw the pleasure in his eyes as his fist connected with my face. He was enjoying it, but he hated himself – it didn't stop him though. Each blow brought me a sense of satisfaction. "Is that the best you can do?" I took pleasure in taunting him. We danced around each other for a bit, fists up and the soggy leaves beneath our feet providing the dance floor. He fell to his knees and I grabbed his hair. A greasy film covered my gloves. "Dirty fucker. Get up, we're not finished yet!" I stood back and held my hand out. He grasped it and I pulled him up with one hand and removed the hammer I had tucked in the back of my jeans. My Daddy's hammer – his prints already on it and my gloves to make sure it was his prints you found. How clever am I?!

'"Are you ready for the next part?" I tried to sound upbeat – give the poor fucker some hope. There was more to come, and Tim didn't know about this part. When he saw the hammer, his face changed. He frowned and then the fear took over. "My what big eyes you have." That made me laugh. He was going to run; I saw his feet shuffle and his eyes look around – clocking whether there was enough space between us to make his move. "Don't be such a dick. Take it like a man!" His lips tightened then. He was angry at that comment. Maybe he had daddy issues.' She looked directly at Maggie. 'Oh wait, that was me.'

Olivia cackled then. A long, piercing scream of a laugh. She stopped almost as quickly as she started and carried on with her confession.

'At first, he stood firm, staring, almost taunting me to hit him but then his lower lip fell. *This bitch is going to fucking cry!* He backed away from me and then his feet slipped from under him. I covered my mouth to hold in the laugh that was bubbling to get out and watched as he tottered, trying to regain his balance while mocking over his shoulder: "You won't get away with this."

'What the fuck does he know? I came close … With the hammer raised, I took a step forwards and gave chase. Tim was unsteady, reaching out to invisible trees in the hope of finding something to help him. I smiled when I heard the CRACK as Tim's skull met the end of the hammer. I gripped the handle tight. Tim was on the ground now. Whimpering. *The fucker was dragging himself towards the car park.* One step. Two steps. I followed behind him. I needed to capture the moment and took out my mobile phone. I looked around the woods – voices in the distance. Fire crackling – they weren't a threat, though, as it was still early enough and they'd all be too pissed to make any sense. That's why I chose this place.

'The flash from my camera was bright. I looked around once more and then hit save. *Memories … we all need something to remember.*

'I walked slowly behind Tim and watched his shaking hands reach forwards. His swollen fingers digging deep into the ground to get hold and then pulling himself forwards. When he had finally reached the edge of the forest, I bent over and whispered into his ear. "Nearly there, Tim. Go on. You can do it." Rasping breaths and spittle of blood drops sprayed from Tim's mouth. He spat but missed me. He certainly was determined.

'A branch snapped in the distance. So of course, that brought me back to reality, right? I kicked him hard in the ribs before I had to go. I wanted to do more but couldn't risk getting caught. Not now. It was too soon. I remember I looked on the ground for Tim's mobile. He was reaching for it. Probably thought he could ring for help. I let him stretch as far as he could; I wasn't completely heartless, you know. Everyone needs that one more second of hope. As he raised his head and turned to look up, another crack to his head and I dropped the hammer.

'Shall I tell you what happened next?'

Chapter Seventy-Seven

'DCI Hastings – or Daddy – looked at me with fear in his eyes. I left him tied up at the house while Tim and I played with Sophia. Neither deserved the terms of endearment that children use to identify their parents. They wanted to lock me away. I was getting out of control, I overheard them say. Of course, Sophia was in denial at first – worried about what people would think.

'WHAT WOULD PEOPLE THINK!?' She shouted those words, and Maggie's ears rang – the whole building probably heard her.

'The selfish bitch. Not concerned at all about what I might think. It had been going on for years. My threats no longer had any hold over either of them. Well, I'd have the last laugh, wouldn't I? And then we'd see what people would think.

'His eyes pleaded with me as I approached him. I think he actually believed that if he gave me that look – the one I hadn't seen since I was about nine years old off him – things would change. I'd change my mind. Some copper …

'"Don't worry, I've a little more in store for you." I bent down and started to untie his ankles from the leg of the chair. "Don't try any of your heroics either or this won't end well for you at all – do you understand?"

'He nodded.

'I pulled a pair of handcuffs out of my pocket and released one of his hands, clamping the cuff on his wrist. He was weak from the drugs. Glad Tim knew some dealers – the drugs really helped, so I guess he hadn't been that useless.

'I picked up the knife I had placed on the table and cuffed his hands behind his back, pressing the knife firmly against the base of his neck. "Now we're going to walk out of here to the car. If you try anything, I will push this knife through your neck … and I'll enjoy every second of it. Got it?"

'I shoved him towards the door and once outside, we walked towards the car. I unlocked the boot and pushed him inside. His eyes still pleading with me. I raised the butt of the knife and knocked him just above his eye before closing the door.

'We used to … oh wait, if I tell you, that might give the game away – who knows how much Daddy shared with his family here? … but where he is, it had been planned for a long time – about two years – I had set up a little home away from home. I found somewhere to escape, and dear old Dad could sit there and think about all his secrets and lies while I finished what I had started.'

Maggie was determined to let Olivia continue without interruption. But something she said, about the location of Hastings, niggled at her. She was sure he had talked about drives in the countryside – but that was all she could remember. It may not even have been him.

'I pulled up close to the building and parked. There was no need to hide the car, as once I dumped him, I'd need to leave the car back at the house.'

Olivia was recounting the details as if she was back there in the moment and her calmness chilled Maggie to the core. She looked over at Nathan and he was just as engrossed in the confession as she was.

'I opened the back passenger door and pulled out my bag of treats before opening the boot and pulling him out. "Walk." I shoved his back forcefully and reminded him of the large knife I still had in my possession by giving him a prod with the tip. He complied.

'Inside the building, I could see the look of shock on his face as he realized that I must have been planning this for some time. We were in the middle of nowhere and even if he did scream, only I would be able to hear his pitiful cry. I tore the tape from his mouth, and he cringed as the sticky bits pulled at his stubble.

'"Sit!" I secured his feet and hands to the chair and then sat down myself, facing him. I couldn't help but smile.

'"Let's see how you like being locked away."

'"Please, sweetheart. Why are you doing this?"

'"Is that all you care about? Don't you want to know where your wife is?"

'"Of course I do. Why are you doing this?"

'"Your colleagues should find her in a day or two."

'"Wha-what have you done, Liv?"

'"*You* did this! Now drink." I removed a water bottle from my bag and held it to his mouth. He turned his head.

'Grabbing his cheeks, I squeezed tightly. "Don't fuck about. I'm not sure when I'll get back to you so drink this now."

'My words must have struck a chord, as he opened his mouth and drank. I reached into my bag and fed him a sandwich and, once he was finished, I tore off some gaffer tape and shut the fucker's mouth.

'Noises emanated as he shook his head. "Mmmmm. Mmmmmm. Mmmmm. Fucksake."

'"I know you don't want me to go but I've not finished yet … and once I'm done, people are going to think you are responsible … how does that feel … Daddy?"'

Olivia stopped speaking then. She stared directly at Maggie.

'And now you'll have to find him. Tick tock … You may already be too late.'

A knock on the interview room door pulled them back into the room and out of the evil they had just witnessed. Bethany handed Nathan a piece of paper and he then shut off the recording.

'Interview suspended. Maggie, let's go.'

Chapter Seventy-Eight

There wasn't any time to process things as Maggie and Nathan raced to the address that Bethany had located in the sat nav device that came from Sophia's car. They found it in Olivia's possessions when she was arrested.

It was an abandoned property located just outside of Markston – about twenty miles from where the Hastings family lived and twenty minutes from Lucy's refuge. That was where Olivia must have been heading when Kat and Maggie caught her. There was no way they would have found the property if it wasn't for the sat nav, as Olivia had hinted it was something from her childhood that only she and the DCI would know about.

'I hope we're not too late.' Maggie bit her nail. She didn't have a good feeling about what they'd find, as Olivia wouldn't give anything away in interview. It was like she was thriving on the worry and fear of his colleagues.

Nathan slowed down. 'Bloody tractors. Move you asshole!'

'He's pulling to the side.' Maggie looked ahead.

'Yeah, I can see that.' Nathan sped up and passed the tractor. Maggie noted the focus on his face alongside the furrowing brows. He was pushing the pool car to its limit.

'It's a left up ahead.' Maggie sat forwards. The area was secluded enough – grassland spread for miles with old barns and buildings scattered about. 'Are all these properties empty?'

'Not sure. I know that there had been some trouble with farming around here at one point. The land had been poisoned and the farmers lost their homes. I guess people just moved on. There! That must be it.'

'The ambulance shouldn't be too far behind. If you pull up at the side of the house, they'll have space to park as close to the door as possible.'

Nathan agreed. The pair exited the vehicle and Maggie felt a rush of adrenaline as well as trepidation. *What if they were too late?* The last thing she wanted to stumble across was the body of her DCI.

'Hang on five minutes and wait for the rest to arrive. We don't know what to expect or whether she has anyone else involved. I don't want to risk anyone else getting hurt.' Nathan looked down the lane and pointed. The calvary was arriving. They walked towards DI Rutherford's car. Kat was with her. No sign of DCI Meechan – Maggie had thought he would want to be there, even if it was only to get some glory.

DI Rutherford waved them over. 'Okay. Let's be sensible about this. We have no idea what to expect when we get inside and, as positive as I want to be right now, we have to face the fact that what we may come across is a body. Nathan and Maggie – I'd like you to go around back. Looks like two floors. You two clear the bottom floor, and Kat and I will head upstairs. The rest of the field team will secure the area and start looking through any of the surrounding buildings. Forensics should be arriving any moment now – but we can't hold off. If there is any chance that Hastings might be alive, I'll be damned if I am going to worry about compromising a crime scene. Watch what you are doing. If there is someone else in there – don't play the hero, okay? Any questions?'

No one had anything further to add. Maggie checked her gear and then followed Nathan through the overgrowth alongside the left side of the building. They crept up the stairs and checked the back door. It was locked. Nathan motioned for the PC with them to use the ram and he called out. 'Police! Open up or we're coming in.' He waited a further minute before banging on the door and repeating that they would enter forcefully if the door wasn't opened. No response, so they stood back as the PC rammed the door.

Dust flew everywhere and the pair coughed as they entered the premises. 'Jesus Christ.' Maggie choked on her words. 'Well, it doesn't look like anyone has been in this part of the house, as we've just unsettled all the dust.' She pointed to the counter where a thin film of dust had resettled. 'I'll check out these doors on the left.' She pointed.

Maggie walked carefully to the first door and opened it. Peering inside she caught a musty smell but otherwise the cupboard was empty. 'Nothing here,' she called out and moved to the next door. The stench of a blocked drain filled her nostrils. She took out her flashlight and peered into the sink. 'Looks like blood in here.' She didn't touch anything so as not to contaminate any evidence. 'Clear.' She turned to face Nathan.

'All clear here too. This was the pantry I'm guessing. A few rusted and labelless tins, but empty otherwise. Let's go through.'

Maggie followed Nathan through to the living room. An old wooden table and a few chairs were all that furnished the room. The curtains had been drawn over. Maggie swept the room with her flashlight. On the table was a file and papers strewn about. Maggie shone the light on the notes – it was Olivia's Social Care information. Circled was the name of her birth mother – Linda Eveleigh – and scratched out was her birth father's name with PRISON written across it. They both noticed something on the floor at the same time and carefully approached what looked like a bloody pile of women's clothing on the manky and stale carpet.

Just as they were heading back out to the hall, they heard DI Rutherford call out: 'He's here! Get the paramedics in here now!'

Maggie raced out the front door while Nathan ran up the stairs two by two.

She called out to the ambulance: 'They've found him. He's alive!' and stepped aside as the paramedics entered. She took a moment to compose herself. Her heart was beating a mile a minute and she made her way back inside, not knowing what to expect.

Maggie went upstairs and joined Kat and Nathan who stood outside one of the rooms. DI Rutherford had remained inside the room with Hastings.

Kat was frowning.

'What is it?' Maggie looked between the pair.

'Fuck. I'm not sure he's going to make it. He could barely speak. His breathing was all … raspy. He's covered in blood … his fucking thumb is missing, and his hand is badly infected.'

Kat gagged and shook her head. 'I don't have a good feeling about this.'

'Well, Olivia had better hope he does survive, or she'll be looking at another murder charge,' DI Rutherford shouted over her shoulder as she followed the ambulance crew out. 'Though let's face it, I don't think she'll be bothered either way. Maggie, Kat, stay behind and see what else you can find out. Nathan, come with me.'

Chapter Seventy-Nine

'While field officers are doing the house-to-house, let's have another nose around here. See if we can figure out what the hell happened in this house. Can you run through what you saw when you found DCI Hastings? Every detail, please.'

Maggie followed Kat into the room. 'He was tied here. Looked like he was bound with some sort of wire on his ankles and wrists – each limb tied separately to a piece of the wooden chair.'

Maggie circled the chair as she pictured Hastings sitting there.

'His head was hanging down. But that contraption there was set up beside the chair, presumably to make sure he was hydrated and didn't die before she was finished with him. But it was empty, and fuck knows how long it has been since he last had anything in him.' Kat pointed at the water bottle crudely attached to the metal pole.

'Why would someone do this to their family?' Maggie

walked to the window and looked out. She couldn't imagine the hate that Olivia must be feeling to torture and then kill her family and anyone else who happened to be an inconvenience.

'I heard how cold she was in the interview with you, Maggie. This is not someone who has any bloody understanding or emotion. The rage against her mother was just awful. I don't even want to think what she had planned for …' Kat couldn't even finish the sentence and rubbed her arms.

Maggie nodded. It was incomprehensible.

The building was visible from the road, but not close enough that anyone would be able to see any movement. Maggie was curious as to why this particular building was chosen from the many others that they had passed on the way. 'This place must hold some significance to Olivia. What do we know about her birth parents, other than the fact that they were abusive? I know that's important, but I can't help but think we're missing something. Her Social Care file was downstairs – or at least a copy of reports from it.'

Maggie heard some noise from the back of the house and proceeded to the window opposite. One of the forensic officers was standing beside a burned-out car and waving to his colleagues.

'Oh shit! Looks like they found something outside.' Maggie didn't wait for Kat to respond and rushed out of the room, bounding down the stairs without thinking about anything but what the forensic officers had found.

Out back, she headed towards the group of people. 'What did you find?' She looked down to where the officer was pointing. A small car, similar in shape to Sophia Hasting's, was burned out. And there was a body inside.

'Bloody hell.'

'What is it?' Kat leaned over and caught her breath. 'Shit – I'm guessing that is not the remains of a large animal?'

The forensic officer smiled. ''fraid not. Just called Dr Blake. She's going to contact a forensic anthropologist – not much flesh remaining, so they can fight amongst themselves.' Maggie nodded. 'I'll radio DI Rutherford. See what she wants us to do.'

Maggie walked away from the area and radioed in to the station.

'Hey, guv. The crime scene folks have found a body in a burned-out car; they've called out a forensic anthropologist to attend with Dr Blake. Not sure if it is linked to this case or not – what do you want us to do?'

'Could this day get any worse? Well, you're not going to learn much more there. Come back here, as we're going to have a briefing before we release any further information. Was there anything with the body to help identify it?'

'Not that I could see. Pretty much burned to the bone; there was some bloody clothing in the house – so forensics may get something off that. Kat and I will make our way back.' Maggie's phone buzzed in her pocket. She looked at the screen. 'Okay, guv. We'll see you shortly.'

'Hey. How are you?'

'Tell me it isn't true. Ronnie – I mean Olivia – murdered her family. I can't believe I fell for her act,' Lucy stammered.

'How did you find out ... never mind. No one could have known. She had everyone fooled. Someone will be around to talk to you, if they haven't been all ready.'

'I was speaking to someone at the DAHU. Word travels fast when it comes to an officer being harmed. Of course, I'll talk to whoever you need me to.'

'Would first thing in the morning be better for you? I can let them know. Whatever works best.'

'Vicki's been released and said she would be here tomorrow, so she'd also be able to help, as she had her reservations about Ronnie from the start. I just didn't see any of it. First Mark – and now … what a mess, Maggie.'

'Don't blame yourself. If anything changes, I'll call – and seriously, Olivia had this planned out for some time, that's apparent. The fact that none of us saw what was right in front of us is no surprise.'

'Thanks. I'm going to stop by the hospital now and see if there are any changes to Mark's condition. What happened with her father? I can't believe I didn't ask …'

'He's on his way to the hospital.' Kat was heading towards her. 'I've got to go now. We'll speak soon.' Maggie signalled to Kat. 'The guv wants us back at the station for a briefing.'

'I'll drive.'

Maggie didn't know what to focus on as they drove back to the station. Maggie could see Kat had wanted to ask her something but for some reason she was holding back. 'Something on your mind? You're biting your top lip pretty hard.'

Kat turned. 'Is it that obvious? I just wondered what other secrets are in Hastings's family. What would drive someone to those lengths and why the hell did the DCI keep that from everyone?'

'Well, Bethany might dig up more from Olivia's phone and the laptop. I was talking to Lucy when we were at the scene. At some point, her statement will have to be taken. Olivia stayed under her roof all this time. I got the impression that Lucy was feeling guilty, especially with Mark in the hospital now too. They were growing close so this must have hit her really hard.'

'I went to see him the other day. Still no change. Though he wasn't getting any worse, so that's something.' Kat's voice caught on the last few words. She had worked closely with Mark, but Maggie admired how professional she remained throughout this whole ordeal.

'Right! Olivia likes to play games. How about after the briefing we finish off the interview? We have a few tricks up our sleeve too.'

Chapter Eighty

DCI Meechan stood at the front of the room. He was rubbing his chin as the team filed in and took their seats. 'I'll keep this as short as possible. DI Rutherford and I will be meeting with the press after this, so let's run down where we're at. I'll share the updates I have and if any of you have anything else to add, shout out. No time for politeness.' He paused. 'Hastings is currently in critical condition at Stafford County Hospital. Some of the injuries he sustained were infected and they are working to stabilize him. It's touch and go at the minute, so let's keep positive and hope he fights through this. I've had a call to confirm that the burned remains found at the crime scene are indeed human – thought to be female – but they have no other information about this yet. Olivia has legal representation now and they are aware that we'll be questioning her again. Maggie and Kat – I understand you will be doing this.'

'Yes, sir. Maybe she'll disclose who the woman in the car is. I don't think it was a coincidence that additional remains were found,' Maggie added. 'Now that we know Hastings wasn't involved, will you be updating the press, as they might want to redact half the shit they put out there.'

'We'll be sharing what we can, but yes we'll be making it clear that we have our suspect in custody and are not looking for anyone else in relation to the murders of Tim Griffiths, Sophia Hastings, and Joe Clayton and the attempted murder of PC Mark Fielding, Vicki Wilkinson, and DCI Hastings.' He shook his head. It was a lot for the team to take on board, but Maggie realized this would be a good closure for his records. She looked at DI Rutherford. Despite the stress, she seemed to have really come out of whatever funk she had been in. Maggie resumed focus on the case. It wouldn't do her any good to start straying now. The interview with Olivia Hastings would be challenging.

'Bethany, do you have any new information to share from Olivia's laptop or other devices?'

'She diarized everything; it's no wonder she lashed out at Lucy when she attempted to help her with her bag. Although she password protected everything in the Dropbox she had created, and I needed the Digital Forensic team's help with cracking them, Olivia took pictures, videos, kept notes – the lot. Looks like she knew Joe Clayton from Tim's estate too – he dealt drugs to the kids to support his own habit and she had a load of info on you, Maggie – conversations she overheard between DCI Hasting's and his wife – so I guess that's why she targeted your house for the listening device.'

'Bloody brilliant! We can use all that when we interview her,' Kat jumped in.

'Hmmm. Well, you could, but other than it being her Dropbox, there is nothing particular that identifies her as the person who wrote the notes or took the pictures. A clever solicitor would point that out.' Bethany shrugged.

'Well, it's at least a start. Can you make sure Maggie and Kat have all the details in time for their interview?' Meechan looked at his watch. 'Unless there is anything else, let's crack on – it's getting late and the sooner we have something to present to the CPS and close this case, the better.'

Chapter Eighty-One

Maggie collected all the notes and images off Bethany and nodded to Kat. 'You ready?'

Kat took a deep breath. The lines across her brow told Maggie that she was nervous about this interview. The high profile of this case could make or break a detective and neither wanted to be on the receiving end of a bollocking. As they made their way down the hall, they bumped into DI Rutherford and DCI Meechan who were heading to the press conference.

'We have every confidence in you both, don't we, Abs?' Maggie noted DI Rutherford's blush, seemingly surprised at what appeared to be a term of affection they once shared.

'Absolutely. You know exactly what needs to be done. We already have enough to charge and hold Ms Hastings, and once we have the latest forensic report back from Dr Blake's team, we can add any additional charges. She won't get away with this.' DI Rutherford squeezed Maggie's hand.

'Thanks. Good luck to you both. Hopefully, the vultures

will get what they need.' Maggie carried on down the stairs with Kat in close proximity. As they neared the interview room, Maggie sensed Kat's nerves and stopped. 'Take a few deep breaths. Don't forget, we have all the evidence we need. Right now, we're just looking for Olivia to fill in some blanks, okay?'

Kat nodded and took a few deep breaths. 'Let's do this.'

They opened the door to the interview room and were greeted with a smirk.

'Did you find what you were looking for then?' Olivia lifted her eyes and stared at Maggie.

Maggie and Kat sat down and nodded at the man who sat beside Olivia Hastings. He reached across the table and introduced himself. 'I'm Jack Durkin from Durkin and McManus Solicitors.' His hand was clammy. 'I was called in, as the other duty solicitor was not available.'

'Poor you,' Kat mumbled and turned on the recorder, reminding Olivia she was still under caution. She hadn't had a solicitor present at the first interview, but she must have had second thoughts once she learned that her father had been found. Maggie wondered how this played into her games.

'You'll be happy to hear that we located your father and he's doing well in hospital.' Maggie knew that wasn't the full truth, but she wanted to gauge the woman's reaction.

Olivia's left eyebrow raised. 'Well, that's not true, DC Jamieson. I had you down as a lot of things, but a liar wasn't one of them. The custody sergeant informed my solicitor of David's condition. Tsk, tsk. Were you hoping I might break down? Cry and plead for mercy?'

Mr Durkin shifted in his seat. Was that a look of

embarrassment on his face? Maggie bet he wished he wasn't the duty solicitor today.

'We found something else of interest at the property.' Maggie dangled the last word, hoping that Olivia would bite.

She leaned back and crossed her arms. 'And what would that be?'

'More remains in a burned-out car. Your mother's car, in fact – identified by the VIN. We suspect it is a female, but we're waiting for more information from forensics; however, if you'd like to tell us more about it, it will go down well with the CPS and the courts noting your cooperation.'

Jack Durkin leaned across and whispered into his client's ear. Olivia responded and then looked at Maggie and Kat. She placed her head on the table and her shoulders shook.

Was she crying?

'It's okay.' Maggie softened, hoping that would convince the woman to open up to them. 'Take your time.'

They heard noises from beneath her arms, shoulders still shaking – but when she raised her head, she wasn't crying at all. She was laughing. And now that laughter was uncontrollable.

'Ms Hastings, do you really think that's appropriate?' Maggie waited.

Her laughter stopped as quickly as it had started, and a cold look came over her face. Her whole demeanour changed as she growled: 'You found her then.'

'Who is it?' Maggie leaned forwards.

'The woman who gave birth to me. Fucking bitch.' Olivia's nostrils flared.

'Your birth mother? How did you find her?'

'That woman was no mother!' she spat. 'She got knocked

up and gave birth to me, but other than passing me between her legs, she was nothing but another adult who used me – as a human ashtray most days. She reminded me every day what a burden I was and then let Social Services take me when her attempts to beat me to death failed.' She paused. 'Did you find the hole?'

Maggie's eyes widened. 'What hole?'

'The grave. Meant for the sperm donor who created me.'

'We were told your birth father is in prison.'

'Yes. The fucker was lucky because if I got my hands on him …' She slammed her fists on the desk. 'All the secrets and lies. David and Sophia thought they could bury them, pretend like I was their child. As if I could forget what happened to me. And then they wanted to lock me away when I got to be too much! No one has that power over me – I'm free, motherfuckers.' She slammed her fists on the table.

Maggie didn't want to interrupt her, as her anger seemed to drive her to share what was behind the killings, but Olivia had stopped talking and was staring at the wall behind them.

'I'm not ashamed of or sorry for anything I've done, you know.' The words sounded like a script. 'Everyone who died and those who should have died deserved what they got. Did you see what I had carved on David's chest? One dot – FREE. That's me now.'

'What about Tim Griffiths? He was an innocent in all of this. Just wanted a friend.'

'Ah – yes. Tim was a means to an end, I'm afraid.' She shrugged.

'You really are a heartless cow, aren't you?' Kat interrupted, and Maggie rested her hand on her arm.

'My colleague is not wrong. Is there any shred of decency

inside you?' Maggie tilted her head and looked at the woman in front of them.

Olivia stood and did a twirl, ending with a curtsey. 'Do you see any?' Laughing, she sat back down.

'Do you have any more questions for my client? I hope you'll note that she has cooperated throughout this whole interview.'

Maggie looked at Olivia who was tugging on her sleeve. 'Is there anything you'd like to add, Ms Hastings?' They had more than enough to charge her, but even with her cooperation it seemed there were some things she just wanted to avoid answering. Maggie hoped it was because she maybe wasn't the psychopath they thought she was. That maybe she had some regret at harming her family. That view soon changed when Olivia pulled a pen out of her sleeve and lunged across the table towards Maggie. Kat jumped across and knocked the sharpened implement out of Olivia's hand, sustaining a cut to her arm in the process. Maggie hit the alarm button and within seconds, a group of officers were in the room.

She stood and as they were leading Olivia away, Maggie read out the charges.

'Olivia Hastings, you are charged with the murder of Linda Eveleigh, Tim Griffiths, Sophia Hastings, and Joe Clayton. You are also charged with the attempted murder of PC Mark Fielding and Vicki Wilkinson and the attempted murder and abduction of DCI David Hastings.'

'Make sure everyone knows the truth or you might find that you're next, DC Jamieson.'

Chapter Eighty-Two

Maggie consoled Lucy Sherwood as they stood and listened to the priest at the burial site. Maggie wasn't much of a crier but even she felt emotional. Nathan winked at her from the other side of the grave and she smiled. No one had expected things to end like this.

He had made some progress and seemed to be pulling through, but eventually his body had given up.

'He was taken too soon, and I can't help but think it was all my fault,' Lucy sniffed and held a soggy tissue up to her nose.

'Here.' Maggie handed Lucy a fresh pack of tissues. 'You can't keep blaming yourself. He certainly wouldn't want it,' she whispered.

'Thanks. I'll be fine. It's just a lot to take in.' Lucy blew her nose.

'Are you coming back to HQ after this? They have one of the large conference rooms set up – food and stuff. I think people will also be going to a pub after that.'

'I shouldn't, I left poor Vicki on her own and we have a lot to do now that the opening was delayed.'

Maggie nodded.

Everyone was silent as they watched the coffin being lowered into the ground.

DCI Hastings would be remembered fondly by his colleagues.

The crowd started to disperse. As Lucy turned to go, Maggie caught her arm. 'How is Mark?'

A smile lit up her face. 'He's much better now and getting stronger every day. I think they'll be discharging him soon, but he won't be back at work for a little while. Once they learned that Ronnie … I mean Olivia had spiked his tea with GHB and then injected him with insulin she stole from his car, his symptoms made sense and they monitored him. There's no long-term damage from her attempt at trying to suffocate him – thank God. He's going to stay in one of the rooms at the haven.'

'Oh yeah?' Maggie nudged her.

'Behave! It's so I can look after him. Just until he's ready to go back to his flat.' She wagged her finger. 'Wipe that dirty smile off your face.'

Maggie held up her hands in defeat. 'Okay. Okay. If you say so.'

The drive to Stafford Police HQ was silent. It was hard to think of anything but the grief felt when you lost a colleague. A few members of both sides of the Hastings's family had appeared but left soon after the joint burial – no doubt to grieve privately and probably question whether they could have done something. A natural reaction. The truth, though, was that because the families had been estranged, there was little for them to know. DCI Hastings clearly wanted to keep what was happening in his family private. Olivia Hastings had manipulated the whole situation so well, that as things had unravelled, even his colleagues had been questioning him. It seemed she had been planning things for almost two years. Setting the scene. Casting doubts. The more Maggie thought about it, the more unreal it all sounded.

'What do you think is going to happen now?' Nathan turned to her.

'You mean about the DCI post?'

Nathan nodded.

'I get the impression that Meechan won't be staying. He definitely loves the glory – he's been involved in more press conferences than Hastings ever was since I joined the team over ten years ago!'

'Yeah. The guv did say he does things mainly for his own success. I wonder if she'll go for the post.' The last sentence was more of an observation; Maggie didn't think DI Rutherford would be interested, but you never can tell.

'Are you going to the pub after this?' Maggie had debated whether she should go or not; it might be easier if Nathan was going. All this had made her more certain than ever to get the home vs work life balance. She wasn't getting any younger and all she seemed to do was work. She definitely didn't want to end up burned out before her time.

'I think I might. You should come too – it would be good to see the less serious side of you. Who knows, people may start to warm to you.' A crooked smile formed and he leaned towards the door; she was tempted to punch him in the arm.

'Funny you should say that! I think I will go – just don't cramp my style.' She laughed.

They pulled into police HQ and once parked, headed inside to where the rest of the police would be.

'I'll see you up there, okay? I've just got to speak to the guv.' He waved at DI Rutherford who was at the far end of the room, speaking with a few other people.

'Sure. I'll let them know.'

Upstairs, Maggie was greeted by people she had worked with over her many years in the force. Small talk mainly as she walked around the room – looking at all the faces. Lots of red eyes, some sad smiles. The drinks would be flowing tonight.

Maggie's stomach fluttered when she spotted Julie Noble, who waved her over.

'Wow. That was some service. So many people. I'll be doing a write-up if you want to contribute something.' Julie looked in her eyes.

Damn this woman. Maggie hoped she didn't realize the effect she had on her. The whole case made Maggie think about her own family and the secret she was keeping from her parents. It might be time for her to share some revelations.

'That's really nice. I'm sure the family will appreciate it … unless you're going to make it quite harsh?' Maggie knew she shouldn't underestimate Julie.

'I know I have a reputation, but even I know what happened was a complete tragedy and the only person to blame is that daughter of theirs. I hope the bitch rots in prison.'

Maggie was surprised at the venom in Julie's voice.

'Sounds like you have some secrets of your own. Care to share?' Maggie reached out and brushed her arm.

Julie's face softened. 'Another day, perhaps. Are you going to the pub afterwards?'

'I think I might, yes. How about you?'

'Is that an invite, DC Jamieson?' A smiled crept over her lips.

'It is. I could use a laugh and as much as you annoy the hell out of me, you have your moments.'

Julie's eyes widened.

'What?' Maggie looked over her shoulder in the direction that Julie had her eyes focused on.

'Holy shit!' Maggie waved and walked towards the door. 'What the hell are you doing here?'

'Sure, it's lovely to see you too, Maggie.' Dr Kate Moloney pulled Maggie in for a hug. The pair squeezed each other tightly.

'I wasn't expecting you. Are you back for good or is this just a flying visit?' A million questions raced through Maggie's mind. Kate looked different. Although her hair was still black, she had cut it into a mid-length bob and coloured the tips purple. Maggie reached out and touched her hair. 'Love the new look. You seem really happy.'

'I am. I took the time I needed and realized how much I missed working in the teams. I'm not saying it's going to be easy, but I couldn't hide away forever. So …'

'What? Don't keep me guessing!' Maggie pulled on Kate's arm, cajoling her to carry on.

'Well, the Domestic Abuse and Homicide Unit is disbanding but merging with the Integrated Offender

Management Unit and I've been asked to stay on and continue working with them.'

'Oh right.' Maggie's shoulders slumped. 'Well, that's good.'

'I haven't finished.' She raised an eyebrow. 'It will be part of the week – two days. The other three days I have accepted a consulting role in the Major and Organised Crime Department. So … once I have got my flat sorted, you'll be stuck with me once again. That okay with you?' Kate's head tilted, and Maggie laughed.

'I think I can learn to deal with that.'

Chapter Eighty-Three

Olivia Hastings had been sectioned for an assessment, as her solicitor was going for a temporary insanity defence. Maggie had no doubt that there were some serious issues with the woman; she was a psychopath, and no amount of treatment or therapy would change her. She didn't want to change. Olivia was wrong. She wasn't free and she never would be.

She had watched her mother cry so often she had mastered the emotion, even though she couldn't feel anything but annoying drips of water falling down her face. The psychiatrist she was being forced to see said she lacked emotion; her motivation to kill was about control and she spent years putting her plan together.

Her adoptive father never laid a hand on her mother – oh no – Olivia was angry that he thought he could just get rid of her by having her locked up in an institution. When he first mentioned hospitalization two years before, she was furious but it kickstarted everything that had led up to this day. No one would lock her up like an animal. Her mother cried – but didn't stand up for her. She paid the price for her deception.

Olivia watched outside the large glass window while she waited for her solicitor. Girlfriends smiling. Children laughing. What makes them feel those emotions? For Olivia, it didn't matter how hard she tried, she just didn't feel anything. Well, nothing good. She blocked out the pain. She felt anger. She wanted to hurt people. Because she could. And she would again. After all, she had some time on her hands.

Chapter Eighty-Four

Six Weeks Later

Sarah struggled with the groceries as she walked up the pathway towards her door. She hoped that Justin was back from his overnight trip – some consultation training – as she didn't fancy having to dig through her handbag to find her keys. She used her foot to knock on the door and shouted: 'Justin, are you in? My hands are full – can you open the door?' She waited and then heard her neighbour call out: 'I haven't seen him come home yet, love. Do you need a hand?'

She smiled at Mrs Burgess. 'Ah no. It's fine. Thank you though.' Sarah put down the bags and searched for her keys. Right at the very bottom. Typical. She unlocked the door and picked up the bags at her feet. Sarah walked into the kitchen and lay the bags on the counter. She picked up the remote when she saw the time, deciding she would catch up on the news as she put the groceries away. She was surprised that Justin wasn't home yet. He was usually the first one in.

She recognized the voice of the reporter on the TV. She couldn't remember her name but knew she had been involved in a few cases that Maggie had worked on. The journalist was standing on the road and behind her were fire trucks – a huge blaze in the background they were fighting to put out.

Sarah stopped what she had been doing and stared at the television screen as the reporter's words rang inside her head in snippets.

Huge fire

Suspected arson

Unidentified body found

Even before the journalist read out the location, Sarah knew. It was her husband's building.

'Oh my god. No!' Sarah looked on the counter for her handbag. She found her mobile and punched in her husband's number.

It rang out and the answerphone kicked in. 'Justin. Oh my god – I've just seen the news. Please ring me as soon as you get this.' Tears flowed down her face. He must have got out. He wouldn't be at work this time. It had to be someone else's body.

She continued to watch the news, hoping more details would be released but even as she stared at the screen, nothing was sinking in. A knock on the door shook her out of her thoughts.

She ran to the doorway, hoping Justin had forgot his keys. 'Oh my god I was so wor—' It wasn't Justin. It was the police.

'Are you Mrs Hardy?' the officer asked.

'Yes. What is it? Is it my husband? Have you found him?'

'I'm sorry, Mrs Hardy, can I come in?' He smiled.

'Of course.' Sarah stepped out of the way and let the officer in. 'Would you like a cup of tea or coffee?'

'No, thank you. Can we go and sit down?'

'Sure.' Sarah showed the officer to the lounge and sat. 'What is this about? You're scaring me.'

'I'm really sorry to have to tell you this – but there has been a fire at your husband's office.'

'I know! I just saw it on the news. Who was in the building? Have you contacted my husband? I can't get a hold of him on his mobile.'

'I'm really sorry to have to tell you this, but we'll need you to come down to the station. A body was discovered in the building once the fire was put out. It was,' he coughed, 'burned beyond recognition; however, we found some items which we believe belonged to your husband and would like you to identify them while we wait for the DNA results to come back. We believe the body is that of your husband, Justin Hardy—'

The scream was deafening.

THE END

Acknowledgments

I'd like to thank everyone who has cheered me on and supported me so far on my writing journey. I'm so grateful to be able to share my stories and I can't do that without any of you.

I'd like to thank my family and friends both near and far, for the tremendous support they have given me – my dad, who I talk to more now that he is gone – I can hear his voice and that gives me comfort. I'd also like to thank my stepmom, Pauline Holten, for continuing to champion my books to everyone she meets in Ireland. My sister Julie and my mom – who fly the Canadian flag along with my brother Tony, Shane and my niece Josianne Boudreau. And to Paula, Christopher and Jimmie – you all mean the world to me.

A massive thanks to my editor Bethan Morgan for her patience, understanding, guidance and belief in me as a writer and to the whole One More Chapter team, who have been fantastic since this crazy journey began – Charlotte, Mel and Claire – you rock!

Special thanks to my beta readers and everyone who has allowed me to use their names! And for the *most* part, their characters are nothing like them in real life … ha ha!

A heart-felt *thank you* to all the authors and festival peeps who have been so incredibly supportive, you have no idea how much it means to me – you know who you are – a thousand #thankyous would never be enough. So many to name, but I love each one of you!

To the crime writing community – do you know how fantastic you are? I wish I could name each and every one of you – your kind words, encouragement, inspiration and overwhelming support continues to amaze me. Don't ever change.

To the blogging community and my blogger friends, I want to name you all, but I can't – so if you are reading this and thinking "is she talking about me?" the answer, as always, is – *Hell yeah, I am*! Love you all. Special mention to Sarah Hardy for organising the most EPIC blog tours via Book on the Bright Side Publicity. And thanks to Berit Lohn for organising the first Instatour for me.

A massive thanks to the Bookouture team (both the authors and my colleagues) for all the amazing advice and cheers!

Of course, I will always mention Tamworth Probation/Tamworth IOM; Stafford IOM; and all my remarkable ex-colleagues within the Police and Probation Service. Your dedication and professionalism astound me – I may be gone but you will never be forgotten.

Finally, a massive thanks to all the readers. There are just no words to convey how much your support and reviews have meant to me. You make me believe I can keep on doing this and give me a reason to write.

A Note from Noelle

I said this in my debut novel, *Dead Inside,* but it is worth noting once again. The book is set in Staffordshire; however, I have used some literary licence by making up names of towns/places to fit with the story.

Having been a Senior/Probation Officer for 18 years, I left in 2017. There are some references to the changes that were implemented in 2015, but I went all nostalgic and some of the work/terms refer to a time when Probation was all one service – though it seems I may have been psychic as the service is coming together under the public banner once again. Regardless, it made things a lot less complicated. Any errors to police procedure/probation or any other agency mentioned within the story are purely my own or intentional to move the story forward. And if you think something sounds unbelievable – don't be so sure – fact is often stranger than fiction!

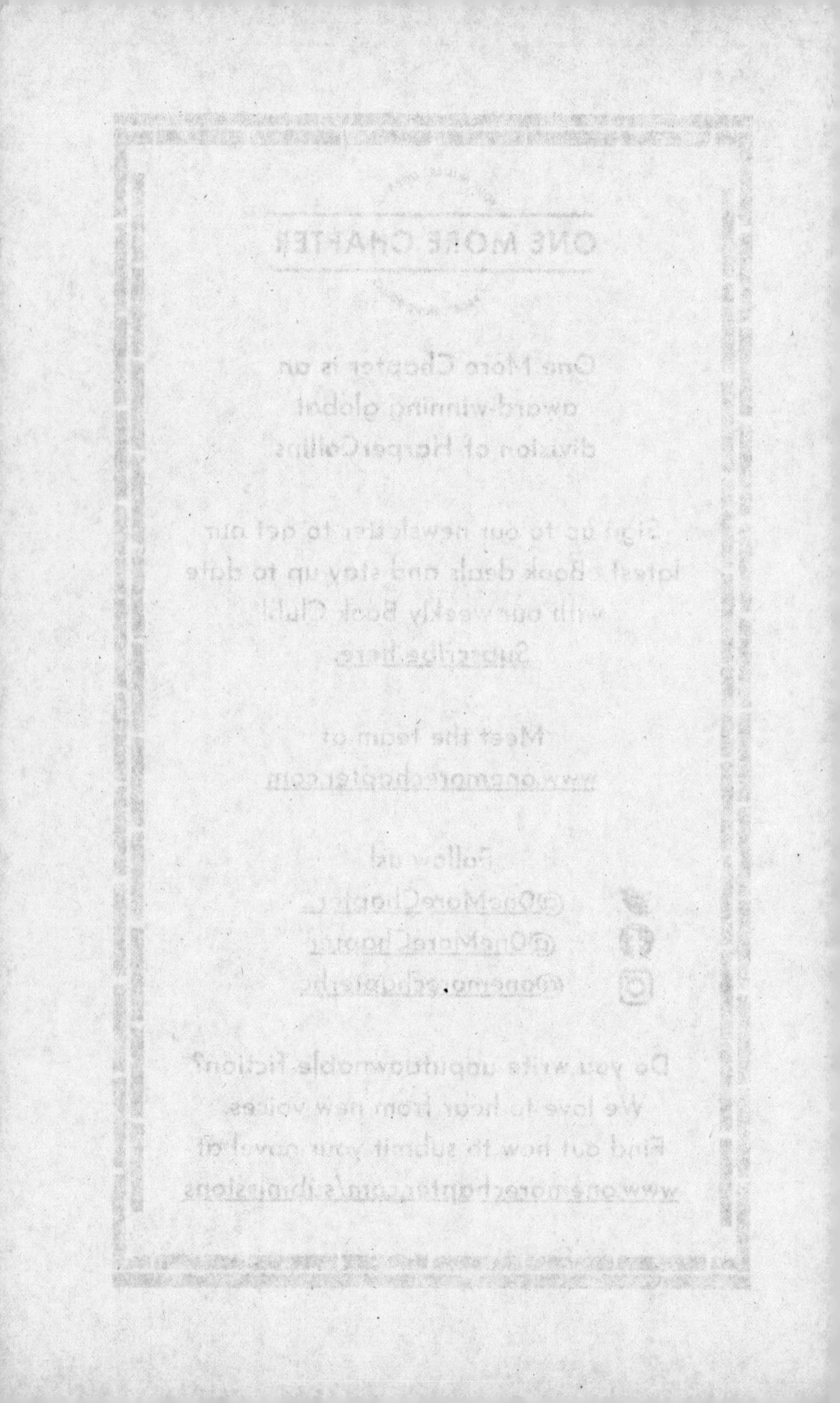